D0734410

The New Aspects program introduces first novelists
of outstanding talent and potential. In our opinion,
THE HIGH HOUSE is an example of the finest
work being created in the fantasy field today.

Betsy Mitchell

Editor in Chief, Aspect

If you have ever cherished and been thrilled
by the classics of high fantasy—William Morris
and Lord Dunsany, Arthur Machen,
William Hope Hodgson, Joy Chant, Evangeline
Walton, *Titus Groan*, or *Little, Big*—then rejoice.
The wonder is back.

"A delightful secret passage of a book, quirky and
exuberant." —Sean Stewart, author of
Mockingbird and *The Night Watch*

"Extraordinary. . . . A delightful, troubling, quirky
book, THE HIGH HOUSE has dragons in the attic,
man-eating furniture in the basement, and both the
dreams and the nightmares of a hundred other
worlds in between."—Diane Duane, author of *The
Book of Night with Moon* and *Deep Wizardry*

more . . .

"A voice of intelligence and amazing literary power. Remarkable."

—**R. A. Salvatore,**
author of *The Demon Awakens*

"This is what all fantasy should be: exciting, literate, intelligent. A wonderful debut!"

—**David Feintuch,**
author of *The Still*

"A real page-turner. . . . Stoddard paints a picture on every page."

—**Bob Eggleton,**
Hugo Award–winning cover artist

JAMES STODDARD
THE HIGH HOUSE

Warner Books, Inc.

ASPECT®

WARNER BOOKS

A Time Warner Company

Copyright © 1998 by James Stoddard
All rights reserved.

Cover design by Don Puckey
Jacket illustration by Bob Eggleton

Aspect is a registered trademark of Warner Books, Inc.

Warner Books, Inc.
1271 Avenue of the Americas
New York, NY 10020

Visit our Web site at
http://warnerbooks.com

 A Time Warner Company

Printed in the United States of America

ISBN 0-7394-0047-9

For Kathryn
For Ever

AUTHOR'S NOTE

Besides being a Story of Adventure this book was written as a tribute to Lin Carter and the "Sign of the Unicorn" fantasy series that he edited from 1969 to 1974. It is hoped that those who recognize herein references to countries chronicled by others will take it for the homage intended. As for myself, having been to neither New York nor Narnia, I must give equal credence to both.

" . . . all the doors you had yet seen . . . were doors in; here you came upon a door out. The strange thing to you. . . will be, that the more doors you go out of, the farther you get in."

—*Lilith* by George MacDonald

The Great House

The High House, Evenmere, that lifts its gabled roofs among tall hills overlooking a country of ivy and hawthorn and blackberries sweet but small as the end of a child's finger, has seldom been seen by ordinary men. Those who come there do so not by chance, and those who dwell there abide long within its dark halls, seldom venturing down the twisting road to the habitations of men. Of all who have lived there, one was born and raised beneath its banners, the man named Carter Anderson, who left not of his own accord, and was summoned back in its time of need. His life and the great deeds he did during the Great War of the High House is told of in *The Gray Book of Evenmere*, but this is a story from long before his days of valor.

He was born in the Lilac Room, where sunlight, diffused between guards of ivy, wafted through the three tall windows, brightening their rich mahogany moldings, casting leaf patterns on the red woven quilt and the dusky timber at the foot of the cherry-wood sleigh bed. The doctor pronounced him a "splendid lad," and his father, waiting beyond the door, smiled and eased his pacing at the noise of his wailing cry.

He remembered his mother only as warmth and love, and slender, dark beauty, for she died when he was five, and he wept many days upon the red quilt in the Lilac Room. Lord Ashton Anderson, his father, the Master of the house, quit his slow laughter after that, and was often gone many days at a time, returning with mud on his boots and shadowed circles around his pale blue eyes.

So Carter grew up, an only child, a lonely boy in the great house, his companions the servants of the manor. Of these, he had three favorites: there was Brittle, the butler, a taciturn man, tall and thin, quite ancient, but still limber; and Enoch, the Master Windkeep, whose sole job was to wind the many clocks throughout the house. Enoch was the companion Carter loved best, ancient as a giant oak and nearly as tanned, older than Brittle even, but burly of frame and jovial by nature, with hair still jet-black, set in tiny ringlets like an Assyrian. The boy often accompanied him on his rounds through the entrance hall, the dining room, the library, the picture gallery, the drawing room, the morning room, and then to the servants' block to wind the clocks in the kitchen court, the servants' hall, the housekeeper's room, the back of the men's corridor, and at the very top of a cherry alcove on the women's stair, where hung a little cuckoo with a tiny yellow wren. After that, they went up the gentlemen's stair to the bedrooms, the private library and others, then on to the sleeping quarters on the third floor.

But on the days when Enoch took the door leading from the top of the third story up to what he called "the Towers," Carter was not allowed to accompany him. The boy hated those times, for the Windkeep would be gone many days, and Carter always imagined him climbing a long thin stair, open on either side, with the stars to his left hand and his right, and he ascending past them to the Towers, which surely lay that far if he must be gone so long.

The final companion of the three was the Lamp-lighter, whose name was Chant. He had a boyish face and a boyish smile, though the gray at his temples bespoke middle age. A bit of the gentle rogue lay upon him, and his eyes were rose-pink, which anyone other than Carter, who knew no different, might have thought bizarre. He had poetry within him; as Lamp-lighter he lit the globes at what he called "the eight points of the compass," and he quoted Stevenson, saying his duties consisted of "punching holes in the darkness." Carter liked Chant, though sometimes his conversation was too complex and sometimes too cynical. He had an odd way of turning a corner on the outside of the house and suddenly vanishing. Carter followed many times, racing around to catch some trace of him, but he never did, so that the boy thought he must be marvelously fast. But magic was commonplace in the house, and Carter saw it often without recognizing it for what it was.

Because there were always rooms to rummage through, closets and crannies, galleries and hallways to explore, Carter grew up an imaginative, adventurous boy, full of curiosity. His father often entertained company during the times he was home, men not in frock coats and top hats, but in armor, or robes, or garb even more grand. There were seldom women, though once a tall, graceful lady came to the house dressed like a queen, all in pearls and white lace, who gave Carter beautiful smiles and patted him on the head, reminding him of his mother, so that his heart ached long after she had gone.

These visitors did not come for pleasure; that was always clear, and they seldom entered through the front door; mostly Brittle ushered them in from the library, as if they had stepped fresh from a book. They ate dinner on the oak dining table, and afterward Carter sat in his father's lap at the head of the table and listened to them talk. They spoke of wars and disputes in far-off countries, of ravaging wolves and robbers. Although the lord was a soft-spoken man, and his chair no higher than the others around the table, they treated him as a king, and implored him to resolve their difficulties. And often, near the end of the evening, when Carter lay sleepy in his father's lap, Lord Anderson said, "I will come." Then Carter knew his father would put on his greatcoat the next day, and his tall hat, and Tawny Mantle, that he would buckle his strange sword around his waist, the one terraced like a lightning bolt, retrieve his marble-headed walking staff, and be gone many days.

One day, a week after Carter's seventh birthday, it happened that he wandered perplexed in the drawing room, looking behind the gray stuffed sofa, crying softly, when his father entered the room.

"Here, now, what are these tears?" Lord Anderson asked, laying his hand on his son's shoulder. He was a kind man, if often sad, and Carter had the greatest confidence in him.

"I've lost my red birthday ball."

"Where did you last have it?"

"I don't remember."

His father thought a moment, then said, "Perhaps it is time to show you something. Come along."

Hand in hand, they left the drawing room, through the transverse corridor to the tall oaken doors into the library, an endless expanse of bookcases where Carter had often lost his way. Lord Anderson did not walk between the rows of books, but took his son through the four-paneled door to the left, into a small study, which Carter did not recall ever having seen before. It was windowless, with a tall ceiling, and a blue carpet with gold fleur-de-lis. There were seven buttercup lights already burning in the brass candelabra, but these were scarcely needed because of the stained-glass skylight, a mosaic in red, blue, and gold depicting an angel presenting a large book to a somber man. The angel looked both beautiful and terrible at once; his long, golden hair flowed to his shoulders and his face was bright where the sun shone through it. A golden belt encircled the waist of his white robe, and the sword strapped upon it gave him a fierce warrior look. Carter liked him immediately.

The study was furnished only with a kidney-shaped desk,

having a leather top fastened with brass hobnails and a matching dark leather chair. Mahogany panels decorated the walls, a fireplace stood beside the door, and a bookcase with blue-leaded glass rested behind the desk. Unlocking the bookcase with a small skeleton key taken from the top drawer, Lord Anderson withdrew a heavy leather book lined with gold leaf. He set it upon the desk, sat himself in the leather chair, and bade his son climb into his lap. But he did not yet open the volume.

"This is the Book of Forgotten Things," his father said gently, but with great reverence. "When you cannot find a thing, when you need to remember something you have forgotten, seek it here. Now open it."

Carter slowly turned the pages. At first, the volume was blank, but to his delight, a picture arose and came to life at the sixth page, and he saw himself in his room holding his red ball. After playing with it a time, he kicked it under the bed and left.

Carter shouted in pleasure, and would have slammed the book shut and rushed to find the lost toy, but his father held him, saying, "Wait, there is more. Turn to page seven."

Carter obeyed, and upon the page, written in gold, were seven words.

"What are these, Father?"

"These are the Seven Words of Power. They are in another language, but we will say them together, you and I."

So they did, the man speaking them clearly, the boy stumbling on their curious sounds, and as they pronounced each one, the gold letters burned like fire, but were not consumed, and Carter felt heat upon his forehead. When they were done, his father said, "You are young and will not remember the Words, but someday, if you become Master of Evenmere, you will find them again in the Book of Forgotten Things."

"Can I see the next page?"

His father hesitated, but said, "Yes, but only one."

When Carter turned the page, it, too, appeared blank, until

the kind, smiling face of his mother gradually rose upon it, her eyes filled with love.

"Mamma," he said softly.

Then she told him how precious he was, and how perfect, and what a beautiful boy, and he smiled as he had when she had once said the words, three years before, though he had not remembered till just then. And then the picture faded, and he looked wistfully at the book.

"It was Mother," he said, turning to Lord Anderson. But his father sat staring at the wall.

"We will go now," the Master said, his voice quavering.

They climbed down from the chair, holding hands. "Father, you didn't look at the book at all, did you? You didn't see her."

His father knelt beside him. "I did not see her, but I heard you call to her. None of us see the same thing when we look into the book, but only that which we ourselves have forgotten."

"But why didn't you look?"

Tears sprang to the corners of Lord Anderson's eyes. "There are some things too painful to see."

Two years passed, and Carter thought little of that day with the Book of Forgotten Things, as he played alone, or accompanied Enoch or Chant on their rounds, or sometimes Brittle. His father had acted less sad in the last year, though his absences had increased.

One day, as Carter was playing with his wooden soldiers in an upstairs room, Brittle came to him. The tall butler looked down upon him in a way that was all Brittle, his eyes quite wise and not unkind.

"The young master will need to accompany me now, to bathe and change clothes."

"But it's the middle of the day, not suppertime."

The butler could be quite stern, but his severe mouth turned up slightly at the small rebellion. "It is indeed not suppertime, but your father has gone for the afternoon, and will be returning shortly with a guest. He wishes you suitably attired."

Mystified, Carter followed Brittle toward his own room, but it was late afternoon before his father returned from somewhere in the back of the house, accompanied by a tall, blond woman, dressed in sky-blue silk blossomed all over with sham daisies, gold bracelets on each wrist, and a carcanet studded in amethyst about her neck. Spiderweb lace, the same color as her dress, descended from a white, wide-brimmed hat, covering without concealing her brilliant blue eyes. Her gloves were white.

"Lady Murmur," his father said. "This is Carter. Carter, Lady Murmur is a friend of mine."

She was very beautiful, but when she looked down her long falcon's nose, Carter saw a gleam in her eyes that made him shiver. Her voice was deep, as if she were always hoarse, and he did not much like it.

"Hello, young man," she said. "I have heard many good things about you. You are not as tall as a nine-year-old should be, nor yet as handsome as your father, though I am sure that will come." She smiled sweetly at Lord Anderson.

Thereafter, Lady Murmur came often, until she and Carter's father were married in the spring of that year, beneath the blue skylight in the long picture gallery, between the rows of yellowed paintings of the former Masters of the house. Many people attended the wedding, until Carter thought the entire manor must be filled, and he saw lords and ladies, and even kings and queens, all splendidly dressed, so that he knew his father must be a great man indeed. He played all day with the children who had come, and it was a wonderful wedding, but that evening, after Lord Anderson and Lady Murmur left for their honeymoon, Carter went to his room, threw himself upon his bed, his picture of his mother clutched between his small hands, and wept.

Everything changed after Murmur came to live with them. She rearranged all the furniture and moved all the pictures; nothing seemed to suit her, not even, after a time, his father. But when they had been married less than two years, she bore him a son, blonde and blue-eyed, who they named Duskin, and things went better for a while. And Murmur called the boy, "the little heir," though never in Lord Anderson's hearing. A nanny was hired to watch Duskin, and Murmur used every pretense to keep Carter away from the baby, so there was no joy in having a brother after all. During the times when his father was gone on business, Murmur acted especially cold to Carter; he could not see Duskin at all then, and her remarks made him ache a bit, deep inside, though she always smiled sweetly as she said them. Carter learned to avoid her. When Enoch was away, and the Lamp-lighter grew too cerebral for the company of a child, he wandered the house, playing alone.

It happened one day, when his father had been gone an exceptionally long time, and Murmur's comments had stuck like a thousand small pins, that Carter retreated toward the back of the house, to the servants' stair, which led to the upstairs bedrooms. Taking his wooden soldiers with him, he opened the narrow door to the alcove behind the stair, a room he had never explored before. To his surprise, a gaslight burned, suspended on the wall about two feet from his head. It was a narrow room, with old hats and coats lying scattered among boxes brown with dust, and at its back wall stood a thin, green door, which Carter tried at once, but found locked. The doorknob was of glass, with the most marvelous miniature inside, an image of Evenmere itself, complete with all its towers and gables, red roofs and brown cornices, colonnades and picture windows. Carter studied it in delight, tugged on it to insure the door was really locked, then sat down before it and looked around. Behind one of the boxes he discovered a marvelous toy carriage, carved with exacting detail in soft pine. Pulling his wooden soldiers from his pocket, he spent a happy hour in play.

Wearying of that, lulled by the warmth of the room and the sputtering gaslight, he had nearly fallen asleep when he heard a soft, scraping sound. Glancing around, he saw the slow turning of the glass knob. He stood up, uncertain what to expect, until the door opened and Lord Anderson squeezed through. Despite his delight at seeing his father, Carter also noticed the wonderful keys the Master held in his hand—the ring was of bronze; a hundred keys slid around it, all different colors, bright as toddlers' toys. The skeleton key that he had used to open the green door was green itself, but dark like malachite, with speckles of blue, as if carved of stone.

"Father!" Carter cried, startling his sire so badly he fumbled for the Lightning Sword by his side. Lord Anderson looked weary, as he often did after his sojourns. There were deep crimson stains upon his greatcoat, and once he recognized his son he appeared little pleased to see him. He locked the door quickly and stuffed the keys into his pocket.

"What are you doing here, Carter?"

"Why, just playing, Father. But you're home!"

Lord Anderson took him quickly by the hand and led him out from beneath the stairs. "I don't want you going in there anymore," he ordered.

Since his father was seldom stern, Carter looked about in confusion. "But, where does the Green Door lead?"

"Nowhere you should ever go! I want you to promise to speak no more of it. Do you understand? And stay away from the stairs! Do you promise?"

"I . . . I promise. I'm sorry, Father." Carter was close to tears.

Seeing his son's distress, Lord Anderson softened. "It's all right. No harm was done. Come now, let's go see your brother."

On the southwest side of the High House, at the garden entrance, a little door led outside from the kitchen into a yard overshadowed by immense oak trees, bordered by a brick fence four feet tall, with short bronze statues of angels with longbows drawn, standing atop the wall at each of the four corners. A wishing well, surrounded by red lacecaps, stood in the middle of the yard, with snails drifting like sailboats up and down its sides, and a bronze plate along its rim that read: *Masonry From the Ifdawn Marest.* A row of tall hedges filled the northern portion of the court, forming a haphazard maze where Carter often played. He loved the yard; it was cool on hot summer days, and when the wind blew, the leaves of the trees rustled like the wings of giant birds. He liked to sit with his back to the well and read books, adventure stories such as *The People of the Mist* or, even better, *The Well at the World's End*, which he thought must be much like this well. Beyond the short wall ran a cobblestone path that circled the entire house, and in its midst stood a black lamppost. Every evening, Chant strolled out the white wooden gate hidden behind the grape arbor, singing snatches of verse as he lit the lamp. Ivy covered the fence; verdigris covered the angels; a heavy layer of peace covered the whole yard.

One day, as twilight slipped gray over the world, when the Lamp-lighter had already done his work, Carter lingered upon the lawn, watching a blue beetle, big as his thumb, making its way along the bottom of the fence. Its shell crackled like papyrus as he cautiously prodded it with a stick.

In the midst of his investigation, a shadow fell between him and the lingering sun. Glancing up, he gave a cry of fear, dropped the stick and backed away, for a man stood, watery as a mirage, on the other side of the fence. In the dimness and the long shadows, when he had first glanced up, he had thought the stranger had no face at all, but a smooth, pink blankness. He saw now this was not so, but it took a moment for his heart to calm. Although he had never actually seen an English bobby, he recognized from illustrations in books the man's tall helmet, dark uniform, and long, wooden billy, swinging on its cord. When he smiled, he had a round, pleasant face.

"Did I startle you, lad?" he asked, in a low, rasping voice, belieing his affable stare. "Terribly sorry. I'm Constable Pratt."

"Pleased to meet you, sir," Carter said, remembering himself. "Has there been trouble?"

"None at all. None at all. I'm simply making my rounds. It's good to check on things." The Bobby drew close to the wall, though he did not touch it.

Carter thought it peculiar that a constable should make rounds so many miles from any village, but he said nothing. His first fear had been replaced by a solid dread, a kind of quiet horror. He did not understand it, but it was made worse each time he glanced away from Pratt, for the illusion of his facelessness returned when Carter saw him only from the corner of his eyes.

"I wonder," the Bobby said, "could you perhaps let me in through the little gate? I'd like a bit of water from that well, if you don't mind."

"I . . . I couldn't do that, sir. Chant keeps it locked. I could get Brittle to let you in if you'd like."

The Bobby exhaled with a noise like a low hiss, but he smiled again. "No, don't trouble him. Perhaps you could bring me a cup of water, then?"

"Of course," Carter said. If anything, his fear had increased. He fought the urge to back his way to the well, as if he were retreating from a viper, yet every step with the Bobby out of sight filled him with panic. He wanted to dart inside, shouting for Brittle and Enoch, but instead he lowered the bucket and drew water from the well. He dipped the tin cup in, filled it, and brought it toward the constable, who waited, hands outstretched.

And suddenly he knew, as surely as he knew the faces of the angels on the fence, that the Bobby could not pass beyond the wall, that it served as a barrier he could not cross. This, then, was the line, and if Carter handed him the cup, he would be crossing it, over into a country where he could be reached. He paused.

"That's a good lad," the Bobby rasped. "Bring it to me."

Carter stretched his hand out and gently set the cup upon the wall. "Here, sir."

Just at the corner of the constable's eyes, so slight Carter thought he might have imagined it, he saw the dagger malice of one thwarted. "Thank you, lad," he said, but he did not take the cup.

"You're welcome. I . . . I have to go in now."

"Wait! Before you go, come closer and let me ask you something."

With all the courage he possessed, Carter stepped toward the fence, not even certain why he obeyed, but quite careful not to cross it with any part of his body. The Bobby, too, drew as near as he dared, and spoke in a whisper.

"What if you took the keys on the brass ring? You could see what was behind the Green Door. Wouldn't that be wonderful?"

Even as he said it, the Bobby leaned closer toward the wall. His hand shot out, clawlike, toward the boy, but struck an invisible barrier above the fence. In that instant, his features went blank again, and he stood like a faceless doll, struggling against the obstruction. Carter backed away and the Bobby did likewise, his features returning.

"Think about it, boy."

Carter bolted for the house, his courage expended. He dared not look back until he had locked the heavy door behind him. Then he peered through the leaded glass. The Bobby stood away from the wall, beside the lamppost, his head turned downward, hidden.

Carter saw the Bobby no more that summer, though many evenings thereafter he looked from the windows, half expecting to see him lurking at the lamppost. Neither did he tell Lord Anderson the tale, though he did not know why. Perhaps it was because he had never thought of taking any of his father's things before, and so wrestled with the temptation the Bobby had placed within him. As time passed, he found himself watching Lord Anderson, to see where he kept the keys, though Carter told himself it was only curiosity. His father had them with him always, in his greatcoat when he traveled, but otherwise in his pocket.

One evening, when the whole family sat down to supper, the Master said to Lady Murmur, "Tomorrow I must go hunting in the country of the Tigers of Naleewuath. I shall be gone no more than a week, I think."

Carter looked up from his roast brisket and cried, "Oh, Father, could I go with you? I've never seen a tiger!"

Lord Anderson paused in thought. "You are nearly twelve. This might be a good time. There are no tigers like those in Naleewuath."

"Do you think it wise?" Lady Murmur asked. "It sounds dangerous."

"There is some danger, it is true, but a boy must learn to be a man, and seeing is a start. We would not be alone there. The tigers . . ."

"Oh, Ashton," Murmur said, looking away at her spoon, "I did not intend to mention it, but I'm afraid Carter has not been a good boy this week, and I told him to spend the day in his room tomorrow."

Carter stared at Murmur in wide-mouthed surprise.

"What's this?" Lord Anderson said, looking hard at the boy.

"I didn't want to trouble you with it," Murmur continued. "It's just that your son is always saying cruel things to little Duskin. He has been absolutely hateful, and spoken back to me as well."

"Carter, is this true?"

"It's not true at all!" Carter cried. "How could I be cruel, when she never lets me near him?"

"You see," Murmur said. "He's quite sarcastic."

Lord Anderson gave Murmur a rigid glance, then looked at Carter in perplexity. "Perhaps tomorrow would not be the best time," he said softly. "You will accompany me to Naleewuath some other day."

As soon as dinner was over, Carter excused himself and rushed up the stair. Once in his room he slid into a corner and wept, understanding nothing. Why had she lied? His young mind could not conceive of her wish to discredit him so Duskin could become the favored son; his only thought was that he had somehow offended her.

The next morning he woke early, dressed quickly, and hurried into the upstairs hall. Far below, he heard his father's voice. Almost without conscious thought, he slipped into Lord Anderson's bedroom, where his greatcoat lay waiting on the bed.

A dim plan, one he had dared not consciously consider, rushed all at once into him. He went to the coat, felt inside the pocket, and drew out the bronze key ring. It gleamed with a hundred colors, but he stared at it only a moment before stuffing it into his own pocket.

He had only one thought: if he could get beyond the Green Door, where Murmur could not reach him, then his father would be glad to see him and they could go together to the Tigers of Naleewuath.

He hurried down the corridor and descended the narrow servants' stair beside the day nursery, which brought him directly to his destination. The stair was straight, but very long; the leering gargoyles on the railing knobs seemed to taunt him as he hurried down. Passing to the floor below, he entered the narrow door beneath the stair. The gas lamp was already on, making him marvel at Chant's abilities. He gave a sudden rush of breath as he stopped before the Green Door. A twinge of doubt assailed him; the door seemed foreboding—even threatening—this day. For a moment he stood uncertain. There was only the gentle swishing of the gas jet, the door before him, and the keys hanging like a heavy weight in his pocket.

"I don't care!" he cried suddenly. "I'll show her!"

His mouth went dry as he took the keys. They shimmered in his hand like phosphorescent stones, all colors, many different sizes, with heads rounded, ovoid, square, triangular, some with angels' wings or faces upon them, and one with an acorn with eyes. Each key brought a different emotion with it: the royal blue, speckled with gray, radiated peace; the golden key excited; the silver spoke of wonders uncounted; the red key of danger; the rusty key, sepulchers and dust. Carter tried to count them, but the number never totaled the same. There was a power, a strength about them that both frightened and thrilled him, as if they had not been made by mortal men.

With shaking hands he took the malachite key and inserted it into the gray lock; it resisted only an instant before turning with a solid click. He opened the door cautiously and peered within. Seeing no danger, he stepped into a gray hall filled with a light mist. An ashen carpet covered the floor and gray pictures of gray flowers hung upon the dull walls. The corridor led to right and left. After some hesitation, he chose the right.

His entire body felt strange and he experienced minute pains—on his arms, his legs, his back, as if every part were being discreetly torn away and rebuilt. A shuddering overtook him that was not fear, and he knelt upon the carpet until it passed. As he did so, he glanced up and realized he could not see the ceiling, which was hidden by the mist.

As he proceeded down what seemed an endless way, the thought occurred to him that he should turn back, lest he miss his father. He did so at once and found he had traveled farther than he would have believed. When he finally arrived back at the Green Door, he found a figure standing there, half-hidden by the fog.

He ran forward, expecting his sire, then stopped short when he saw the Bobby, his face a smooth nothing save for a crescent-moon grin.

Carter backed away in horror, but when he turned to run, his path was blocked by a man clad in black, who seized him at once, bound him by the hands, and threw him over his shoulder.

The Bobby approached. The grin had given way to the kindly face he had worn in the yard. Smiling, he searched Carter's pockets until he found the bronze ring. As he held the keys, they dulled in his pale hands. "Thank you, boy," he rasped. "You have given us a great gift."

Carter cried out, but the man holding him thrust a gag over his mouth.

"Should we lock the door?" the man asked.

The Bobby grinned. "No. Leave Anderson a clue. He will suffer all the more for it."

For what seemed to Carter like hours, his abductors carried him through endless halls, up winding stairs, then down others, through rooms great and small, until he thought they must surely be traveling in circles; no house could be this large. Yet on they went, past bookcases with shelves carved like serpents and nightstands sculpted like dragons. Carter was carried facing backward, so he could not see their direction of travel, but only where they had gone. So miserable was he that his disobedience had brought disaster, he did not think to memorize his path until it was too late.

The men began a long descent, down a stairway woven in

shadows and spiderwebs, that creaked in protest at every step; ebon carvings of angels of darkness stood in alcoves to the sides—proud, arrogant, their wings like vultures, their hawk noses cruel. Carter whimpered and closed his eyes.

That stair seemed to go on indefinitely; they passed dozens of landings lit by green gaslights in braziers carved as skulls. Carter only once caught sight of the Bobby during that time, his face blank, ghastly in the eldritch glow.

At last they came to a four-paneled door formed of black marble. The Bobby drew out a long, rusted key, though not from the bronze ring, and unlocked it.

"In you go and in you stay," he said, taking the gag from Carter's mouth and the rope from his wrists. "This is the Room of Horrors. You will never leave it."

With rough hands, they cast him into the darkness, skinning his knees as he slid across the hard floor. He flung himself, too late, back at the door; the lock clicked shut before he ever touched it. Through the heavy marble he did not even hear the men depart. He beat upon the door with his small fists, until he heard an odd, scraping sound behind him.

He turned to face it and screamed.

A ghost stood before him, wrapped in insubstantial white, chains fastened to its gossamer arms. It moaned as it approached, like wind blowing through rafters. Carter backed against the marble, paralyzed with terror. The specter drew near and abruptly thrust its face three inches away from Carter's own, its mouth and eyes gaping darkness. The boy screamed and bolted, feet pounding against bare boards, fleeing through utter blackness.

He smashed against something hard, and fell back, dazed and weeping, trembling like a fawn. Gradually, he recovered himself, controlled his sobbing, and sat up. No matter how he strained his eyes, he could detect no trace of light.

A low growling rose at his left ear. He leapt to his feet and ran again.

Hours later found him cringing in a corner. He could run no

more; he had been pursued through every waking moment by visions and monsters, some visible, others hidden in the night. He had no more tears for crying; he wanted his father, who he now knew to be involved in dangerous business indeed. He wondered how the Bobby could be so cruel.

Finally, he slept a twitching, trembling sleep, a brief cessation from the horror.

When he woke, he found the face of the ghost thrust before him once more. He screamed and ran again.

In years after, he remembered nothing about the Room of Horrors except its night and terror, for it was indeed filled with fears of every sort that sent him scurrying across the boards, hiding in closets and crannies, sleeping when he could, only to be awakened by the things of nightmare. He found food sometimes, for it was never the purpose of the chamber to starve its victims. There were moments and even hours of respite, but these were always broken by tramping feet, hideous howls, or leering stares.

He could not have lasted long there, in such dread, not without being broken in spirit. Whether he remained a week, or only a single day, he never knew; it seemed eternal, but eventually he heard the sound of thunder. A blast shook the chamber, blinding him; he thought it only a new peril. But when he could see again he found Brittle, holding a lantern aloft, standing before the marble door, which lay broken and smoking, sundered by a mighty blow, the smell of sulphur roiling from it. Beside the butler stood Lord Anderson, his jagged Lightning Sword held high, fury burning in his eyes. In that moment, Carter understood, perhaps for the first time, that his father would have dared the devil himself to save him. He swept Carter into his arms in one swift motion, wrapping him in his cloak as if he were an infant. Wasting no time on speech, but weeping as he went, he rushed the lad up the stair.

Carter cried in his father's arms until he fell asleep, so that he did not even remember being tucked safely into his own bed.

He had nightmares for several weeks thereafter, and his father stayed close, neglecting the business of the house to be with his son. Carter remembered those days as happy ones, despite the lingering fear, because of Lord Anderson's attentions. Murmur, if anything, was even less kind, and often, as the Master held his son's hands to help him say his nightly prayers, Carter would see, between half-closed lids, the lady standing at the doorway, glaring.

It happened shortly after Carter's twelfth birthday that he wandered back into the walled garden, which he had avoided since his encounter with the Bobby. Still, looking out the windows, the sunlight against the leaves beckoned him, and he followed after, to play among the hedges, knowing his father was in council with visitors and would be busy throughout the afternoon.

With a carved wooden sword and a hat made of paper, he charged among the hedges, playing games of war, fancying himself a brave captain, leader of a host. The tall rows of privet provided fortresses, enemy lines, and corners for turning and falling on the foe, and he played while the cool breath of morning lapped his brow.

He was bent down upon the ground, drawing a map in the dirt with a stick, when a shadow suddenly crossed above him. Looking up, he saw the Bobby grinning unpleasantly.

He shrieked in terror and leapt up, but the hedges pinned him roundabout, and the Bobby grasped him in his cruel grip. He cupped one hand over his mouth and dragged him across the yard. They were at the well, heading toward the gate behind the grape arbor, when Carter got his teeth into the thick hands. The Bobby growled in rage and the boy screamed for help as loud as he could. His captor cuffed him sharply, then continued dragging him toward the gate.

At that moment, Brittle bounded out of the doorway, a broad-axe in his hands, running with an agility Carter had not thought possible in the ancient butler.

Seeing himself pursued, the Bobby gave a cry of rage, lifted Carter, and flung him into the well.

He tumbled into darkness, fortunate not to strike his head on the way down, but hitting the water hard. He descended into the depths a great distance; had he panicked he would have drowned at once, for he did not know how to swim. Instead, he clawed his way to the edge of the well, where the uneven rocks gave him a handhold, and pulled himself up toward the bright circle of light hovering far above. The air had been knocked from him during his plunge; only an effort of will kept him from opening his mouth to breathe. He felt his pulse hammering in his temples as he narrowed the distance; after his terrors in the Room of Horrors, this seemed a return to that endless nightmare; part of him wanted very much to give in to the lure of the waters, to breathe in once and never again, a subject of sleep eternal. He struggled all the harder.

Then his head broke the surface. He pulled air into his lungs, went under again, then rose coughing. He clung to the rocks; it was all that saved him from a bad blow as the wooden bucket splashed directly beside him. Beyond the noise of the water, he heard Brittle frantically calling his name. He managed to shout.

"Grab the bucket!" the butler ordered.

"I have it!"

"Hold tight! Can you hold? Help is coming."

"I can."

What seemed like a long time passed, during which Carter thought he saw the walls of the well closing in all around him, the circle of light becoming smaller and smaller, as if he were at the end of a long tube that was gradually squeezing shut.

Looking around, he saw this was not so, yet the claustrophobia nearly cost him his grip on the rope. He closed his eyes to shut it out, found that little better, then concentrated instead upon a patch of rust on the handleplates of the bucket, which resembled a butterfly, wings outstretched. The water was icy cold.

He gave a cry of fear as another rope flopped into the well, mistaking it at first for a water snake. A man followed the rope, descending hand over hand, his feet slipping against the slick sides. Seeing it was not Brittle, he imagined for a moment that the Bobby had overcome the butler and was coming to seize him once more. But when the figure looked down, it was the slender face of Chant. The lampman lifted the boy from the water, one-handed, with surprising strength. Still, he could not support Carter all the way up, but placed him with his legs astraddle the bucket. At his word those above raised both bucket and boy, while he supported them from below. They ascended rapidly, and once above the lip, Carter found Enoch and two other servants manning the handle, while Brittle stood beside, biting his lip.

Enoch swept the boy into his arms, and they carried him inside, where he was given new clothes and taken swiftly to bed. His last memories before he fell into a troubled sleep was of his father, bending softly over him, examining his bruises and kissing his cheek.

Several hours later, after he had roused and eaten, he was brought into the dining room, where, to his surprise, he found all the many members of the household assembled: the House Steward, the Groom of the Chambers, Brittle's assistants, the housekeeper, housemaids, laundry maids, nanny, hall boy, the usher, even the valets and footmen. Enoch and Chant were there as well; Brittle stood by his master, still biting his lip. Lady Murmur sat imperiously in the little gold chaise; Duskin was not present.

Lord Anderson sat at the head of the dining table, the household seated down its length, Carter to his right. The silence of the room was palpable; the Master's eyes held everyone so, with a simmering look like the fire Carter had beheld in them within the Room of Horrors, but mixed with another emotion he could not comprehend. When the lord spoke, his voice was flame and ash.

"You know what has happened. The Enemy gained entrance to the yard. He did so because the gate was left unlatched, unlocked. Whose neglect caused it?"

The company remained silent, eyes down, not in guilt, but that their master, who they loved, had been ill-served.

"Speak!" he cried, rising to his feet and striking the table a thunderous blow with his knobbed staff. All were startled, including Carter, and the maids gave little shrieks.

The fury diminished in the lord's eyes; he sank back into his chair and rubbed his hands across his face. His voice softened. "You will forgive me if I am distraught. He is my son. I do not ask the question seeking retribution; I assure you there will be none. It is important to know. If the gate was not left open through neglect, then there is a traitor in our midst."

Carter saw shock and horror on the servants' faces, but his father's blue eyes were cold now, and they stared straight at Murmur as he spoke. "I will interrogate each of you now, one by one, to see who might have passed through the gate. We must ascertain the truth of this."

"I will speak first," Chant said, "for I can say with certainty that the gate was locked last night after I lit the lamps. I am always careful, but yesterday evening more so; I do not know why. A premonition was on me, as sometimes happens."

"Very good," the Master said. "Then it was opened between the hours of eight o'clock yesterday and ten this morning. We must see who else used it during that time."

He questioned each of the servants, one after another, but always the answer was no; none had approached the gate, and this was little surprising, for it was seldom used, save by Chant. When all had been interrogated, he turned toward Murmur, saying, in a hard voice: "What of you, my lady?" A slight intake of breath went around the room, that the mistress of the house should be questioned.

"Am I a hired girl, to carry wash buckets beyond the yard?" she replied, her voice unnaturally jovial. "I never leave the house."

Lord Anderson nodded. "Very well. Then I tell all of you to be watchful. The gate was left open not by accident. If you hear anything, no matter how trivial, bring it to me, or to Brittle. My son's safety depends upon you all. You are dismissed. Carter, you will remain."

When all the servants were gone, and the room empty except for the boy and his father, Lord Anderson drew his son to him. He held his small hand in his own two hands and spoke softly but earnestly.

"I have chosen poorly in Lady Murmur. You know that, don't you?" Without waiting for a reply, he continued: "Duskin is my son as well; I love him equally, whatever his mother's heart. Carter, you do not know the forces aligned against us; the Bobby was but one, the head of the Society of Anarchists, a group seeking to undermine the whole house. They wait beyond the Green Door, but I had thought to keep you safe within the Inner Chambers. I see now I cannot. Thus, I must send you away."

"Away?" Carter cried. "Away where? For how long?"

"I do not know. Perhaps for many days."

"But why? Have I been wicked? Is it because I took the keys?"

"No. Even with the Master Keys the Bobby cannot easily enter here, not even into the garden. But the gate was left unlocked, and he was invited in. You were the target, you alone. It was not your fault that the keys are gone; you were tempted and I was not vigilant, but there are consequences: I must seek the keys now; they are too valuable. I have forces and armies at my disposal, but still I must be away often, perhaps weeks at a time; I must walk difficult, sometimes dangerous ways. With a traitor in the house, I cannot leave you unguarded; you must leave. We will tell no one where you are, save Brittle. You can always trust Brittle or Enoch. Chant as well. I will write, if I can. If the matter is not resolved, you may never see this house again, unless you become its Master."

"But, am I not to be the Master? I am the oldest."

"This is not a common house. It is not for me to say who will be its lord, though you would surely be my choice; you are your mother's son, and I see her goodness within you. If you are worthy, you will be chosen; the house itself will choose. Murmur has never understood this, though I have tried to tell her often; her hunger for power is too strong. We will speak no more of it. One week we will spend together; I can afford no more, then you must go."

True to his father's word, they spent the week in sport. They held picnics in the walled yard, rode horses across the wide lawns, fished in the wide pond to the west, hunted fowl in the woods to the east, though they never left the yard through the narrow southern gate. They played hide and seek through the rooms of the house and tag amidst the hedgerows. They wrestled on the lawns and threw one another, exhausted, upon the grass. And if a sudden sorrow came into the eyes of one of them, the other teased it away, and they played again. So they gave each other a going-away present.

At the midnight hour, when the week was passed, Brittle woke Carter from a sound sleep, carrying a meager lantern. "Your bags are packed, young master, except for the things you most treasure. Fetch them, for we leave within the hour."

So Carter got his wooden soldiers, his wooden sword, and his small, framed picture of his mother, and put them all with his other things. Then he and Brittle went downstairs together, the lantern making their shadows bob.

His father met them in the drive, and clasped his son roughly to him. "Brittle will drive. You will stay with an old friend of mine. He and his wife will treat you like their own. You must always be careful; if *they* know where you are, they will seek you. Remember I will always love you."

So saying, he kissed his son, helped him into the carriage, and nodded to Brittle. The horses trotted forward, their hooves clopping on the cobblestones. Carter's last sight of Evenmere was the shadow of his father, standing before its great shadow, until both man and house were lost in the shadows of the night.

He would not see it again for fourteen years.

Return

The carriage rolled along the dirt lane, past stands of
hawthorn and larch, rising gradually with the low hills.
Monarch butterflies, big as blowing mulberry leaves, passed
back and forth through the windows, heralds of Carter's return. One stopped to rest upon his knee, and he and Mr. Hope,
the lawyer seated next to him, admired it a moment before it
flitted away. The grass was green; sweet william and alyssum
grew beside the road; it was summer. Carter sniffed the air,
fragrant with coming rain from the clouds building in the
west, breathing in his own nervous excitement.

"The hills look right," he said. "From the time I was old
enough to travel I have searched for Evenmere, both while I
attended Bracton College, and later, while serving as secretary to Kraighten Manor. I've become quite a hiker because of
it. I had despaired of ever returning."

"And your father never corresponded with you, not in all
those years?" Mr. Hope asked. He was young, with a pleasant, round face, dark hair, serious gray eyes, and a short laugh

like a barking dog. They had met only the day before, briefly, in the attorney's office.

"At first he wrote often, weekly at least, but the tone of his letters became increasingly darker; he was traveling, you know, down grim paths. He was . . . searching for something. His last letter spoke of a Great Sea; he said he was considering crossing it, though he knew it would be foolish. It was his final correspondence."

"There are no seas hereabouts," Hope said. "He must have been far away."

"Yes," Carter said, his blue eyes fixed on the advancing storm clouds, but lost in limitless horizons beyond. "Very far."

"Shortly after that, he must have vanished," the lawyer said. "According to my instructions, he has been gone just over a decade. As I said in my office, I was informed by correspondence to deliver you, along with your father's will, to the house. Nothing more was made clear. It is somewhat irregular."

Carter gave a grim smile. "I have discovered, living outside of Evenmere, that much which occurred there was irregular, perhaps impossible. As a child I accepted the amazing as commonplace. Sometimes I think it was all a dream."

"So your guardians never brought you here?"

"Mr. and Mrs. MacDonald were old friends of the family. I think my father must have saved his life at some time, though I'm not certain. They were kind; I love them dearly, but they never spoke of Evenmere, nor even admitted knowing its location."

The road gradually narrowed as old Ransom, who had been Lord Anderson's driver when Carter was small, coaxed the horses up a long hill. Although the countryside appeared familiar, nothing else stirred Carter's memories; truly he had never before *approached* Evenmere, but only left it. So, as they crested the incline, curving round it to the left, passing through a narrow belt of Corsican pine trees, he drew a sharp breath at the sight of the house, standing in the midst of a long heath, surrounded by monstrous oak, poplar, and willow, with birds flying everywhere between the branches and the rooftops, and trains of ivy sweeping up the walls. Tears sprang unbidden to his eyes as he looked upon the skyline of turrets, gables, and stacks, the chimney-breasts and bay windows, the twin mulberry trees beside the front doors, the single lamppost beyond the drive. As they rode, the house unfolded before him, in his mind large as a faerie castle. Time had not diminished its splendor as he had supposed; if anything he saw it with the appreciative eyes of an adult. For the first time he realized it was a truly beautiful pile of building, all masonry, oak, and deep golden brick, a unique blend of styles—Elizabethan and Jacobean fused with Baroque—an irregular jumble balancing the heavy spired tower and main living quarters on the western side with the long span flowing to the graceful L of the servants' block to the east. Innumerable windows, parapets, and protrusions clustered like happy children, showing in their diversity the mark of countless renovations. Upon the balustrades and turrets stood carved lions, knights, gnomes, and pinecones; iron crows faced outward at the four corners. The Elizabethan entrance, the centerpiece of the manor, was framed by gargantuan gate piers and pavilions, combining Baroque outlines with Jacobean ornamentation.

He stepped out of the carriage before it had gone all the way up the drive, so he might approach the manor more slowly. At the main entrance stood the tall, gray marble sculpture of a figure dressed in the robe of a monk, his hood thrown back from his face, his long locks rippling over his shoulders, eyes to the sky, his muscled arms held before him as if he faced a great northern storm, more like a god of thunder, despite the cross hanging from his neck, than a pious pilgrim. Green tiger beetles meandered along the powerful shoulders. Goldenrods grew at his feet. Overhead, the clouds swept across the westering sun.

Returning to himself, he realized the carriage had reached the porte cochere at the main entrance, where a familiar figure stood beside the horses. Removing his hat, Carter hurried toward him, barely containing his urge to run and shout. Neither could he resist throwing his arms around the smiling Brittle, and suddenly bursting into tears. Only Mr. Hope saw the butler squinting hard against the light wind to hold back his own emotions. Patting Carter on the back he said hoarsely, "Now, now, young master. Proper decorum. But it is good to have you home. The boys will take your things."

Carter drew away, slightly embarrassed, but Brittle smiled. "You have grown into a handsome man. I see both your father and mother in you. Come along. You must be tired. If you and Mr. Hope will follow me?"

They walked beneath the cool shadows of the porte cochere, up the marble steps, to the tall, rounded, oak doors. Carter drank in everything—the eight fluted pillars, deep gold as butter, set in pairs; the rough stones and the four smooth steps; the red rose in the blue-stained glass in the fenestra by the doors—yet it was not enough. He could not take it all in. He saw the iron lion-head knockers; the polished, white stone; the glint of a cobweb beside the threshold. They passed into the entrance hall, paneled in mahogany, where Brittle took their hats, then through archways leading to the right, down the transverse corridor lined with flying buttresses with kittens carved upon them, through double doors into the drawing room.

The room looked exactly as it had when Carter had played with his wooden soldiers beneath the French mirrored console, though he had forgotten the magnificence of the ivory plaster on the ceiling, wholly Baroque, fluted, with opulent, dangling pendants, like upside-down towers, swarming Atlantides, seraphs and flowery festoons, with a border of somber ancients peering out from the wall. The golden damask curtains, embellished with deep fringes, matched the chairs and low couches; the carpet was royal blue. In true Victorian style, the room massed its furnishings like a general hoarding for battle, with squadrons of chairs, battalions of occasional tables, regiments of bric-a-brac, and companies of pillows and damask draperies, all bivouacked together in mutual defense.

The only two occupants of the room were Lady Murmur, seated upon a high-backed chair, and a young, blond-haired man standing protectively before her, who could only be Duskin, since he possessed Murmur's hawk nose and the blue eyes of Carter's father. Murmur had aged; her hair was gray now, clipped in short curls. She wore a shimmering, golden gown, with heavy rings upon her fingers and a gaudy diamond necklace. As he entered she rose and embraced him, while his arms remained limp by his side. Dimly, he recognized that once he had tried to love her, because she had been his father's wife, but her cruelty to a little boy had made that impossible.

"It is so good to see you," she said, smiling in her cold way. "You have been gone a long time. A shame that your foolish prank with the keys kept you from seeing your father the last time he was here. I will never forget that day; I think of it now as a farewell breakfast. I think he knew that he would not return, though we did not know, Duskin and I. Still, he told us good-bye for the last time. Duskin, come shake hands with your brother."

Duskin stepped forward warily, as if approaching a viper, not bothering to shake hands, his eyes smoldering. "You were the one who drove Father away. Why did you come back? What do you want?"

"Now, Duskin," Murmur said, "he returned because he was called. Brittle had orders."

"How old are you now, Duskin?" Carter asked. "Fifteen, I suppose?"

"Sixteen last month," Duskin said. "Old enough."

"Not old enough to be civil," Carter replied. "But you won't spoil my homecoming. Many nights I prayed to be brought back to Evenmere." He turned from his half brother as if dismissing him from his thoughts. "Brittle, might I have my old room?"

"It has already been prepared," the butler replied.

"I'm surprised you don't want the Master's chamber," Duskin said.

Carter felt heat upon his face, but he said, "You've learned nothing if you think there is competition between us. If there is to be a Master here again, the house itself will choose. That was Lord Anderson's last words to *me*. For myself, I believe our father still lives. I intend to do my best to find him." He nodded toward Murmur and followed Brittle from the room.

They walked back up the transverse corridor, past the morning room to the right, and the dining room to the left, to the main stair, all of dark oak, with eagles' talons for decorations, and an ironwood eagle with a six-foot wingspan hung upon the highest landing, ready to dive upon any daring to walk beneath it.

As they ascended to the second floor, Carter said, "It seems Duskin is now her sword, while she stands behind, gloating."

"I would not know, sir," Brittle said. "She insisted on greeting you first. Things have been . . . difficult since your father departed."

"Of that I am certain."

They turned left at the top of the stair, down a long corridor paneled in oak, carpeted in vermilion, its rafters wrapped in shadow, that brought them quickly to the familiar door of Carter's room. To his surprise, two old friends waited within. Seeing him, both Enoch and Chant sprang from their seats. The ancient Windkeep defied all propriety by laughing and throwing his arms about Carter. His grin made his olive skin crinkle all around his eyes. "Murmur wouldn't allow the servants to meet you in the drawing room," he said. "She wants us to know our place, so we arranged a meeting here. You look tall. You look handsome. You were scrawny when you left; now you are the brawny one. How are you?"

"Wonderful!" Carter cried. "Especially now, to see all of you. This is a homecoming indeed!" He clasped Chant's hand. "You each look exactly the same. I thought you would be shorter, or older, but you're not."

In truth they seemed wholly unchanged. Chant's hair retained the same touch of gray, while Enoch had always appeared ancient as a great oak and just as stout—his dark eyes were merry as ever; he walked like a young man. Carter scarcely constrained himself from weeping once more.

"Fourteen years is not so long," Chant said. "Not when you live in a house old as time."

"So you still light the lamps each night?"

"Of course." Chant's rose eyes twinkled. *"Then I'll come when I'm a man, With a camel caravan; Light a fire in the gloom, Of some dusty dining room.* As always."

"And you wind the clocks?"

Enoch laughed. "Every one."

Carter sat upon the silk coverlet, stroking it with his hand. "You've left the room the same. I thought it would be altered."

Enoch sat beside him and looked intently into his eyes. "We have been waiting for you. We need you now. Your father has been gone ten years; will he ever return? But the house must have a Master. You have been brought back to see if you could be the one."

"There is Duskin," Carter said.

"Yes," Enoch replied. "Perhaps. He, too, is an Anderson. But things do not work that way in this house, to be passed from father to son. The Master must be worthy. His mother makes Duskin bitter; many years may pass before he learns better. But who knows? You are home! What could happen? Anything!"

Carter looked at the three smiling faces surrounding him. "I have learned one thing while I was away, that the High House is unlike any other. In the outside world, guests do not appear dressed in medieval garb, bobbies all have faces, and houses do not have infinite corridors. I learned not to tell my tales; even my foster parents thought me filled with fancies. Or did I simply dream those things? What is this house?"

"That will be explained," Brittle replied.

"Would you learn it all in a day?" Enoch asked. "It is too long for that. Today you should remember. Walk the familiar ways. See if the house fits you." He pulled a pocket watch from his coat and groaned. "I have clocks to wind; they cannot wait."

"And I, lamps to light," Chant said.

Just then thunder boomed overhead. Brittle peered outside and shook his head. "It will be a great storm tonight. Twilight will come early."

They said farewell and left him to reminisce among his old things. And if they departed abruptly, Carter thought little of it, for he knew they were thinking of his father, and that made the meeting, however joyous, hard as well.

He sighed, opened his suitcase, and drew out four wooden soldiers, a notched wooden sword, and a picture of his mother, all of which he placed on the dresser. Then he lay down on the bed and gazed at them.

Later, he wandered amidst the rooms, looking at all the old things: the picture gallery, with the portraits of the former Masters hung in long somber lines down its length; the conservatory, fragrant with lilacs and roses; the morning room, happy in yellow and gold; the gentlemen's chamber, drab as an old man; the library, ponderous and strange—and all the other rooms, except only the dining room, which he wished to save for later. There was much he had forgotten, and much he saw with new eyes. Most of all, he remembered the last week he had spent with his father. Lady Murmur's words had stung him, yet as he considered, he realized he, too, had said goodbye in those final days. She could not take that from him, not even with cruel insinuations masked behind pleasantries.

Near twilight, he wandered out the garden entrance into the yard. With a trace of anxiety he looked at the old well, slightly smaller than he recalled, its stone worn as ever, the verdigris creeping over its brass plate, and he gave a shiver, remembering the fall, the cold water, and the fear. But he did not dwell upon it long, for he had spent too many happy days in that yard, and his mind drifted toward those times.

Large, sparse raindrops descended as he made his way to the low brick wall. For an instant he was tempted to step over it, to defy the barrier, but instead he wandered into the grape arbor, though not without casting a sideways glance to insure the gate was locked. The wall ascended to meet the top of the arbor, making of the gate a white wooden door. The shading leaves left the arbor in shadow; he could hear the rain pattering against them, soft as angels' feet. He listened a moment, his mind empty and joyful at the same time, watching the water rill down the branches.

Thunder rolled in the distance, and the rain increased. He shivered violently from a sudden chill as he left the arbor and strolled to the porch. Looking back, he saw the dark figure of the Bobby standing beneath the lamppost light, faceless in the obscuring rain, as if he had waited there all through Carter's exile. Sudden anger seized him, that his enemy remained while his father was gone; he wanted to launch himself over the wall, to destroy this evil with his bare hands. But he restrained himself with cold determination, saying softly, "You no longer deal with a boy. I will uncover your secrets." He would confront the horror when he knew what he faced. He glared at his enemy a long moment, then strode back into the house, bolting the door behind him.

Supper that night was a pleasant affair, since neither Lady Murmur nor Duskin joined Carter and Mr. Hope in the dining room. Both sorrow and joy swept through Carter as Brittle ushered him into the room where his father had dined and kept council with numerous lords and ladies so many years ago. He saw with new eyes the splendor of the room: in some remote time the inglenook had been transformed into a formidable construction of white marble, with a tall, fluted arch adorned with plaster grape clusters, a two-foot bas-relief border above it depicting a pandemonium of squirrels bounding between maple branches, and a heavy stone apron below, descending nearly to the fireplace mantel. It made a romantic hideaway beneath, with hooded chimneypiece, patterned tiles, and pre-Raphaelite ladies in Morris stained glass. Two cushioned benches rested to either side of the fireplace, so that one could sit within the nook, under the shadow of the heavy arch. Upon the mantel, carved in wood, was written: "Gainsay Who Dare" above a triple-towered castle with an armored hand holding a sword rising from the topmost turret. The floor was covered with Persian rugs of royal purple, with great golden sunflowers. The ceiling and walls were paneled in ornamental oak, and held a built-in sideboard with a curved top. The rectangular oaken table, with massive clawed legs and a leather edging, seated sixteen. Etchings of little mice scurried around the borders of the crystal chandelier.

Brittle brought him to the head of the table, to his father's black leather chair, but he took the seat beside it. Mr. Hope sat across from him, there being no other diners. They ate a vegetable broth of shredded cabbage followed by center-cut salmon steak covered with a spread composed of fresh herbs, egg yolks, butter, and capers, alongside large loaves of brown bread, and it seemed a better feast than any Carter had eaten since he left.

"A lovely dinner," Hope said, between mouthfuls. "And a beautiful manor as well. I've never seen a house quite as grand."

"Yes," Carter said. "It remains so beautiful and unchanged. Now that I am here, my life away seems a fading dream, as if only the house was real."

"I understand. It is truly compelling; I hope to have time for a full tour before I leave. But Brittle said the will is to be read tomorrow, so I've spent most of the afternoon examining it."

"You sound concerned. Is all in order?"

Hope hesitated as he tore at a loaf. "I *am* somewhat anxious. Before we came, I took it upon myself to check the tax records. They are paid in full, but both the land and the house are deeded to a trust, which makes no mention of your family's name, neither your father, nor his father before him. It's almost as if the house belongs to no one at all, and never has. Don't be alarmed; I'm certain it is nothing, and my secretary is working on it. I was hoping your father's will would shed some light."

"And it doesn't?"

Hope gave his short, barking laugh. "Perhaps I should say no more, but you'll know soon enough. The will allows you and Duskin to remain in the house as long as you desire. It also makes you Steward of the house, 'until the Master is chosen.' That's the exact wording. You have the rights, but not the property. Neither is the Master given title to the house, but is to 'serve' as its lord. Quite unusual. I hope I haven't alarmed you."

Carter smiled. "No. Nothing about this house surprises me. It is very old, and its customs very strange. I am unconcerned."

They sat smoking cigars and talking late into the evening. Carter found William Hope to be much to his liking; he had an honesty, almost a naivete, of thought not normally associated with lawyers. Probably the man could never pursue a successful career because of it.

Afterward, they bid each other good night, and Carter retired to his room. He sat down on the bed where he had not slept for many years, touching the posts and the comforters, taking off his shoes and socks to run his bare feet upon the wool carpet. The thunder rolled outside, the flashes lighting the windowpane. He looked at the scarlet azaleas on the wallpaper, the carved angel on the mahogany fireplace mantel, the saber in the silver sheath above it, and the heavy dresser with the oblong looking glass. He put out the lights and sat in the darkness, listening to the rain beating against the windows, to the creaks and groans of the ancient manor, to the wind rushing through the great trees outside, the old commonplace noises of his childhood. He was home, who had never thought to sleep in this room again.

He went to the window, pulled back the damask curtains to view the storm, and gave a start. For an instant, a face seemed to press against the glass, gone at once, so he could not be certain he had seen it. His first thought was that it was impossible; he was on the second floor and there was no balcony. With his heart hammering in his chest, he moved his head about, seeing if some trick of the shadows had caused the effect. He suddenly saw the Bobby, standing beside the gaslight beyond the yard, looking up at Carter's window, heedless of the rain, his face vacant in the distance, a pale blob beneath his helmet, the lightning flashes turning him all black and white. Carter shivered. For a moment the darkness of the well, the darkness of the Room of Horrors, filled him, an unthinkable terror, like a great pit threatening to engulf him. He gave a sharp breath, almost a sob, and clutched his fist, infuriated by his own weakness. "I never should have returned," he murmured. Then, "I never should have left!"

He forced himself to close the curtains, climb into bed, and pull the comforter around him.

He awoke late in the night, filled with deep foreboding, uncertain for a moment where he was. Recalling himself, he peered out the window; the gas lamp cast its comforting glow across the yard and it had ceased raining, though lightning still flashed overhead. The Bobby was gone. Drawing the curtains, he lit the oil lamp beside his bed and watched its flickering flames cast shadows across the room. The mantel clock said quarter past two.

Although the night was warm enough, he considered lighting a fire in the hearth for comfort, for he found little inclination to return to sleep. As he reached for a candle on the mantel, he pushed against one of the fireplace bricks, which slid in at his touch.

A slow, scraping noise sent him scooting across the chamber and up against the bed, as the entire hearth swung slowly outward, revealing an opening three feet wide and tall enough for a man. Gathering his courage, he lifted the lamp and gazed into a small, dust-laden chamber, empty, with wooden floors and a narrow stair leading upward.

He ran his hands over his face. Three things he feared most, feared them even though he called them childhood terrors not fit for a man: closed places, drowning in deep water, and darkness. Though he remembered little else about it, he knew the Room of Horrors had been filled with Things in the Dark.

"Only a fool would go up there at night," he muttered. But even as he said it, he knew he would do so, if only because he *did* fear it. After a moment's debate, he put on his clothes, drew the saber from its sheath above the mantel, and mounted the thin steps, holding the lamp aloft.

His shoes left tracks in the dust; the stair creaked; the paneled walls ran smooth on either side, unbroken by any design. He felt his heart pounding beneath his shirt, but as the stairs went on and on, the repetition calmed him. He wished, too late, that he had bothered to count the steps.

Eventually, the stair opened directly onto the wooden floorboards of what felt like a vast, empty chamber. By holding his lamp high he could just see the center beam of the sloping roof of a great attic, its walls lying beyond the circle of his light. Boxes and trunks lay scattered across the floor with bits of forgotten finery and ceramic dolls.

A cloud of small bats skittered away from the light, startling him, their soft cheeping loud in the silence, their flapping wings whirling like bolos. He crouched while they passed and waited till the stillness returned and his heart subsided before drawing a deep breath and rising again.

Since he could not pierce the blackness on either side far enough to glimpse a wall, he proceeded straight ahead, the better to retrace his steps by his tracks in the dust. He passed old hats and kettles, brooms and wooden trunks, books written in strange, unrecognizable tongues, and flags from countries he did not know.

He had not gone far before he found the dirt before him disturbed. At first he thought a wind sometimes blew through the attic, but closer inspection revealed an animal print many times greater than a man's. He shivered, then chided himself on his fantasies; no brute so large could live in an attic. Still, it did resemble the four-clawed foot of some beast.

He proceeded again, but halted abruptly, thinking he heard a soft, lowing moan. At the same time, he found another footprint, exactly as the first, spaced to indicate a creature capable of twenty-foot strides.

The stillness of the place rushed into him all at once, and he became aware that he heard neither wind nor thunder, as if the room were cut off from the whole world; he knew if he died there no one would ever know his fate. He started to turn back until he saw what appeared to be a massive piece of fallen sculpture, gray and cold beneath the wavering flame. It had a curious, oily look, and he tapped it with his foot. It was strangely resilient.

Slowly, terribly, the form quivered, unfolding itself, lifting into the darkness, while the floorboards groaned in complaint. A serpentine head, filled with rows of massive, sharp teeth, with red eyes large as his fist, and a flickering red tongue raised itself nearly to the ceiling. He had kicked the monster's whiplike tail, which now slid reptilian across the floor, forcing him to avoid being struck by leaping over it.

It stood on two legs, balanced by its tail, its short, front claws dangling before it. He had no thought of using his sword, but fled across the attic floor, back the way he had come. The beast roared behind him, a sound like a whole jungle howling at once. Leviathan feet pounded at his back.

His flight was a madness, a desperate whirl across that nightmare junkyard. He had a slight lead, and the monster was slow; its footsteps did not sound often, but it covered a great distance with each stride.

He banged his knee against an old trunk, stumbled and nearly fell. Great jaws snapped shut just to his left, crushing the trunk like an egg. He dodged to the right and ran on while the beast worried the trunk.

The respite lasted but a moment before the pounding footsteps resumed. Hot breath blew across his back as he spied the stairwell. He cast the lamp and sword behind him and gave a desperate leap.

He made the last of his headlong lunge in darkness, as the beast trampled the lamp, snuffing it out. Carter's breath was knocked from him as he bounced over the threshold of the stair and rolled down it face first. He covered his head with his hands; the fall seemed to go on and on as he skipped across the steps.

At last, he came to rest, sprawling in blackness upon the stair. He crawled on all fours, twenty steps farther down, then stopped to listen. Above him, the monster shuffled and growled its frustration. Fetid breath blew across him; fire gushed down the stair, a blast of flame falling short by inches, its heat singeing his brow.

He scrambled down the steps, finally pausing to take stock of himself. His shoulder, arms, and ribs were badly bruised, but nothing seemed broken. Pain throbbed through every part of his body, but he was alive, if he could only make his way back to his room.

He cringed as a voice like rumbling thunder boomed down

the stairway. It was a moment before he recognized the words within it.

"Who is the little man who enters my attic, the fillet buttered in his own oils?" it asked. "Speak. Tell me your name, the name of your kin, the name of your station."

"I am . . . the Steward of the house," Carter called, for so his father's will had named him. "Who—what are you?"

"I am Jormungand, the Last Dinosaur, destroyer, devourer, ravager of kingdoms and epochs, all greed and covetness, brooding loneliness. Once I was Dragon, but in this scientific age that is no longer stylish. The flames I kept for high drama. Now I, who was once Behemoth, am only pieced-together bones, first believed to belong to biblical giants, fresh-dug by nearsighted archaeologists, given flesh by faint intellects, made poorer by lack of imagination. But you aren't the Steward of the house. If you were, I would have seen the Seven Words of Power within you."

Carter paused, uncertain where he had heard of the Seven Words before. "I became the Steward only recently."

"A Steward without the Words of Power? A fish in a bucket, a duck in the desert, fodder for your enemies. But you are fortunate. I know the Words well. Come up here and I will teach them to you."

"Perhaps you could tell me while I sit here."

Jormungand chuckled mirthlessly. "Perhaps we could sit together with little pastries and tea and play bridge. And afterward, harmonica on the front porch."

Another torrent of fire poured down the steps, but fell far short of Carter. Through his fear, he faintly wondered why the staircase did not ignite.

"Still there?" Jormungand asked.

Carter lay very quiet, not daring to speak.

"I can see you, unblackened like a missed marshmallow. Conversation *is* a lost art. You're like all of them, skipping up the stair, hoping to steal my hoard of Wisdom, perfectly willing to skewer me for it, cowering when things don't go well.

And what did I ever do to you? I suppose now you'll go whining about your mistreatment. But if you flirt with monsters you should expect an occasional nip on the nose."

Carter crept slowly downward, wanting to hold no more conversation, since it only allowed the dinosaur more time to consider how to reach him.

"Leaving, I see," Jormungand said. "It's been lovely. Come back sometime. Bring your friends. If you have the Words of Power I might even answer questions. If you knew them once, but do not recall, you might look in the Book of Forgotten Things. But if you return without them I will use your bones for those little toothpicks normally found in less-fashionable dining establishments. This is my attic and my kingdom, the dominion of the Last Dinosaur."

Carter heard Jormungand tramp away, his massive frame shaking the whole stair. He made his way carefully downward, feeling as he went. Between his bruises and the blackness it seemed a long age before he finally reached his room, where he groped his way to the fireplace mantel, and with shaking hands lit a candle. He moved the brick that returned the hearth to its original location, then sat on his bed and examined his battered limbs.

Throughout his childhood this had been his room, but in all his play he had never found the concealed chamber. He wondered if it had always been there. With the danger past, the full magnitude of his peril filled him. But even through the fear and pain, a joy like a tiny flame ignited his thoughts, for the dinosaur had reminded him of that forgotten day, so long ago, when he first looked at the Book of Forgotten Things.

He awoke late the next morning to the low rumble of thunder, the soft patter of rain against the windows, and diffused light falling upon the blue comforter. For a time he lay, unwilling to think, watching the curling paint upon the sill, the drops of water upon the pane, the gray moth battling to reach the light outside the glass. Slowly, he recalled his own mad flight across the attic floor and, rising, touched the hidden mechanism opening the passage, to reassure himself of its existence. But he did not dare ascend back up those murky steps.

He dressed and made his way downstairs to find Mr. Hope at the dining-room table, successfully pursuing a quarry of French toast, scrambled eggs, and marmalade.

"Good morning," Hope said. "I must commend the chef. The meals here are wonderful. My father is portly and I'm afraid I've inherited his love of food. I haven't a chance, I suppose."

"I'll join you," Carter said as Brittle appeared from the kitchen, a young assistant by his side. "May I have the same?"

"Of course, sir."

"Brittle, do you know of any secret passages in the house?"

"Passages, sir?"

"Yes, you know. Hidden rooms."

Brittle glanced down at the table. "And did the master sleep well last night?"

"Not well at all. I discovered another outlet from my chamber."

Brittle smiled knowingly. "And you followed it?"

"I did, to the attic. There was something up there."

Brittle's smile turned into an absolute grin. "And you survived."

Carter frowned. "You astound me. I survived by chance, but I don't know what it all means. We need to talk after the will is read."

"All the Masters of the High House have faced a baptism of fire," the butler replied. "I am delighted you escaped." So saying, he turned back to the kitchen.

"He's a bit brisk for a servant," Hope said.

"I've known him a long time. He is more of a granduncle than a butler to me. If he pulled my ears and sent me to my room, I would probably go."

Hope laughed. "Sounds like you had a night of it."

"How long do you plan to stay?" Carter asked. "What I mean is, I know your business is concluded after the reading of the will, but I wonder if you might remain a time? The rain has ruined the roads, no doubt; traveling through mud will be tedious. I could provide a retainer for your time, of course."

"In what capacity am I to serve?" Hope asked. "You speak of restitution, so you offer no holiday."

Carter's breakfast arrived just then, and he buttered his toast before continuing. "I need your advice and your keen eyes. I told you yesterday this house had many strange customs. Could I dare relate a fantastic tale, not just from last night, but from my youth? First, you must agree to stay, a week at least. The roads should be dry by then."

Hope reflected, frowning. "I am unmarried, but I will need to send word back to my office. I love this old house; I have the most marvelous dreams sleeping in it. I find it compelling, both legally and romantically. How could I resist?"

The two shook hands and Carter launched into the tale of his father's many visitors, of the Book of Forgotten Things, even of the Bobby, though he did not mention the creature's lack of a face, and he related his loss of the Master Keys and his being sent away. Then he told of the dinosaur in the attic. The attorney appeared scarcely disturbed by the bizarre story, although Carter wondered if the man wore the same face when confronted by the lies of an accused murderer.

"Can you believe a word of it?" Carter asked.

Hope gave a warm smile. "It is incredible, and I would require tangible proof, but you appear sane enough, and I see no purpose in an elaborate hoax."

"You surprise me, sir."

"Because I concede the possibility of the fantastic? But I have heard utter fancies spoken in the courtroom. And as a boy I observed many things unfathomable to a child; could that not also occur as an adult?"

"You indulge me, surely," Carter said. "I saw it myself, and I scarcely believe it."

"I do not make light of the matter," Hope replied. "I am not a credulous man; remember I have only acceded to the possibility. All my life I have lived by the law. Laws can change from moment to moment, simply by the way they are interpreted by the magistrates. Why should the laws of the universe be any more irrevocable? You tell me you have discovered a behemoth in the attic. However implausible this seems, should I follow you into those upper reaches, I would be unsurprised to discover myself in the verdant forests where such creatures dwell. A matter of interpretation, that is all."

"You have an unusual outlook for a modern man."

"I have simply thought through the ramifications of the law. I tell you, sir, the world is a strange and mysterious place, full of oddity and coincidence beyond the ken of mortal flesh. Why should I be surprised by a dinosaur, when I have been transfixed by the wonders of an octopus, a steam engine, and a sunset, miracles all? Why should I debunk magic, when I have gaped at the enchantment of clouds billowing unsupported in the sky? Is a tree, a splayed wooden stick with the appearance of an upside-down root covered with green fur, a credible thing? Keep an open mind—there is my motto. I consider a giant lizard hardly less likely than that a house should have no owner, though it *has* been owned for many decades, or that a will be drawn which gives away nothing."

"Thank you for giving me your trust," Carter said with a relieved smile. "Can you also give me counsel?"

"I might suggest we poke around the library after the proceedings, to see if we can discover any old records concerning the mansion. There seems almost a conspiracy of silence among the servants. We need to know more."

"I would be grateful," Carter said, feeling he truly had an ally.

The reading of the will proved a dreary affair, the only ones present being Hope, Carter, Lady Murmur, and Duskin, while

Brittle bustled in and out, bringing tea. As the attorney had said, the document made Carter Steward of the house until a Master was chosen, a wording that troubled both the lawyer and Lady Murmur greatly; Mr. Hope because it was vague, the lady because she had wished for more.

"Is there nothing for my son?" she demanded, while Duskin glared at his half brother. "Is he to live in the house at Carter's discretion?"

"The document is specific," Hope said. "Both the Anderson sons have the right to dwell in the house, but the Steward controls its assets. The method of choosing a Master is not specified. I can only assume there is some unknown mechanism for doing so, one that might eventually surface. I intend to research the matter further."

"Perhaps you will, and perhaps another attorney should be summoned," she said. "You seem to know Carter too well."

"Madame," Hope replied. "If you insinuate tampering, it is preposterous. This document, along with several others, was deposited with our firm nearly a decade ago. I am a junior partner at Dyson, Phillips, and Hope, having worked there only six years, but the facts are attested by my associates. Mr. Carter and I met day before yesterday. Do you deny that this is the signature of your late husband?" He held the document up for her inspection, while she squinted down the planes of her sharp nose.

"I deny nothing!" she said, rising to leave. "See that you do, indeed, 'research the matter further.' We will await your results. Come, Duskin, let us return to our rooms."

Duskin followed his mother out, all anger and malice.

"She seemed unsurprised that your father made no provision for her," Hope said, once she was gone. "He left her entirely at your mercy. You could have her removed."

"Yes, but my father loved her for a time, though I think he knew at the last what she was. And Duskin is my brother. She has poisoned him to me already. Why repay evil in kind?"

"Quite right," Hope said, rubbing his hands together, as if

cleansing them. "Best to take the high road. And with that task done, perhaps the library will offer some clues."

They left the dining room, and passed down the transverse corridor to the tall doors of the library, which were made wholly of heavy oak, with such herds of seraphs and hippogriffs circling their embroidered edges that it took the servants a whole day to polish them. Despite the weight of the oak, at the turning of the jade knobs the doors swung easily on soundless hinges, revealing the room Carter had always thought the most mysterious, misty gray as a marsh, the watery edges of its walls borders he had often approached as a child, but never quite reached. Heavy carpet, all russet cattails on olive fronds, ran between the stacks. A small sitting area lay to the left of the entrance, its verdant couches stretched long and sporting carved hunting hawks arching down mahogany armrests. Gray dolomite pillars supported the low ceiling there, which was also gray with tendrils of yellow and brown. Beyond the couches Carter saw the narrow door that led into the chamber of the Book of Forgotten Things.

Past the sitting area, tall oak shelves formed intricate mazes on the main floor. Beyond these, a curved staircase led to a gallery, also filled with bookcases, bordering all four walls of the upper story.

"Formidable," Hope said. "Or perhaps I should say ephemeral; it doesn't seem quite substantial."

"There is a card catalogue," Carter said. "But what exactly are we looking for?"

"Clues as to the traditions of the house, specifically the way the title is passed down. I need to find the legal section."

The card catalogue was thirty feet of dark cherry. Hope quickly identified several volumes and the two men wandered the aisles to find them.

Walking amidst the stacks was like plunging into jungle shadows, with the slow running of a stream, the cries of birds, the lowing of oxen, the stamping of warrior feet just beyond hearing, and dark leather all around. The pungent odor of books surrounded them, old, forgotten, ponderous with words, deep antiquity in rectangular form. Carter saw a centipede flowing across the carpet.

"Odd," Hope said, stopping before a section with FICTION carved upon the top of the shelves. "Everything is out of place. The legal books are here." He searched a time before choosing a tall, moldering tome.

Carter, who had moved farther down the aisle, gave a chuckle. "You should see the HISTORY section. *Vathek* by Beckford, *The World's Desire*, even the *Orlando Furioso*, fantastic books all. Why, here's even the dreaded *Krankenhammer* of Stefan Schimpf, the mad cobbler of Mainz, a book of magic outlawed in most countries. Bad filing, you think, or an odd sense of humor?"

As Carter scanned the misplaced editions, he saw a small gold book wedged between a pair of larger volumes, with the prestigious title: *The High House, Evenmere, Being a Genealogy and History From Its Founding.*

"I might have something here." He took it and sat in a red velvet chair, in a small alcove built into the nearby shelves, with a modest desk and a green lamp overhead.

"I'm going to poke a bit farther on," Hope said, disappearing between an opening in the stacks.

Carter's excitement on finding the book lessened when he discovered the chronicles ended more than a hundred years before his father's birth. The genealogical list, though dull, was of amazing length. The names and the history proved enigmatic, the events and references being of an obscure nature, although he did find mentioned the *Tigers of Naleewuath* and the *Master Keys*. But mostly the book told of the times when the Masters of the house were summoned to various countries to perform inexplicable services. It reminded Carter of the strange folk who used to visit his father, dressed as if from another age.

Pondering the volume, thinking of the past while the soft lapping of water trickled unaccountably at the edge of his hearing, brought a heavy drowsiness upon him, made worse by his previous sleepless night. His head soon drifted to the top of the desk; the book fell from his hands. His last conscious thoughts were that there must be a fountain somewhere in the room.

Dreaming, he raised his head and found himself still at the desk, although the dimness had given way to a soft mist high up on the paneled ceiling. He looked down at the table, where the book lay open to the last page, and saw his father's signature upon it, proceeded by a brief history.

"Why, that wasn't there before," he said.

"Of course not," Brittle said, causing Carter to start. The butler stood slightly behind Mr. Hope, both men looking down upon him, their faces waxen pale. "It was not there because you are only dreaming now," Brittle continued. "You fell asleep on the table. Yet, we are all here together."

Carter looked around, perplexed and suddenly suspicious, uncertain if people in dreams say you are dreaming. He shut the book quickly and stood. "Perhaps I should read this alone."

"Very well," Mr. Hope said. "A most interesting dream. I think I will poke about a bit." Turning, he walked into the dimness between the shelves. Brittle had vanished as well.

Carter tried to leave, but discovered the library all changed, the bookshelves no longer in neat lines, but at various angles, more a maze than before. He walked a short distance, turning right, then left, following the labyrinth until he reached a dead end. An ominous whispering fled around the shelves, but when he looked, he saw nothing but the books. The sound grew louder until he could almost understand it, and he became afraid. There was something menacing about the way the bookcases leaned toward him, threatening to pounce.

With the logic of dreams, he decided to push the books off the shelves and make his way out of the library by crawling between the spaces. He withdrew a handful of volumes at eye level.

The blank face of the Bobby stared at him from the other side, a white emptiness without eyes, nose, mouth, or ears. Carter bellowed in surprise and fled back against the shelves.

"Come to me," the Bobby said, low and earnest. "Join us. Or do you want the Room of Horrors again?"

Carter rushed back down the rows of books, the whispering all around him. "Join us," it said. "Join us or die."

He tried to turn a corner, banged into a shelf, and fell to his knees. Far away, he thought he heard the growling of a large animal, a hunting beast. Looking up, he saw the bookcases changed, half-organic: leaves branched from the volumes, moss grew down the tops and sides of the shelves. *A jungle of books*, he thought, rising to run again.

Around the next corner he found Brittle stalking along the aisles, poking between the books, a bright sword in his hand. Gold specks danced on its point.

"What is it?" Brittle demanded, seeing Carter's expression.

Carter halted. "Didn't you hear the noise? The Bobby pursues me. Come with me."

Brittle stood and listened. "It is very faint to me. And it is hard to see as well. They are controlling the dream, but they won't have it all their own way. You should hurry."

"Come with me," Carter urged again.

"Not yet. You go ahead. Find Hope. He is in danger as well."

Carter paused, confused. It *was* a dream, wasn't it? It even *felt* like a dream. Yet, he could not escape the inordinate sense of fear. What was the saying, that if a person dreamed they were falling and hit the bottom before they awoke, the shock would really kill them? But who had ever hit the bottom and found out?

He continued down the maze, turning right, left, then right again, nearly colliding with the man waiting for him, a long knife in his hand, the very same man who had helped abduct him many years before.

"Been looking for you," the man said.

Carter backed up, while his assailant followed. Reaching to the side, he grasped a book and threw it with all his force, striking his opponent in the forehead, sending him reeling. Carter fled once more down twisted aisles resembling more and more a wildwood; branches drooped from the ceiling; bird calls filtered down through heavy foliage.

He turned another of the endless corners and found Mr. Hope standing perplexed.

"Carter, what the devil is happening?"

Carter had no time to reply before one of the bookcases toppled toward Hope with a loud rumble. He yanked the attorney away, saving him from being crushed as a whole row of shelves fell in domino fashion. Out of the dust and rubble, Brittle came running, brandishing his sword before him.

"They are right behind me!" the butler cried. "Continue ahead! Seek the second floor; there is a door to the north."

From behind the fallen bookcases came the Bobby, the other man with him. A large black beast proceeded them, like a great cat, but a shadow creature with a continually shifting form. The chandeliers rattled as it roared.

"You can't stay here!" Carter cried.

"Someone must hold them off," Brittle said. "You are the one they want. Hurry!"

Carter turned, Hope with him. He thought himself a coward, leaving Brittle like this. But wasn't it all a dream? They rushed down the aisle, dodging and turning through the maze. They had gone no more than fifty yards when they heard the scream of the dark animal, this time crying in pain, and Brittle's ancient voice, shouting, "For the High House!"

A thunderous crash followed, and then silence. Carter and Hope kept running, straight into another dead end. They exchanged frightened stares. Hope was dripping with sweat, looking terrified; Carter was certain he looked the same.

"Over here," a gruff voice said.

A center section of one of the bookcases slid forward, opening like a door into a dull, shadowed chamber. Within it sat a lanky man wrapped in penumbra. Even in the darkness, Carter saw his clothes were old, mismatched like a vagabond's. His face remained hidden by the wide brim of his stovepipe hat. The collar of his patched coat hid the rest of his features.

"Who are you?" Carter demanded.

"The Face Outside the Window. The Thing the dog barks at in the night, which it cannot see. I am the Thin Man. In here, quickly."

Despite his reservations, driven by need, Carter followed, Hope behind him, and the door slid into place at their backs. The stranger held a tiny candle, which barely illuminated the way before them, revealing a rounded tunnel, with a stair angling upward.

"Where are we?" Carter half whispered.

"Headed away," the Thin Man replied.

They climbed one flight of rickety steps, but then descended as if toward the basement. Carter wondered if he could defend himself in this narrow way if the Thin Man meant them harm.

They came to a door, and the stranger grasped Mr. Hope's sleeve. "You go through there," he ordered. "You will be safe."

Hope looked at Carter and licked his lips. "This is just a nightmare, isn't it?"

Carter attempted a smile. "Yes, I suppose it is."

Hope disappeared behind the door. The Thin Man led Carter farther along to the end of the stairs, into a vaguely familiar room.

"I will leave you now," the stranger said. "You should be fine."

"Yes, thank you." He turned to look around, but when he turned back, the Thin Man was gone. "Where are you?" he cried. And though he had vanished, his voice echoed in the room, as if far away: "Happens this way in dreams."

Part of the wall slid outward, revealing an opening. To

Carter's shock, he found himself back in his own room, entering from the fireplace again. Yet, the staircase had led down, from what should have been the attic, not up from the library. He pressed the brick that rolled the hearth back into place. A great weariness was upon him, despite his fear, and he lay upon the bed, intending to close his eyes only a moment.

A loud knocking on the door roused him from sleep. He stood groggily.

"Just a dream, after all," he murmured, relief sweeping over him.

As he went to the door, he abruptly halted, for if this were a dream, why hadn't he awakened in the library, instead of in his own room?

He opened the door cautiously and found Mr. Hope looking grim.

"Something wrong?" Carter asked.

"You better come down. It's Brittle. In the library. He's been murdered."

The Tigers of Naleewuath

A hard rain fell as they laid Brittle to rest in the servants' portion of the ancient cemetery south of the house. All the staff was gathered around: the housemaids, ladies' maids, the housekeeper, valets, butler's assistants, cooks, the groom of the chamber, footmen, ushers, the hall boy and others, some gaping, some weeping, some biting their lips so as not to weep. Most of the grave markers were modest, but a marble statue of a young boy stood in the center of the stones, his hand above his brow, as if gazing into the distance, and though Carter thought its significance obscure, it gave him comfort to look upon it, and there were flowers on many of the graves. The mounds were nearly level, for no one had been buried there in many years. Brittle's marker was unassuming, for Enoch said he would have wished it so, and it bore the words *Trusted Servant*, and gave the date of his death, but not of his birth. Carter asked Chant about that, but the lampman said, "No one really knew when he was born, he had no kin, and no one would believe the number of his days, anyway." Since Chant was sometimes poetic, Carter asked no more.

Others attended the service, a mysterious assortment of strangers in all manner of garb, from light armor to long robes, as if they had stepped from another century. Many spoke languages Carter found unrecognizable, and made mysterious, holy signs over the coffin. Over two hundred mourners assembled to honor the humble butler and Carter was both touched and amazed that so many had come.

He stood with Duskin and Lady Murmur to his left, Chant and Enoch at his right, beneath the sheltering pavilion, as the minister, who must have traveled a considerable distance to reach the house, said the final words. Enoch wept openly as the wooden coffin was lowered into the ground. Carter dropped a handful of mud into the hole, and moved away, misty-eyed, nearly stumbling against Duskin on his way out. His half brother's eyes were red from weeping—a momentary rush of sympathy ran through him—he had known Brittle until he was twelve, but Duskin had been with him all his life. He glanced at Murmur. If there was moisture on *her* cheeks it was from the rain.

Mr. Hope approached, extended the cover of his umbrella, and shook Carter's hand. "A terrible blow. I'm sorry. Can I walk with you back to the house? An awful day for it— stormed ever since we came, hasn't it? We could all use some hot tea."

They made their way across the small hill toward the manor, the others following after. Carter walked with his head down, feeling the rain, the storm, and the heavy weight of Evenmere upon him. It was late afternoon; the clouds hung nearly to the ground; all the world lay shrouded. He thought it fitting.

"It's probably a strange time to mention it," Hope said, "but I've had no chance to speak with you since the murder. Did you . . . by chance . . . I mean . . . well, did you happen to have a dream about any of this?"

Carter stopped, turning sharply toward him. "I did! I've been trying to put it all together."

"As have I. I fell asleep in the library; at least, I thought I was in the library, though I awoke in my own room. I failed to mention it at first. I think I was afraid. I wondered what the police might think. But then, the inspector was an unusual man; I never quite caught where he was from. We should compare notes."

"But not alone. As soon as we are warm and dry I want the two of us to meet with Enoch and Chant in the drawing room. It is time I learned what the High House is about. I think they know."

Standing by the hearth, Carter warmed his hands and studied the intricate pendants of the plaster ceiling, which trembled with each roll of the thunder. The meeting had been postponed until after dinner, and night had fallen before the four men gathered together; the gas lamps cast shadows thick as rough wool, which wrapped around the light like east-end thieves. Enoch sat in the high-backed chair; Chant sprawled across the golden sofa. Mr. Hope stood in the center of the chamber, as if in a courtroom, and was just finishing his tale, following Carter's own account.

"Then, this 'Thin Man' let me into my room. I lay down on the bed and was almost immediately awakened by one of the maids. It had the unreal quality of a dream."

"Yet we shared the same dream," Carter said.

"A premonition of Brittle's death?" Hope asked.

"No, not at all," Chant said. "It was more."

Carter turned. "You must tell us."

The lampman glanced over at Hope. "It may be too much for an outsider."

"I have hired Mr. Hope to counsel me on these matters," Carter said. "I did so because everyone here is unwilling to speak. Tell us."

Chant looked at the floor.

"Were we the Master, to presume on Brittle's position?" Enoch asked reluctantly. "It was his place to show you these things. That is why they killed him. Who knew more about the house? Only your father."

"They have many powers, the Society of Anarchists," Chant said. "In the past we have been protected; they could not come here. But now, though it takes great strength to do so, they have entered the library through your dreams. It shows how vulnerable we have become."

"What is it all about?" Carter said. "If I am to help, I must know. What is the High House?"

"A poem," Chant said. "A mystery. A Force of Nature. All of these and more. *I stretch lame hands of faith and grope, and gather dust and chaff, and call, to what I feel is Lord of all, and faintly trust the larger hope.* Do not look so. I am answering as best I can. But Enoch is older. Perhaps he can say it better."

The old man sighed and stared into the shadows and the fireplace; the sound of the burning logs mingled with the patter of the rain against the eaves, while the angels in the architecture bent their heads above the men, quite frightening in the darkness, all shadows and staring eyes. Carter cast an anxious glance around the room. As a child he did not recall being bothered by the weight of the gloom.

"My story is the only one I know," Enoch said, his swarthy features deepened by the night. "I was born, son of Yarad, six thousand years ago in the country once named Aram. You would call it Syria. As a young man, I used to walk with the Lord God among the fields and forests. Do I deserve that look? Such things were common in the Old Days. And I know what you are thinking: what was He like? Don't ask. I can only tell you He was beautiful. We would talk. Mostly I listened, which is a good thing to do when you are walking with God. People lived longer then, and one day, when I was three hundred sixty-five years old, we strolled until the evening. The stars came out, the pearls of heaven. I suddenly thought:

I am far from home. My feet are sore. I should have thought of this. The Lord looked down at me and said, 'See, your house is far away, but Mine is near at hand. Come stay at My home awhile and I will give you work to do.'

"So He brought me here, and showed me how to wind the clocks. Then He went away. And not a word since." Enoch shrugged. "Maybe He is too busy. I miss our talks.

"The house was different back then. The styles changed; the architecture changed. But one thing is the same: it is His mechanism. He uses it to run the universe, and the clocks must be wound and the lamps lit, or it will All run down."

"And I thought Chant a poet," Carter said. "So the Bobby and his brood wish to replace order with anarchy?"

"Do not be deceived by their name," Chant said. "The anarchists use order or chaos at need, for the universe requires both and they must remain in balance. The anarchists oppose the *idea* of the universe. On the surface, they seek power, but they are the Great Destroyers, and our real enemy is Entropy. Sometimes, if I cannot light a certain lamp, or if Enoch cannot reach a clock to rewind it, then suns perish and segments of Creation die. *The bed was made, the room was fit, By punctual eve the stars were lit.* The anarchists will do anything to master the Balance. What they cannot control, they will destroy."

Carter and Hope exchanged skeptical glances. "Here, Mr. Hope, is a behemoth even you may have trouble swallowing."

The lawyer smiled. "Yet we have dreamed of faceless men, and death has passed from sleep into the waking world."

"But what are we to do?" Carter asked. "Can they assault us anytime we slumber? How will we rest tonight?"

"I do not believe they can reach us so easily," Chant said. "The library is a most unusual place; it is their beachhead. There, they focused their powers, causing both of you to fall asleep so they could enter your dreams. Apparently, Brittle was caught in it, and was probably their true target. But I think we will be safe in our beds this night, so long as we are far from the library."

"Why Brittle instead of me?" Carter asked. "They have made attempts on my life before."

"The High House will have a Master," Enoch said. "Perhaps you; if not it will choose another. By killing Brittle, who could have taught you much, they have delayed us. They want to overwhelm us before the new Master is ready."

"Then I must learn what I can, as quickly as possible. But one thing still troubles me: how did the Thin Man transport us to our rooms? And why?"

"The why is simple," Chant said. "To take you beyond the anarchists' control, so you could wake."

"Yes," Enoch said. "That must be true. And I have known Masters who possessed the power to enter the world of dream and to transport the physical body along the paths of the dream self. It is difficult and seldom done, but perhaps this man has the talent as well."

"Intriguing," Mr. Hope said. "We must learn more of our unknown benefactor."

A knock sounded on the door just then, and a hall boy, made timid by having to perform the butler's services, entered and bowed.

"Sir, there is a man named Duncan to see you. He was at the funeral today."

Carter looked at the others. "Send him in."

The man entered, a stout fellow, with eyes cat-green in the firelight. He wore a dark coat, black trousers, and carried a black hat, clothes too fine to suit his weathered face and hands. He was surely older than fifty, and he looked miserably uncomfortable.

Giving a half bow with his shoulders he said, "I'm Duncan. I've come from Naleewuath."

Carter started, not having heard that name since the day of his kidnapping. Looking closer, he thought Duncan might appear familiar if fifteen years were taken from his face. Rising,

Carter shook his hand and introduced the others. "I believe I remember you, sir. Did you not visit my father?"

"I did. Many years ago. You were only a lad." The man warmed slightly. "You favor him."

"Sit down. Tell us why you have come."

He took a chair across from them, facing the fire; the dancing flames made crags of the planes of his face. He smelled vaguely of cedar.

"Perhaps you remember our story, then," Duncan said. "Every few years, the wild beasts become too many in Naleewuath. Sheep begin disappearing, and if it isn't stopped, then children. As we came to your father and your father's father, we come to you now, asking your aid. Bring those you can and help us, as agreed in the treaty between my people and the Inner Chambers."

Carter sat silent so long Duncan grew nervous. "My lord, is there anything to consider? We have promised fealty to you in return for your protection. Will you come?"

"Forgive me," Carter said. "The name of Naleewuath stirs old memories indeed. The tigers—"

"Yes," Duncan said. "Several handfuls of them. You must come."

"You realize I am only the Steward, not the Master of the house?"

"But if there is no Master, the Steward must do. We have waited longer than we should, during the time when there was neither Master nor Steward, while your father was away. It seems he is dead; someone must perform the task. Will you come?"

"I will come," Carter said softly, remembering how his father always said those same words before donning his heavy boots, his Tawny Mantle, and his Lightning Sword; and taking up his gnarled walking stick.

"I thank you, lord," Duncan said, rising from his chair. Carter shook his hand once more, and saw him out the drawing-room doors.

"Was that wise?" Hope asked. "With all our troubles should you be going off?"

But Enoch beamed and said, "Maybe we will have a Master, after all."

Carter was too lost in his own thoughts to reply. Without information, without skill, knowing nothing of how his father would have conducted such a mission, still, his heart beat hard against his chest. He was finally going to hunt the Tigers of Naleewuath.

But that night, when the others had gone to bed, doubt guarded the gates of his slumber. How could he hunt in Naleewuath when he did not possess even his father's Lightning Sword? Near midnight, filled with resolve, he rose from his bed, lit a candle, and left his room, padding down the hall past mirrors and statues with gray, glistening eyes. Flashes from the endless storm, bursts of light and dark, lit the benighted house, baring furniture lurking like wild beasts. The stairs creaked beneath his feet; the thunder rolled in the distance; a brilliant flash revealed the taloned eagle, shaped from wood, squinting down upon him from above the landing. He took a deep breath and descended, feeling the familiar banister against his left hand. Traversing the transverse corridor, he made his way to the library, where he opened the great doors with some trepidation. The clatter of the knob made an awful commotion to his own ears. He stood at the entrance and listened. The weight of the cavernous room flowed over him, air currents smelling of old books, musty as the opening of an Egyptian tomb, all dust and antiquity, deep velvet silence. His courage failed him; he longed to flee back up the stair, so that he hesitated, indecision lapping round him like deep water. Yet that same fear drove him onward; he would never surrender to it, for he knew he had walked these same corridors many times as a child, with the same frightened thoughts, and always he had persevered against them, even after the Room of Horrors.

He crept into the chamber. Lightning against the upper windows outlined the bookshelves, monstrous and hulking, grown clever from the knowledge resting on their shelves. He avoided looking upon them, but walked quickly to the four-paneled door beside the study. A thin lance of light slipped between the frame, causing him to think someone waited within, until he recalled that the lamps had been lit when he and his father entered long ago; perhaps they remained perpetually so. Still, he turned the knob half expecting to encounter an intruder, perhaps even the Bobby, sitting at the desk.

The door opened with a creak; the room lay empty. The buttercup lights burned their soft song and shadows slept where their rays did not reach. The room remained unchanged from his recollection of it: the royal blue carpet with gold fleurs-de-lis, the kidney-shaped desk, the leather chair. The stained-glass angel looked down from the ceiling, muted except when the lightning flashes revealed him as a fiery avenger, grown terrible in the midnight hour, his golden hair transformed to silver, his face like a son of God. Carter's wonder of it had not abated with the years.

He ran his hands along the mahogany panels, over the white marble fireplace. Reaching into the desk drawer, he retrieved the skeleton key and opened the bookshelf doors; their blue, leaded glass glistened with the lightning. Slowly, reverently, he withdrew the leather book lined in gold leaf. Old memories rushed to him as he sat down in the chair and laid it upon the desk.

He feared this book. As he had grown older, when he thought of it at all, he had convinced himself that his first encounter had been a childhood illusion. Now, holding it before him, he was no longer certain. He exhaled softly and his hands trembled as he turned past the cover page. He thumbed through the leaves, but saw nothing until page six, where a picture faded into view of him and his father riding horses across the low hills. He wore red riding boots and an ivory jacket. Lord Anderson, going slightly before him, turned back and sent him a quiet grin.

"I had forgotten this day," he murmured, smiling to watch the younger version of himself, riding beside his father, laughing, enjoying the wind and the rough clatter of the horse's hooves. Almost, he felt the cool breeze upon his face.

The vision faded. Carter sat silent a moment, warmed by his father's voice and the look of his eyes.

Recalling his mission, he reluctantly turned to the next page. There, written in gold, were the Words of Power, but to his surprise there were not seven, but only two.

He said the first one, softly, rolling the r's across his tongue as his father had taught him. *Rahmurrim.* The gold letters burst into flame but were not consumed; the heat of the burning warmed his face. He spoke it again, slightly louder, and felt it brand itself into his mind. He would not forget.

He spoke the second, *Elahkammor.* Again, the letters flamed, again the majestic release of power flowed through him, and then the characters went cold, and he found himself utterly exhausted, filled with such weariness as if he had carried heavy sacks all day. The Words were there, but they had taken their toll.

He started to shut the book, but a strong desire to look upon the next page made him pause. It had been good to see his father again.

Slowly, he turned the page, not without effort, for it felt leaden. A vision came almost at once of great darkness. He was in a room, though he did not know how he knew, since it was completely obscured. From a long way off, a white figure approached, and a terror preceded it. Carter suddenly knew it had a face too horrible to look upon, so frightening he might die to see it. As it drew near he saw its head was shrouded in a white cloak, yet gradually, with studied movement, it removed the shroud and raised its visage toward the dim light. Though he did not want to watch, Carter could not turn away.

He gave a shriek and the vision vanished, leaving sweat beading his brows. "Room of Horrors," he murmured, slamming the book shut.

"There is worse," a voice beside him said.

He shouted and leapt up against the wall, clutching the book, ready to batter his way past whoever stood between him and the door.

"No need for violence," the stranger said. "I saved you once, didn't I?"

Carter hesitated, his fighting instinct nearly overwhelming his reason, until he recognized the figure as the Thin Man.

"What do you want?"

The ragged man moved away from the door to a less threatening position along the wall, his face submerged in shadow, always outside the circle of lamplight. "We need to speak. You barely escaped with your life before. If not for Brittle and myself . . . ."

"I never thanked you properly," Carter said.

The man raised a hand, almost violently. "Do not bother. It was probably wasted effort. You play the fool, coming into the library late at night, where your enemies have already struck once."

"I assumed they had withdrawn."

"Assume nothing!" the man cried. "A fine disaster, this, a boy made Steward, without training, without hope. They will tear you like wolves. If you value your rescue, then grant my request: leave this house, and take your half brother with you; he, too, is in danger. If you abdicate, another will be appointed. You do not have to follow this road."

"How can I abandon my childhood home? The responsibility is mine. And more, I want to discover my father's fate. I cannot leave. But what is your concern with this? Who are you?"

"For now, a friend. If you stay, I will oppose you if I can. Go away. Your father is dead. Go away."

"You know this?"

"He is dead. Heed my warning. Leave Evenmere."

Carter looked down at the Book of Forgotten Things. "How can you be certain he has perished?" But when he glanced up, the Thin Man was gone and the four-paneled door stood open just a crack. He flew to it and flung it wide, but could see nothing in the cavernous murk.

Thunder rolled overhead as he put the book back in its resting place, locked the cabinet, and dropped the key into the desk drawer. His candle had burned low; he had been within the book much longer than he imagined. Shaken, he made his way back into the library, resisting an urge to run as he crossed to the double doors. Down the transverse corridor he went, up the stair, and into his own room, where he bolted the door behind him. He sat down on the bed and shivered, awash in questions and doubts.

He slept poorly that night, and dreamed of the Thin Man and the Bobby chasing him through endless halls. But these dreams were no more than dreams, and he woke with the morning sun, thinking he had not slept at all.

When he made his way downstairs an hour later, he found Mr. Hope already awaiting him, looking as bleary-eyed as Carter felt. They dined together in the breakfast nook, on the round, claw-footed table with gulls carved around its border, on wooden plates and pewter goblets, with silver spoons etched with butterflies. The nook looked west through a long picture window, and there were patches of sunlight between the clouds; the rain had abated, though it appeared it might soon start again. Carter told the lawyer of his midnight trek to the library.

"The motives of this Thin Man bear studying," Hope said. "He saved our lives, yet he threatened you. We should be wary of him. For myself, I've spent the night reading. After leaving the drawing room, I had Chant escort me to the library, where I found a few books large as houses on treaties and compacts. Duncan said there was an agreement between Evenmere and Naleewuath, so I thought I should look it up. Seems there are *hundreds* of treaties between Evenmere and Everyone. You, sir, are the Last Baron in the world, judging by it. Within those volumes I found oaths of fealty, treaties of mutual defense, trade agreements—all with places and peoples I had never heard of: Gwyve, Naleewuath, Keedin, Westwing, Aylyrium, Ooz—scores of others, some exotic, some not. It is like a secret kingdom, vast as all the world. But where are these places? Where is Naleewuath, in fact? You speak of dinosaurs in attics; I speak of nations."

Carter raised his eyebrows. "It explains my father's visitors all those years. But did you find the Naleewuath treaty?"

"I did. It is quite specific: we promise to come when called, and they agree to be part of the White Circle, a ring of defense surrounding Evenmere, comprised of kingdoms bordering the house, and participating in a mutual defense pact. The most interesting thing is that the treaties were signed not just by your father, but by Brittle as well."

"Brittle?"

"There's much you don't know about the man. I had the opportunity to poke about when Enoch was helping to dispose of his personal belongings. He lived four lifetimes, at least, or I miss my guess. He held five degrees, was knighted by Queen Victoria, fought in two wars, was ambassador to Japan—the list goes on. If he was only a butler, then I am a dentist."

Carter leaned back in the chair, his breakfast growing cold. "I did not know. Brittle could be articulate when he wished. What do you propose? Should I consult Jormungand once more? The thought terrifies me."

"I wouldn't advise it, not yet. Let me attempt to research the dinosaur a bit before you risk your life. I think you should go to Naleewuath, to find out where in the world it is. The need is urgent, and Enoch has already said he knows the way.

Meanwhile, I want to try to contact some of those in the White Circle, to see if they can protect us from whatever killed Brittle. Perhaps Chant can help with that."

"So you won't accompany me to Naleewuath?"

"I want to," the lawyer admitted, his eyes shining. "It sounds exciting, but I should remain here. You need information and I feel pressed for time—whatever struck at us may return. At any rate, you have more the physique for hunting wild game, but eventually I would like to witness evidence of these wonders firsthand; the dream was convincing but something more tangible would be appreciated. Perhaps you could show me the dinosaur."

"Perhaps," Carter said, laughing, "though I fear he might eat you."

After breakfast, Carter discovered preparations for his journey were already under way; it seemed several of the servants would accompany him as they said they had done with his father. Though Enoch would lead the way, he could not stay to help in the hunt, for he had clocks that would not wait. Carter was given a pearl-handled pistol unlike any he had ever used, a single-action similar to the designs of Mr. Colt but far heavier, so that it was necessary to grip it with both hands to contain the recoil; a heavy cloak, and a four-foot spear with wide, ornate guards meant to halt the charge of a wild beast.

"Will we carry rifles?" he asked.

"You will not go through wood or marsh," Enoch said. "This is all close work. Jorkens knows his way about Naleewuath and will be your best guide."

Enoch indicated a tall, slender man with a ruddy complexion, who was tossing gear into a pack.

"I am ill-equipped for this," Carter said. "I have hunted small game on my foster parents' land, but nothing of this sort."

The burly man nodded heavily. "But do not forget: it was

in your father's blood; it is in yours as well. And remember this is no sport, but to rid Naleewuath of the most terrible of beasts."

They left soon after, a party of less than twenty, Enoch at the lead, Jorkens beside Carter, all marching swiftly to the back of the house. To Carter's surprise they went directly toward the door beneath the servants' stair. Chant waited for them upon the fifth step, and leaned over the balustrade to say, "*And sometimes for an hour or so, I watched my leaden soldiers go, with different uniforms and drills, among the bedclothes, through the hills.* Good hunting, my lord. And remember: *The graves a fine and private place, but none, I think, do there embrace*, so be careful." He gave Carter a wave and a wink as the Steward followed Enoch through the door, into the room he had not seen in over a decade. As always, the lamp within was lit, and Enoch proceeded directly through the Green Door, which had apparently remained unlocked from the time Carter had taken the Master Keys those long years before. Tears of shame sprang unbidden to his eyes as he stepped through the portal and stood once more in the misty halls, as gray as he remembered them—the gray pictures of gray flowers on the gray walls meeting the gray carpet, the ceiling hidden in fog. It even smelled gray, like smoking ashes. Enoch led them to the right, down the wide corridor. Once again, as it had been those long years before, Carter experienced pain and shudderings all over his body, as if he were being remade. The grimaces of his companions showed they suffered as well, and all paused until the aching passed.

"This is the Long Corridor," Enoch said.

"Well named," Carter replied. "How far does it go?"

"How far does a circle go? It loops back upon itself and has no end," Enoch replied. "Only it will not always be so colorless. It connects all the members of the White Circle. We are in the Great Block of the house now; the smaller portion we left is called the Inner Chambers."

"What lies beyond the White Circle?"

"Other kingdoms and countries, some loyal to Evenmere, others not. The White Circle is the heart of our strength."

"And if the anarchists could seize the Inner Chambers?"

"It would still not be enough. Their road to power requires more. But the loss of the Inner Chambers would be a bad blow. It is the core of the High House."

"Am I foolish to leave when we are so endangered?"

Enoch laughed softly. "And if you stay, what will you do? If you are to be the Master, you must act the part. And a Master is needed now; we have been too long without one."

"Last night the Thin Man found me in the library, and warned me to abdicate my claims and leave the house."

"You went to the library? Brave, but foolish after Brittle's death. Who is this Thin Man to tell you your place? I do not know him; Chant does not know him. Why should we believe his words?"

"Was my father a happy man, Enoch? Would he have wanted me to be Master? I think his life was very hard."

"Happy? He was a great man," Enoch said. "Great men often suffer. Sometimes they fall the farthest. But he never turned from a task that was his. Neither would he want you to. If you do not try, if you turn away, you will sit in your dusty chair in your old age and say: 'Ah, what could I have been? What did I miss?' Evenmere is a grand adventure, after all, and you were ever curious, poking here and there, looking for who knows what. How could you leave?"

Carter smiled, buoyed by the Windkeep's words. "It's true. I have certainly always longed to see Naleewuath."

They passed down the gray passage until noon, when they stopped to eat lunch beside one of the brick fireplaces scattered along the corridor, this one having a stone bench beside it. Carter and Enoch sat together, while the other men rested on the floor, their backs against the wall, eating bread and cheese. The walls were not so gray now; little patches of color appeared in the paper, which had tiny, light orange zinnias upon it, and the carpet was almost peach. After a short rest, they continued throughout the afternoon, until Carter's feet ached from walking. All the color had returned to the passage by the time they came to wide double doors, opening onto a large chamber. A portly man and two stout lads, all dressed in green, bowed as they entered. The man said, "Welcome to Halfway Hall. Ansbok at your service, sir. There are rooms to the sides to refresh yourselves. Dinner will be ready in one hour."

"They knew we were coming?" Carter asked.

"We sent word," Enoch replied. "These halls are spread throughout the Long Corridor, for the benefit of travelers."

"Like inns," Carter said.

"Yes, but tonight, this will be reserved solely for us."

A great fire burned in the hearth, sending goblin shadows large as horses prancing across a room lacking windows for their escape. Plaster gargoyles and gryphons peered down from the rafters of the high-beamed ceiling. A table sprawled like a dragon the length of the room, ending at the mouth of the fireplace, which was carved like a bear's head. The oak floors were pocked by dancers' heels; the air smelled of oil, deep and thick, and women's curls on winter nights. It was a dark hall, warm and comfortable as house shoes.

Carter retired to his room, made elegant with heavy oak furniture and a canopied bed with more gryphons carved into the posts, their claws outstretched. He found hot water for washing in a basin, steaming water for bathing in a tub, and a change of clothing lying across the bed, including a pair of gray boots, silken soft on the inside, scarcely heavy, but of stout leather without. He bathed and changed, finding the boots so perfect a fit he wondered if someone had measured his foot while he slept.

One of the lads called him to supper shortly thereafter, and led him back into the main hall, to a chair set at the center of the table, made more ornate than any of the others. Ansbok bustled about, talking to the lads in a soft, firm voice: "Young

Swelter, bring venison for the Master. Yanuk, fetch more bread. Nothing must be cold."

With Enoch, Jorkens, and the others around him, Carter ate a happy feast beneath the gryphons' wings. In his soft, rumbling manner, Enoch told tales from long ago, some he had known, and some he had lived. Carter had heard many of them before, while walking with the Windkeep as a boy. Hearing them again, in his friend's rich accent, he saw the wind in tall fields of wheat, the sunshine on antediluvian plains, the heavy timelessness of water and stone, and recognized what he had overlooked as a child: the utter antiquity of Enoch's tales, the names of Akad and Sumer, Elam and Nod, as if the man truly came from a time when Nimrod the Hunter was young, and Baal Puissant was worshiped in the High Places.

When dinner was done, they sat around the fire, but not too long, for all were weary. Enoch blew smoke from a red pipe, carved slender and small, and the scent of tobacco, fragrant as Eden, filled the hall. For the first time in a long while, Carter felt a great contentment. After basking in it a time, he stood and stretched, thinking he must either go to bed or sleep in the chair.

"Will we see Naleewuath tomorrow?" he asked. "And the tigers?"

"Naleewuath? Yes," Enoch replied. "We will reach its borders by evening. The tigers? Not till the following morning. We have been on the Gray Edge today, no one's kingdom at all. Tomorrow we will pass through little Indrin. The hunt, it worries you?"

"A bit."

Enoch's eyes grew grim. "When the beasts come at you, their roars freezing your bones, you must act all by instinct, to fire or stab. Do not let the terror seize you. There is only a moment, for your very life."

"I will try to remember," Carter said. But that night, though he knew the next days might be treacherous, he went quickly to sleep, content to be on his way.

The following day's journey was much like the last. They met a few other travelers passing down the Long Corridor, dark men in dark robes carrying ebony staffs; and once, a fat ancient pulling a little cart, who offered to sell them jewelry from Westwing and scarves from Kimmunkissee.

After a time, the passage gradually widened. The zinnias on the wallpaper slowly changed to deep green leaves and the carpet darkened from peach to dusk gold, with patterns like autumn leaves scattered across it. The light lessened until they proceeded through a half twilight. In the dimness, Carter's eyes betrayed him, so that the leaf patterns on the floor and wall appeared real, as if the branches of trees extended into the passage.

To his wonder, he gradually became aware of the noise of the crackling of crushed leaves beneath his boots, and he bent down to retrieve a golden maple leaf, its capillaries brown, its edges crumbling. Branches descended from the ceiling ahead of them, which lay once more in shrouds of mist. Water dripped from above and light fell in square patches, as if from unseen skylights. He touched the branches on the wall, then turned to grin at Enoch.

"Yes," Enoch said. "The border of Naleewuath."

"How is it possible?"

"You want to know how, you should have asked Brittle. Perhaps he didn't even know. Much is possible within the High House; it opens into worlds, and parts of worlds creep into it. I am just the keeper of the clocks."

They reached a fork in the corridor and passed to the right between a pair of tall arches adorned with life-size statues of tigers on either side, and snails drifting between the green ivy growing at their base. The tigers' teeth and claws glittered in the twilight, and Carter suppressed a slight shudder. Beyond the arch was a rectangular room, with two doors on each of its three walls. A willow grew in its center; thin slits of sunlight fell between the branches.

"Here we camp," Enoch said. "All of Naleewuath is like this, small rooms, close for fighting. We could go farther, but we are less likely to meet the beasts here."

They cast their blankets beneath the willow and made a fire in the small hearth. From the packs, Jorkens produced enough food for a banquet: slices of beef, green vegetables, even warm tea. They ate on the ground, their blankets spread beneath them.

"We certainly dine well," Carter said. "It is nearly a picnic."

"Such is the way in the house," Enoch said. "But once we reach the beasts, that will be no picnic. No picnic at all."

They spent the evening inspecting their guns and gear, and talking, as men are wont to do when they have too much time. At last, the sunlight haze dimmed above the trees; the lamps were extinguished; the fire popped its final rounds and dwindled to a soft glow. A chill came upon the air, and the company cast their blankets around them and fell into slumber, leaving one to watch.

Carter dreamed uneasy dreams, of falling leaves and gray halls, and giant voices calling down from a limitless ceiling, so that he thought himself in the library again, pursued by goblins and tigers, and someone calling his name. He woke with a start and found himself lying on his back, looking up at the willow's branches, like clawed hands reaching over him. He sat up and glanced about, but all remained quiet save for the sounds of the men's breathing; the sentry sat hunched in his cloak against the tree, looking half-asleep himself. Yet far in the distance, Carter thought he heard the dream voice still calling his name, just at the edge of hearing, intermixed with the sounds of distant waterfalls. He rose and walked to the doors, thinking it came from the middle one on the east wall. He opened it softly and slipped inside.

A narrow corridor awaited him, all ivy along the rose walls, with wooden floors and a single gaslight at a distant door. As he took his first step, he was startled by the sentry's touch on his arm.

"Your pardon, sir," the man said. "It's best not to walk Naleewuath alone at night."

"Do you hear a voice?"

The man listened carefully. "I've heard nothing during my watch. If you want, I'll wake some of the others and we can have a look."

"No, let them rest. I'd like to walk at least to that next door."

The man looked uneasily back at his comrades. "Then I'll accompany you, sir. We should only be a minute."

The light flickered and the boards creaked as they passed down the hall to the door, which proved to be farther away than it looked. The voice sounded louder to Carter now.

I will not play the fool, he thought to himself. *We are still within shouting distance of our camp and if there is danger beyond the door we can retreat.*

He gripped the knob firmly and gave it a turn. As if he had pulled a lever, the floor suddenly dropped from beneath them, plunging them into blackness. They managed no cry, for they landed immediately, with their breath knocked from them. Even then they did not come to rest but found themselves entangled together, rolling down a steep chute. Carter struggled, but could not reach the sides to slow their descent.

They slid into an area lit by lamps, and struck the bottom with a crash. Both men rose slowly, battered and breathless.

"Are you injured?" Carter asked.

"I don't believe so," the man said. "You?"

"Bruised, but unbroken." Carter looked around at what appeared to be a drawing room, with a heavy wooden mantel, long bookcases, and the largest sofa he had ever seen, stretching half the length of the room, all mottled green, like a reptile, with massive clawed feet. The other furniture was just as large: an armoire ten feet tall and nearly as wide, with wooden pegs like bulldog's teeth; a French buffet, ponderous and square, yet petitely legged as a great spider; a lamp with a shade like a Mexican hat and a base round as a Buddha. Despite his fall, he was immediately struck by the incongruity of the ghastly furnishings, for none went together, nor were they all meant for a drawing room.

The other man gripped Carter's arm. "I don't like the looks of this. Best we climb back up."

The armoire, standing to their left, made a sudden, swift movement. Carter did not see it change, for it happened too quickly, but it transformed into a lumbering beast, its arms large as wooden posts. The sentry pulled his pistol, but the monster knocked it from his grasp, and him to the ground, as it pushed itself between the men and the chute. A blockish head had formed from the center of the armoire doors, and it looked more animal than wood now, with glinting yellow eyes above a square snout, huge, flapping ears, shoulders no longer square but just as massive, its clawed feet true claws. Carter reached for his own pistol, but a hand like a wrapping tendril took it effortlessly from his grip. He turned to see the couch transforming, its figure a rapid blur as it rounded to serpentine slender. Hundreds of arms, writhing like snakes, and dozens of eagle-claw legs, sharp-tipped, shining like adamantine, bulged from its frame. When done, it had grown a blunt nose, thick, grinding teeth, and a snake's tongue, flicking like fire in the light. The tendrils held both men in a heavy grip.

The French buffet came skittering beside them, wholly spiderish, with dark fur, long quivering fangs, and multiple eyes. The lamp strode forward on two rounded legs, its shade a horned crown, its porcelain skin pearl beneath the lights, its eyes and grinning mouth the color of blood.

"Has 'em," the couch hissed, tongue gliding in and out. "He the one?"

The lamp reached to touch Carter's face with hands pudgy as blubber. "It is, Taka. The Master's son. Hold very tight."

The serpent squeezed Carter's breath from him. "Do we eats?" it asked.

"Foolish to eat!" the armoire boomed, sniffing the other man with its long nose. "You know bargain. Bobby wants 'em."

"Bobby no friend of ours," the spider-buffet said, its voice feminine, liquid haunting. "Let me wrap 'em."

"No wrapping," the lamp insisted. "With this one gone and Bobby's help, we own all of Naleewuath."

Other smaller beasts crept around the men's feet, umbrella holders and ottomans like dachshunds. A thing resembling a huge tomato worm, two feet long, slid around Carter's shoe, leaving green slime across the carpet.

Far away, a door slammed.

"Hear it?" Taka, the couch, hissed. "The Bobby, he comes. Wish I could eats 'em."

Carter closed his eyes, trying to shake off his panic. The Bobby would arrive in moments to kill or imprison them. Cold sweat ran down his back as he thought of the Room of Horrors. He could not reach his weapons; the tendril arms wrapped him like rope.

He recalled the two Words of Power he had learned from the Book of Forgotten Things. He had not understood their meaning as he read them, but now one came to his mind, burning brightly upon the page, lit with a flame that did not consume, and he knew it as the Word Which Brings Aid. He had only to speak it.

He opened his mouth, but no sound came. He coughed, tried again, and failed. It was not that he could not speak; it was the Word itself that denied being spoken—it was too powerful, too full of meaning; it would not pass the lips. He saw the truth of the old expression that words were power, and the right words, used at their proper time, were potent indeed.

A door opened at the far end of the drawing room, the Bobby silhouetted against the light from beyond, his rounded helmet a bullet upon his head.

Carter closed his eyes, knowing instinctively that once he was in his enemy's hands, all ability to use the Word would be lost. He searched within himself for the strength of will to speak, the will his father had surely possessed. He wished someone had taught him, even as he knew it was not a thing that could be taught, but must be found. He brought the Word burning to the forefront of his mind, held it there a moment, then opened his mouth, willing it forth with all his heart.

"Elahkammor!"

It boomed, low and powerful, granting his voice a vitality it did not normally possess. The monsters gasped and hissed and cringed at it. The tendrils constricted around him until he could not breathe.

"Not say it!" the serpent cried. "Not say Terrible Word, or I eat 'em."

Carter looked around. The last echoes of the Word had dissipated, yet nothing had changed. He did not know what he had expected, the death of his enemies perhaps, the appearance of the angel on the stained glass, sword in hand. The Bobby strode chuckling across the room.

"We have 'em for you," the lamp said, teeth bared in a dog's grin. "Bargain finished."

"It is indeed," the Bobby said, standing before Carter, his faceless face more horrible than ever, his mouth visible only when he spoke. "Why were you fool enough to return? We will have more fun. Unpleasant fun. I will send you back to the Room of Horrors."

Carter said nothing.

"Yes, the Room of Horrors again. I see the fear of it in your eyes. There is a way out, of course. You could swear fealty to the Society of Anarchists, change sides, become one of us. We have great power. Under my tutelage, you could rule the High House in a new way. Nothing would exceed your grasp. You could wield the Power your ancestors never dared use, re-make Evenmere in your own image, do great good. Don't look so surprised. You must listen to me. We are involved in a war against powers and complexities you cannot understand. Good, Evil, Chaos, Order, Entropy, these are only words. You think us faceless bombers, madmen bent upon destruction. There is more. The anarchists wish to tear down, it's true, but only to rebuild, to create a better house. Has it never occurred to you that all the universe is wrong? Haven't you felt it? The world is full of pain, sorrow, injustice. Children go hungry; the poor remain poor while well-meaning governments stand helpless, their leaders corrupted by the love of power and material gain, controlled and coerced by those seeking the acquisition of wealth through hypocrisy, cunning, or brute force. If things were better managed, such indecencies would never occur. We seek not simply to annihilate, but to escape from the bondage of time itself, to give mankind the chance to control its own destiny. Imagine, a world where the ravages of the years caused no harm, where corruption befell no one, where death was abolished, where no accident ever harmed man or beast. A world of flowing rivers, endless summers, never the dropping of a single leaf. Where greed would not win the day, and capricious fate have no hold. A planned world, wholly devised, patterned for the good of all. A universe without ugliness, where all were truly equal not just in vain prattle, but in every way—equal in love, temperament, beauty, intelligence. This house holds the power to arrange it so. We will have to destroy much, rebuild from the ground up, but when we are done, time and space will do our bidding. We are called anarchists, and rightly so, for we rage against the injustice of the universe, against God Himself, if you will, and this reality where so many have suffered so long. You could aid us. Join our cause! Fight no more for the balance, the status quo; be bold, innovative, seek a new thing. Those who are rebels today can become the Founding Fathers of a new age, the patriots of eternal justice. Will you be one of us? Against us, you have only the Room of Horrors; with us you have ultimate authority. Make the pledge and I will set you free."

"Don't listen to him, my lord," the other man said.

"Silence!" the Bobby hissed, thrusting his blank face before the man's eyes. The soldier quailed, and the Bobby turned back to Carter. "This has nothing to do with your servants. I offer you only one chance. Otherwise, we travel back down the Dark Stair. And there is no one to rescue you now."

For a moment, and only a moment, Carter was almost persuaded by the Bobby's idealistic fervor, for he had indeed thought the anarchists mindless zealots, intent on destruction for its own sake. In that instant, they seemed the most humane of men, holding a way of escape against the dread of the Room of Horrors, which filled Carter so that he would have promised anything to escape the rising nightmares, the images he had fought to forget, the memories he had forced to retreat, the visions long locked in the deepest vaults of his mind. Almost, they overwhelmed him, made the Bobby's words reasonable. But in the midst of his despair, his utter capitulation, he recalled the sight of his father, standing at the shattered door, holding the Lightning Sword aloft, calling his name.

"You are wrong," he said softly, though his voice trembled. "You cannot do evil in the name of good and expect it to stand. I will defy you."

Before the Bobby could reply, a door sprang open to the left and there were instantly tigers.

They slid into the room in one continuous string, tall, sleek beasts, orange and white striped, whiskered and long-fanged, green-eyed like jade, ferocious and wise. Power rippled across their shoulders, down their lean frames, through their supple flanks. Like kings of the earth they came, all lightning war, dancing claws, darkling rage. One pounced on a yelping footstool, splitting it like a tomato. Another leapt across to the armoire, ripping it from throat to shoulder. The spider-buffet skittered up the wall and out the back door, followed quickly by the porcelain lamp.

Carter was flung across the room and slammed against the far wall. By the time he could sit up, the room was a fury of animals. Taka was centipede-sliding out the far door, while tigers tore at his back. Two of the great cats rolled over the carpet, wrestling with a love seat. The Bobby had somehow vanished completely. Those pieces of furniture unable to escape were caught in a rapid slaughter. One of the cats pounced on a nightstand sliding by Carter's feet, forcing him to hug the wall to avoid the tumbling teeth and claws.

He drew his pistol and kept it close, though he could not see a proper target. The last of the furniture monsters gave a final, perishing cry; the cacophony died; the room fell silent. Carter glanced around, wary, expecting the tigers to turn on him next. He found his companion sitting on the floor a few feet away, dazed, and he was just edging toward the man as another of the side doors flew wide, and Jorkens and Enoch burst in, followed by the entire company.

"Beware!" Carter cried. "Go back!"

But Enoch grinned broadly and hurried over. "Are you injured? You look unharmed."

The great cats, more than a dozen in number, sat staring at the men, and the men stood staring back. Then the largest of the tigers, a tremendous creature with a long scar down his left side and two white spots upon his breast, raised his head and roared, shaking the room with the sound. Carter quailed and raised his pistol, but Enoch restrained his hand.

In answer to the tiger's roar, Jorkens lifted his head and gave a howl of his own, like a wolf, then laughing, approached the great beast, holding his arms bent at the elbow, palms upturned. The tiger placed his massive paws upon the man's hands, claws sheathed.

"Mewodin, you old rascal!" Jorkens cried. "As usual, you're right on time."

"I cannot take credit," the tiger spoke in a voice between a growl and a purr. "We were summoned by a Word of Power. I heard it in my den; we came swiftly. Has Master Anderson returned?"

Enoch led Carter to the great cat. "Not the father, but the son," he said. "Mewodin, this is Carter Anderson. Mewodin is lord of the Tigers of Naleewuath."

The tiger looked at Carter with wise jade eyes, and gave a bow of the neck. "I am honored, young master. But if you are going to shoot me aim for the chest."

Carter looked down and saw he still held his pistol in both hands. He put it quickly away. "S . . . sorry. Pleased to meet . . . I mean . . ." Exasperation took him. "Don't we hunt the Tigers of Naleewuath?"

A shocked silence followed. Jorkens turned pale and several of the men stood openmouthed. Then Enoch began a soft, deep laugh from behind closed lips that grew until he held his sides to contain it. Mewodin watched a moment, turning his head from side to side as if to comprehend, and then a low, rumbling laughter erupted from him as well. Then everyone began to laugh, while Carter's face reddened to crimson.

"Where in all the White Circle did you get such a notion?" Enoch asked.

"But . . . but, my father," Carter said. "He said he went to hunt the Tigers of Naleewuath."

The laughter gradually subsided. "No, young Master," Enoch said. "He went to hunt in the land of the Tigers of Naleewuath. Did he never tell you? The tigers help us hunt the gnawlings, the chameleon beasts you saw here. When their numbers grow too large, even the tigers must have help. They are natural enemies, and when the gnawlings are not surprised as they were tonight, they can even slay the great cats."

Carter looked at Mewodin. "I must apologize," he said. "I did not know. I have been . . . away from the house a long time."

"We are all kittens at times," Mewodin said, his green eyes

unreadable. "But the night is not yet old, and men prefer to sleep in darkness. Let us return to our places. Tomorrow we will speak."

Carter gave a slight bow and the cats slipped from the drawing room in a long, sleek line.

They awoke the next morning before sunrise, and Carter soon found himself, sleepy-eyed, standing with several of the men around the hearth, warming his hands and sipping hot tea. Enoch departed after breakfast to wind his clocks, leaving Carter in Jorkens's keeping. Still embarrassed by his behavior from the previous night, he determined to keep silent and learn the ways of the hunt. Duncan, the man who had originally requested Carter's aid, soon arrived with a handful of men, this time dressed not in gentleman's garb, but farmer's breeches, looking much more comfortable because of it.

"Thank you for coming, my lord, you and your men," Duncan said. "Last night a full-grown steer was killed. The gnawlings grow too bold."

From Duncan's maps Carter saw that Naleewuath was not all house, as he had begun to believe, for Evenmere opened out onto wide terraces beyond which lay fields and hill country. He learned that most of the people lived in the house itself, much as men dwell in towns, though there were always a few who built their homes upon the hillsides. Still, they would not hunt the gnawlings in the open; the creatures' dens lay in that part of the house called the Low Cellars. It would be close work.

The tigers appeared, thirty-eight in all, and Carter thought them thirty-eight works of art, beautiful, noble, posed like velvet statues, sitting on their haunches, lying down to lick their paws, stretching their tawny shoulders, yawning like cubs—the younger ones pouncing on one another, the older ones king-eyed, seeing everything, scenting the air with a delicate lift of their noses, rumbling their excitement for the love of the hunt. In changeling form the gnawlings were shells of wood and cloth, but in their true shapes they were meat and bone—most excellent fare for a tiger. The gnawlings had not always dwelled in Naleewuath, but had been introduced by the anarchists, who had given them their chameleon abilities. But the tigers had taken what was evil and made a meal of it, which had only strengthened their treaty with the folk of Naleewuath, for they not only kept the gnawling numbers down, but had more to eat and were less likely to snatch a sheep or cow.

Two days earlier, the tigers had driven any stray gnawlings down from the hills into a part of the house called the Puzzle Chambers, a vast array of small rooms, with doors all interconnected, forming a maze. The hunters would begin there, driving the gnawlings through the rooms, down into their dens in the Low Cellars.

The company made its way down a lengthy corridor, where the walls and the forest became even more indistinguishable.

"Are all the countries of the White Circle like this?" Carter asked Jorkens. "The outdoors and indoors all mixed up?"

"No, sir. Naleewuath is somewhat unique. It is the tigers that bring the magic, they say. And that is all any man knows of it."

At last they came to a large chamber with booths set up in long aisles. There congregated the short, stout peoples of Naleewuath, the women in long robes, their heads covered, with gold rouge upon their eyebrows and dark sienna on their pouting lips, the men in breeches and woolen shirts—their passions close to their faces—all scowls and loud laughter, bawling voices and bursts of song, selling eggs, tomatoes, bread and fish, goats and beans, leather and iron. They displayed brilliant quilts made on tall looms, silver rings shaped like frogs, beetles with agate and malachite for eyes, and clever wooden toys.

"It looks like a market," Carter said.

"That it is, sir," Duncan said. "Naleewuath is a little country. We are not soldiers and the Farmers' Association is the closest thing we have to lords. This is where we bring our goods, and we sell little to anyone but ourselves, except for jade and copper to Indrin and Nianar. Beyond the booths, we can show you the Terraces, if you like."

"Very much."

They passed between the rows of stalls, through another corridor into a narrow room opening onto a balcony. Carter stepped through the double doors, unprepared for what lay beyond. Beneath was spread a fair green country, all long, terraced hills. The sky looked very blue after his long stay indoors, and he blinked against the rising sun. He stood midway on a high wall, gray and cracked with age, with other balconies both above and below him, and the whole countryside stretched before his face. Oaken stairs led down from each of the balconies into that fair land. Of one thing he was certain— this country was nothing like that surrounding the main portion of the house.

"It's beautiful," he said.

"Yes," Duncan said. "Almost a paradise, if not for the gnawlings."

Eventually, they returned back to the house, with its leaf walls and trees, and sultry sunlight dimly permeating the mist, yet Carter now knew there could not be skylights above them, because of the upper stories, so he thought it must indeed be enchantment as Jorkens had said. The trees grew thicker as they passed through large chambers more like forests than halls, but after a while the rooms became smaller again, and the light less diffused, leaving shadows everywhere. Patches of gray plaster ceiling became visible, and they walked in a wildwood twilight, all ginger and dry leaves, with hulking furniture scattered against the walls.

"How can you tell a gnawling from an ordinary hassock?" Carter asked.

"It is in the way they don't move," Jorkens said. Seeing

Carter's look, he said, "No, sir, I do not jest. Regular furniture merely sits, but gnawlings have a way of sitting still, a sort of quivering. You will learn to recognize it."

The Puzzle Chambers were all their name implied, hundreds of interlocking rooms, never more than fifteen by twenty, with a door on every wall. A long, narrow corridor bordered the rooms, and the men and tigers drifted down it and waited before dozens of doors, the tigers roaring, the men's feet tramping on the floorboards.

"The gnawlings are within," Jorkens said. "As we hunt them we will drive them toward the Low Cellars. They've no other way into the house, except through these rooms, and we won't let any slip past. The men are ready."

Mewodin came bounding up. "The Tigers of Naleewuath are ready. We begin at your command." His eyes gleamed with an excitement Carter found disquieting.

Carter brought his pistol up and clasped his spear. He felt a momentary dread in his stomach, but said, "Let the hunt begin."

Jorkens made a gesture, the men opened the doors all along the corridor, and the tigers sprang into the lead. Carter and Jorkens, preceded by Mewodin, entered their first room, while the men poured in behind them. The chamber was dim and Carter squinted at the furniture, looking for any sign of the "quivering" Jorkens had mentioned, but he saw nothing.

He now realized why so many men were needed, as they divided into three groups, each opening one of the three remaining doors out of the room. Carter stayed with Jorkens and Mewodin's party as they exited into a chamber quite similar to the first, and equally unoccupied. In such a way, the men splintered off, until Carter found himself alone with his two companions and Duncan, but to right and left he heard the opening and closing of doors, so that he knew all the parties now moved straight ahead, assured of comrades on either side.

The next hour was a tense affair, Jorkens opening the doors

ever so slightly, and Mewodin sniffing through the crack before bursting into the room, claws unsheathed. Yet, they saw no gnawlings, and Carter began to think they had all escaped.

But finally, as Jorkens eased yet another door, Mewodin gave a low growl; Duncan hissed through his breath and clutched his pike. The tiger sprang into the room, slamming the door against the wall with his weight, and Jorkens followed after, pike and pistol ready. As Carter entered, he heard a low squealing and saw Mewodin pursuing a small scurrying thing, little larger than a dog, that bore a resemblance to a night stand. It scrambled up a bookcase like a monkey while Mewodin pounced furiously after, stretching on his back legs to reach it. He missed the creature's mahogany tail by a fraction. The prey lurched to the top of the bookcase, leapt to the doorknob, opened it with a swinging motion, and slid inside. The tiger followed, as men shouted in the next room.

Carter was about to follow, when he glanced back and saw a flowery fainting couch trembling as if in an earthquake. He gave a shout to Duncan, who stood between him and it, and the man turned just in time to meet the monster's assault, as it transformed into a tawny, pouncing beast. Duncan blocked its iron claws from his throat with his pike, but was thrown against the wall by the force of its charge.

Without breaking its stride, the beast bore down on Carter. Barely, he brought his own pike into line, as the gnawling leapt half the length of the room. Its green-gold head filled his sight: long ripping fangs, slavering mouth, blood-red eyes. He was driven off his feet as it impaled itself upon the pike right up to the guards. It bit at him, inches from his face, even as it died on the edge. Its gore spilled down his legs; its claws vainly batted the air; its last breath, the stench of rage, blew into his nostrils, making him gag. He kept the beast from him with all his strength, until it was finally still. Jorkens helped him rise.

"Are you hurt, lord?"

He stood stiffly, inspecting himself. "Bruised only, I think. Where's Duncan?"

The farmer rose, grimacing in pain. "It . . . knocked the breath from me," he said. Then recovering a little, he looked gratefully at Carter. "You saved my life."

Mewodin bounded back into the room, proudly shaking the dead monkey-thing between his teeth, but he dropped it when he saw the slain gnawling sprawled upon the pike, all flower-scaled like an alligator.

"A great feat, young master," the tiger said in admiration. "This one will make a good rug for your drawing room."

All day they hunted the gnawlings through the Puzzle Chambers, and often the dealings were close, though never so near as that first encounter. Mewodin dealt mostly with the larger beasts and Carter quickly learned that the pistol, which he had considered his first defense, was not so at all; the quarters were too close, and he feared shooting either his fellows or the tigers. Though they slew several gnawlings that day, they met none as large as the alligator-thing, though other members of the party did.

After several hours, they entered a final door opening onto a landing, with a long stair leading downward to the Low Cellars. They descended, following steps that twisted and turned. It was an evil path, all dark wood and carved gargoyles, marred by slime and the bones of the gnawlings' victims, which were mostly animal, though some looked dreadfully human. Carter was reminded of his descent to the Room of Horrors.

At last they came to a red painted door, eight feet tall and nearly as wide, with a red eye carved at its center.

At Jorkens's order, the men distributed torches.

"The rest of the beasts have fled down here," Jorkens said. "This will be harder labor, and less certain, for it is a lightless place. We must fan out in a straight line across the room, and drive our prey toward the far walls. The tigers will go in front. Pistols are useless so put them away. Keep your pikes before you."

"Are you ready, my lord?" Jorkens asked.

Carter clutched his pike. "I am."

Jorkens grasped the knob and tried to turn it. His face went pale. "The door is locked, sir," he said, looking at it in bewilderment.

"You must use the Master Keys," Duncan said.

Carter's face reddened. "I do not have them. They were lost, several years ago."

Duncan grimaced. "I had heard stories, but I didn't know they were true. Only the Master Keys can lock or unlock these doors. Then the anarchists have them?"

"They do," Carter said.

"Then they are learning to master them," Mewodin said. "It must be a hard thing for them, for the keys would not easily bend to the will of such men. The gnawlings are safe from us then, and can strike when they wish."

"Can't we force the lock?" Carter asked.

Jorkens looked at him, obviously astonished. "You must recall, sir, no force on earth can budge a door secured by the Master Keys."

"What will become of Naleewuath?" Duncan asked, his face white.

"What will become of all the High House?" the tiger said. "Is anything safe from the anarchists now, young master?"

"I do not know," Carter said. "But I intend to find out."

It took two restless, dispirited days for Jorkens to lead the company back through the winding passages out of Naleewuath into the Long Corridor, through the Gray Edge to the Green Door into the Inner Chambers. As he looked upon the stains on his cloak and boots, Carter knew he had walked in the footsteps of his father, who had often come home looking the same. But Lord Anderson had always had an air of triumph about him, where Carter knew only defeat.

Both Chant and Enoch were upon their rounds, but Mr. Hope met Carter in the dining room, and together they dined on roast fowl, butter and bread, strawberries and potatoes, all tasting like dry dust in Carter's mouth. When he was done telling of the hunt, he said, "Will I never cease paying for the one crime of an errant child? When I took the keys I meant no harm, yet it was an arrogance far beyond my years."

"No," Hope said. "It was only a childish act, such as all of us have done in our boyhood. It is true the consequences are greater, but you had no way of knowing that. If I may say so, the fault lies with your guardians, even your father himself. To forbid a boy entrance through a particular door is to guarantee he will seek it."

"I have to find the Master Keys, you know," Carter said. "I need them, along with the Lightning Sword and the Tawny Mantle if I am to fulfill the office of Steward. There is no other way."

"I thought as much myself, though how you will obtain them, I don't know. But I have spent my time trying to rally help. You recall my mentioning a White Circle? Chant knew a little about the matter, and with his help I sent out messengers seeking to speak with the representatives from the surrounding kingdoms. I hope that was all right; I felt a need for haste. From what you tell me of Naleewuath I must assume all these countries border the house. Of course, that is impossible by natural laws; it is as if a whole other world opens out from the Green Door."

"It does, from what I've seen."

"Then perhaps our allies can help us, both in protecting ourselves and in finding the keys."

Carter sighed. "I don't know. Father must have commanded every resource at his disposal in his search, and he found nothing. Still, you've done good work. Ten years have passed; perhaps we will succeed where he failed."

Carter retired to bed early that night, worn thin with worry and labor, and fell immediately into a restless sleep filled with gnawlings and tigers. He woke early and came downstairs to find the servants looking very grave. Mr. Hope met him at the bottom of the steps.

"Is something wrong?" Carter asked.

"It's the Green Door," Hope said grimly. "It has been locked from the outside. The anarchists are gaining more power over the keys."

Beseiged

Enoch came weeping down the stair, great racking sobs that shook the banisters and resounded all the way into the breakfast nook, where Carter, Hope, and Chant, still morose at the locking of the Green Door, ate a meal of despair around the claw-footed table, in the form of marmalade, toast, and scrambled eggs. Outside the picture window, the wind buffeted the Corsican pines; the rain fell in heaps; the morning lay twilight. Carter and Mr. Hope stood, but Chant sat, head down, staring at his food.

Enoch burst into the room, rending his garment in grief, his face suffused in pain. Before anyone could speak he flung himself into one of the chairs, threw one hand over his eyes, and pounded his fist against the swarthy table. "They have us now!" he cried. "We are doomed, and the whole house with us!"

"What is it?" Carter asked.

Enoch looked beneath his hand into the Steward's face, his brown eyes bleak. "They have locked the door to the Towers."

Chant sagged in his chair and slowly traced his finger along the carvings of gulls embellished into the table.

"What does it mean?" Carter asked.

"Everything! Unless I can wind the clocks in the Towers they will run down. All of them!"

"Can't they be rewound?" Hope asked.

"It is as we told you," Chant said softly, "though you scarcely believed. The house is the mechanism that propels the universe, the clocks, like the lamps I light, one of its components. If the Towers' clocks are not wound their portion of Creation will fall to Entropy. Imagine hundreds of stars winking out in the night sky. *But now the whole Round Table is dissolved, Which was an image of the mighty world.*"

Enoch buried his head upon the table and moaned.

"This morning when I went outside to extinguish the lamps, I found the Bobby waiting at every lamppost, and his minions with him," Chant continued. "They have surrounded the house, and learned enough of the Master Keys to lock many of the important portals. We are besieged."

"What can we do?" Carter asked.

"Who but Brittle might have known?" Enoch murmured. "How could we learn his duties, when we were kept so busy with our own?"

"If I might," Hope said, retaking his seat and spearing his eggs, "I couldn't begin to take Brittle's place, but I have been reading, especially the *History of the High House*, and I have found references to the Seven Words of Power. You said you had learned two of them, the Word Which Brings Aid and the Word of Hope, but there is also a Word of Secret Ways, which *opens doors not always seen.* If we need to reach the Towers, perhaps the Word could reveal a passage."

"It is a chance!" Enoch said, brightening.

"It would be worth a try," Carter said. "But the last time I opened the Book of Forgotten Things I got a taste of the Room of Horrors. I dread doing so again."

"But someone must," Enoch said. "If not you, who?"

Carter sighed. "A good point, I suppose. If that is the case,

I would rather go at once and be done with it, but only if one of you will accompany me."

"Enoch and I will both go," Chant said. "The Bobby attacked from the library before; it may not be safe."

"I will remain and continue my reading," Hope said. "Perhaps I can find something useful."

"Reading, or eating?" Carter asked, managing a slight smile. "But at least you have an appetite."

"Actually, I'll try to do both," Hope said, buttering a scrap of toast. "Armies and attorneys march—and research—on their stomachs."

They proceeded down the transverse corridor to the library doors. As they entered, Carter momentarily thought he heard soft voices echoing among the shelves, but the sound receded so quickly he dismissed it as mere fancy. The room appeared as unchanged as ever, like a desolate valley or forgotten corner of the world lost in slumber. Clouds streamed beyond the tall windows, and dreary, diffused light crept through the glass. Thunder rattled in the distance as they crossed to the study door.

"Does the sun ever shine here anymore?" Carter asked.

"I do not think it will," Chant said. "Not until the Bobby is sent on his way. He is Stormbringer, Disrupter of the Old Ways; the tempest fits his mood. *The ancient one lives in the east in the Wood of Iron and there gives birth to Fenrir's brood, one of them all, especially, in form of a troll will seize the sun.*"

"Always comforting, eh, Chant?" Carter said as he opened the door and entered the small study. He glanced around at the kidney-shaped desk, the dark leather chair, the white marble fireplace. The day shone dully through the stained-glass angel; the gas jets in the buttercup lamps sang their soft firesong.

"Do you light the lamps each morning?" Carter asked.

"I see they remain lit, but they are always left on," Chant replied. "All the Masters have required it."

Carter refrained from asking Chant how old *he* was. Instead he used the tiny key from the drawer to open the bookcase and retrieve the Book of Forgotten Things, which he set carefully upon the desk.

Despite his reluctance, he sat down immediately, gathered his resolve, and opened the book. The scent of dust and leather rose to meet him; the textured pages felt like papyrus beneath his hands. He intended to avert his eyes until the seventh page, but at the sixth he was halted by the rising image of his father and himself, sitting at the drawing-room table, in a time before Lady Murmur came to live in the house. His father looked sad and pale, his face like chiseled alabaster.

"There is a sea," Lord Anderson said, "a vast endless sea, that no man living has ever sailed, with waves all the colors of the rainbow, and a sky of copper and bronze, where flashes of blue lightning pass between azure clouds."

"And can we sail there?" the little boy asked, his eyes all wonder.

"Oh, no," his father said. "No one can sail it, though it is very beautiful to see. But sometimes, when I stand beside its banks, I think perhaps your mother has gone that way, for it seems to me quite close to heaven, and I see the wind in her hair, and her standing on a fair green shore, waiting for me."

There were tears in his father's eyes, and Carter, looking down on his younger self, suddenly remembered there had been tears in his own as well, so that this must have been shortly after his mother's passing.

Gradually, the image faded, leaving his throat tight. He sighed and turned to page seven.

Four words slowly appeared upon the paper, their letters burning in fire like hot brass. The first two were those he had learned before, the Word of Hope and the Word Which Brings Aid; as his eyes passed over them he felt reassurance and power welling within him, and the thought, *These are mine*, came unbidden. His confidence waned at the third, which was more difficult to look upon, as if it burned brighter, and at first the letters were strangely indecipherable. Under scrutiny, they gradually became clear, and as the Word filled his mind, he had the odd impression that it expanded within him, a looming pressure begging release. It seemed he must speak it or burst, yet it took an effort of will to bring it to his lips: *Sedhattee*. A deep rumble, somewhere overhead, shook the house. He said it again, feeling it burn into his memory. The Word Which Gives Strength.

Already he was weary, as if carrying heavy chains up a steep hill, but he cast his eyes upon the fourth Word and repeated the process. *Talheedin*. He spoke it with effort, wrenching it from his mouth, wrestling it as if it were a man, and as he did he knew it was indeed the Word of Secret Ways, as if the book had known what he sought.

He was drained down to his bones, and his hands trembled as he shut the book. This time, having learned the danger, he felt no temptation to glimpse another page.

He glanced up and found the door closed, neither Chant nor Enoch within the room, and all silent save for the gas jets. Startled by their absence, he quickly locked the volume back within the bookcase and flung the door wide, calling their names. Chant answered from the library and came meekly forward, Enoch trailing behind him, their faces pale.

Enoch cast his eyes down in shame. "I am sorry, Master; the Words were too powerful. They filled the whole room. They crowded us out, though we kept watch from the library."

Carter, suddenly aware he was drenched in sweat, wiped his brow and gave a wan smile, astonished that such force had been released to drive his trusted servants from his side. "I have never doubted you. Come, cheer up, you have done no wrong, and I have what we need. Perhaps it will help."

He shut the study door and turned to go, but as they crossed the library, he noticed an odd stirring among the shelves, like a heat mirage rising between the aisles, shimmering, the wan sunlight soft upon it, making the fronds in the carpet appear to flutter. He paused to watch the luminance splash across the bookcases, waving like feathers in the breeze, uniting and dispersing, until a shape began to coalesce. Both Enoch and Chant stepped quickly in front of him, and the Windkeep drew a long dagger from somewhere in his breast pocket.

Gradually, the form of a man emerged within the gleaming, an armored figure wearing a peculiar helmet, with metal strips rising from its sides like thin horns squared at the ends. He stepped from among the shelves, a tall fellow, all in white, wearing a close-fitting pearl hauberk, its intricately woven rings glistening as he walked. He had a sword hanging by his side, a shield strapped to his back, and an ivory-handled pistol in a leather holster at his waist. As he approached, glints from his blue eyes flashed in the gloom. He halted a few feet from the men and raised his hand in salute, but Enoch had already put his knife away.

"Greetings to the High House. I am Glis, captain of the White Circle Guard. We have received word from the man, Hope, that we were to come."

"The White Circle!" Carter said. "Yes, Hope spoke of it. I am Carter Anderson, Steward of the house. This is Enoch and Chant."

Glis bowed at the waist to Carter, then hurried forward, grinning, to clasp Enoch's hand. "These I know. How are you, old lion? And you, Chant, have you any more of your splendid poetry for us?"

Enoch returned the grip enthusiastically. "I rejoice to see the face of a friend. The anarchists have locked the passage to the Towers. The Green Door is shut as well."

"I expected no such news," Glis said, sobering at once. "I brought only a handful, thinking this a meeting of introduction. Others will be sent for at once; we will rally the entire Circle."

As he spoke, other warriors, all garbed in white, emerged from the mists of the aisles, lean, powerful men such as Carter had seen in his father's house as a boy. They numbered less than twenty, but it heartened him to see them. It scarcely surprised him that the library was a passage to other countries; books had always been his route to other lands, at least in spirit, and enchantment had ever lain heavy on the room. He recalled emissaries to his father often emerging from its doors.

The captain gave a message to one of his subordinates, who left at once, passing back between the aisles, fading away among the stacks.

"Have your men eaten?" Carter asked.

"We could use a bit of breakfast. Our coming was more difficult than we expected; all a part of your troubles, I'm certain. There were Things in the darkness last night, fanged beasts and shadowed faces; we slept little, and woke twice to drive them off. I thought it a random attack. I doubt now that it was."

They led the soldiers out of the library, down the transverse corridor to the dining room. Hope was there, taking notes on a gray pad, with a large volume propped upon the table. He rose quickly at sight of the company pouring like white lions through the doors, and approached the captain without hesitation.

"Captain Glis, I presume? You have the look of command about you. William Hope. Glad you could come. Things are a bit more dire than when I first sent word. Let me find a servant and we will have food brought around."

Carter sat at the head of the table, Hope to his right, Captain Glis to his left, with Chant and Enoch, having stayed at Carter's request, farther down among the men. The captain removed his helmet, revealing a dark-haired, handsome face, marred by a three-inch scar across his right cheek, Carter's elder by less than half a dozen years.

"You will pardon my ignorance," Carter told him. "Hope tells me the White Circle represents the countries surrounding the Inner Chambers."

"Correct," Glis said. "These twenty are my elite guard, one

from each of the kingdoms. Blade, there, is from Naleewuath; I understand you recently visited that country. I am from Aylyrium. At need, we can rally a sizable army, whose duty is to protect the whole of the Circle, and, of course, the Inner Chambers. Tell me your situation."

With Hope's help, Carter recounted their crisis, after which the captain looked grave. "Much of this is beyond our power to relieve. The loss of the Master Keys has been a terrible thing; since your father's day we had no luck finding them. But clearly they must be retaken. We will do what we can. Our first priority is the defense of the house. I will station guards at the Green Door and the stairs to the Towers, as well as the library doors, since the previous assault came from there. We can at least prevent the situation from worsening."

With nothing more to be decided, Carter questioned the captain concerning the White Circle, and Glis told him of that fair ring of countries, of the halls of Aylyrium, its palace walls mosaics of silvered splendor, its princes tall but delicate as porphyry; of Moomuth Kethorvian, its monolithic standing stones, expansive halls like deserts, and gaping idols made by a people no longer remembered; of High Gable, built on shelves upon the rooftops like eagles' aeries; of Westwing, which has two kings and where no man may carry a sword; and Himnerhin where are the best craftsmen in iron and leather, and where sweet peaches grow indoors in orchards spanning leagues; of many-spired Ooz where all the shutters are crimson; and the harbors of North Lowing, where wide rivers run right through the house and wild deer are hunted upon the stairs. All these he had witnessed, for he had traveled much in his life, and Carter realized what a great unseen land stood roundabout, a true circle of countries, with the High House as its hub. Beyond that, the captain said, were stranger lands, such as Ephiny Edge and Darking, some desolate wastes, some controlled by allies to the anarchists, others great kingdoms of their own, but even these were connected to Evenmere as well, in what Carter could only imagine as another, outer circle. And still the house went on, into legends and stories, and kingdoms beyond the ken of men.

They spoke through the morning, with Hope taking notes, so that when Glis finally left to inspect his men, the lawyer had filled eight pages. Everyone else had departed, and Carter slumped in his chair.

"A bit overwhelming," Hope said.

"More than a bit," Carter said. "I begin to see how important Brittle was to the entire house. He must have been my father's ambassador, his counselor, and his friend. Odd that I never knew; I saw him simply as an old servant."

"Ahh, but aren't the oldest friends the best servants?" Hope asked. "What do we do for our friends but serve them, even as they serve us?"

"I suppose so, but I find I haven't made any close friends in my life. I was considered strange to those outside the house; I shouldn't wonder why, growing up here. What should I do?"

"You must find someone you trust to fill the opening. I can do initial research for you, but eventually you will need to hire a permanent butler."

"That may take some time. But perhaps you might consider staying on as ambassador and advisor?"

Hope frowned thoughtfully, his round face open and honest. "I hadn't considered it. You haven't known me long. As your advisor I would advise you not to hire anyone too hastily."

Carter laughed. "You already give good counsel. I feel we could work together. I am certain I could offer you a decent wage, and, of course, room and board. Consider it. We could attempt it on a trial if you like, to see how it works."

Hope smiled. "Following my current course, I am unlikely to become an ambassador to anywhere. I should like to give it a try. Of course, if it works out, eventually I will need to return to Dyson, Phillips, and Hope to conclude my business and retrieve my personal things. But here is an opportunity I cannot refuse!"

The two shook hands warmly. "We're in it together, then," Carter said. "But you haven't seen proof of my claims yet. No behemoths in the attic."

"But I have seen a battle in a dream and a company of knights in mail. I have also been looking out the windows since Chant told his story this morning. At each of the four cardinal points I saw an English bobby stationed beside the lamppost. From a distance, every officer appears identical. Can our enemy be in more than one place at once? Or are these his servants, similarly guised? I will not require the dinosaur. Honestly, I've come to fear the thought of seeing him. What will you do next?"

"I need to use the Word of Secret Ways, to find a new passage to the Towers, but I don't know if I have the strength. Reading the Words has wrung me out completely. When I spoke the Word Which Brings Aid, back in Naleewuath, it was like hurling a shot. I believe attempting to speak a Word of Power and failing to bring it forth could be dangerous, perhaps catastrophic. Am I being cowardly? The need is urgent."

Hope pondered a moment. "Having no other guide, you should follow your instincts and recuperate a bit. I will do my best to monitor the goings-on in the house. Captain Glis appears competent, and there is little more to do."

Carter complied at once, and found himself actually stumbling as he made his way up the stairs. At its top he encountered Lady Murmur and Duskin coming down the hall. He had not seen them since his return from Naleewuath, had scarcely seen them at all since their first meeting, in fact, and had no desire to do so now.

"Lady Murmur," he said with a nod, hoping to simply pass.

"Carter," she said, smiling, reminding him of a fox. Only the fangs were missing. "I understand there has been trouble in the house."

"Somewhat."

"If only your father were here. He would know what to do. A pity he did not train you. If we can help, let us know. Despite Duskin's earlier, regrettable words, he wants only what is best for Evenmere, as do I."

Duskin, scowling, did not look like he wanted the best for anything.

"Thank you," Carter said, striding past them.

"Oh, Carter," she called, forcing him to turn. "We have not heard how things went in Naleewuath."

"They went well," he said, and continued to his room, determined to ignore her if she spoke again.

Once behind his door he sat down on the bed, fists clenched, wanting to pound the dresser. He blew his breath out, the anger burning in his chest. "Calling me back like a child! As if the whole house were not abuzz with the news of Naleewuath!" As a lad, when she had treated him as a vagabond, he had not known how to respond, had not realized her remarks, cast like stones from behind her smile, were meant to draw blood. Respect for his father and naivete had kept him from retaliating. She, who had been his parent, had used her position of power for spite. What further mischief did she intend?

He forced himself to relax. Weariness prevented him from remaining angry long. He went to the window; it was raining still, soft drops against the pane, though the wind had abated. The Bobby stood beneath the lamppost, head down, heedless of the storm.

Carter cast himself upon the bed and fell into a deep sleep. Though he feared slumber with his enemies all around, he dreamed only ordinary dreams, visions of Hope and Murmur, Enoch and Glis, with the Tigers of Naleewuath chasing themselves round and round a tree, in an ever-narrowing circle, until at last there was nothing to be seen of them at all.

When Carter awoke, the room was dark, save for a narrow sliver of light slipping beneath the door, and it took him a moment to know where he was. He sat on the side of the bed and lit the lamp. Squinting against the flames, he discovered by his pocket watch that it was after ten o' clock. He moaned softly at having slept the entire day away, rose, and went down the stairs in time to meet Hope ascending.

"Hello," the lawyer said. "I was just coming to make certain you were alive."

"I was more washed out than I thought," Carter said. "Has Enoch been pacing the floor?"

"No, he understood. He has a great deal of confidence that you can find another passage to the Towers."

"I wish I did. Now that I have the Word of Secret Ways, where should I speak it? Or do I just stand in the middle of the house?"

"I don't know, but come eat a late supper. A bit of food for thinking might help."

They passed through the dimly lit corridor into the dining room, where the butler's assistant served up heavy slabs of roast beef, with steaming potatoes, gravy, and fresh-buttered bread. The plates and glasses, which reflected tiny suns beneath the lamps, were all of emerald, made darker by the dyed malachite tablecloth. Ladybugs circled leaves upon the handles of the silverware. Finding himself suddenly ravenous, Carter set to at once, while the fireplace cast shadow-monsters of him and Hope against the far wall.

Just as he was finishing his meal, one of Glis's men burst into the room, a naked sword in hand. "Sir, we must rouse the house! The anarchists are attacking from the library!" The man was gone before Carter could frame a question, so he turned to the butler's assistant. "Go spread the word, boy. Tell all the house to arm themselves."

Wide-eyed, the lad raced away, and the two men rushed quickly after, down the shadowy length of the transverse corridor to the library doors, where nearly all of Glis's force was already assembled. Several of the men struggled to hold the doors shut against the heavy pounding of an instrument from the library side, while Glis made preparations for a charge. At the captain's signal, the warriors stepped back, flinging the doors wide, and the whole company pushed through the portal, shouting, swords and pistols flashing. An answering roar, as of many men, rose from within. Shots rang out, steel clashed, and soldiers screamed. Carter drew near and glimpsed countless figures within the library, silhouetted against the moonlight flowing through the high windows, in a room otherwise dark. He heard animal snarls like those of the black beast in his dream, when Brittle was slain.

All but five of the white knights had poured into the chamber. Carter moved up beside them just as a man in gray mail, shrouded in a hood, leapt through the doorway, a mace in one hand, a pistol in the other. He swung his bludgeon at Carter's head, but a knight parried the blow with his sword. The assailant shot Carter's savior in the stomach, and the man toppled to the floor, doubled over in pain. Another soldier stepped forward and killed the attacker with a quick thrust to the throat.

Carter knelt beside the fallen knight. "Lay quiet," he ordered, but to his surprise the man waved him away.

"I am well, just winded. The gun kicks hard."

"You've been shot," Carter said, but to his surprise, he saw the bullet had not penetrated the armor. He had no time to consider the forging of mail capable of deflecting a shell, for another assailant burst through the doorway. While his comrades engaged the enemy, Carter helped the knight up, then retreated, certain he could do nothing without a weapon.

A handful of servants appeared, armed with pistols, rifles, a mattock, and even an ancient blunderbuss. Carter and Mr. Hope both took pistols, though the lawyer turned green and held it as if it were a viper.

"Stand three paces behind the knights," Carter ordered the

men. "Be careful not to shoot any of our comrades, but watch for anyone trying to break through."

Scarcely had he spoken, when a heavy, gray figure bounded out the doorway into the light. Five shots erupted as he stood revealed, and he dropped to the ground, bloody with holes. Carter was relieved to find the enemy's armor less resistant to bullets than the plate of his allies.

Two others rushed the door, and the knights downed one, but the other broke through and charged straight at the Steward. Carter raised his pistol, and saw the man's features clearly—sky-blue eyes, sculpted nose, square, handsome chin—before he fired, point-blank into the face. The anarchist reeled away. Carter felt the blood drain from his own cheeks; he had never killed anyone before.

As quickly as they had charged, Glis's knights poured back into the corridor, their captain at the rear. A dozen of the men forced the doors shut.

"Bring a table!" Glis bawled. "The doors will not hold them!" Seeing Carter, he sprang to his side. There was blood on his left shoulder, though Carter could not tell if it was his own or another's.

"There must be half a company in there," Glis said. "We cannot hold this position. You are the Master; you must speak the Word Which Seals to barricade the library doors, else we are lost."

Carter felt his face pale. "I have not yet learned that Word."

The captain opened his mouth but said nothing, then set his jaw in firm resolve. "We can expect no other aid, then. The messenger I sent returned moments ago, unable to break through. I need as many of your staff as you have. Once they hew down the doors they can only come at us a few at a time. We will make them pay for every inch."

"My people are coming," Carter said.

The table was brought forward and nailed into place with sledgehammers and long spikes, its top flat against the facing. Just as the work was completed, the library doors shuddered and began to splinter from the blows of many axes. A hole appeared; a face popped up, only to be driven back by a pistol blast. The axes struck again and a large upper portion of the door fell away. The anarchists pressed against the table, while the white knights thrust their swords around it to force them back.

A horn sounded, and the attackers suddenly melted away, but a moment later a heavy battering ram made of wood and iron broke the table in half, sending the knights reeling. Glis ordered his men forward, but it was difficult for them to resist the press. More and more gray forms filled the doorway. Carter thought they must break through at any moment. He took careful aim with his pistol.

Before he could fire, a tremendous explosion rocked the house, a detonation originating within the library. A flash of light, blinding bright, shot through the doors, and the concussion blew the combatants off their feet. Carter found himself tossed backward against the corridor wall.

Dazed and winded, he stumbled up and saw smoke billowing from the library. Not a single anarchist remained standing, though a few vainly sought to rise; those who had been at the door were gone, utterly vaporized. Several white knights lay moaning, but Captain Glis was already on his feet, helping others to stand. It was he who first looked into the library.

"Someone bring a light!" he ordered, and Chant, who Carter had not noticed previously, hurried from the crowd of servants, lamp in hand. Carter joined the captain, and together, surrounded by their men, they entered the room.

The carpet, the stones, the shelves, were scorched, as if a great heat had passed over them, but the books were untouched and nothing was truly damaged, except for the glass in the high windows, which was completely blown out. Helmets and broken swords lay on the floor, and the smoking remains of the battering ram, but no sign of the men could be found.

"What has happened?" the captain asked, incredulous.

"Some power was released," Chant said. "We have been saved, but I do not know how. Did they attempt to use a weapon they could not control, or do we have unknown allies? Whatever the answer, we have been spared this night. *Here again, here, here, here, happy year! O warble unchidden, unbidden! Summer is coming, is coming, my dear, And all of the winters are hidden.*"

"*Something* is certainly hidden," Carter said. "Questioning the survivors may provide answers. But I am sick of lacking the strength to serve as Steward. If only I had known the Word Which Seals!"

"But how were they able to enter the library?" Chant asked. "There are powerful wards against it. It is one thing to send a dream, another to appear in person."

Carter stopped, struck by a suddenly realization. "There is only one answer. When I was a child, when the Bobby came into the yard, it was because he was invited."

The Secret Ways

While Captain Glis constructed a new barrier for the library doors and prepared the night watch, Carter searched down the butler's corridor, past the shadowed back stair, through the men's corridor, until he found Enoch in the servants' hall, which served now for a temporary hospital. The room was all of paneled oak, with a wide border at the top of its high ceiling, carved with apples and daisies, milkmaids and dashing horses. Rose petals were etched around the borders of the polished floor where pallets were now being laid; servants scurried in every direction, scouring for supplies, escorting the wounded and tending their injuries, fetching lanterns to brighten the begloomed hall, all a bedlam of shouted orders and the cries of the hurt. Remarkably, only one of Glis's men had died, though five others were wounded, and three of the servants. The old Windkeep had played his part in the fight and received a long, but shallow cut across his shoulder, which one of the maids, *tsking* in pity as she worked, was dressing with a white bandage. The old Hebrew gave Carter a fierce grin.

"Did we give them a battle?" he asked.

"One we would have lost if not for the explosion. What did you think of it? Did the anarchists misuse some weapon?"

"Would it have killed only them? That was power aimed with intent; it scarcely harmed our forces. We have a friend. What will you do next?"

"On that I need your counsel. I am ready to use the Word of Secret Ways, but I do not know how. Where should I speak it? In what part of the house should I stand? Also, this battle has shown me I need to command my father's full authority to survive. I need his Lightning Sword, his Tawny Mantle, and the Master Keys. I need all the Words of Power. Only then will I have a chance. What would you advise?"

Enoch thought a moment, wincing as the woman tightened the bandage. "Where to speak it? A good question. Anywhere? Everywhere? Experiment! But doing so will tax your strength. I do not know. Your father took his things with him. Find him, find them. As for the remaining Words, they will be revealed to you in their proper time. Am I helping? No. You should ask these questions to the beast in the attic."

"You know of the dinosaur?"

"He is a dinosaur now? My people called him Behemoth. He has watched the wide world for a long time. He knows much."

"In our last encounter, he told me not to return unless I knew the Words of Power. Are four enough?"

Enoch shrugged. "Four, five, who can say? I am certain he will recognize your authority. But you must be careful. He is very old. He thinks his own thoughts and speaks the truth he sees, but a truth other than that of men. A wrong word and he will kill you. Is this good advice? You should have gone to Chant."

A dread fell upon Carter as he thought of ascending the steps to the monster's lair, yet his need was great, and he considered Enoch the wisest of men. By the time Hope came tramping up, he had made his decision.

"I am going to visit Jormungand," he said to the lawyer. "You could come partway, if you want to see him. Enoch has offered enough comfort to make me long for company."

"Tonight?" Hope's face was suffused with excitement, the battle having worked an unexpected change in him. A fierce light burned in his eyes. "But I hoped to bring you more information on the beast, and my research has turned up nothing."

"Then I must go, trusting in the best," Carter said. "Time is short, and I have slept the day away. I have already conferred with Glis; he has things in hand."

"I'm ready," Hope said. "You know, at first I was frightened when the men charged through the library doors. I knew it was a deadly business, but I found it more of an adventure than I expected."

Carter slapped him on the shoulder. "Good. Your stout heart can bolster mine. The monster up there terrifies me. We go at once." Carter lowered his voice. "But while I have you together, I want you to know I suspect a traitor in our midst."

Hope raised his eyebrows. "Do you? On what grounds?"

"I believe the anarchists could not have entered the library unless invited. Chant agrees."

"Your father's old question!" Enoch said. "Who left the gate open to the yard?"

"Precisely," Carter replied. "I will not voice my conjectures at this point, but we must all keep alert. Speak of this to no one else. We will discuss it further when I return. Are you ready, Mr. Hope?"

"I am."

They bid Enoch farewell, delaying only long enough to speak with the other servants who had been wounded; neither were badly injured, a housemaid with a broken collarbone, trampled in the press, and a footman with a cut to the thigh, both quite happy to recount their part in the battle to their new lord. Before Carter and Hope departed, they were surprised to discover Chant meticulously removing shot from the shoulder of one of Glis's men, working with a calm professionalism while the patient grunted in pain. The Lamp-lighter glanced up and gave Carter a wink with one rose-pink eye. "We'll lose no more tonight."

"You appear experienced," Carter said, grimacing at the sight of the open wound.

"I hold a degree in medicine. *I had the eagle in my bosom erst: Henceforward with the serpent I am cursed.* A dreary business. I practiced a number of years until I found more useful work."

"Amazing," Hope said, and they left him to his task.

Back down the men's corridor, up through the servery into the dining room they went, into the transverse corridor; the lamps were still lit, and two of the knights stood watch at the library doors, while servants hammered heavy lumber across the shattered opening. As they ascended the main stair, Carter glanced up at the carved eagle upon the banister, taloned power wrapped in the shadows of the upper reaches, sighting down its beak, merciless, murderous, a symbol of the hunter and the house itself; he gave an involuntary shudder.

"What is it?" Hope asked.

"I was thinking about the wounded. Why is blood so unmoving in a fireside tale, yet so dreadful in real life?"

"Because in real life it could happen to us."

They reached Carter's room, where they lit two lanterns. Carter peered out the window, but since Chant had been unable to light the lamps, he could not see if the Bobby still lurked beyond the house. Lightning thrashed across the sky, and he thought he detected a black form beside the lamppost, head tilted back, staring at their window. The flash passed too quickly for certainty, but he drew the curtains before turning to the fireplace.

He depressed the brick, half expecting the mechanism not to operate, but the entire mantel slid away with a groan, revealing the small room and the narrow stairway. As if in answer, the thunder rolled above the house, sounding like water poured across a hot pan, and the rain beat harder against the panes. The secret chamber stood foreboding as a tomb, the dust already obscuring the footprints from Carter's previous visit.

"I must have been an unobservant child," he said softly. "It is remarkable that I never found this during all my boyhood."

"More than remarkable if you played in your room much. I daresay you weren't *meant* to find it."

"What do you mean?"

"Everyone speaks of the house as if it had a will. Perhaps, somehow, it does. Perhaps a "fate" is a better description. Shall we enter?"

As the two men left the bedroom and climbed the steps, the noise of the storm died into silence, as if they had entered another world. Carter supposed the high attic ceiling insulated against the din; in the hush their boots resounded heavily on the boards.

The bare steps, the unpainted walls, the space far above, the lantern light dancing, the fear of facing that which waited above, all sank into Carter's soul, as if he walked once more in nightmare. He dared not consider the possibility of failure, lest it send him fleeing back down the stair. He kept his eyes focused at the edge of the light, fearing they might reach the top unexpectedly; as it was, it surprised him when they attained it so soon, the distance having shrunk as it does when the unknown becomes familiar. He ordered Hope to wait a few steps farther down while he ascended the remainder of the way. Bereft of the company of his friend, he felt the fear clamp over his heart.

He stepped forward slowly, raised his light to illuminate the ceiling joists, and gave what he intended to be a loud hallo, though his voice sounded thin and small in the expanse. Only dust, old toys, and silence greeted him.

He walked a dozen feet farther into the attic, called again, and heard a heavy exhalation behind him. He whirled and found two red eyes staring down at him from a great height. An involuntary cry escaped his lips, but he stood his ground. "Jormungand."

The voice of the dinosaur rumbled above him. "The little steward has returned."

Carter heard the hissing of the monster's breath, the soft slapping of the heavy tail across the floorboards. The dinosaur stood like a stone gargoyle, all gray, his eyes lidding and unlidding rapidly, like the tongue of a frog taking prey. This close, the pungent smell of reptile was nearly overwhelming.

"I have come to ask your help," Carter said.

"You have gained four Words of Power," Jormungand said grudgingly. "I see them in you, floating like flies in soup. But not all seven. Perhaps I can eat you. Or at least chew on you a bit. The fare has been slight of late."

The dinosaur moved closer, bending his slavering jaws down, his hot breath blowing on Carter's face. He stood perfectly still, afraid to run, afraid to stay, his whole body trembling before those eyes, large as melons. "I am the Steward!" he cried, angry in his desperation. "I command the Words. Do you require further proof?"

For a long moment the dinosaur stared at him. Carter saw ages of wisdom and power, discernment beyond measure, and indifference toward men. Jormungand was like living rock, oiled with reptile sweat, teeth sharp as spears.

Slowly, condescendingly, the monster withdrew. "You *are* the Steward. Have you come for entertainment? Do you hope to place a hook in leviathan's mouth; hoist me up by my tail so we can take a photograph together, me dead and you smiling? Later, dinosaur for dinner, leftovers for six weeks, and a Jormungand rug your children can run back and forth across on bare feet, to get the feel of real Jurassic leather? What do you want?"

Sweat beaded on Carter's forehead. "I possess the Word of Secret Ways, and I need to use it to lead Enoch to the Towers. But where should I speak it?"

"You disturbed me for this? You should ask the skinny butler, Rattle, who used to accompany the Masters."

"Brittle. He's dead."

"Ah. Already? I should have known. But it's difficult to keep track. Men are like buzzing gnats, swarming on a summer day, burned by the sun before noon, mating and dying in the air, buried in the grass by sunset, their offspring rising with the morning light. The dust in this attic is older than you, and less ephemeral. But Jormungand has been since the beginning. As for your question: speak the Word of Power at the door leading to the stair of the Towers, and the hidden way will appear. But you should also use it at the bottom of *this* stair, to find passages that will bring you knowledge."

"I also need to find my father's Lightning Sword, his Tawny Mantle, all the old things which he once used, including the Master Keys which the anarchists possess."

The dinosaur turned from side to side in contemplation. "And do I look like a crystal ball, mechanized fortune-teller bought for a pence, Ouija board tyrannosaurus, circus gypsy stored with the trunks, unwrapped like an old suit on All Hallow's Eve, moth-eaten, ill-fitting, a comical diversion for the children? You tread a thin line. Is this the best you can ask?"

Carter felt his whole body trembling. "I believe so."

"Very well," Jormungand hissed. "A harder puzzle, at least. If I were to seek the old lord, I would go to Arkalen beside the Rainbow Sea. You might find his things there."

"Do you know if he still lives, then?"

Jormungand shook his great head. "Nothing is certain, but being who he was and what he wanted, that is where I would look. He sought death, though he did not call it such. He yearned for someone from the Other Side, even as he looked for the Master Keys. Go to Arkalen. There you will also begin your search for the keys. Do you have a fourth question?"

"No."

"Too bad. If you had asked another I would have been entitled to devour you. There is a balance, and a tally kept; no one ever asks more than three things at once of the Great Worm. You have passed a test, little steward, and you did not even know. Because of it, I give you a present. But first, tell me what you fear."

Carter stood silent, but beneath those great eyes he found he could not dissemble, and the answer came unbidden from his lips. "Darkness and deep water. Closed places. I nearly drowned in a well as a child."

"Yes. I see it within you. Then to find the Master Keys you must go through those things. Perhaps even to the Room of Horrors."

Carter flinched. "No," he said softly. "I will never go there again. This is a miserly present. You give me little comfort."

"Comfort, you say? I should have bought you a banjo. One does not keep a dinosaur in the attic for comfort. Or merely to frighten away the birds. Did you come for packages wrapped in pink bows, so we could open them together, slap each other on the back, and squeal like girls? Where *have* I put my candy dishes? All out of bonbons. But there is always a price to speak to me, and the present and price are the same. Someday I will be released from this attic, for I am prepared for a time and a place, and a battle beyond measure. Perhaps a battle for the end of the worlds. I have seen much, but I am never pleasant to converse with. Go now, so I do not have to paw after the man who came with you, whose flesh smells a little like that of a lamb."

"Thank you, Jormungand."

"Oh, no. Thank you. I was waiting, bated breath, for your call."

The behemoth sat back on his haunches, and curled up with his long tail about him, as if preparing for sleep. The red eyes closed, leaving darkness where they had been.

Hope and Carter walked back down the stair, silent until they reached the little room at the bottom, when the lawyer said, "Do you intend to do as he said? He gave me goose-flesh all over. Can he be trusted?"

"We will find out beginning now. I will use the Word of Secret Ways here, in this room, as he instructed. You might want to go downstairs, for your own safety."

"I'd rather stay and see the show."

"Very well. It will take a moment."

Carter concentrated, recalling the Word, bringing it before his mind until he could see the flames dancing like sprites across the letters, each character standing bright upon blackness. He held it there, studying its majesty, absorbing its full meaning, the ponderous weight of its being. Its existence belied the words of Jormungand, suggesting that because the Word *was*, that men were more than dust, that there was Purpose, and perhaps, even, Justice. Carter could have remained there forever, mesmerized by that single Word, as a man in a hashish trance ceaselessly studies the lines of his hand, but the nature of the Word was either to action or quiescence; it could not be held long. Sensing he must use it or see it wither, he slowly opened his mouth, dragging the Word from his throat, sending it clawing into the world.

"Talheedin!" Released at last, it roared into the small chamber. The room shook; Hope went pale. Carter found himself trembling. He looked around expectantly.

At first nothing occurred. Then, a dim rectangle of blue luminescence slowly appeared upon the east wall. He approached it warily, dropped to his haunches, and ran his fingers over its surface, but except for the unnatural glow, it remained unchanged.

"What do you make of it?" he asked.

"I . . . don't see anything," Hope replied.

Carter looked up, thinking he was joking, but the lawyer remained impassive. Carter described it.

"I can't detect a trace," Hope said. "But surely it's the Word at work; there must be a hidden door. We simply have to find the mechanism."

They began a thorough search and soon discovered a tiny button upon the top of the baseboard. At Carter's touch, the center of the blue area rotated sideways on a metal rod, revealing a lightless passage wide enough for a single man.

Carter went first, slumping to avoid brushing the low ceiling. The smell of mold pervaded the corridor; the bare boards creaked beneath their feet. The walls curved gracefully to the left, smooth except where the plaster had fallen away, revealing the slats.

As they followed the curve, they saw a single shaft of light, no larger than the end of a finger, shining on the wall to the left. This they discovered to be a spy-hole, complete with a leather rest for the chin and forehead. Carter looked through it and found himself staring through strange glass into Mr. Hope's bedchamber, the Rose Room.

"Here's news," Carter said. "Take a look. I could have spied upon you at any time."

Hope pressed his eye to the glass and grinned. "Not that there is much to see, but it does speak unkindly of the architects. We are standing where the portrait hangs over the mantel, probably looking out from one of your ancestor's eyes."

"We should use my coat to shroud the lantern, in case we discover more of these peepholes. We don't want our light to be seen through the glass."

With the lantern partially mantled, an illumination crimson beneath the coat, only the nearest floorboards were lit. They advanced farther down the curving passage until they came to another spy-hole. Through the opening Carter saw

Lady Murmur sitting at a low table, clothed in a yellow, silk day dress, studying her face in a mirror. Duskin sat to the side on a sofa. Carter could hear him clearly: "You should have let me go, Mother, to help defend the house. I am sixteen, no longer a child."

Murmur gave a low chuckle, but did not take her eyes from the mirror. "We cannot risk the future lord of Evenmere being injured in an absurd battle. War is for others; you were born to lead."

"No leader was ever respected who would not command his men in war. I saw Carter in the very midst of it. If I did not hate him so, I would admire his courage."

"You speak your father's nonsense," Murmur said. "It is the idealism of youth, which he never outgrew. You must learn to be practical."

Duskin shook his head. "Mother, I must learn to follow my own way. Perhaps Father was idealistic, but he was brave and kind as well."

"You were only six when he vanished; you do not remember him clearly."

"I do! There was strength about him, whatever his faults. Let me be an adult!"

Murmur's voice hardened. "Very well, if you wish to be an adult, then let us speak of adult matters. The anarchists could never enter the library on their own, not even with the keys, unless they were invited."

Even through the spy-hole, Carter saw his half brother's eyes widen. "Mother, you cannot mean . . ."

"They will be the force which makes you Master. Do you think we can simply stand around and wait for Carter to relinquish his title?"

"What have you done?" Duskin was on his feet. "The anarchists, invited here? How can we control them? How could you do this to the house?"

Murmur rose to meet him. "How could I not? You must become the lord of the manor. When I married your father, I was a princess of Meszria; I came here thinking to live in a world of high politics, of great riches. But he would not rule that way, speaking always of what the house wanted, what the house needed, as if it were a living thing. Power must be used; there are many kingdoms beyond the White Circle owing no allegiance to us; treaties must be made, kingdoms must be broken if they will not deal with us. We are close for the first time; the anarchists can help our cause."

"Say no more!" Duskin cried, tears in his eyes. "I will not hear it! Are we traitors to all I have ever known? Did Brittle die on my account?"

"Brittle was an old fool, and there are always casualties. But I did not know he would be harmed."

"Brittle was my friend! I will not hear it!"

Duskin lurched outside Carter's view, and a moment later a door slammed shut. Lady Murmur looked down at the carpet a moment, frowning, then sat back in the chair to study her eyebrows.

Carter withdrew from the spy-hole. He motioned to his friend and they moved farther down the passage, out of earshot.

"I heard it all," the lawyer whispered. "We have found our betrayer."

"Let us see what lies beyond," Carter said.

The passage continued to curve, and the men looked into many rooms, so that Carter realized they were making a slow circle all along the second floor, past the Rose, Lilac, Marigold, and Daffodil bedrooms, the drawing room, boudoir, day nursery, night nursery, sick room, into the women's servants' quarters, around past the workroom and the schoolroom. At last they reached a narrow stair, which he knew must be built opposite the wall running beside the main staircase. Tattered brown carpet covered the steps, less for decoration, he thought, than to muffle the footsteps of any going that way. Through a spy-hole he discovered he could indeed see the ebony banister and the green carpet of the main stairway.

As they descended the stair, the ceiling, constructed of cedar planks, sloped so as to remain slightly above their heads, making it seem they walked down a long tunnel. The sweet cedar scent buoyed their spirits, and they quickly reached a landing, with a portal leading to their right, while the stair continued downward into darkness. Carter's lamp revealed a long passage, much like the first, which he felt must allow viewing of the ground floor. He decided to follow it at once, and to return after to explore the lower regions.

Once within the passage, he saw another corridor intersecting from the south, so that he suspected the course made a complete circle around the entire floor. This was later confirmed, as they passed the rooms in a slow circle, beginning with the main stair, then proceeding to the gentlemen's room and the picture gallery, where hung the portraits of all the Masters of the High House in neat, orderly lines; through the spy-hole Carter saw his great-grandfather, Ethan Anderson, in his white navy uniform and gray moustache. Beyond the picture gallery they passed the morning room, the drawing room, then east beside the transverse corridor, gentlemen's stair, the entrance hall, the dining room, the butler's bedroom and pantry, north along the housekeeper's corridor and room, east beside the scullery, kitchen court, and kitchen, back south along the servants' hall, then west beside the men's corridor, the footman's room, and the gun room. There were other rooms as well, but these lacked spy-holes.

"The library should be next," Hope said. "Is it safe to go there, do you think?"

"It is the reason I came this way. Captain Glis has barred the doors, but I want to get a glimpse."

They had gone quietly before, but now went with even greater caution; the floor was bare wood and creaked at every step. At this side of the house the ceiling opened above them to ten feet, and they could hear the rain against the eaves, so that they knew they were under the lower roofs to the south. It made it more difficult to hear, but the soft beating muffled their footfalls as well.

Behind the first spy-hole lay the foyer area just inside the library entrance. Beneath the light of a lantern stood two men with cruel eyes and hawk noses, dressed in gray mail and heavy, black boots. One carried a truncheon in his left hand, the other was casually desecrating a dolomite column with a long, glistening knife. From his viewpoint, Carter saw that none of the anarchists were near the hallway doors.

Carter led farther down the passage, to the next observation point, where he found himself looking across the bookshelves. A dim candle burned upon a small table, and three more of the anarchists sat there, eating from oily leather bags and spilling wine across a pair of books stacked on the table. Carter could just see their faces within the circle of light.

"How did they manage it?" one asked, in a worried voice.

"They have an amplitude of armaments," another said, a portly, bearded man, with close-set eyes like a boar.

"But the whole company disintegrated in a twinkling, and not a book destroyed," the first said. "It could easily have been us. I don't like it. I will not be fodder, not even for the Bobby."

"I wouldn't let him hear you say it," the third man said. "At any rate, consider the remuneration when the house is ours. Not just monetary rewards, although those will be ample; we will be the harbingers of the New Order. It will be glorious. Those that are dead will have no share, leaving more for us."

"If we live to see it," the frightened man said.

"Hush, he comes," the portly man said.

The Bobby entered Carter's view, his face devoid of ears, nose, or mouth, but possessing large, dark eyes under heavy brows.

"We have discovered a way into the basement," he said, though no lips moved. "I want two of you to come with me. We have a task there."

"Are two enough?" the frightened man asked.

"There is little danger. We simply have to open a door. We can't reach the Entropy Door in the attic; the dinosaur guards it too well, but this one has no watchmen at all. Come quickly."

Two of the men followed the Bobby away into darkness, while their timid comrade remained at the table, drinking his wine.

"We have to follow," Carter whispered. "Down the stair."

They hurried along the passage, and turned a corner, only to discover that the way opened into a small room, with a metal canister lying upon the floor.

"Is this familiar?" Carter asked, halting to inspect the chamber.

The lawyer looked around. "Perhaps. I'm not certain."

"Do you remember, in our dream, when Brittle was murdered? The Thin Man brought us into a room behind one of the bookcases."

"You're right! Could this be the same?"

Carter bent down and examined the canister. What do you make of this?"

"It looks like the materials to construct a bomb. Here is a timer. I've seen such in the courtroom, though none quite like this. It isn't armed; I'm certain of that."

"Could it have caused the explosion in the library? If so, who set it? The Thin Man?"

"If he did, it raises many questions. He threatened to oppose you before, if you remained in the house. Why would he help us? And if not him, then who?"

"We will leave it for now; the matter of the basement is more urgent."

They hurried on, up a rickety flight of stair, the way they had gone in their dream, but this time, instead of leading to

Carter's bedroom, it wound back to the wooden stairs where the men had begun, completing the circle of the ground floor.

The thunder, which had been a soft rumbling above their heads, died away into silence as they descended into what could only be the basement. The musty odor of damp stone and earth rose to meet them; the walls and ceiling gave way to mortar and brick. Beetles and slugs patrolled along the granite steps. Carter pushed through the cobwebs and warily studied the holes in the brick, gaping like vipers' dens. The close proximity of the walls, which had been tolerable before, seemed to enfold him, as if the weight of the whole house lay upon his breast, and he suddenly found he could hardly breathe.

"Are you all right?" Hope asked softly.

Carter gasped for air and fought the sweeping panic. He nodded and went on, not certain if he was "all right" at all, trying not to consider how much the walls resembled the sides of a well, and he descending to its bottom.

A pinpoint light, shining like a tiny star, marked another spy-hole. Carter looked in, expecting to find nothing, and at first all appeared indistinct, but when his eyes adjusted, he found the Bobby already arrived, accompanied by his two servants, standing before a gray door beside a dusty stair, beneath a sallow light. In his hand, he held the Master Keys. Had there been a way, Carter would have smashed through the wall, attacked the monster, and seized the bronze ring, but he could do nothing except watch.

The Bobby brushed the dust off the front of the door, exposing cryptic runes carved across its face. With a soft, ugly chuckle, he said, "This is the one, the Door of Endless Dark. None have opened it before. We will see if I have the strength."

He searched the ring and selected an ebony key, one Carter remembered well, for its head was carved into the shape of a skull, with hollow, foreboding eyes; as a child he had found it both exciting and disturbing. The Bobby seemed to grapple with it as he dragged it to the lock, as if it resisted him with human strength. Clutching it with both hands, groaning from his efforts, he twisted the handle with his thumb, and the lock opened with a loud click.

"All together," he rasped. "We must pull it wide."

All three anarchists grasped the heavy knob. Their first pull opened it the tiniest of cracks. A single sliver of blackness slowly oozed out from between door and frame. The room was dim, filled with shadows, but this substance was not the absence of light, rather the presence of Dark itself, the emptiness before the making of the worlds and the weaving of the first suns, a Dark of the abandoned soul, and of despair. Already it covered the door frame, and as if in doing so, caused it to cease to exist.

"Make haste," the Bobby commanded. "Open it wide!"

Carter suddenly knew it was imperative the door be opened no farther. "Scream," he hissed to Hope. "Wail like a banshee at the top of your lungs. At the count of three."

Together, the two men bellowed, and then ceased abruptly at Carter's command. In answer, one of the anarchists turned and fired a pistol, even as Carter pushed Hope down. The bullet struck the stone, but did not penetrate, and Carter raised his own firearm to the spy-hole, which was only large enough to fit the barrel. He pulled the trigger, hoping it would not backfire. Looking quickly, he saw the portly anarchist clutching his shoulder—a fortuitous strike from an unaimed gun.

"Away!" the Bobby cried. "They have found us. Away!" He bolted up the stair, leaving the other man to help his wounded comrade.

"We must return to my room," Carter said. "We have to reach the basement and shut that door."

They made a furious dash back up the steps, and by the time they reached Carter's bedroom, both men were panting, but they continued into the corridor and down the stair, calling for Captain Glis.

It took time to locate the captain, and even longer to make their way into the kitchen and through the narrow door leading to the basement. With Glis and Enoch in the lead, and a dozen men behind, they rushed down the stair. The light had gone out, but they carried several lamps. Halfway down, Glis abruptly halted, and all strained to see.

The Dark had risen halfway up the stair, covering the floor with a vast nothingness that did not reflect the lamplight, like a starless night sky. Carter reached down and dropped a coin into it, where it sank without a splash, as if passing out of existence.

"We cannot cross to reach the Darkness Door, and the liquid is rising," Glis said.

"Will the door above contain it?" Hope asked.

"The High House is unlike any other, so perhaps it will," Enoch said. "Or maybe the Dark will squeeze out between the cracks into other parts of the house. Brittle once told me the basement goes under everything, even Naleewuath and distant Capaz."

"The Bobby spoke of another door, in the attic, that he called the Entropy Door," Carter said.

"I have heard of it," Enoch said. "Then this is indeed the Door of Endless Dark. The Entropy Door allows the heat of the universe to escape; the Dark Door lets the Darkness enter. Either will bring the house to ruin, and Creation with it. It is said that someday both doors will be opened wide, and then all will end."

"I will seal the basement and place guards beside it," Glis said. "Is the Entropy Door safe?"

"From what the Bobby said, it has its own guardian, one they will not easily pass," Carter said.

"We best retreat. It continues to rise," Glis said.

They returned to the kitchen, where the captain shut and bolted the door. "It is the best we can do," he said.

For an hour they kept watch, and when it seemed the Dark could not pass the door, Carter glanced at his pocket watch and found it was quarter past two. "Captain, I am bone-weary, though I slept half the day away. If you promise to keep me notified, I want to turn in. Mr. Hope, would you see I am awakened early tomorrow? We have to deal with a traitor."

"Why have I been summoned?" Lady Murmur demanded as she sat in the wicker chair in the drawing room, Duskin standing by her side. Carter thought his half brother had not slept well that night; dark circles lay under his eyes, and his face was so pale he looked ill.

It was early morning; the remainder of the night had passed untroubled; the cellar doors had contained the Dark for a time. Despite his weariness, Carter had slept little, and had risen with the gray, cloudy dawn, nervous but prepared for the coming confrontation. Mr. Hope, Chant, Enoch, and Captain Glis were seated around the room, restless, uncertain what would occur.

"Lady Murmur, I will waste no words," Carter said. "Last night, through means I will not reveal, I discovered you have collaborated with the anarchists. It was by your invitation that they entered the Inner Chambers of the house."

Her face flushed, and Duskin looked as if he had been struck, but she managed a slim smile. "That is nonsense! Why would I do such a thing?"

Carter felt old resentments rising within him, but he kept his voice level. "For the same reason you invited the Bobby in the first time, when he nearly drowned me in the well—for power, for greed, for all the things my father abhorred. Denial is useless; Mr. Hope and I heard it from your own lips."

"You have spied upon me, then!" she cried. "And in doing so you have erred! A chance comment—"

"A full confession, you mean," Hope said.

Murmur looked from face to face, suddenly sly as a wounded wolf. Her eyes fastened on Enoch. "You have lived here longest," she said. "Will you believe this boy, who gave the Master Keys away?"

It was more than Carter could bear. "And if you hadn't lied about me, I would have gone to Naleewuath with my father and not been tempted to take them!" His face grew hot, but he quickly mastered himself. "I will accept responsibility for my actions, and hold you responsible for yours. I can do nothing to punish you legally, but as Steward of the house, in the interest of Evenmere, I can banish you from its doors. The will stated Duskin was to dwell here; it made no mention of you. I find no guilt in him, at any rate. Is there anything you would offer, to redress the ills you have caused? If so you may find me merciful, if only for your son's sake."

Her face changed then; that which she had hidden behind the corners of her eyes slipped out—the malice, the envy, the hatred of a small, wicked mind. "*I* married your father! *I* was his queen, and he gave me nothing! The *servants* and the hired help sit in our drawing room like rats upon new cheese, and you treat them like old friends!"

She halted, containing herself, and a low smile spread across her face. "Very well," she said, almost sweetly. "If you choose to send me into the rain, I will depart the house. I will go to my allies, who will soon possess Evenmere anyway. Come along, Duskin."

As he took her hand to help her up, Duskin gave Lady Murmur a sad, pitying look, one Carter thought no man should have for his mother.

"You do not have to go with her," Carter said.

"No," Duskin replied, his eyes down. "I do not, but I will

not allow her to go to *them* alone. I am sorry we damaged Father's house. I am sorry for . . . everything."

With Captain Glis on one side of her, and Chant on the other, with Carter, Enoch, and Hope leading the way, they marched to the front door. Beyond the statue of the monk, beyond the hedgerow, beneath the lamppost, stood the Bobby, a light rain running down his helmet. Carter opened the door, and perhaps for his father's sake, handed Murmur a white parasol. She glared at it a moment, then took and flung it back to him, where it bounced harmlessly on the floor. But Duskin, a trace of gratitude in his eyes, retrieved it and held it over her as they made their way out the door, to where the anarchist stood. Her dress was white, and she moved with elegance down the walk.

Carter closed the door and quietly locked it, feeling triumph and grief, together as one.

The Path to the Towers

$\mathbb{A}$ blast of thunder shook the house and the air crackled with power as Carter spoke the Word of Secret Ways, and it was difficult to know which was the stronger, the force of nature or the spoken Word. The windows rattled; the pictures trembled, and to Carter, wielding that mighty utterance, shaken by its use, it seemed both were the same kind of power, harnessed but never mastered.

He stood beside a door tucked away in a corner of the second floor, the gateway to the Towers that the anarchists had locked. But upon his speaking the Word of Secret Ways, the portrait-length painting upon the west wall, depicting an eerie house and the sinister figures from Machen's *The Three Impostors*, began to glow with a faint blue light, giving the characters a spectral appearance.

By the time Enoch, Chant, and Hope peered cautiously around the corner, they found him sitting on a stool, his eyes closed.

"Are you all right?" Hope asked. "You shook the rafters with that one."

"I shook myself. It made me weak in the knees. I don't

know why it was so strong this time. Perhaps I'm learning to use the power. I'm fine. Just give me a moment."

"I see no hidden doorways," Chant said, turning in a slow circle to survey the corridor. "*I saw the different thing you did, but always you yourself you hid.*"

"Only the one who uses the Word can see its work," Carter said. "Help me up and I'll show you."

With Chant's aid, he went to the portrait and felt along its back edge, where he quickly discovered a latching mechanism. With the clamp released the gilded frame slid to the side on silent rollers, revealing a square opening, tall enough for a man, draped with the silver webs of spiders.

"*Where shall we adventure, today that we're afloat, Wary of the weather and steering by a star? Shall it be to Africa, a'steering of the boat, To Providence, or Babylon, or off to Malabar?*" Chant quoted wistfully, peering into the dark passage.

"I really wish you would let a few of Glis's men accompany you," Hope said. "Or some of the servants."

"No. Enoch and I have discussed it. Glis intends to retake the library and get a messenger to the White Circle; thereafter he will liberate the path to the Towers, hopefully in time to provide us a safe escort home. He will need every man, and ours is not a military expedition. We have to go swiftly and in stealth. They may guard the Towers if they think we can reach them, but they can't yet enter there; it is a place of tremendous power that they cannot master. Only Enoch and I will go."

"It seems vaguely wrong," Hope said, "but I do have something to give you, an article Chant helped me find."

He handed Carter a thin scroll, with sculpted rosewood handles. "It looks small," Hope said, "but it will surprise you."

The material was soft as damask, dyed with blues, greens, and yellows, still brilliant for all its obvious age.

"A map!" Carter said.

"Let me show you," Hope said. "We are here. It won't

show the secret ways, but it reveals the main passage to the Towers. I've even found Naleewuath and Arkalen."

"Thank you," Carter said. "This will be useful. I only wish I were going to Arkalen now; I desperately need to find my father's sword and cloak. Sufficient for today is today's troubles, I suppose, but I must reach there soon."

As he put on his pack, Carter glanced out the window at the morning; water stood in pools upon the muddy ground; the gray clouds left all subdued, drained of light and life, the kind of day he normally thought good for curling up with a book. But the constant dreariness had sunk into his soul and he would have given much for a real ray of sunshine.

Far below, the tiny figure of the Bobby stood beneath the lamppost, like a wooden soldier in the rain, and Carter shivered suddenly, wondering what had happened to Murmur and Duskin.

Enoch gave him a lamp and a wink. Carter already had his pistol in his coat and a short dagger about his belt, and if he had possessed the Lightning Sword, he might even have felt eager, instead of only half-equipped. Still, he returned the tall man's grin. They shook hands with Hope and Chant, and the Lamp-lighter said, "Godspeed, Master. *I can but trust that good shall fall, At last—far off—at last to all, And every winter change to spring.*"

They stepped into the shadows of the secret passage and murmured a final farewell as Hope slid the painting back into its place, caging them in darkness, save for the tender light of Enoch's lamp. The floorboard slats, which were layered with dust, creaked beneath their steps; spiderwebs thick as twine caught their arms and hair. The plaster had crumbled in parts, leaving piles against the border and bare boards upon the walls.

"Sneaking like rats," Enoch said softly. "To a place where I have always walked proudly. Will this teach me humility? Maybe so. Humility is a good thing. Tell me it is, so I do not pound the walls in anger."

Carter glanced at his friend, but saw only humor in his eyes. "It is a very good thing. At least, so Father always said."

"He was a wise man, your father. Wise and foolish as are we all. I miss him. Do you think you will like the Towers?"

Carter chuckled. "I hadn't considered it. As a child, I always thought of you climbing a long stair with the stars in-between; I never imagined your arrival."

"A tower to heaven? My descendants tried it. They were unsuccessful. The Towers are nothing like that."

"Why did you never allow me to accompany you?"

Enoch stepped over a bit of debris on the floor. "Your father would not permit it. He was cautious, as fathers sometimes are. He feared something might happen to you. It lies outside the Inner Chambers, where the anarchists sometimes go."

"Did they ever attack you?"

Enoch drew his greatcoat aside, revealing a long, silver scabbard, heavy with runes, inlaid with topaz and lapis lazuli, with ivory and pearls adorning the guards of the gleaming hilt of the wide sword. "Those who did, did not again."

Carter fell silent, amazed at the innocence of youth, that had perceived a dangerous journey only as a forbidden holiday, and a grim warrior as a laughing uncle.

The bare corridor continued only a brief time before ending at the base of a wide stair, which ascended to a gallery leading to the left, its end lost in the darkness. The steps were gray marble, and monks were carved upon the balusters, their mouths wide as if in song, their faces all turned toward the top of the stair. The wall beside the steps had been papered long before, and the material puckered and sagged from accumulated moisture. A faded painting of a ship on a restless sea hung at the bottom of the stair and Carter reported the presence of another hidden doorway beside it, marked by a blue, luminous rectangle.

Enoch paused a moment in thought, looking at the staircase.

"Does it feel right? No. It must go up, yes, but see how it leads back east? It cannot reach the Towers unless it crosses upon itself."

They climbed to the gallery, which terminated before ornate double doors opening into a long, straight corridor. Enoch shook his head. "Who knows which way a passage may turn? But this leads the wrong direction. Should we try the secret way?"

The two men went back down and examined the walls for a device to open the panel. They soon discovered a spy-hole hidden beneath the painting. Enoch peered through it and declared that the main stair to the Towers lay on the other side. "There must be a way between there and here," he said. "It is most sensible."

Carter explored the stairway, and eventually realized that one of the carved monks was turned slightly more to the right than its companions. It rotated easily at his touch, and a distinct click emanated, like the opening of a latch, yet the doorway did not appear. He was momentarily mystified, until he discovered that the banister knob, previously secure, now lifted effortlessly from its position, revealing a hidden compartment, with a small valve within. He turned it with some labor to overcome decades of disuse, and a hissing, like running water, flowed through the valve. He could not guess if it were truly liquid, or jets of gas that powered the mechanism, but the wall slid slowly aside, revealing by the light of a single lamp in the room beyond, green, golden-flowered carpet wrapped around the bottom of a wide staircase. They entered cautiously, the circle of their lantern eclipsing the ring of the other light.

The room was paneled in dark oak, with a door facing the stair and another on the far wall. Above the shadows of the high ceiling a faint rain tapped against the roof. The stair, seen from its bottom, stretched long and straight into the darkness, and Carter sensed vast heights above him, the massive weight of wood and stone ascending as if indeed to the stars.

He slowly perceived that this was not simply imagination, but a true communion with the leviathan architecture, and he knew, somehow, that it was connected with the Words of Power.

"Enoch, there are other secret ways above us. Do you feel them?"

"I know only the single stair. You see more than I. But I do smell tobacco in this room, which I have never done before. Our enemies were just here. They must be very close, perhaps behind that far door. Or perhaps above us. If we climb the stair, we may meet them."

"You say the other stair does not go to the Towers?"

"Am I a wise man? Who am I to say what goes where? I say only it does not seem to, but it might wind and curve and so bring us there at last."

"We should use this one, I think. But first, there must be a way to shut the passage behind us. We should guard our secrets."

"The first lever was hidden in the banister knob. Why not the second?"

Carter inspected the rail of the main stair. "Why not, indeed?" he said, finding and turning a valve identical to the first, which closed the sliding door.

They followed the flowered carpet up the stair; Enoch held the lamp low, and little else could be seen except the steps and the dark wood at the bottom of the railing. They listened as they went, but heard only the rain above them.

"Is it always this dark?" Carter half whispered.

"Not usually. Chant keeps the lamps lit to the first landing, which is hundreds of steps above us, but he does not go beyond it. The anarchists have extinguished the jets. For what reason? I cannot guess."

They fell silent once more, hushed by the stillness and the obscurity, the soft footfalls on the cushioned stair, the dim light on the dusk wood, the pounding blood through their chambered hearts, the bending knees and the quiet breath.

After a time of straining to peer beyond the circle of the lamp-light, it seemed to Carter they walked not up, but down into cavernous depths, and only the pressure in his calves told him otherwise. He saw the lamp as a sliding serpent, eating the ebony before them, spewing it back behind, and he a rider balanced on its frame.

After what felt like many hours, though less than two by his pocket watch, he saw an indistinct shining before them, which Enoch could not discern. They approached warily and discovered the glowing blue rectangle indicating a secret doorway.

"Should we take it?" the old Hebrew asked when Carter told him what he saw.

"We haven't seen the anarchists. If you've smelled no more tobacco, we should continue on the familiar way."

They had gone only a short distance before Enoch abruptly extinguished the lantern, plunging them into darkness. Both men stood frozen on the stair, swaying slightly for balance, Carter ignorant of what his companion had seen, until he detected a pinpoint of light like a distant star, far above them. They crouched on the stair, the carpet soft beneath their hands, their eyes transfixed on the light until it became apparent it was descending. Muted voices drifted down. There was nowhere to hide.

"Back to the hidden door," Carter whispered.

They made a creeping retreat, as swiftly but silently as possible. It became apparent, from the increasing footfalls and the growing light, that they would soon be overtaken if they did not find haven. Carter strained to locate the illumination marking the hidden door, unwilling to glance away lest he overlook it, fearful that the Word of Secret Ways had run its course. His heart fluttered like a bird's, his breath fluttered like a fluted reed. For an instant, he despaired. And then the cold blue rectangle was there.

Still crouching, they searched the banister below the illumination for the secret catch. Carter ran his hands over the top of the wood, but discovered nothing, then felt his way to the bottom while Enoch searched the wall.

"Did you see something?" a voice above them said loudly.

"What? Where?"

"Down there! Something moves!"

The clamor of numerous feet jolted the stair. Carter felt frantically around the banister base, trying to rotate one of the balusters, but they remained unyielding. A panic seized him and for a moment he could not think. Then he realized that one of the banister-pole carvings felt slightly lower than the rest. He pulled straight up; it lifted with a firm click; the blue rectangle slid down, revealing a dark shaft lying at a ninety-degree angle from the wall. Carter crawled in quickly, knowing Enoch would never agree to enter first. The dull crack of a pistol reverberated down the stair as he squirmed into absolute ebony. For a fearful moment he held his breath, thinking Enoch had been shot, until he heard his companion following after.

His hand brushed against a short lever.

"Are you in?" he asked softly.

"I am."

Carter pulled the lever and heard the soft sliding of the panel.

Beyond the wall, feet clambered past, then abruptly halted.

"Where are they?" someone asked. "Did you hit one?"

"I don't see anything," another said. "They must have descended."

Gradually, the noise of the pursuers diminished, leaving the men to the silence and the dark. Carter crawled forward.

A fear took him then, quite apart from the fear of the anarchists. With the four walls enclosing him, narrow as a coffin, a rushing panic brought cold beads of perspiration over his whole body, and suddenly, desperately, he wanted to flail the walls until they gave way. It were as if he was in the well again, a narrower well, with water about to pour in at any moment and the Bobby waiting above to drown him. He bit his hand to keep from crying out and forced himself to push forward with precise slowness, fighting the panic.

Every inch was an agony, and when his hands at last touched empty space, he grasped the lip of the shaft and swung himself down onto a wooden floor with such force that he scraped his head against the top of the shaft.

A moment later, breathless and faint, still in darkness, he helped Enoch down, though he could scarcely stand himself. "Are you wounded?" he managed.

"For that, we were frightened?" Enoch said, close to his ear. "Those were no marksmen, missing us on that slender stair. Should I dare the lamp? I think I should."

They moved away from the shaft and after some fumbling, managed to light the lantern. They stood in a narrow room, with a wrought-iron, spiral stair winding its way to the floor above. Finding no other exit, they ascended quickly; a thin film of red rust darkened Carter's hand where he held the railing. Enoch popped his head up to the next floor, glanced around, then mounted to the top. Carter followed after, into a narrow room with a short passage that turned a corner to the right. Pursuing this, they found another corridor, just wide enough for two to walk abreast. Judging by the feel of the air currents, Carter supposed it to be quite lengthy, though their lamplight did not penetrate ten feet. The floor sloped steeply upward and they labored as if climbing a hill. The carpet, unraveling at its edges, was the dull brown of sand. Patches of plaster had fallen from the walls and ceiling.

"Enoch, are we above the main stair?"

"You must be correct. Why else would it slope? We are following the rising of the steps. All the years I walked the stair, there was another way just overhead. Who would have thought? Not I. But is it safe?"

"I doubt the anarchists know of it. That was a close thing down there. You seem unshaken."

"Inside I still tremble. I have not been fired upon in a long time."

They fell into listening silence, hearing nothing but their own soft footfalls; even the rain did not reach to this passage, a fact Carter found curious since they were now closer to the roof. Its timelessness awed him, as he might have been awed by a desert plain with the stars shining all around, or a forest glade unexplored by man; it was the lure of the desolate places—surely no one had walked this corridor for many years, perhaps many lifetimes—yet it remained, unmoved by its own emptiness. In his wonder at such solitude, his fear of being pursued and of being trapped in the shaft faded. He suddenly felt very young, embarked on the greatest of all adventures.

The monotony of the continual passage and the quiet soon brought his mind to another state, however, lulling him until he forgot himself, and thought he was once again the small boy following his old comrade down the great passages, with all the summers of childhood before them. Carter remembered that Enoch used to sometimes whittle when they walked, and had made him whistles and tops, and even the wooden soldiers now standing on the dresser in his room. When such a relationship between a man and a youth is forged, it is not easily changed, and though Enoch now called him Master, the Windkeep's words still warmed Carter like sunshine and warm honey, and he thought him wise as any oracle.

So he asked Enoch if he remembered their walks and the man chuckled softly and said yes.

"I suppose I was a great deal of bother," Carter said.

"No, you were not, for you asked good questions and you did not talk too much. You were company for me. I enjoyed it. I have had many good walks in my long life."

The brown carpet in the shadowed hall, the dim flame on the plaster walls, the slow tread and the slow breaths—there was nothing else.

"Enoch, did you mean it when you said you use to walk with God, long ago?" Carter inquired sheepishly, thinking it a boy's question, for he believed the man had spoken figuratively. Yet, this was a strange house. . . .

"Yes," he said. "Those were good walks as well."

"What did He look like? What did you discuss?"

Enoch was silent so long Carter thought he had not heard the question, but at last the Windkeep said, "What did He look like? The truth. I cannot remember. His face was like our faces, I think, but when you looked at Him, it was as if our faces were not faces at all, but only masks, as if we had never had faces and only His face was real. Would I call it a good face? That says nothing at all. Or wise? Or kind? No. It was goodness and wisdom and kindness. From the day I met Him, I always wanted a face like that. I do not believe we can truly meet Him face-to-face until we have such faces.

"What did He say? It was of clouds and wind and rain, of grass and hills and the wide places between the stars. It was a time before science when men thought the trees had voices, and the rocks and every other thing, so I did not ask Him the questions a modern man might, such as how the universe was shaped, or how hot the sun was, or if the world was round, for I thought it was not. I told Him I thought His mountains were nice, and that I liked the taste of His fish. And I asked Him foolish things like if it would rain that day, or if the wind would blow. Sometimes I asked His help with my grandchildren. He always said He would see what He could do, but that He had made them with their own opinions to make the decisions they thought best. He spoke of simple things as I would speak to a child, because any others would have been beyond my understanding. I liked Him! I thought Him splendid. And sometimes I long to see Him more than anything, and there is no loneliness like the loneliness for Him. I think He liked me, too. Why? I do not know, except He is that sort of person, for I was foolish in His presence, though it did not seem so at the time."

Enoch paused and looked up at the ceiling, then chuckled softly. "Have I told you anything? No. But it is all I can say."

They traveled another hour in silence, listening always for sounds of their enemies. At last the ceiling veered down toward them and the corridor ended in an alcove containing another spiral stair leading down. To the men's surprise, a pentagonal window adorned the ceiling, inviting a soft column of light to rest, like a will-o'-the-wisp, on the worn carpet.

Carter examined the window and found a brass latch, but did not try it; it had probably never been opened and the drops of rain on the glass dissuaded him from making the effort.

"A fine place for lunch," Enoch said. "It is good to see light, even if through clouds."

From their packs they produced bread and cheese and a slab of roast beef, and Enoch even made tea, warming it by the heat of his lamp. During their walk Carter had little noticed the damp and cool of the air, but he did now as the hot tea and the good bread warmed and filled him. They sat on the floor together, around the small patch of light, as if it might cheer them, and Carter felt quite content, as if there were no danger at all, and they were simply having a picnic. And looking upon the old leather face of his companion, he suddenly found tears at the corners of his eyes, feeling he had truly returned to the innocent days of his past, and that they might, if they wished, curl up on the carpet after lunch and take a solemn nap. And he knew then that Enoch had raised him as much as his father, and perhaps he had been with the old Hebrew more.

They had just finished packing their things, when they heard a noise from the bottom of the spiral stair, a loud clang and then a curse. Both men were on their feet at once, listening.

"Be silent back there," a voice commanded softly. "We may encounter them at any time. Be diligent."

Carter and Enoch exchanged glances; somehow the anarchists had found their way into the passages. If the companions remained to fight, they might become trapped, but retreat would only take them farther from the Towers, perhaps into the hands of their enemies.

Carter grasped the brass latch on the overhead window. At first it withstood him, until Enoch added his own strength. It unhooked with a thud, and the window creaked open. Enoch gave Carter a boost, and he had to squeeze his shoulders together to penetrate the narrow opening. Once through, he gave his companion a hand. Enoch scrambled up with amazing spryness. Carter pulled the window shut, but there was no way to latch it from the top. It would leave the anarchists a clear trail.

Looking about, he beheld a breathless panoply of skyline, festooned with legions of assorted towers, more than could possibly belong only to Evenmere. Battlements and bastions, crags and crannies, the roof ridges and the roofs of slate, spires like spears aimed at the heavens, the long balconies, the deep quadrangles, the gables and domes, the summits and the inclines—their shapes seeming to form before the eyes, popping out from amidst the conglomerate stones like boiling cloud banks, presenting the faces of the stone gargoyles, goblins, angels, and friars, views forever changed by the slightest tilt of the head. And across it all, a path of paving stones, ocher and gold, leading from the window, like a bread-crumb trail through the masonry forest.

They set off at once across the hills and valleys of that insurmountable heap; the stones were slick from the rain, the roofs were sometimes flat but often sloping, with fountained courts or walled gardens sleeping far below and a single treacherous footfall between. They quickly lost themselves amidst the towers, and when Carter glanced back he could not even discern the roof of the pentagonal window; every movement shifted that vast landscape. Were it not for the path, no pursuer could have followed them, yet it was only by it that they hoped to find their way.

They slowed their furious pace to a more cautious stride as they approached a narrow bridge between two ridges, lying at the bottom of a sloping roof made treacherous by the rain. Enoch went first, sliding down on his back, but the slippery surface carried him more swiftly than Carter thought possible. He tilted toward the bridge pole, missed it by a handsbreadth, and disappeared beyond the ridgeline.

With a cry of terror Carter followed after, standing upright but leaning far back, even as a noise whizzed by his ear. Hearing but not heeding, he slid down to the bridge, caught the railing in both hands, and came to a stop on his knees, fearing to see his friend's crumpled form lying on the flagstones below. Instead, he found Enoch clutching a metal stanchion a foot below the roof, his legs dangling in space.

Before Carter could grasp the old servant's hand, a bullet tore at the roof beside him, and he realized the first shot had passed close by his head as he slid. A single man in a dark coat stood upon the ridge crest, revolver in hand.

Hot wrath erupted within him for the sake of his ancient companion, and he drew his own pistol and fired three times quickly. The assailant dropped like a rag, rolled down the roof, and then to the ground, but Carter did not see him fall; noticing no other anarchists, he cast his eyes back to where Enoch was bravely pulling himself onto the bridge. Carter gave him his hand and helped him rise.

"Across the span!" Enoch cried. "The others will be behind him."

The bridge was little more than a steel walkway, wide enough for one person, with metal railings for safety. There was little chance of falling, but the slippery metal and the long drop below, augmented by the fear of a bullet in the back, left Carter glancing from his feet to the roof behind. They were nearly across when he saw two dark figures reach the peak. The first duplicated Enoch's slide down the roof, but failed to catch the railing. Carter gripped the bars as he watched the man dwindle to doll size, all flailing arms, greatcoat, and terrified scream, resembling for an instant a thrashing gray bird, before the earth took him. The other man hesitated, obviously shaken by his comrade's plunge, then he, too, slid down, catching himself on the bridge. He leapt to his feet, his long strides overtaking his victims, his gun already out of his pocket. "Halt!" he cried. "I can't miss from here."

Enoch reached the other side, and Carter turned at the end of the bridge. At this distance, shooting between the rails, the man was correct; he could scarcely fail to hit them. He approached slowly, certain victory in his cruel grin.

"You'll stop there!" he ordered. "Drop the weapon. Be swift, or I'll blow you open."

As Carter dropped the revolver onto the flat roof, he noticed a peculiar mechanism built into the end of the bridge. At first glance he did not fathom its purpose, but after a moment, its function became clear.

"Take it easy," the man was saying. "No one wants to die, though you may desire to before it's over."

Carter kicked the lever at his feet, and it unlocked a pair of heavy pins, releasing the walkway from its moorings. The bridge dropped away from the side where Carter stood, and the anarchist lost his pistol as he clutched frantically for a hold. It did no good; as the walkway slammed against the opposite wall he was hurled screaming to the ground.

"It was designed for that!" Carter cried. "Can you believe it?" A pair of cables and a hoist were built into the wall to bring the bridge back up at need.

"The Masters of the house have often required speedy retreats on their journeys through Evenmere," Enoch said. "Various factions have always opposed their rule. But come away quickly. A bullet can still reach us."

They soon left the bridge behind, lost in the maze of stonework and statues, and came to a roof covered in flagstones, large as a cathedral, with a tall tower lording over its center, having four yellow clock faces, each displaying a different time, none of them correct. Years of spiderwebs bound the hands of the east face in gossamer ropes, nearly obscuring it. The trail of ocher and gold paving stones, which had continued through the flat waste, ended at the bottom of the structure, where a metal ladder led up to the clocks.

"Do I know where we are? Yes!" Enoch grinned brightly against the stormy sky. "This is Four Dials Tower. Until now, I have always reached it from below and wound it from within."

"But surely it no longer runs," Carter said. "None of the times are correct."

"The east face was ruined half a hundred years ago," Enoch said. "But I did not claim that all the clocks were set to the same time we know. Surely it is different times in different parts of the world. I see they do not run down, but I do not reset them; that was not the task given me. Come. We should climb the ladder and look for a way to descend."

Enoch led up the metal rungs to the north face. It was higher than Carter had expected; from his perch he could see above most of the surrounding towers, and it made him uneasy, since he knew they were targets for any who could witness. The ladder ended in a narrow landing, with a tottering, wooden railing, rotten from the weather. The landing itself was more sturdy; their heads were level with the bottom of the clock face, which was eight feet across and sheltered by a stone lip.

Enoch ran his hands as high as he could reach around the rim of the clock. Finally, he stepped back and scratched his head. "It is not wound from the outside. Does the ladder lead nowhere? I doubt it. There must be a way in."

Carter examined the clock face. It was white, with black Roman numerals. He noticed the six was slightly crooked, so he reached up and gave it a hopeful twist. It turned with a click, and the whole face opened outward, swung on a long hinge. They pulled themselves over the brink with an effort. Before he shut the face, Carter looked out once more. He could not be certain, but he thought he saw a cluster of black-garbed figures, like blown rags, moving between the cloistered shadows. Beyond that, the clouds had parted, and a single shaft of sunlight shone silver off the rooftops, like coins on the water.

"They cannot maintain the storm forever," he murmured, grinning ruefully.

The clock face shut with a dull clang.

By the lances of light entering around the border of the four dials, they found themselves in a chamber large enough for the timepiece mechanisms, with enough space for them to stand comfortably. The room resonated with the noise of the ticking.

The two companions thumped one another on the back in triumph. "Who could have given a better run?" Enoch asked. "And your quick wit saved us on the walkway."

"We did it together. I'm still trembling all over. I wish we had time to celebrate with some hot tea, but they surely know our location."

"They do. Once they arrive, it will not take long to decipher the locking mechanism on the clock. And we still must reach the Towers before they block our way."

Enoch lit his lamp to dispel the shadows, drew a long key from an inner coat pocket, and wound each of the clocks. By the time he was done, Carter had discovered a trapdoor leading from the tower by way of a rickety ladder.

They wasted no time, but departed hastily, climbing over splintered wood, and tearing through spiderwebs to reach the narrow room at the bottom. A stair covered in frayed, red carpet led from there, a short descent into a delicate room, with French furniture, green damask curtains, and needlework pictures covering one wall. It must once have been beautiful, but the dust lay thick upon the white linen tablecloth and covered the furniture like gray frost.

"Anyone ever live here, I wonder," Carter asked, "and where have they gone?"

"Since the day I first wound the clocks, it has been empty," Enoch said. "But there are many living in this great house. It is not unusual to find a poet or a hermit, dwelling in some back room, obtaining their food who knows how. Some have been alone a long time."

"Will this route take us back to the main stairs?"

"Back? No. By climbing the rooftops we have bypassed it and much more. Had I known of this way, I could have saved my weary feet many times."

"Did none of the Masters ever accompany you on your rounds?"

"Several, including your father, but they never used the Word of Secret Ways. I always suspected alternate paths; there are more hidden passages than termites in Evenmere, but the Words of Power are not used for convenience. I never needed a new route until now."

They left the room through a paneled door and entered a narrow passage, with chrome-yellow carpet and oak baseboards twelve inches high. Doors lined either side of the corridor and unlit chandeliers hung down its length.

"Where do the doors lead?" Carter asked softly, lest he be overheard.

"Where? Many places. I have not explored them all. Some open to rooms like the one we just left; some lead other ways, some into strange, curious countries. When I was young I traveled them into many kinds of trouble or adventure. I am less inquisitive now. You could spend many lifetimes wandering and not see it all."

One of the doors opened before them, and a figure stepped out, holding a red lamp aloft. Carter drew his revolver, but Enoch placed a hand upon his arm. The man was ancient, and dressed in pajamas and a nightcap. His eyes glowed yellow like a cat's, giving him an elfin appearance, but when he drew nearer, he cried out in alarm, and hurried back through the door. Carter heard the turning of the lock as they passed. He wondered if the man would care that he was the Steward of the house, or if he even knew there was one.

For three hours they traveled past the endless rows of doors, and they saw neither inhabitants nor anarchists, though

Enoch assured Carter that their enemies would know their destination and guard every known route. Their advantage lay in the size of the house, and in its many connecting passageways, for the anarchists could not patrol all of them at once.

They reached an intersection, new passages arranged identical to their own. Enoch hesitated. "I must think. We should go to the left; it will lead us away from our goal, yet we can use it to circle back. No, that is not the way. It would take us past routes the anarchists would think to guard. Straight ahead is my usual route; it will be the most watched. Should we go to the right? It will lead to the area called the Winelderwist, and it is a maze." His eyes suddenly blazed as he spoke. "Beyond it is a narrow way, little known, that might be our best chance, if only I can find it again. What do you think?"

"If it is the least guarded, I say we try it," Carter said.

"Ha, spoken like your mother!" Enoch slapped him on the back.

"I would have thought rather my father."

"No, no. He would have pondered upon it, being a precise man. Your mother made her decisions briskly, with a quick mind."

They were hushed by a sound from the left, and Enoch extinguished the lamp at once. This saved them from discovery, for a party of men turned the far corner a moment later. The companions ducked back behind the junction and began testing the nearest doors. The first two were locked, but the third opened with a dull creak, and they hurried within, their way lit by the approaching lamps from the intersecting corridor. No sooner were they inside when the intruders turned the corner, so close they dared not risk the noise of shutting the door. Carter watched through the narrow crack as six anarchists filed down the hall, their shadows bobbing behind them like goblins. At the intersection, two of them continued down the right branch, while the other four halted directly in front of the door.

"This is it," one of them said. "They must advance through

here if they approach the Towers. I want lights extinguished. We will spot them by their lamps."

"Two of us could proceed farther down," another said.

"Ineffectual," the first said. "There are innumerable doors. They would observe your party and simply seek concealment. It is preferable that they come to us."

Perspiration slid down Carter's back. The anarchists' lamps shone through the crack in the door, granting a half-light to the room, which was small, with little more than a desk and a pair of chairs. At its far end stood another door. He turned toward his companion and gestured toward it, unable to remove his hand from the knob, lest it shift and creak.

Enoch slipped back to the door and opened it by inches, silently, until it was wide enough for him to slide through. He vanished into its shadows.

Carter faced a dilemma. If he followed, he would have to release the door; it would certainly move, creaking as it had when opened. Yet, he could scarcely stand here for hours, and the light would soon be extinguished. After a moment, he determined his course.

The anarchists' lamps went out, plunging all into utter darkness. Only then did he shut the door, quickly, and it did not creak, but gave a slight click, sounding to his ears as loud as a hammer.

"What was that?" one of the anarchists asked.

"Numerous folk wander these halls," another said. "Nothing to be alarmed about."

"Relight the lantern. I say it's worth investigating."

Carter had done his best to memorize the path to the far door. He groped his way through the darkness until he reached it. Once there, he entered and shut it carefully behind him.

"Enoch," he whispered.

"Here," his friend replied, just to his left. "There is another way out. Do we dare make a light?"

"Not yet. They may be coming."

Carter listened, ear to the keyhole, and heard the door to the corridor open. Lamplight trickled over the threshold crack. By its light, Carter spotted another exit, and was about to try to reach it, when he heard the anarchist say: "There's no one in here. Should I search the rooms beyond?"

"Don't bother," another voice hissed. "We can't pursue every noise. If our quarry has already reached these rooms, we will never find them. Our hope is in surprise; every moment with the lanterns lit spoils our chances. Come back to your place!"

Carter heard the door close; the room was immediately plunged back into darkness. He waited several moments before groping his way to Enoch.

"With two doors between us and the corridor, I think we can dare a low light," Carter whispered.

The soft glow of the lamp gradually rose, less than a sliver, barely revealing another room much like the first, with a door on the opposing wall opening into a drab bedroom with tatters for blankets and cobwebs between the posts. Within that room, they found two other doors, and took the one opposite the way they had entered, into a deserted drawing room. So far they had moved in a straight line; the next door stood on the left wall, so Carter knew it would probably exit into the corridor once more, past the intersection where the anarchists waited. This was precisely the direction the men needed to go, yet they would be scarcely two doors away from the ambuscade. After some debate, they decided to douse their lamp, wait thirty minutes for the anarchists to settle, then attempt to slip down the passage.

The wait in the dark grew eternal. Carter could not say how long they actually delayed, for he could not discern his pocket watch, but Enoch seemed to know the exact time, as if winding so many clocks had made him a living timepiece. At first Carter was anxious, but the monotony of staring into blackness soon made him sleepy. He was nearly dozing when

Enoch touched his knee to signal their departure, and he struggled from his stupor, reminding himself of their danger.

At Enoch's insistence, Carter went first, and he knew it was because the old servant wanted to place himself between the guns of the anarchists and his master. He slid his hands over the knob and tested it. At first he thought it would prove resistant, for it did not turn easily, but as he gradually increased the pressure the striker slid soundlessly away. As he opened the door, it gave the barest creak. He stood frozen, listening for a hundred heartbeats, yet the passage lay silent.

He stepped out onto the soft carpet. Gratitude swept through him that he would not have to cross bare, cracking floorboards. It was dark with the complete darkness he had feared as a child, that he feared still, and for an instant he wondered if he had the courage to go on, for he wanted to turn and flee back into the room until the anarchists departed. He could see absolutely nothing. He drew a deep breath, knowing himself a coward, and began inching his way down the hall. Enoch followed, guided by clasping Carter's shoulder.

Almost at once, Carter brushed against a picture. He rushed to steady it with his hand, lest it fall from the wall. It struck the plaster with a light tap; he stood holding it for the space of a minute, knowing the anarchists would hear and investigate. When they did not, he gradually released it, and continued his trek, his mouth dry, his heart beating hard within him.

He was terrified that the Bobby would come at him from the darkness, and he clutched his gun in one hand and doubled his other fist into a knot. At first it was hard to make himself stir; he trembled and could not move his feet; then as they drew farther from their enemies, it was difficult to go slow, for he wanted to run. He caught himself walking too fast, making too much noise, and restrained himself only with an effort. His mind raced. What if there were other anarchists down the corridor? When would they be able to relight their lamps?

After what seemed like hours, the wall to his right ended. He felt around, trying to ascertain if this was truly the turning of the corner. He stopped and listened again, praying they were not about to walk into their enemies, as they took the passage to the right.

Step by step they made their way through the darkness, not knowing what was before them, feeling their way again along the right-hand wall. Spots of color faded into Carter's view, illusions from the lack of light. Finally, when they had gone twice the distance they thought necessary, Enoch knelt with flint and rags and lit the lamp. But as he stood to his feet, a voice called out, "Stop right there!"

Glancing back, Carter dimly saw the shadow of a man at the corner they had passed; they had slipped by him without knowing.

A bullet struck to Enoch's left, and they bolted down the corridor. If the corner had not been near, they would have certainly died, but they ducked behind it and sped down another, shorter passage, Enoch's lamp, half-mantled, stretching their frenzied shadows long across the walls. At any moment Carter expected to feel lead burning through his back. He doubled his efforts and reached the goal before Enoch, and so turned and fired twice to keep the anarchists at bay until his friend was safe.

He had been on the track team at Bracton College, and had tried to stay in condition since then, but the run left him breathless; he had been a distance man and no sprinter. Enoch fared a little worse, but there was no time to pause. The next corridor ran into the endless dark, and might be forty yards or four hundred.

To their good fortune a way opened to the left almost immediately. As they took it, Enoch gasped, "I know where we are. We're almost there."

This corridor branched in three directions, and they ran back to the right, then left again, where they came to a circular room, the intersection of eight separate corridors. In the red glow of the lamp, Enoch grinned. "We've reached the Winelderwist. Come with me."

The passage they took lasted less than a hundred steps, before angling to the right; Carter rejoiced that their light could no longer be seen from the circular hall. Still, they did not relent until they took three more turnings, when they slowed to a walk. Gasping, red-faced, they looked at one another and softly laughed.

"I thought my galloping days were over," Enoch said. "Necessity gives wings to age."

"Will they be able to trace our steps?"

"There were ten separate branchings we could have taken. Of those, four are unlikely, if they are familiar enough to know it, for they lead away from the Towers, not toward them. If there were six men and each took one corridor, we could indeed be followed. But just ahead is our salvation, if only no more guards await us."

"Do you think it likely?"

"Not much. The Winelderwist has too many branchings for the anarchists to guard them all. But we must be wary."

They came to three doors and a spiral staircase at the end of the passage. Enoch took the door to the right, which opened onto a long, wooden stair leading downward, with a landing and a doorway every dozen steps. He led through the door on the third landing, down a narrow passage with doors on either side. Halfway down that hall, he took another door, which led down another stair, carved all in wood, with the heads of eagles chiseled on the posts.

"If I wasn't before, I am wholly lost now," Carter said.

"Fortunately, I am not. This will lead us past the Room of Statues, once I find two more portals."

At the bottom of the stair were four doors. Enoch tried them all and found the first one locked, the second only a closet, the third a stair scarce two-feet wide, leading upward by rickety steps, and the fourth a straight passage. He chose the third, and they plunged into a country of spiderwebs and creaking boards, railings of rough wood, the smell of mold in thick air, and no walls at either side, so that Carter's childhood fancy of Enoch ascending a stair between the stars seemed true. The floor was soon lost to their lamplight, save for rugged support posts rising from the darkness, and the ceiling remained indiscernible. The echoes of their footsteps fluttered around them, indicating that they climbed above a great chamber; cool air wafted across their brows. Their whispers skittered all about the room, returning to them as soft sibilance.

They came to a landing, with a rusted metal door intruding out of the void, supported by a tunnel of brick. Enoch stood before it a time, hand to chin.

"Should we open it?" Carter finally asked.

"Some doors in Evenmere are best untried," Enoch replied. "I do not think this is the one, nor the next."

They continued upward. It was a long while before they passed the next door, which appeared identical to the first, and even longer before they reached the third. Enoch wiped its surface with his sleeve and uncovered four marks scratched into the metal.

"Is this it? Yes!"

It was a massive door, and they struggled together to lift the heavy latch and strained to pull it open. At last, it budged with a loud groan, its hinges shrieking, and the entire chamber roared back, reverberate, like Jormungand in his attic. Once loosened, it moved freely. Within, the passage was red brick on all four sides, and tall enough for a man. They closed the door after them, its echoes muffled behind the massive plate.

"This leads to the Room of Statues," Enoch said. "We will be safe here."

The passage ended soon enough, and they stood within another cavernous space. At Enoch's suggestion, they lit Carter's lamp for additional light. As the flame sprang upward, Carter gave a start and fumbled for his pistol, for a massive face loomed out of the ebony. Enoch restrained him, and he soon realized it was the statue of a warrior, helmeted and plumed in the Roman manner, cast of black marble, armored, his sword flung outward in a gesture of vengeance.

"There are many of them," Enoch said. "The chamber is filled, though most are not so tall. There are windows at the end of the room, but night has fallen. I believe I can lead us through."

The next hours were those Carter remembered best, of all that journey to the Towers, for there was a sepulchral quality in seeing the statues rise into the circle of their lamps, faces noble, foolish, cunning, or beautiful. They were carved mostly from white stone, unlike the dark warrior, and none were as tall as he. Carter found himself giving them names as he went, so that they became the Magician, the Juggler, the Princess, the Piper, the Magistrate, the Counselor, the Beggar, and the Thief. The Lamp-lighter even resembled Chant a little, and the Unicorn was cut from a rare stone sparkling blue fire. Enoch used the statues to mark his way, and he turned left beside the Merchant and right beside the Gatekeeper.

They had neither eaten nor rested for many hours, and the oppressive night left them bone-weary, but need spurred them on to the Towers, lest all the ways become guarded. They halted only long enough to eat a cold meal of dried fruit and strips of meat, with lukewarm water from a flask.

At last they reached a doorway leading through a narrow corridor, with faded flowered wallpaper and wooden floors. They ascended several slender stairs, like ants climbing out of their den, and emerged onto a flagstone courtyard, built upon the highest roofs. Moonlight pierced the storm clouds, casting a pallid light across the expanse. A light mist was falling, so that a halo crept around their lanterns. Carter breathed the cool air; its sharpness drove away the torpid half sleep that had enveloped him as they walked the ragged ways. They stood at the lowest of several levels of the courtyard, each of which ran into the base of four towers, built like a candelabra, with a single supporting column. Stone trusses led up to the outermost towers, and walkways intersected the others, so there was clearly more than one entrance.

Enoch hastily doused both lamps to avoid detection. "They will not expect us from this direction. Rather they think we will arrive from below the central tower, up a long stair. But all ways may be guarded."

An overhang provided concealing shadows, and they made their way cautiously around the courtyard's edge, pausing often to watch for the anarchists. They were halfway around when a bullet ricocheted off the brick beside them. Carter searched the skyline until he spied a figure, half-silhouetted in the moonlight, standing on the second-floor landing. He fired his pistol; dust rose up from the stones where it struck, and the man vanished behind the masonry.

The two companions bolted as gunshots erupted from two separate directions. They raced between stone columns, remaining always in the shadows. The moon shone onto the base of the Towers, with a wide, open stretch surrounding it. For a moment they stood wavering, unwilling to leave their shelter. But both knew they could not remain long; the men above would soon outmaneuver them. In wordless agreement, Enoch clapped Carter on the back and they sped toward the door at the bottom of the Towers, their guns blazing.

Despite his fear, a strange euphoria passed over Carter; as bullets bounced all around his main emotion was excitement, as if he were living the fictional adventures of some American cowboy. None of it seemed real, and he suddenly knew they would reach the Towers unscathed, heroes passing through a hail of lead. A wild, exultant cry sprang from his lips. The door was almost within reach.

Just then, a cloaked figure, which in the dimness had appeared as a pile of rags, half raised himself from before the door. Orange fire erupted from his revolver. Carter cried out involuntarily as burning pain seared his left leg. He and Enoch fired as one, dropping the assailant to the flagstones.

The door was smooth metal, without a handle, its seams

bare outlines, but Enoch spoke a word, and it sprang open. A shot whizzed by Carter's neck as they plunged into the darkness. Enoch pulled the door shut with a solid clang.

"Are you hurt?" the Hebrew asked.

"It's my leg," Carter said.

He heard the striking of flint, and a narrow flame appeared. "I'm getting a bit faint, old friend."

Enoch lit the lamp and Carter saw blood running down his own arm. His head felt moist, sticky, and when he touched his hand to his temple, he found blood on his fingers as well. The world did a slow circle; his legs would no longer support him, and then Carter fell into darkness.

The Clock Tower

Carter woke to the smell of warm blankets, and diffused illumination through a clear skylight that cast a dull white square on the patchwork quilt of his bed. He roused in a gradual way, as if parting layer after layer of translucent curtains. His first realization was that one of his toes was sticking out of the blankets, though he did nothing to cover it. He wondered where he was, decided it did not matter since he was safe, and drifted back into slumber.

He woke more fully sometime later, to the sounds of Enoch puttering around the room, brewing hot tea on a decrepit stove. Carter sat up on one elbow.

"Hello, is it morning?"

Enoch smiled, but his eyes showed he had not slept. "Closer to afternoon. How many fingers do you see?" He held up his hand.

"Four. Why are you testing me?"

"A bullet grazed your skull. I was hoping you hadn't lost any brains."

"Too deeply embedded for that," he muttered, feeling his own face. There was a bandage above his left ear and a tender lump at the back of his head. "I was shot in the leg, too, wasn't I?"

"I tended it. You will not use it for a time, but it will heal. Is it a miracle we survived? More than a miracle. I should have planned better."

"There probably wasn't a better plan. We knew the Towers would be watched. We are there, aren't we?"

"In the highest, the Tower of the Eternity Clock."

Carter glanced around and discovered a clock face, tall as a man, in the wall behind him, beside the head of the bed. "Does it run? I don't hear it ticking."

"It does run. It even ticks, but so slow you could stay a hundred days and not hear it. It is called the Eternity Clock, either because it displays the pulse of Eternity or because it shows how long until midnight, when Time itself ends. I do not know which."

"I hope it isn't the latter," Carter said, for the clock read 11:50. "How long to make a minute?"

"Three seconds have passed during all the years I have served the High House. I brought you to this room because nothing can harm you here; even sound cannot cross the threshold from outside. Also, wounds heal faster beneath the clock. No one knows why. Your leg requires recuperation."

Carter nodded, not yet ready to face a paradox. He glanced around the chamber, made homey by an odd assortment of furniture. There was even a linen tablecloth on the short table.

"Did you bring all this?" he asked with a wave of his hand.

"A little at a time. After winding the clocks I usually stay the night. No one else ever comes here; probably only I know the word to open the doors. Would you like some hot tea? Something to eat? You should eat. I have soup and bread."

"Yes, please, I am hungry."

Carter ate the soup and bread across from the pleasant crackling of the fireplace. His leg ached where it was bandaged above the knee. He found himself ravenous, and when he was done, the torpor had lifted from his brain. "Now that we are in, we will have to find a way out again," he said.

"Yes. They will try to detain us, for there are other clocks to wind in the house. And in thirty days I must return here again."

"We barely made the journey this time. Glis will retake the path to the Towers as soon as he receives reinforcements from the White Circle, but we don't know how long that will be. Perhaps I could use the Word of Secret Ways to find a new exit, if there is one. Otherwise, we will have to wait for him to catch up with us."

"He is a good man. If he says it, he will do it."

"Yes, but I intend to do more, myself. I cannot simply return to the Inner Chambers, not without my father's things. Do you believe Jormungand spoke true? Is my father in Arkalen?"

Enoch looked unusually bleak. "Do not hope too much. Ten years gone! What but death could keep him so long? Yet, it is uncertain; he might be imprisoned, or ensorcelled. Perhaps his memory has been stolen from him. As for his sword and his mantle, they surely still exist; they were cast of sterner stuff."

"Would you counsel me to go, Enoch? Should I leave the house when it needs me most?"

"On its face, it seems foolish. But the thing most foolish is often wisest. No one can see everything. If your heart says go, then go. Perhaps you are led to do so."

"Yet, if I am wrong . . ."

"Then you are wrong, as your father was wrong more than once. But think it through! Your position is grave. The whole house depends on your decision."

"Yes. I learned how tragic consequences could be the day I took the Master Keys. I want no more mistakes."

"That was a hard lesson, not yet paid. But looking back in remorse, blaming yourself—senseless! Have you learned that as well?"

"I have tried. But it is hard to get it under the skin."

Carter's wounds did not heal quickly and he remained always anxious. Enoch kept busy cleaning the mechanism of the Eternity Clock, oiling its gears with precise care, but Carter could not help with that. He found a copy of MacDonald's *Phantastes* and spent a few happy hours, but it was soon done and there were no other books. The tower above the clock room had seven windows, and he spent many hours sitting in a gray, stiff-backed chair watching the anarchists skulk in the courtyards below, beneath the stormy sky. As the days wore on, he began to wonder if his old friend was deceiving him about the recuperative powers of sleeping in the chamber of the Eternity Clock, lest he become too impatient of his recovery.

He learned the truth one night when he could not sleep. A long stair swept down from the clock room to the lower levels, and since his leg was already much improved, he decided to exercise it upon the steps in the hopes of growing drowsy. No sooner did he cross the threshold when he heard a rapping on the door situated on the landing immediately below the chamber, a door leading outside the Towers. He descended the steps slowly because of his injury and peered through the spy-hole, where he saw a ruined face, ash-gray beneath the candle the figure held, suffused with an anger made horrid by the liquid quality of the whole visage, that changed like dripping wax even as Carter looked. Without opening the door, he called out, "Who are you? What do you want?"

The voice, too, had a quality of insubstantiality. "Let me in, let me in! The Dogs of Doom! The Open Mouth, the Clinging Face! I must come in!"

Except for the stranger's bizarre appearance, the urgency of the request would have sent Carter's hands speeding to the lock. "Why do you want entrance?"

"Don't you know? The Red Rose in the Blue Stained Glass! I've seen the Ancient Sea, the Sea No Man Can Sail. I was there with him. I saw him!"

Carter's heart beat faster. "With who?"

"Your father! Lord Anderson! I sailed with him. I've been Over the World's Edge. I can tell all!"

It was more than Carter could bear. He unlocked the door quickly, but it opened less than six inches before a weight slammed against it, and a grotesque claw slipped through the aperture, black and slimy, like lizard leather. Even as it reached into the room, it reshaped itself, its palm becoming a face, with black eyes fixing a predator's gaze on Carter, and a thin mouth with spiked teeth. It seemed to enlarge itself, almost as if it sprang at him by growing, the mouth expanding, the fingers extending like tentacles, seeking to grasp and draw him into its maw.

He would surely have died because of its swiftness, had an axe blade not severed the hand at the wrist. The monster howled and withdrew; the amputated member scampered back through the crack in the door like a spider, and Carter and Enoch put their weight against the door, slamming and locking it.

The Windkeep dropped the gory axe to the ground.

"What was it?" Carter asked.

"I should have told you. Why didn't I tell you? I did not want you to worry. It has knocked every night for the last week; you did not hear it in the clock room, which exists in another time. It is a servant of Chaos, sent by the Bobby."

Together, they climbed back up the stair. Carter threw himself on the edge of his bed. "What did it want? Why would it aid the anarchists?"

"Are Chaos and Order living creatures? No. Forces of nature. The Master of the High House must maintain a balance between them, lest all be overcome by Entropy. Like any force, they can be harnessed, and the anarchists have no scruples against doing so. Once inside it could have killed us both."

Carter sighed. "You saved my life, and I am grateful, but you mustn't keep things from me. You can't protect me that way."

"Are you right? You are right. I am sorry. You still seem young to an old man. Once I dangled you on my knee. But that is the past. I should remember. I will remember."

Thereafter, when Carter crept from bed each night, he heard the voice of Chaos and the hammering at the door. Sometimes it spoke in Enoch's voice, and sometimes in Chant's; once it used the warm timbre of his father, bringing tears to his eyes, sending him fleeing back to his room. He never stayed to listen long, for it had a wheedling quality, an air of shared secrets, which he thought dangerous to heed.

As he became stronger, he wandered among the four towers, but there was little to see. Most of the rooms were empty, as if they had been sacked, and the remaining furniture was ruined by water and age. Plaster had fallen from the ceiling in parts.

Several days passed before he felt strong enough to use the Word of Secret Ways. It strained him more than he expected, and when he was done, he crawled back into bed and slept a day and a night. When he finally awoke, he found six separate exits scattered about the Towers. He decided to try each in turn.

Enoch accompanied him on his first journey, out a sliding panel into a series of chambers that promised excitement, but proved unrewarding; they were empty, arranged in a square block, all connected by halls, with no other exit from them. It was a place to hide, but nothing more.

The second way led by ladder down a trapdoor into a lower chamber secured by a smooth, white marble door. Carter looked through its spy-hole and saw it opened directly onto the courtyard guarded by the anarchists. Likewise, the third way was but a secret compartment, but the fourth and fifth opened to long halls and dim passageways that Enoch was certain would lead them from their enemies. Since an escort would lessen their danger, and because Carter was not fully recovered, the men agreed to wait five days more for Captain Glis to arrive before setting out alone.

For Carter, the sixth secret way seemed the most interesting. Hidden behind a false bookcase in the chamber above the clock room, it opened upon an attic space, with dust on the wooden floors and the wall studs bared. It had a deserted feel, so he little feared meeting the anarchists, and he resolved to exercise along its paths. To one who had spent his childhood alone, poking amidst the nooks of desolate spaces, it held a warmth and wonder unknown to those who find no joy in solitary things. There were narrow, gabled windows to admit the dim sunlight, with borders painted faded green, and worn carpets scattered upon the floor, with yellow tulips stitched in rows. There were many doors, set in disarray, scattered at random against corners and outcroppings.

He returned the afternoon following its discovery, determined to reach its end if it did not go too far. Because Enoch was anticipating the arrival of Glis, he came alone. Rain fell on the windows, the continuance of the endless storm, but the air was warm, and he felt a cheerfulness he had not known for some time. He did not understand the feeling, except it was good to walk again, and to see the anarchists could not control everything, even if it were only this empty attic.

He traveled much of the afternoon, testing doors and poking into open spaces, seeing no one but often finding signs of humanity: children's toys, discarded jackets, a glove or a gnarled walking stick. Despite the solitude, he felt no unease, and he examined the discarded articles as if they were treasures, musing over the children who must have made war with the carved cannons, and the grandfathers who had steadied themselves on the broken canes.

After several hours, a weariness overcame him, a reminder he was not yet as hardy as he wished. He sought a resting place, and soon found a rounded room jutting into the attic, whose door had fallen from its hinges long before, with four grimy windowpanes looking out into the gray sky. Within lay a cot, dusty, but otherwise sturdy. Carter lay down to rest his leg. The attic was still, the gray illumination comfortable. He closed his eyes, intending only a moment, and drifted into thick slumber.

Whether hours or seconds passed, he did not know, but he abruptly sat up, a premonition of danger upon him. The room had another window, besides the one facing outdoors, that looked into the attic, its casement shuttered, its panes shattered. He crept to it, moved the shutters enough to see, and beheld the face of the creature who had sought entrance into the Clock Tower, the thing he had come to call Old Man Chaos. Seen in full light, it was even more horrible, its body all gray, misshapen like a clay doll, its shoulders humped and uneven, one thin arm longer than the other; it walked with a limp. The melting-candle look of its face made it too long; blue and black circles inhabited the hollows of its gray eyes. The hand Enoch had severed was restored. It muttered incoherently and moved without purpose, like a lost ghost.

As it approached Carter's hiding place, it stopped, seeming to stare right into his eyes, and the wild glance made the Steward's heart recoil within him; it was all he could do to keep from shrinking back. The creature sniffed the air, like a hunting dog.

Then the abominable head turned away and Carter withdrew into the deepest shadows of the small room, though he doubted it was dim enough to conceal him. A coatrack draped with mildewed garments stood against one corner; he slipped behind it and pressed himself against the wall.

Between the tattered folds of the clothing he saw the Old

Man thrust its inhuman head into the room, still sniffing, grinning the crooked snarl of a rabid wolf. Carter's terror of the monster went beyond physical appearance, for it was surrounded by a palpable aura that spoke of endless space and swirling gases, of forces and energies beyond control and infinities beyond comprehension. Its face was that of the Void, and Carter pressed himself harder against the wall.

Suddenly he found himself swinging away from the coatrack, performing a gentle circle that he could not control. He saw the side of the wall, then rotated into darkness. After a breathless moment, he realized that it was the corner of the room itself which had turned; he had been leaning against a secret panel, built to revolve floor and corner alike, so that he now stood on the opposite side, removed from the other room, facing darkness. He stepped forward cautiously, then turned back to discover the familiar blue glow indicating a secret way—apparently he had missed seeing it on the other side because of his haste. He also noticed a spy-hole, which he used to look into the room he had just left, where he saw Chaos still grinning. The creature came right up to the coatrack, brushed it aside, and seemed to stare straight into Carter's eyes. But to his great relief, it turned away, apparently having detected nothing, and departed the room.

He turned to examine his surroundings, and as his eyes adjusted, found it not as pitch as he had first thought. He was in a long corridor, with a soft light providing bare illumination from around a corner. He crept to it, peered out, and was surprised to find four long windows, each with a window seat before it, and a little girl sitting at one of them, softly weeping.

"Hello," he said quietly, trying not to frighten her. She looked up from beneath black curls, her eyes large and blue. She appeared to be about eight. She did not try to run, but sat up expectantly, saying, in a voice like rung crystal: "Please, sir, my mother told me not to go far, but I was chasing Campaspe, and got lost."

He smiled at her innocence and approached her. "And who is Campaspe?"

"My cat, but she has been very naughty, leading me so far away. I will scold her when I get home."

"You should certainly not be alone. Perhaps I could take you back to the Clock Tower with me."

"Oh, no, sir, please!" she cried, tears welling up once more. "We would have to go through the halls of the Crooked Man. Mother says I must never go there!"

"Very well." Carter spoke hastily to fend off the tears, fairly certain she referred to Chaos. He dropped to his haunches to be on her level and deliberated. Up close, she possessed a face of exquisite beauty, its symmetry wholly unmarred, a loveliness found often in illustrations, but seldom in real life. He questioned her to find out how long she had been gone and through what portions of the house she might have passed. She had no idea, and in the end he could do nothing but lead her down the hall, she taking his hand in utter trust. He told her his name, which she said she liked, while she was called Anna.

"I usually bring my dolls, Gwalchmai and Corenice, if I leave my rooms," she said. "They would have known the way back."

"And do you leave your rooms often?"

"Oh, no, because Mother does not allow, but if I did they should come with me. They are very lovely, except that Corenice has lost an eye. It was not her fault. I dropped her when I was little. When we get home, we will have a tea party, you and I and Gwalchmai and Corenice, and we shall invite Mother and Granmama. We will have crumpets. I have a very nice tablecloth and white dishes with red flowers."

They came to the first intersecting passage, and Carter saw the slender figure of a woman gliding toward them. "That's my mother!" Anna declared.

As the woman left the shadows and the light fell upon her, he gave an involuntary gasp, for perfection lay upon her like a tiara, and the comeliness of the daughter, mirrored in woman's form, achieved an exquisiteness he would have thought impossible. So alike were the two, they might have been duplicates, separated only by age. The mother appeared unconcerned by Carter's presence, but said in a voice like tinkling bells, "I am Anina."

Her hair, her eyes, and her lips were dark, and her face exceptionally pale, and if she had told him she was Aphrodite come to earth, he would have believed. Her gown was raven, and her earrings crescent moons. She met his eyes unflinching, and he suddenly realized he was staring.

"Carter Anderson," he said, giving a slight bow, a thing he had not done since a boy. "I found her wandering lost," he added.

"There are no chance meetings," Anina said. "If you will return to our apartments, we will offer hospitality."

In that moment Carter discovered there was such a thing as beauty both great and terrible, for he found himself afraid to walk beside this woman, with a fear beyond shyness, as if she were holy and he merely mortal. No logic could account for it, no cynicism dispel it, and if it would not have shamed him, he would have declined her offer and bolted down the corridor, completely overawed. As it was, he managed a smile and nodded heavily.

Anina took Anna's other hand and together the three of them marched down the passage until they came to ocher double doors, with brass lions for knockers. Anina unlocked the door with a gold key, and ushered him into a chamber with sunlight streaming through skylights. Puffy clouds dotted the blue sky. "The storm is passed," Carter said, surprised.

"I do not approve of gloom," Anina said, as if in explanation. She crossed the white marble tile and reclined upon an ivory couch, while Anna disappeared into the back rooms. Carter glanced around the chamber, which was large as a small hall and adorned solely in white. Sculptures of frost lions sat on their haunches in the four corners, a chandelier hung from the festooned ceiling. Pearl dolphins sported in a pearl fountain at the center of the room, and white tapestries of jousting white knights covered the walls.

"Come sit beside me," she said, indicating a nearby chair. She rang a silver bell taken from a marble table and a servant appeared, also clad in white, her face pale and white as well, bearing silver goblets and a bowl of fruit upon a silver tray. The clouds overhead stood still as if painted; the sunlight warmed his feet.

"I am fortunate you found Anna. Old Chaos has been about. It would like to have her."

"I've seen the monster," Carter said. "It almost came unawares upon me as well. A vile creature."

"More horrible than you can know. It would ruin every good thing if it could. I, who would have beauty and truth always about me, am ever plagued by it. Often it walks these very passages, and I am forced to bolt the door."

Carter sampled the beverage in the silver cup, and found it to be apple juice sweeter than any he had ever tasted before. "This is wonderful!"

"There is a walled garden beyond this chamber, and I plant every type of berry and fruit there; it is my greatest joy, to cut away the wild things and reveal a beautiful landscape. Later you will come with me and I will show you."

The fruit was as good as the juice, apples red and unblemished, peaches of perfect texture, strawberries sweet as kisses, grapes larger than Carter's thumb, ripe and succulent. There were slabs of bread and cheese brought as well, rich as the good earth, and he ate until well content, while she nibbled daintily.

Afterward, she played a harp that glistened like alabaster, its notes resonating off the marble floor, the music rushing from her hands and then returning from every corner of the room, sonorous and manifold. When she sang, her voice was snowfall on the hillsides, each flake identical in its perfection, green grass in a well-tended garden, lilacs and roses all in rows, each note unerringly accurate and sweet as young corn. He did not watch her much, for he feared her beauty still, though her kindness had put him more at ease.

And in that music, as he lay almost dreaming beneath its tenderness, he saw himself truly the Steward, and perhaps soon the Master, of the High House, with the rights and position of such a one, lord of a vast domain, who might be bold enough to seek the hand of a woman such as this.

When she ended her playing, he roused himself from his trance, smiling sheepishly upon her, but her eyes were very bright, and she began to tell short, exquisite tales, so that he saw she was not just a musician, but a storyteller as well, each account a small polished gem, its facets revealed one at a time, always in the proper order, with a nicety and compactness of description. At the end of one he laughed aloud, at another he sighed, at a third he found tears brimming his eyes.

"Is there nothing you cannot do?" he finally asked.

"There are many things," she replied. "But what I do, I do well."

So they sat through the long afternoon. When she had told her tales, she asked of his, and he found himself confiding all: his wondrous childhood and the great house; his father, and the mother scarcely remembered; Brittle and Chant and old Enoch. He even confessed his taking of the keys, and spoke of the years of exile in his foster home and of his return. She seemed to find him amusing, for she laughed at his small jokes and nearly wept at his sorrows. And she amazed him, this skilled storyteller who also possessed the art of listening, for he knew few who could do both.

Later, they walked in her walled garden, where Carter felt the undiluted sun upon his face for the first time in days. He breathed the soft fragrance of countless flowers, set out in precise design; the pink hollyhocks in the heart-shaped beds; the purple hyacinths in the ordered squares; the tree peonies in the oval rings; the red roses in the well-kept rows. There was sweet alyssum, petunias, marigolds, zinnias, and many more. Orange trees guarded the four corners; hydrangea picketed the borders. Even the ivy upon the walls lay not in tangles, but in sculpted patterns shaped like balloons, clown faces, and the signs of the zodiac. She took his hand and led him around the low hedges, showing him each plot, surrounded by its white stones. His heart beat strong against his chest at her touch.

"You could not do all the labor yourself," he said.

"Almost all," she said, "since I trust no other. But perhaps you would like to help."

"Yes, I would. Do you mean now?"

"The garden must be attended each day, else the wilderness will overtake it."

She did not excuse herself to change her garments as he would have expected, but simply slipped on a pair of soft white gloves. From behind the hedgerows she produced gardening tools, and they soon set to work on a patch of periwinkles. At first Carter could not see what to do, for the beds were already immaculate, but under her tutelage he discovered her desires, and was soon making minute progress. She hummed sweetly, pausing occasionally to indicate areas requiring attention, and they spent a pleasant hour.

Anna appeared in the midst of their labor, but remained very quiet. She did not play as children normally do, but sat silent on a little white stool and watched them.

At last, as the shadows lay long across the hedges, Carter rose and stretched. "I fear I must return to the Clock Tower."

"There are quarters if you would like to stay the night," she said.

"Please stay!" Anna burst out. "You haven't had tea with my dolls yet."

"I am sorry, I cannot. Enoch will be concerned."

"Then perhaps you could come again tomorrow," Anina said, smiling.

"Yes, I would like that very much."

Patting Anna on the head, he reluctantly took his leave. As

he marched down the drab halls he whistled softly under his breath, his heart light for the first time in many days. But as he approached the secret doorway he slowed and fell silent, remembering Old Man Chaos. He peeked through the spyhole. To his consternation, he discovered the creature peering into the room, as if it had remained there all day. Carter drew back hastily and paused to consider. There would be no returning to the Clock Tower so long as the monster remained, and he had no way of sending Enoch a message. Yet, if the old servant came seeking him, he might run headlong into the beast. He determined to linger awhile to see if the horror departed.

But when he looked through the spy-hole again he discovered Chaos lying on the floor just beyond the doorway to the room, apparently preparing for slumber. He watched for a long hour, until the fading rays of the sun no longer breached the attic rooms, and shadows gloomed the spaces. When he could no longer even discern his enemy's form, he decided to return to Anina's apartments and seek the Clock Tower at first light. He departed reluctantly, burdened by guilt at having spent such a pleasant day at the expense of possibly placing Enoch in danger. Yet, he doubted the old servant would dare the attic at night; Enoch was a man of endless patience and wisdom; he would not brave the dark unless in urgent need.

Anina greeted him at the door, showing no surprise at his return. When he explained how Chaos blocked his path, she only smiled and said, "Accompany me, and we will allay your concerns." She led him into an inner chamber, as spacious as her garden, all carpeted in gold, with gilded bird cages hanging from ceiling chains, occupied by many kinds of fowl, from white doves to resplendent peacocks. She drew a gray pigeon from its golden stockade. "These birds will go as I direct, and this one knows its way to the Clock Tower. We will tie a message to its leg."

"Why, this is wonderful!" Carter said. "I won't have to worry then. I've seen carrier pigeons, of course, though it is remarkable that the bird could find its way to the tower. I thought no one went there but Enoch."

"I have lived here many years, and the birds are easy to train. One never knows when it might be necessary to send a message to nearby parts of the house."

Mollified, Carter wrote a hasty message saying: *All is well. Chaos prevents me from returning, but I am safe. I will try again tomorrow. Carter.*

She took the bird into the garden and released it. It circled once with fluttering wings and then vanished beyond the walls. Afterward, she fed him a splendid dinner of chicken breast, coated with egg and bread crumbs and fried in butter, with steamed cabbage, brussels sprouts, green peas, and miniature potato soufflés washed down with an apple nectar better than wine.

He slept that night beneath a covered, four-poster bed, in a red-carpeted room with massive furniture and a picture of a yellow dwarf upon each wall. The mattress was comfortable, and he fell asleep thinking he might like to remain his whole life in that house.

Anna woke him the next morning, her little face peering up to the high bed. "The yellow birds have come into the garden. Will you see?"

He smiled, said he would, and sent her off while he dressed. Sunlight poured through the windows, which he found curious after the endless storms. He glanced out and saw he was on the seventh story of a square tower built of dark green stone. Shorter buildings lay below his window, and he could see the Clock Tower nearby, across a sea of flagstones.

Anina greeted him at the foot of the stair, took his hand, and led him to an enormous breakfast of boiled eggs, sausages, bacon, and muffins with coffee, on the wrought-iron table in the garden. As Anna had said, a migration of yellow wagtail had landed within the walls, and were resting and cheeping on the branches, specks of sunlight given wing.

"They came at dawn," Anina said. "I love to watch them play."

"At the moment they aren't very playful," Carter observed. "They look ready to roost."

She seemed briefly annoyed. "Their play is the quiet of Being. Nothing else is required."

"No, I suppose not."

After breakfast they sat sipping cinnamon tea, watching the sun climb above the walls until it heated the flagstones. Wearying of the warmth, they moved indoors, where Anina took her place once more upon the ivory couch. She was dressed exactly as the night before, though the clothes looked fresh, as if they had been laundered in the night. The new day stole none of her dark beauty.

"I have not sufficiently thanked you for your hospitality," he said. "Yesterday was the first peaceful day I have had since I returned to Evenmere. I dreamed last night I was a child again, rocked in my mother's arms. I have seldom felt so comforted."

"It is nothing; there are no chance meetings. I hope it is only the first day of many. Now come, sit beside me." She indicated the chair where he had rested the day before. Taking the silver bell, she summoned her servant, who brought another tray of fruit, with bread, cheese, and apple juice in silver goblets.

"It is fortunate you found Anna," Anina said. "Old Chaos would like to have her. Ever it tries to ruin all I have, and ever I must defend myself."

"Why does it hate you so?"

"It hates anything which is well ordered; it hates all the good things."

They spoke a long hour, and finally she drew out her small harp, and played again, as beautifully as the day before, though Carter noticed she played no new songs, but the same ones in the same order. Once more the music touched him, evoking images of himself as the owner of this emerald-stoned tower, spending the days with her, each hour as lovely as the next. With her by his side, he would sweep the anarchists away, and together they would establish a reign that would last a thousand years, greater than King Arthur's, for Carter's Guinevere would never fail him.

When her playing ended, he shook himself, abashed by the arrogance of his daydreams, but she gave him little time for reflection as she plunged once more into storytelling. Again, the tales were masterpieces of narrative, recited with the genius of an artisan, but Carter soon realized these were the same stories as the day before, told in the same sequence and manner.

When she finished, he sighed and said, "You have marvelous gifts, your singing and your tales."

"I cannot do everything," she replied. "But what I do, I do well."

They sat through the rest of the long afternoon, and she questioned him once more, asking him to tell again of his childhood in the great house, of his father and mother, Brittle, Chant, and Enoch. Because he had done so the day before, he began reluctantly, but she prodded him, insisting he leave out nothing he had said before. He saw in this a childlike quality, a desire to hear the same story again and again, and he thought it flattering, though he became hesitant when she demanded the tale of his theft of the Master Keys again, and of his subsequent exile. Still, she laughed at his humor and nearly wept at his sorrows, so that he thought her extraordinary.

As the afternoon waned, and she invited him into the garden, he insisted upon seeking the Clock Tower once more. He went alone, and again found Chaos sitting before the secret doorway, as if guarding it. With a chilled heart he returned to her apartments.

She escorted him around the garden once more, showing him all her flowers, her ivies, and her shrubs. Afterward they worked in the tulips, which he found somewhat frustrating, for she was precise in her desires, and he did not believe nature should behave so symmetrically.

Anna came and quietly watched them work, though she said little, and Carter realized he had not seen her since she had woke him that morning. He guessed she had been playing alone in her apartments.

More than once that evening he sought a path back to Enoch, but each time Chaos blocked his way. Finally, he had no choice but to dispatch another message by way of pigeon. He slept that night in the same room, though not as well as before.

Anna roused him with the same words of the previous day, her face aglow, "The yellow birds have come into the garden. Will you see?"

She departed and he arose. With a sigh, he opened the window and measured with his eye the distance between that tower and the Clock Tower. By traveling the rooftops, he thought he saw a way he might go, given rope from his pack and good fortune.

As on the morning before, Anina met him at the bottom of the stairs and brought him to the garden for breakfast, to listen to the cheeping of the yellow wagtail.

"They came at dawn," Anina said. "I love to watch them play. How was your rest?"

"Why, I had a most peculiar dream," Carter said. "I dreamed I was taken to heaven, where I stood before God and worshiped Him, and was filled with ecstasy. And the worshiping and the ecstasy were endless, so my face was turned always toward Him. And I never did anything else. And though I was filled with delight, I kept thinking there must be more to heaven, that He would expect us to serve more purpose than this, and that perhaps I had gone to hell instead."

Her face darkened at his words, but she said, "In this you

err, for the repetition of ritual is the highest calling, and true
joy is found only within it. I will show you much concerning
this."

Then Carter knew for certain with whom he dealt, and he
vowed to be firm in his resolve.

The day proceeded as the one before, and what had been
pleasure became only tedious. They sipped the same cinnamon tea, watched the same sun rise above the walled court,
and retired indoors as the day grew warm. Anina sat once
more upon her ivory couch, dressed exactly the same, while
they ate the same meal of bread, cheese, and fruit. Despite the
goodness of the apple juice, it tasted as ashes of disappointment to Carter, and the harp music that had entranced him before left him cold. Though he became impatient at her
moribund tales, he sat impassive.

Apparently, she saw none of this, for when she was done
she took his hand, kissing it, and said, "Three days we have
spent together, and three hundred more would not be enough.
You must know by now I love you, for I see in you all I have
desired. Stay with me forever, and we will live a life of pleasure. I will give you your every yearning, over and over, in its
time and place. You will never want."

"And could you give me passion, lady?" he asked softly.

She kissed him fiercely then, a kiss like hot wind, and for a
moment, as it took his breath away, he desired only to possess
her beauty. But he knew even this would become wearisome,
and he drew her from him, though it took all his will.

"I must see if Chaos still waits at the door," he said. "We
will speak of this later."

"First, speak again of yourself. Tell me your whole story,
for I can never hear it enough."

"When I return, I will."

He departed quickly, lest his resolve fail him, stopping only
long enough to fetch his pack. He did not go back to the room
where he knew Chaos surely waited, but found a stairway
leading down from the corridor of the window seats to the

next floor, which contained a similar passage, with long rows of glass. He chose one and unlocked it; the window opened with a screech. He took a rope from his pack, secured it to the head of a gargoyle, slid himself over the sill, and began a careful descent toward the rooftops below. From there, he hoped to cross to the Clock Tower and find a way to Enoch.

He was not particularly bothered by heights; if his position had not been so serious he would have enjoyed the climb. Numerous statues and outcroppings provided bountiful purchases. He was surprised to see the cloud cover had returned, threatening further rain, leaving the air refreshingly cool, but not cold. For a moment he felt wildly free, and he knew he had escaped an exceedingly subtle trap.

He had climbed only a few feet, and was still high above the roofs when he heard a voice above him. Little Anna leaned out the window, the glistening blade of a knife poised against the rope.

"Please come up, sir, or I will surely cut it," she said.

He glanced around, but saw no immediate handhold. Two men, dressed in white helmets, stood beside her.

He kicked off with his legs, and released the rope slightly, repelling down the side of the building, his hands burning from the friction.

He had covered almost half the distance to the rooftops below when the line went slack, dropping him like a stone.

Captured

He reeled downward, partially breaking his fall with his hands upon the smooth sides of a stone stallion, an effort that nearly pulled his arms from their sockets before he slipped away, continuing his plunge, every moment of the descent filled with agonizing detail. He saw his own flailing hands, the pink of his fingernails in the sunlight, the leaves of ivy upon the receding windows, the cracks in the mortar of the building fleeing past. He saw the blue sky and the wisps of cloud.

He landed on his back upon a wooden housing that buckled beneath him. His senses fled.

When he revived he was no longer on the rooftop, but lying on an ivory couch in the white chambers of Anina, while she bathed his brow with a cool cloth. He was wholly surprised to be alive, though it was a time before he could recall himself to speech. He moved his hands, arms, and legs carefully, and though they gave him pain, he did not think anything was broken. He poked his own ribs, and even curled his back slightly; though all was a mass of bruises he seemed mostly whole. He slept for a time.

When he awoke she was still with him. She fed him fruit juice mixed with honey, bending over him, tears in her eyes. Almost he loved her again for it.

"Why did you flee me?" she asked. "I, who would have given you everything?"

"Because I know who you are, and I feared you."

"Only my enemies need fear me. And what do you know of me, truly?"

"You are Order Incarnate, or something of the sort, no more human than Old Man Chaos."

"It only means I can offer you even more. Not just love, but eternal life, for I am immortal, and you could reign with me in my kingdom. Am I not pleasant to look upon? Did we spend these past three days in bliss? I could show you Love Unending, for I am perfect in my love."

"And in your hate as well, I suppose? I am sorry. You are a tool of the anarchists; I will not become one as well."

She looked at him with sad, cold eyes, and as she looked, a vapor rose about her, steaming from her clothes and garments, until they became the steam, and all of her evaporated away, leaving only her face lying on the floor like a flat piece of dried leather, her eyes inanimate as a mask. As Carter drew back in horror, Anna entered the room, quite prim in a white dress with matching shoes, gloves, and hat.

"She is of no further value," the little girl said.

His throat was dry. "You are the one behind it all, then?"

"She and I are both the same, manifestations of Order. As you have guessed, we are Primeval Force. But Order is always a child."

"Serving the anarchists."

"Serving our own ends," she said sweetly. "When the Bobby comes to power he has promised us certain . . . territorial advantages over Chaos. It is our most ardent desire, for the Old Man is bedlam, dissolution, the Void. We would bring complete Order to the universe."

"Yet Chaos blocked my path and aided you."

"Perhaps the Bobby has promised him something as well. That is not my concern."

He watched her, and after a time she said, "Why do you sit silent? Will you not reason with me?"

"Better reason with a flooding stream. I don't believe you are aware, at least in the way of men. You are a form of power, like magnetism, that the Bobby is using, as I would use a hammer. Discourse is useless. What will you do with me?"

"I had hoped you would join us. Failing that, we will keep you here until the Bobby comes. It is not an easy journey for him."

She had him bound, though gently because of his injuries, and she placed a leather band over his mouth so he could not cry out. Then she left him with a white-cloaked guard at his side, possessing eyes with neither pupil nor iris.

He had seldom felt so miserable, and he stared at the empty mask of Anina and wept bitterly the tears all spurned lovers must shed. But after a time his anger focused on the Bobby, and he resolved to escape before his enemy appeared. It occurred to him that he had been gagged so he could not speak the Words of Power. These, he enumerated to himself: *Talheedin*, the Word of Secret Ways: *Sedhattee*, The Word Which Gives Strength; neither seemed useful here. *Rahmurrim*, The Word of Hope. It would not help. Only *Elahkammor*, The Word Which Brings Aid, could be useful, though assistance might be too far away.

He emptied his mind of all thought, gradually instilling a calm bereft of any consideration of either Anina or the Bobby. Then, he slowly summoned the Word into his mind. At first, he could not hold the image, but it eventually grew more substantial, its letters blazing like fire, and as its power rose within him, he tried to release it, but it came out only as a muffled breath behind the gag. A backlash of power followed, a squeezing force so mighty he could not breathe. Darkness and light flashed before his eyes; he felt as if he were being ripped apart one molecule at a time and for an instant he thought all of his blood vessels would explode at once. He must have screamed behind his gag, for the guard cuffed the side of his head with an armored hand, turning his pain to anger, so that he strained against his bonds to strike back.

The ringing in his head and the rage subsided together, leaving him dissipated. He could not master his thoughts for a time thereafter, but sat uncomprehending as a man on opiates. When at last he returned to himself, he trembled as if from cold, and sat forlorn, every muscle aching, sweat stinging his eyes, his hands chafed from his struggles against the bonds. A long hour passed before he had any strength at all, and then another before he could conceive of a plan.

He had only one hope, and that a slim one, to use the Word without speaking it aloud. He rested for the space of a dozen breaths, drawing his strength around him once more.

Again, he summoned the Word into his mind. At first it was dim, but gradually it grew within him as before. He knew he must make it real, call its power into the world as if it had been spoken, and he centered all his being upon it, bringing it this time not into his throat, but into the midst of his mind, holding it there until it seemed he held a fiery brand, the Word of Power written across it like a banner.

And suddenly, he no longer held the brand, but had become it. Or rather, it had become part of him, as if the Word had burned itself upon his soul. Before that moment, the Words had been tools; afterward they lay, deep as his bones, within him. Now, he was truly their master, and for the briefest moment he reveled in the power that filled him.

When he released the Word the room shook, the air *roared*, its power coming not from him, but from everywhere at once. The guard, thrown against the wall like a wooden soldier, lay broken, senseless, one arm bent at an impossible angle. Carter's chains dropped from him, and he knew he would never be held against his will again.

He seized the guard's sword from its sheath and flung the door wide, but it no longer led into the chambers of Order. Instead, a dark passageway beckoned, layered with dust, tattered paper hanging from its walls. A figure stood within, shabby and ragged, a thin taper in hand, his face lost beneath the shadows of his tall hat.

"When last we spoke you claimed you would oppose me," Carter said.

"There is no time," the Thin Man replied. "Come this way."

Carter fell in line behind the dark back. "How did you arrive so quickly?"

"It is easy here, and I was not far. I have been blocking the Bobby's path to you."

Carter stopped him with a hand on his shoulder. "There is something familiar about you. Who are you? Why do you help me?"

The Thin Man shrugged off the grip and continued on. "It doesn't matter who or why. You could repay me by leaving the High House, taking Duskin with you. No man should bear this burden. Go away! Leave it to others."

"What others? My father did not raise me to run from a fight."

The Thin Man paused and looked back. "He did not raise you to die, either."

"You knew him!"

"I did. Will you leave the house if I tell you he wanted it?"

"Only if I hear it from his own lips."

The Thin Man gave an irate grunt and strode on. The passage opened out into what felt like a large chamber, for a cool wind brushed Carter's face, and the echoes fluttered around them like bats, but he could see nothing beyond the circle of his benefactor's candlelight.

They had gone only a short distance when a small form stepped into their path, startling Carter badly. She was still dressed in white, but her eyes were sad. "We could have given you everything," Anna said.

The Thin Man shied from her presence, holding his hand

before his eyes, unable to look upon her. "I cannot withstand her. You must help me."

Carter raised his sword and stepped between the Thin Man and Anna.

"This sad Thing which aids you is of Chaos," she said. "It should be destroyed."

He did not hesitate, lest she find some way to recapture him, but struck her hard, with greater anger than he intended. She was not pierced, but broke into myriad pieces, each an exact circle no larger than his thumb, which rolled like coins across the floor, before spinning slowly into silence.

"Hurry," the Thin Man commanded as Carter stood dumbfounded. "She can never be truly destroyed." He led across the boards until they came to a narrow stair leading up to a gray door. The Thin Man paused at the landing.

"This will bring you back into the halls. You will find further help there." He blew out the candle, plunging the passage into ebony. Carter fumbled for the knob and thrust open the door; daylight rushed in from the other side. The Thin Man was gone.

He now found himself in the same passage where he had first met Anna. The light fell diffused from the windows, and looking out he saw the storm clouds had returned. It was a moment before he accustomed himself to the brightness, and when he did he saw a man sitting at one of the windowseats, looking out the glass, his back against the wall, his knees up against his chest. Carter approached slowly and called a greeting.

Hope turned toward him, his face pale in the pale sunlight. He did not appear startled but said, "Hello, Carter, what are you doing here?"

Carter came forward, his hand clenched on his sword. "I could ask you the same. We are far from the Inner Chambers."

"Not as far as you might think. I found myself here, and I've been trying to recall how it came about. The last I remember, I was reading a grueling tome in my room, and growing monstrously sleepy. Therefore, I have fallen asleep and this is all a dream."

"Like the one we had before? Then I am sharing it with you?"

Hope's brow wrinkled, but he did not sit up. "I only have your word on that, since you might be part of the dream. I could be the same, from your viewpoint. Where are we supposed to be?"

"In an attic space off the Clock Tower."

"So you made it! I should tell you then, before I wake up or some such thing, that Glis has contacted the reinforcements, and should be reaching the Towers soon, assuming he can follow your path."

Carter moved across from Hope, but did not sit down. "If what you say is true, I haven't really awakened from my nap on the cot in the attic, but only think I have, and the last few days have been a dream. More a nightmare, actually."

Hope formed a steeple with his fingertips. "The work of the anarchists, no doubt. But why now? We have to assume they can't do this anytime they wish, or they would have renewed their attack long before. And why am I in the dream?"

"I can answer the last question. I used the Word Which Brings Aid. It has brought you to me, even in the land of sleep. I suspect they could not strike at me until I left the room of the Eternity Clock. And they did it through dream because they could not reach me physically. And *that* means both Lady Order and Old Man Chaos are not physically in the attic either."

"I don't follow that last bit."

Carter related the previous days' experience. When he was done Hope said, "But why couldn't the Bobby manifest his minions directly in the dream, like he did when Brittle was murdered, instead of sending Order and Chaos?"

"The Thin Man said he had prevented them from reaching me."

"That suggests our unknown friend may have uncanny abilities of his own, doesn't it?"

"Perhaps. We don't understand any of the rules. Do you realize three days have passed for me in this dream? I've slept twice. How can that be?"

"To sleep within a dream? I don't know. But the Thin Man surely cannot hold the Bobby back forever, and when he comes for you again, you will be in grave danger."

Carter shivered, thinking of Anna. "I have already passed a terrible test, just scraping by. I have to wake up. But how? It isn't as simple as pinching oneself."

"There may be a way," Hope said, brightening suddenly. "As you recall from before you left the Inner Chambers, I had stumbled onto a volume naming the Words of Power. I have done further research since then and learned the names of another: the Word Which Masters Dreams. If you could return to the library, and find it, you could protect yourself."

"But I am *in* a dream!" Carter said.

"Yes, but the halls of dream, though fluid, seem to be basically the same as those of the physical world. And the anarchists would never expect you to go back to the library."

"You are assuming they do not see all that occurs in this dream world."

"If they did, they would have caught us in the library the first time. There are two dangers: one to your body sleeping in the attic, and one to your dream body. We know from Brittle's death the dream body is as important as the corporeal. As far as we know, your physical body is lying vulnerable right now. You are in double danger."

Carter paused to reflect a moment, then said, "I will seek the library as you suggest, but I must find another route. Chaos undoubtedly still blocks my way to the Clock Tower."

"Yes, but there is a courtyard below us, which you should be able to reach. From there you can work your way back toward the Inner Chambers."

Carter paced the floor a moment. "The Thin Man told me I

would find another who would help me. From that I can assume you truly are Mr. Hope. But I can expect no other aid; though Glis's soldiers might recapture the whole path to the Towers, they will not walk the corridors of dream. We need to go swiftly, and I know only one route back to the library. It may be guarded."

"As likely not," Hope said. "Creating these dreams, and sending his lackeys into it, if that is what he does, must take great power, else the Bobby would use it more often. He can't afford to waste it posting dream guards everywhere. It is all guesswork, of course, but everything, even magic, must have its laws. He will concentrate his forces where he thinks you are, near the chambers of Lady Order."

"I see no other recourse," Carter said. "I cannot wake, nor wait to be captured."

He walked quickly down the hallway to the spy-hole, to ascertain if Chaos still patrolled the attic. He gave an involuntary start to see the hideous form standing directly before him, its eyes fixed on the spy-hole. Carter had never seen it so close, its skin like gray clay, stretched and distorted, its crooked teeth, half missing, yellow in its tortured mouth. The smaller of its yellow eyes stared straight at Carter's own. Almost, Carter thought he could smell it, even through the wall, a scent of both graveyards and lilies. It mumbled and slavered, then addressed him in a rasping voice: "Her beauty did not sway you, eh? I knew it would not, else I never would have sent you to her."

Oddly, Carter found the creature both repellant and yet attractive in its strangeness. By this, he knew it was more than a monster, but a force to be feared, for there was strength in that ghastly voice. He answered carefully. "So you intentionally blocked my path so I would meet her. I thought you were enemies."

"Oh, yes," the twisted face said. "Oh, yes, indeed. The Bobby made promises, to give up whole rooms of the house if I helped him. Enough, even, to make up for your loss. But

I knew, as Chaos always knows, that you would not turn to her; man is attracted to the infinite ever-change. Order is a myth, a false cat, clawless. Can you not see? All will return to disarray; all will be as it once was, when I ruled, boundless and unchained—no Master in the house then. Can you see?"

Carter saw it indeed, for the words cast a spell upon his mind, a vision that threatened to overwhelm his senses. He saw vast darkness and swirling cosmos, star matter burning bright and dying, all the universe a frantic dance, with Order nothing but a dilettante seeking to thrust a waltz step upon the spinning anarchy. And in the turmoil he saw its beauty, the endless kaleidoscope of never-order. He gasped in wonder and stepped back, and the vision passed.

"It can be yours, yes," Chaos said. "I have many names and faces, and you can see them all. I can make you Master; I can give you the Hymns of Ecstasy. Order does not have this power; she is limited by her boxes and division bells. Anything, anything can be yours. Do you think me ugly? Know that all the beauties are within me, seen at the chance moment, never at the expected time. I am spontaneity, creativity, the abrupt satiation of desires undreamed. You wish to walk these halls as Master; I will give you these and others, ever-changing, rearranging, always yours. Babies breath and flame tongues, colors and delights."

Again Carter saw it, images bursting in his mind like flares in a night sky. He saw himself, striding above the shaken stars, order turning into exquisite bedlam beneath his feet. Colors he could not name, of piercing beauty, transforming even as he watched.

The monster's voice continued, no longer rasping, but smooth: "Side with me and I will show you the Sea No Man Sails, under a rainbow sky, where once your father paced the shores. I saw where he went, and what he did. I can give him back if you wish."

"Tell me!" Carter demanded, for he saw Lord Anderson upon the prow of a small ship, deep water beneath him, the wind blowing in his hair, his eyes fearsome and fearful. An awful ache clutched his heart. "Tell me if he lives still."

"Living and dying are nothing to me; they are all as one. But I can tell all. I can give your heart's desire. Promise to serve me and it will be done. Otherwise I tell you . . . nothing."

Thin tears obscured Carter's sight; he leaned against the wall, helpless, having no means to force the monster. "Blackhearted beast!" he said bitterly. "Have you no mercy?"

"None. But I can be your friend—"

"You are no man's friend!" Carter shouted, his voice shaking. He backed from the wall. Almost he returned, to tell the monster he would do anything, serve anyone, to find his father, but the memory of the man would not allow it. And the next instant the spell had passed, and he knew Chaos's promises were empty deceits.

Chaos slammed its fists against the walls, apparently unaware of how to activate the secret panel, as if it had no skill with ordered devices. "You are not done with me yet. Oh, no. We will find you!"

Carter and Hope hurried down the corridor.

"Are you all right?" Hope asked.

"I will be when we escape this nightmare. Let's see if the road back to the library is the same as the one in the real world."

It took several minutes to locate the stair and descend to the flagstone court, which appeared empty. Recalling the maps Hope had given him, Carter retrieved them from his pack. "Do you think these of any value?" he asked.

Hope shrugged. "In an ordinary dream, no, but here they could be. Still, it is a gamble; the anarchists might be able to change them."

Carter studied the map. "That, too, could be beyond their power. I say we go back to the right, a more direct route than Enoch and I took to get here. It should bring us straight to the Long Stair."

They took a door leading into a series of ample corridors lined with crimson carpet, illuminated by lamps at every turning, with many shadows between. The wallpaper was yellow with age, the baseboards dusty with neglect. They spent two hours traipsing down the halls, squinting for want of light, and found the intersection shown on the map just when Carter had given up hope.

"This is the way Enoch would have come, had we not been waylaid," Carter said. At the lawyer's request he gave an account of their journey, of his injury, and of their time in the room of the Eternity Clock. Mr. Hope, in turn, related the events in the Inner Chambers of the house.

"After you left, we had a devil's time against the anarchists. They tried to come out from the library shelves three times, but Glis had secured the room and met them with pistols and swords. Then they found another way, from a trapdoor leading into the heights of the house; they held half the upstairs wing before we discovered them. It was bloody fighting to drive them back. Our soldiers were on their feet two solid days and nights. But then reinforcements appeared, from Naleewuath and Keedin."

"I wish I had been there, instead of waiting for my leg to heal," Carter said. "There's proof this is a dream, by the way; my injury hasn't bothered me during all this time. I should have realized it earlier. What happened next?"

"Once the anarchists were driven back, and our position reinforced, Glis led his men through the secret panel, following your path, and set about clearing the way to the Towers. He's a brave man. But there is little you could have done if you had been there. Bringing Enoch was more important."

They came to a door opening onto a wide banister, with balustrades on either side, carved with the slivered figure of the man in the moon, his nightcap on, looking out over the top steps. This was the beginning of the Long Stair, and it descended like a train tunnel, sporadically lit by lamps like porter's lanterns trailing into the darkness. On the ceiling above the landing stretched a grand, stained-glass portrait of an angel, brother to the one in the room of the Book of Forgotten Things, though much larger. His hair was fire, his eyes night; his sword gleamed golden as he sat, hand on hilt, his gaze sweeping down the steps. And if he were the guardian of that way, Carter wondered that any evil dared pass.

"Quite splendid," Hope muttered as they stumbled downward, craning their necks to see it.

They spent many hours descending, allowing themselves no rest or stops for food, for if they were truly dreaming, why would they require either? But their feet grew sore nonetheless, their legs and backs ached, and their stomachs began to grumble. After a time they grudgingly drew dried beef from Carter's pack.

"This really isn't a dream as we know one," Hope said. "In a dream one can be frightened, and even have a similitude of running, but not this sort of weariness. And the detail is that of life."

"It's like another state of being, as if we have entered another dimension."

"Perhaps we have. That might explain why the Bobby cannot control all of it; it takes on a life of its own."

After nearly six hours, footsore and aching, they acquiesced to their situation and sat on the steps for a brief respite. As they ate dried fruit washed down with water, they noticed a peculiar smokiness to the ceiling not far before them, as if a low fog hung there.

"What do you think it is?" Carter asked.

Hope opened his mouth to reply, but the sound never came out. To Carter's shock, the attorney grew transparent and vanished, a look of astonishment on his face. For an instant, through his weariness and loss, he could not think what had happened. Then he realized Mr. Hope had awakened. He pulled himself to his feet, feeling lonely and a little betrayed. There was no one to help him now.

He marched on, and reached the mysterious mist sooner

than he expected, for it traveled toward him, and was soon passing above his head, billowing like a dark cloak, spectral in the lamplight. It became more dense, until it resembled storm clouds in summer. Wind tugged at his collar.

A fat drop of water struck his nose, harbinger to a heavy curtain of rain. He was soaked in seconds, and the wind rose to a hollow howl. Beneath the pelting deluge he stumbled like a sailor on a pitching ship, clutching the banister for support. He buried his face in his sleeve to avoid breathing water. His lantern went out, plunging the stair into darkness.

Water from above rolled down the steps in waves. He took several nasty spills, and was nearly swept away before he realized he could not continue. He pulled a bit of rope from his pack and tied himself to a railing to weather the tempest.

Whether he was there for minutes or hours, he could not tell, but he began to believe he would drown. The water ran in a stream down the stair, roiling around his thighs, and Carter expected it to inundate the entire stairwell. He could see absolutely nothing, hear only the rushing of the water; he remembered nearly drowning in the well as a boy, and fear gripped his heart. It appeared his enemies could do anything, command any force, yet he knew this to be untrue, else they would have simply killed him, or materialized on the stair and taken him captive.

Between shivering and struggling for breath, he found the courage to consider his encounters with both Chaos and Order. Each had sought to persuade him to join their side. Had Order wished, she could have killed him while he was in her chambers. Yet, she had not. Likewise, Chaos had been unable to access the secret panel to reach him. But the monster had known it was there, and the mechanism was simple. Had its pounding on the walls been only a display? If so, then Chaos and Order either did not wish to slay him, or were prevented. If the former, it was because they desired rather to use him; if the latter, then who or what restrained them? He was not the

Master of the house, but he did hold some of the Words of Power. Did that somehow thwart their harming him?

He breathed a nose full of water and fell coughing against the banister.

The Bobby had certainly killed Brittle in the dream world; Carter believed he could have killed him as well. But the Bobby was surely answerable to different natural laws than those controlling Chaos and Order.

Who caused the storm, Chaos, Order, or the anarchists? Carter doubted it was the Bobby; in the library the anarchists had attacked directly. And this was not an orderly attack; Lady Order would have nothing to do with anything so untidy. It was Chaos that had threatened him; the Old Man was causing the deluge. If that was true, and if his assumption about their inability to slay him was also correct, this storm was but a diversion, meant to keep him on the stair until the anarchists came. With an aching heart he realized the storm might never end, that Chaos could hold him here indefinitely. He chided himself for not thinking of it sooner, but quickly realized it was because he was used to natural, not dream, terms; in the real world a storm eventually ceased.

After some thought he untied himself and began making his way downward once more, clutching the banister with all his strength. A barrage of water knocked him from his feet almost immediately, and he tumbled hard. For what seemed an eternity, he was beneath the waves, rolling down the stair. He panicked. This was the well once more, the water and the dark. He thrashed, pushed against the steps, slipped and fell again. Every bit of air was knocked from his lungs as he slammed against the banister, once, twice, then once more before he regained his grip and pulled himself above the surface.

Low sobs escaped him, the involuntary reaction to death. But as he came to himself, a new determination took him, a defiance of the forces and powers allied against him. Chaos could divert him, batter him, discomfort him, but it would not stop him. A low laugh crept from between his pallid lips.

He descended again, less fearful, and when he was washed from his feet once more, he rode the stream. Nonetheless, it was terrifying in the dark, unseeing, roaring down the waterfall, his back and head striking the stair, gasping every moment for air. After long, hard minutes, he struck a wall. The impact rattled his bones, and he dog-paddled furiously before he realized the flood was only waist-deep even at the bottom, instead of wholly submerged as it would have been in the real world. He thrashed about until he found the door, but it was locked.

He struggled back to the stair, and pushed his way to the left banister post. Without light, finding the mechanism to open the secret panel was difficult, but at last he turned the valve and entered a passage where the rain did not follow; neither did the water rush through the opening as would have been expected.

He fell on his knees, gasping, too cold to feel relief, too weary to continue, and if his enemies could have taken him then, he would have been helpless before them. He had lost his pack with all his gear, but he found a handful of dried fruit in his pocket, which he stuffed in his mouth. He might easily have fallen asleep where he sat, water dripping off him, but he forced himself to rise, knowing he was nearly to his goal.

There was still no light to guide him, but he knew this corridor ran straight. He followed the left wall and came quickly to the secret panel behind the painting in the upstair hall. The mechanism stymied him for a time, until he fumbled long enough to release it. The painting opened with a creak, and he stepped into lighted halls.

As he saw all the old, familiar things, he had to remind himself this was not his true home, but only a semblance in dream; he would find no Chant, no Glis, no servants to help him. The chambers were empty.

Though he sorely wished it, he did not stop to change garments, but made his way downstairs toward the library.

Halfway down, he saw Old Man Chaos standing at the base

of the stairs, one yellow eye fixed upon him. Carter's fear lasted only an instant, replaced by hot wrath at being bearded in his home after fighting through so much. He drew his gun and fired at close range, but Chaos only laughed. "I have brought all my forces, all my furies!"

A Word sprang to Carter's mind, the Word Which Gives Strength. He spoke it at once, not knowing what its effect might be. *Sedhattee!* The stair shook even as he felt power rush through his limbs. He leapt toward Chaos, intending to rend it with his bare hands, but the Word had an even greater impact on the monster; horror danced through its sallow eyes; it threw its arms before its face, and then was gone.

Carter rushed down the banister and dashed toward the library. He flung the doors open and gave a shout of fear. The room, which lay in twilight, was filled with creatures from nightmare—witches and goblins, trolls and dwarves, wielding axes and swords, uttering spells and incantations. A hag rushed toward him, seeking to drive him back, but he dove to the left, firing his pistol into those who crowded nearest. He was glad indeed for the Word Which Gives Strength after that, for only it, and his anger, gave him the might to thrust his way past the rotting skulls, the vampire jaws, the hands that clutched and clawed. Perhaps the fury of his charge surprised even these vile monsters, or perhaps they truly had no power over him, but he drove them back and reached the door to the study of the Book of Forgotten Things.

He hurried in, and bolted it behind him. Unlocking the cabinet, he opened the book without ceremony and went directly to page seven, while the horde hammered and yowled beyond the door.

Immediately, the flaming Words appeared on the page, all seven together. He read the last three carefully, forcing himself to allow time for them to burn themselves upon his memory. As he did so, a new awareness came upon him concerning the purpose and meaning of the Words, and he knew that so long as a single Word of Power lay within him,

Chaos and Order would find it difficult to slay him in the world of reality, and impossible in the land of dream, for they were subject to the Words, and the Words had been made to give the Master the power to maintain the balance between Order and Chaos. And now, with all seven Words in his possession, it was he who was their master.

Three words at once was a terrible trial, and when he stood moments later, his knees felt liquid.

He put the book away with deliberate slowness, trying to absorb his new understanding. Then he focused his thoughts on the one he needed, opened the door quickly, and spoke it.

"Ghandwin!" he cried, and the Word Which Masters Dreams shook the library.

Chaos was suddenly there, standing before its witches, its warlocks, all its minions, but its jaundiced eyes looked uneasy. Carter raised his hands. "No more," he spoke softly, but his voice rang through the room. "Begone."

"The red robe in the gray pool!" Chaos cried. "The golden sun on the yellow buds! You will never defeat us!"

But Carter saw he had defeated it, for its minions were melting behind it, like wax candles left too close to the hearth, turning to puddles, writhing and swaying as they went, even more ghastly in their death cries.

Smoke rose where the minions had stood. Chaos itself looked smaller, almost shriveled. Carter strode to it. "Understand," he spoke with soft authority, "the Words of Power are mine. You will no longer toy with me in the dream world, for I can master it, and you within it. And you will no longer disturb me in the real world, for I can master you there, as well. Do not speak, but go from me, and do not return here again unless I give you leave."

No emotion passed across Chaos's face, though it turned and slipped out the library door. Its movements were not those of a defeated foe, but rather, as a river diverted from its course continues on its way, or a mountain, blasted and tunneled by explosives, yet stands unperturbed—passionless force, given passion by the wiles of the Bobby. Was it so with Lady Order as well?

Carter shivered, then reached within himself and commanded his own wakening.

He opened his eyes and found himself lying on a cot staring at the ceiling of the attic room he had been investigating before weariness drove him to slumber. He sat up quickly and fumbled for his watch; if this was the same day he first fell asleep, he had slumbered less than three hours, not three days, as it felt to him. He was no longer wet, or sore, or even weary; all his adventures in the dream world he recalled through a haze, yet he knew they had been real. He strode to the corner of the room and verified the existence of the spy-hole, though he did not use the secret passage; he searched his memory and discovered he knew all seven Words of Power as well, so that learning the three and utilizing the one in the land of dream had cost him nothing in exhaustion in the waking world.

He rose and entered the main hall, where he heard soft scratching noises. The source proved to be a distant door, and he soon recognized furtive, muffled voices and the scraping of metal as someone tested key after key against the lock. He concealed himself behind a corner in the center section of the attic, and followed a wall away from the door, hoping to circle back around to the other side and return to the Clock Tower.

Though he could no longer see the door, he eventually heard it flung open and the scuffling of boots upon the boards. He drew his pistol and hurried, silent as he could, across the creaking floor.

Someone uttered a loud curse; apparently the anarchists had discovered he no longer slept in the side room. This, then, had been the reason Chaos and Order had sought to hinder him, so the Bobby could capture or kill him, if not in the dream world, then upon the cot as he slept.

He heard scurrying feet, passing in different directions, the echoes making them seem so ubiquitous he doubted he could long escape. He slipped into a room and made his way from chamber to chamber, until he could go no farther, and so returned to the corridor. Soft footfalls at his back, just behind an intersection, spurred him to hasten around the corner, where he encountered the Bobby, barring him from the secret panel leading to the Clock Tower. He started to flee, saw it would avail nothing, and aimed his revolver at the heart of his foe.

An anarchist turned the corner to Carter's left just then, gun in hand, cursing in surprise. Reacting instinctively, Carter downed him with a single shot, then retrained his sights back on the Bobby.

"Guns will not harm me," the Bobby said, his face only a caricature of dark eyes and scowling mouth.

Carter pulled the trigger. The explosion reverberated through the attic; smoke roiled from the pistol. Though the shot struck him full in the chest, the Bobby did not flinch.

"We will take you back with us," he said with a wicked smile.

Carter wanted only to flee, but there was nowhere to go; the other anarchists would be upon him in a moment. He felt within for the Words of Power, burning like brass, chose the proper one, and let it rise within him. *Falan*, the Word Which Manifests. It burst from him in a radiance, transforming his face, projecting a brilliance from his very spirit. The Bobby threw up his hands to shield his eyes.

"Stand aside, or feel its full weight," Carter said. "I am the Master of the Words now. I am coming to power. So far you have bested me because I was unprepared; you will do so no more."

Gradually, as if pressed back by some force, the Bobby withdrew from the portal, but as he did he laughed. "You are nothing! The Words are nothing! You do not have the Tawny

Mantle, or the Lightning Sword of your father, and you will never hold the Master Keys."

As Carter approached the portal, he caught a movement from the corner of his eyes. Another anarchist had appeared, his revolver aimed at Carter's head.

The man smiled a snarling grin from beneath a thick moustache. "Dispense with your weapon," he commanded. "You won't have it all your own way."

Carter dropped his gun.

"What should I do with him?" the subordinate asked.

"He knows all the Words of Power," the Bobby rasped. "It is too late to indoctrinate him. Kill him."

The anarchist drew his arm taut, aiming carefully.

A shot rang out, and for a moment Carter thought it was he who had been struck, but his assailant crumpled to the ground, felled by another, who stepped from behind the corner.

It was Duskin, now standing waxen-faced, staring at his own pistol as if it were a scorpion. Carter turned back to the Bobby, but he had already fled.

Carter rushed to the panel leading to the Clock Tower. "Quickly!" he cried.

Duskin looked blank, as if he had not understood. Blood pooled beneath the anarchist's body.

Carter darted to his half brother, took him by the arm, and guided him to the exit. "We must hurry. There may be others."

Duskin nodded vaguely. "Yes, of course."

Once inside, Carter locked the panel carefully behind him, and together the two made their way upstairs to Enoch.

Kitinthim

When they entered the Clock Tower Enoch embraced them both, so that Carter realized the old Hebrew loved Duskin well, and he wondered if, like himself, his half brother had followed the Windkeep on his rounds as a child.

Enoch seated them at the table, and set to work preparing biscuits and scrambled eggs upon the ancient stove, humming softly under his breath. The first scent of food smote Carter with ravenous hunger, so that he thought dreaming must be hardy labor. They said little as the meal was prepared and when Enoch set plates before them, they fell upon them with purpose, Duskin as hungry as Carter, saying between mouthfuls: "The anarchists spread a penurious table." He had a bewildered look about him, as if he had seen much disagreeable to him; his previous arrogance had fallen away, leaving his eyes sorrowful.

"What happened after your mother left the house?" Carter finally asked as they worked on seconds.

Duskin gave a look of distaste. "The Bobby treated us like compatriots in some glorious revolution. I went along, wanting to see some glimmer of decency in Mother's actions. But he is vile; his words were sweet but meant nothing. He promised me lordship of the house, and fiefdoms and lands for her, and she believed because she desired it. I stayed with them, wanting to obey her, and they told us they had trapped you here. They required me to accompany them, to help in your capture, I suppose to insure my loyalty; they knew I hated you, and thought I would be no trouble. But when I turned the corner, and saw the man's weapon trained upon you, you looked so much like Father. I remembered how he kept your picture on his desk, and how fondly he spoke of you. Blood called to blood, I suppose, and I knew beyond doubt the anarchists' plans were all for evil. I . . . I never killed a man before."

"Nor I, until I returned to the house," Carter said. "Defying your mother was a courageous act."

"It was the act of an Anderson." Duskin's face took on the determined look of his father, making Carter wince inwardly, but the next moment the younger man's countenance fell, and tears filled his eyes. He looked down, seeking to control himself. "How could she do this? Brittle died because of her. He was my friend. I could forgive her anything but that!"

"She is blinded by ambition," Enoch said. "I saw it in her early, when she could not understand why Lord Anderson would not use the power the house granted him. It has caused much pain. But what will happen to her now you have gone?"

"I have no doubt she will prove valuable to the anarchists' cause," Duskin said. "Mother has made a point of gaining the confidence of all the most influential people in Evenmere."

"She may become a terrible enemy," Carter said.

"It is quite possible," Duskin said. "At first, when she told me she had invited the Bobby into the Inner Chambers, I couldn't believe it. I thought there had to be some justification. But it was only greed. I am ashamed, both for her and myself." He glanced bleakly across the room, as if struck by a new thought. "I've turned my back on her. I have nowhere to go now."

"You could come with me," Carter said. "To find Father."

"Do you really believe he still lives?"

"I cannot rest until I know the truth. You say you are ashamed of what you've done—I betrayed him. I gave away the keys, and he is gone because of it. I did not desire to be lord of Evenmere, but I have the Seven Words of Power, and I must serve as the house demands."

"I . . . don't think I want to rule anything now," Duskin said. "I don't know what I want. Mother always said it was my right, that Father wanted it . . ."

"There is no truth in that," Enoch said. "Your father loved you both, but he knew the ways of the house. The Master has great responsibilities; it is not easy. Often he told me he thought you would be happier if neither of you became lord. But Carter is right. The house chooses who it will."

"You speak as if it were alive," Duskin said.

"Have you not heard its breathing, late at night?" Enoch replied. "Do you feel its windowed gaze upon you, the lamps of its eyes, its gargoyle faces watching? Its heart, blood pumping through gas-line veins, behind its plaster skin? The perspiration in its water pipes, the lit tobacco pipe of its chimneys? Have you never walked in a room and felt its soul, regal as its grand arches?"

"You can't be serious," Duskin said.

"Yet, surely you've felt it, too," Carter said, "when you played in its halls as a child—a presence, a spirit—but it is only after coming back that I recognize it. As a child, I did not sense it always surrounding me; departing Evenmere I did not know what I longed for; returning, I feel it, though I could not have put words to it till now. I doubt it is alive, but there is something uncanny in it, as if it were a favorite grandfather."

Duskin smiled for the first time, but it was a sad smile. "Father spoke that way sometimes."

"He did," Carter admitted. They fell silent, bound suddenly by the bond of blood and memories.

"I will go with you," Duskin said finally. "I am sorry I have hated you."

"You had the right," Carter said. "I took away your father."

Sunrise found Glis banging on the door where Chaos had once sought entrance, a company of men behind him. The captain, resplendent in his white armor, gave Carter a low bow, shook Enoch's hand, and threw a doubtful nod toward Duskin. After ordering his band to disburse along the halls, he followed the three up to the Clock Tower for breakfast. Taking the offensive had left him cheerful, and he spoke enthusiastically over poached eggs of strategies and troop deployments.

"The way up was hard but steady, once I received reinforcements from Nianar—Prince Clive's people—I know him well, though he did not come himself. The anarchists massed on the stairs and we had to fight our way through. Bitter work. They lacked the numbers to stop us, but they keep our forces occupied; we must guard the liberated corridors, leaving the Bobby free to strike elsewhere. Nonetheless, our casualties were light and I am content. The only incident was a strange message brought to me by a runner from Hope, saying you had reached the Towers but were in danger, and urging us to hasten."

"He was correct," Carter said. "He and I have been . . . in contact."

Glis waved his hand. "I needn't know all the Steward's secrets. I *will* inquire as to the correct deportment toward Duskin, as the last time I saw him he was accused of disloyalty."

Glis did not bother to hide his suspicious glare, while Duskin turned an angry crimson.

"Not he, but his mother," Carter said. "He has had his fill of the anarchists."

Glis dropped his eyes. "That, too, is the concern of the Steward. I, for one, will remain alert as the operation unfolds. Since we cannot use the Green Door, our connection with the White Circle is tenuous; the path to Keedin and Naleewuath involves ladders and precipices. I want to locate another route into the Circle from here."

"That should be possible," Carter said, drawing his maps from his breast pocket.

"There is one thing more," Glis said. "The Darkness which the Bobby released from the cellar has been seen throughout the house."

"It breached the cellar door?" Carter asked.

"No, but perhaps it seeps between the cracks in the bricks into other parts of Evenmere. There have been no sightings in the Inner Chambers, but thin streams have been reported in other corridors. And where it passes it leaves only Emptiness. That door must be closed."

"I need the Lightning Sword, if ever I am to regain the Master Keys. I intend to seek them at Arkalen."

"I can't tell you your affairs, but Lord Anderson has been gone ten years. The sword may be lost."

"Lost? Not lost," Enoch said. "Such devices have a way of turning up. It could not remain lost long."

"I've been to Arkalen," Glis said. "A fay country, terrible and splendid. And a great sea. If the sword lies at the bottom of that brine, it is lost indeed. And I can scarcely afford to send men with you; we are stretched thin."

"Then Duskin and I will go alone. Force of numbers would be of little use, anyway. We are not going to war, but on a quest."

"I little like this," Glis said. "From the beginning the Bobby has kept you off-balance, forcing you to defend the library, forcing you to come here, now forcing you to seek the sword. And the more time passes, the more he learns of the Master Keys. You may return home to find ashes."

Carter sighed. "You are right. But he has not had it all his way, else he would have subverted or destroyed me by now. I have grown as well. We will leave as soon as my leg is fully healed."

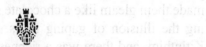

The day of their departure was as cloudy and rainswept as any other, and there was no one to bid them farewell. Having positioned his soldiers, Glis had moved on to other matters, and Enoch, needing to wind more clocks, had left two days before. The old Hebrew had hugged their necks, traces of tears swimming around his eyes. "Take care of one another," he said. "You are the last of your father's line, and it should not perish from the earth."

They had spent nearly a week in the Clock Tower together, time Carter had found profitable, for he had marked the ways of his brother. If he had not witnessed, through the spy-hole, the exchange between Duskin and Lady Murmur, he would have doubted him; as it was he let his misgivings rest, and so learned the joy of his sibling, who was too direct for dishonesty, and too serious for gentle teasing. His upbringing must have been harsh under cold Murmur, without Lord Anderson's tender humor. Yet he was bright and quick, though restless as a ship seeking its course.

They studied the maps carefully, and found a path leading into Arkalen through districts Enoch called barren. When all was ready, they left the Towers by the same door Glis had entered, which led into wide, open corridors, with neither rooms nor doors on either side, as if it had once been a banquet hall. The floorboards shone as if recently burnished; light drifted down wide skylights; altogether it was a cheery place, though the echoes of their boots made them anxious and they spoke only in whispers. The morning passed while they traversed the passage.

During the afternoon they followed a winding path up and

down stairs, across bare chambers, and through endless corridors, traveling through a country (for so Carter thought of it) of deep oak, heavy and ponderous. These floors, too, were polished to a high finish, and the light across their surface made them gleam like a chocolate sea, the wood patterns giving the illusion of gaping faces. The map named the area Kitinthim, and there was a richness about its wooden beams and carved gryphons that drew the men, so that they spoke of refurnishing the halls and making them habitable once more.

They spent the night within a barren chamber, once a drawing room, beside a fireplace of black obsidian, which to their surprise still had wood stacked in its firebox. With the sunset, Kitinthim lay brooding and ancient, the shadows of its shadows lost in the high-beamed ceiling, their fire the only light visible across the myriad halls. The gryphons poked their cruel beaks from the mantel and the arches; crickets rattled in the corners; a monstrous loneliness shrouded the empty rooms, yet neither Carter nor Duskin were afraid, but rather awed. They found a table and brought it before the hearth, brushed the dust from it, and made an altogether merry meal in a room that dwarfed them, ignoring the descending gloom and the sculpted monstrosities peering from the shadows. They spoke of things they had both done within the High House, each in their own time, of playing in the closets and stairwells, rummaging across the lawns, pretending to be Wellington at Waterloo in the yard. The hot tea had left them content, their soft laughter echoed around them, and Carter thought it a fine adventure, to sit together in the warm dark, so far from humanity. He discovered their upbringing had been similar, for Duskin, too, had been raised alone, his only companions Brittle, Chant, and Enoch, and if Carter had lost his mother, Duskin's father had been absent much of his youth.

"But I never knew where he went," Duskin said. "He never spoke of it, and avoided all questions."

"In his letters he mentioned the Sea No Man Can Sail," Carter said. "I think he went there to think of Mother."

"And that is why we seek him at Arkalen?"

Carter sighed. "So the dinosaur in the attic said. It is a place to start."

They unrolled their bedrolls before the dining-room fire. Lying there, listening to the soft cackling of the flames, Carter felt an odd contentment.

"What are you thinking?" Duskin asked.

"Oh, many things, strange things. I love these halls, the crannies and endless passages. The secret panels. The promise of adventure. I think there is something wonderful in all the desolate places. It's like being a child again, walking outside at night, with the wind stirring the trees, and the sudden fear that something would leap out before I reached the house. But beyond the fear there was a question, a mystery of what inhabits a land when no man is there. What do the trees do when they are alone? And the stones? And this is another desolate place. Think of it, year upon year, and perhaps we are the first ones to walk her halls in many lifetimes. Have you been outside the main portion of the house much?"

Duskin ran his hand over his blond hair. "Mother used to take me to Westwing, which is part of the White Circle. She has relatives there. That was only after Father disappeared. He never even told me about the house; I learned of its special properties from her."

Carter nodded. "It was much the same for me. Father did not want us to venture away from the Inner Chambers." Carter gestured at the blackness around them. "Do you love such lonely places in the house?"

Duskin's eyes looked golden in the firelight. "I hadn't really considered it. Not in the way you mean. I love the familiar part of Evenmere, where we grew up, but out here everything is too vast. As a child I always feared I would become lost, and never find my way home."

The thunder rumbled overhead, the first for a long time. As

its last echoes died away, the rain followed, pattering upon the windows.

"The Bobby said the storm wouldn't cease until he gave the word," Duskin said. "He said when he appointed me Master I could control the elements as well."

"Quite a promise."

"It did not tempt me. I recognize a lie. He would make me Master only as long as it suited him. He uses everything he touches. Carter, why did you ask me to accompany you?"

"You saved my life."

"Yes, but that could have been a ruse to gain your confidence. Surely you've thought of it."

"I have. But, for what reason? The Bobby wishes me dead or controlled. I was in your hands. What would be the purpose of such a deception?"

Duskin shrugged.

"Besides," Carter said. "I want to trust you. Enoch was right; Ashton Anderson's sons should not be foes."

Duskin stared at the flames for a time, then said, "You know, Father used to speak of you often. As a child I always wished you had stayed at Evenmere, so I could have had a brother. My mother never knew, but I used to sleep with your picture beneath my pillow, especially on the nights Father was away. I wish we could have grown up together."

"Yes," Carter said. "I would have liked that as well."

They fell asleep gazing at the fire.

All the next day they traveled the halls of Kitinthim, but the passages became increasingly debased, the banisters no longer polished, dust thick upon the threadworn furnishings, table legs and broken chairs scattered in the corridors. Only the floor retained its lustre. As the decay increased around them their spirits sank. Motes swirled thick within the sparse sunbeams through the smudged picture windows.

For several hours they walked in silence, constantly refer-ring to their maps, for the way was winding. Kitinthim was built like a funnel at its northernmost edge, all the rooms and passages narrowing to a single, large door, which they hoped to reach by the shortest route before twilight. Beyond lay the country of Ril, and beyond that, across the White Circle, Arkalen.

By midday they had made good progress, but toward late afternoon they became lost, and had to retrace their steps, which cost them an hour. When they finally found their way they were frustrated and weary, and the light through the win-dowpanes was fading. They pressed onward, knowing they neared their objective, and soon began to hear the sound of a torpid stream.

At last, with night nearly upon them, they discovered a wide corridor into which all the other passages converged. Signs of care appeared once more; the oak-paneled walls glis-tened, spotless chrome-yellow carpets covered the floor; all trace of dust was gone.

The passage was not long, and the heavy noise of the stream grew steadily louder. As the shadows massed thick with nightfall, and they approached a doorway twenty-feet tall, a horror crept upon Carter, for the source of the flow was a dark mass, too wide to be hurdled, barring their way, drift-ing with the lassitude of sludge. Duskin, thinking it water, would have waded across, but Carter restrained him and lit the lamp.

In the gaslight, the stream that whispered across the rugs was utterly black, and where it flowed the objects it touched were swallowed in its murk. It discharged from a widening rift in the left wall, coursed into the channel it had cut into the floor, and exited through a gap in the wall to the right.

"What is it?" Duskin asked.

"A Darkness the Bobby released from the cellar," Carter said. "Is it coincidence it blocks our way? We cannot cross, and this is the only way out of Kitinthim without going a great distance around."

Disheartened, they retreated from the passage, wishing to distance themselves from it. They found a hearth but no wood, and resigned themselves to a cold meal and a dreary evening. They rested only fitfully, and arose to a bleak dawn. By Carter's map, their closest route was to the south, and they set out at once, chewing bits of dried fruit as they went.

The passages, no different in appearance from those seen on previous days, led them without incident or deviation down their long lengths. As the morning wore on, their tempers improved, for it seemed the detour would not detain them as long as they had thought. This proved false hope, however, as they soon found their way blocked by debris. Part of the upper floor had collapsed along the corridor, dumping tons of masonry, and after some scrutiny, they soon realized they could not pass. This led them back to their maps, where they quickly located another passage perpendicular to their own, which promised a return to their course.

It proved to be an unlit way with few intersecting doors, and after forty minutes tramping down its length, having found no way back to their original corridor, they began to suspect a cartographer's error. Slightly farther on, they discovered this passage had also suffered damage—a solid mass obstructed its center, leaving questionable tunnels open to either side. They tried the right, but it was wholly blocked five feet from the opening, while the left way appeared unobstructed as far as they could see. With noon approaching, Carter slunk down with his back against a wall. "I intend to have lunch before I brave it."

"You look pale," Duskin said. "Are you ill?"

"No, I'm fine. It's . . . closed places make me nervous."

Duskin sat down beside him and took a sip from his canteen. "Have you always been that way?"

"Yes. Well, no, I don't think so, though I'm not certain. The Bobby caught me in the yard once, when I was twelve, just before father sent me away. He threw me into the well. It goes back to that, I suppose. I have too many foolish fears to be Steward of the house. Closed places, drowning. Even darkness still frightens me."

"Because of the well?"

"No. Because . . ." He suddenly grew very still, and his voice was low when he spoke again. "I don't think of it much. The Bobby took me . . . to a room. He called it the Room of Horrors. Father and Brittle rescued me from it."

"You are white as a specter," Duskin said. "What did you see? No, I'm sorry. You don't have to talk about it."

"No, I . . . It's all right. I don't remember much. Faces. Terrors. Darkness. More darkness than even here. Sometimes I have dreams." He looked around at the gloom and gave a violent shiver. "There's no point in talking of it. It was long ago."

"We could go back, find another route."

"It would take a week to reach the next one; it's at the exact opposite end of Kitinthim. And it might be blocked as well. The tunnel probably extends less than fifty feet, at any rate. We'll scoot right through."

They ate the rest of the meal in silence, Carter feeling vaguely silly, wondering if his half brother thought less of him for his confession.

The roof of the tunnel was tall enough for a man to walk upright, though there was only a foot between the debris and the wall. The lantern revealed rusted nails, splintered boards, and silken spiders fleeing from the light.

"I can go first," Duskin said.

"No," Carter said, feeling suddenly stubborn. He pushed his way through the cobwebs. Immediately it seemed the whole world closed around him; his stomach tightened involuntarily, and he could scarcely breathe. He closed his eyes momentarily, willing himself to remain calm.

Half-stooped to protect his head from low boards, he stepped farther in. His breath returned to him, allowing him to

better observe his surroundings, the half-shattered stone gargoyle, the bits of masonry and plaster, the mahogany boards,
once beautiful, scratched and splintered by the fall. He was
able to move freely enough, and the way looked open as far
as his light could penetrate. The air was hot, stuffy, and
smelled of molding plaster, and trickles of perspiration ran
down his neck. He pushed forward.

The farther they went the lower the ceiling became, until
both men were bent over, almost on their haunches. The rubble became a greater obstacle then, with less space to maneuver, and their pace slowed almost to a standstill. When half an
hour had passed, with the sweat burning Carter's eyes and the
dust irritating his lungs, he began to doubt the possibility of
an exit, as if they were burrowing deeper and deeper into the
vitals of the house. He forced such thoughts away, lest anxiety give way to total fear.

A section of cornerstone barred their path; Carter could
pass only by moving to the side and squirming by. For a moment he was caught between the rock on either side, blinded
by perspiration, and panic welled within him. He clawed his
way forward desperately, scraping his elbow and cheek
against the stones, and reached a wider space beyond. His
lantern toppled and went out, casting them into darkness. It
was almost more than he could bear. With shaking hands, he
groped till he found the lamp, drew the match, and relit it,
feeling all the while that only light could keep the roof from
crashing down upon them.

Duskin's begrimed face popped out from between the
crack. For an instant they stared eye to eye, the same thought
evident in both their faces, that neither wished to go on, that
neither wished to go back. Carter turned and pressed forward.

The next barricade was a post wedged between floor and
debris, too wide to be circumvented. Together they pushed
against it, and it moved more easily than they had supposed.
Dirt and wood hailed upon them, and Carter scrambled past,
fearing a cave-in. Both men made it beyond the deluge, but

the post suddenly tipped farther down, and sand poured in, followed by heavier stones. While they scrambled out of the way, the passage behind filled with wreckage. The whole rubbish heap groaned above like a tree in a violent wind.

Carter saw his own astonishment mirrored in Duskin's face. "What idiots!" he hissed. Before they had only thought of getting through, or failing that, retreating to find another way. Carter suddenly saw their foolishness in seeking such an unlikely path. But they had believed it would be but a few feet and then out.

As is often the way when men face a horror, they did not speak of it, but pressed forward. Carter forced himself to move with deliberation, to resist the urge to push frantically ahead, yet his heart pounded in his chest, while the way before them narrowed even more, until they could not remain on their knees, but were forced to crawl.

This was the worst of it for Carter, squirming forward, unable to even raise his head without bumping the ceiling, crawling between rocks and wood that pinched him cruelly, fighting panic, wanting to weep, wanting air, holding on only because he knew he must. His scraped knees and elbows hurt; his left cheek and forehead were bleeding; he could not keep the burning sweat from his eyes. Time wore on interminably and always there was the tunnel before him, like the mouth of a well. He cursed his own stupidity, blaming himself for leading Duskin into danger. He wondered, when the tunnel ran out, as he thought it surely must, whether he would be able to back his way to the cave-in, so they could attempt to dig themselves out. He wondered if any oxygen reached through the rubble.

He crawled through a particularly narrow way, while a protruding nail tore at his shirt and scratched his back, halting him. He tugged, the cloth ripped, the nail bit deep, then came free, making him groan. He crawled between the boards. Beyond, the tunnel widened slightly, though it became no taller. He pushed ahead and his hands struck stone. Brushing the perspiration from his eyes he saw solid masonry before him, and no exit to either side. He stared in despair, speechless, and pressed his hands helplessly against the rock.

His brother elbowed through the narrow way and was soon beside him. Duskin moaned softly. "What now?"

"We have to go back and dig through the sand," Carter said. "Dig our way out."

"We can't dig our way through that collapse! That's asinine!"

"It's all we can do!" Carter cried. "Unless you have another suggestion!"

His brother glared at him and he glared back, all their fear turned to anger.

Duskin lay his forehead in the dirt. "Sorry."

Carter softened and nodded. "Would you like some water?"

They both took a brief swallow from the canteen, wiped the dirt and sweat from their eyes, and looked around.

"We just have to dig our way out," Carter said. The resolution gave him courage.

"Perhaps we could dig our way up from here."

"But we don't know how much rubble is above us. We could be wasting our strength. And there is so little room to maneuver."

In answer Duskin pulled himself onto his back. "Perhaps if I could reach up through the cracks, feel around a bit."

He pushed his hand between two boards and thrust upward to the elbow. Carter could see nothing, but after sifting the wreckage for a time Duskin said, "I've pressed aside a metal sheet. I see light above us!"

Carter twisted himself sideways to catch a glimpse, and saw the faint glow of diffused sunlight.

"If we disturb it, the whole pile may collapse on us," he said. "I could use the Word Which Brings Aid, but who would come, I wonder?"

"Or what?" Duskin asked. "We just have to shift enough away so we can crawl out."

"Very well, but let me dig while you slip back down the passage."

"I want to help."

"I'm not being heroic. If it collapses you need to be free to drag me out."

While Duskin reluctantly retreated, Carter turned onto his back and cleared away a few loose stones. A solid piece of masonry blocked any path to his left, but to the right the debris was smaller. Dust rattled into his eyes and mouth; a small rock rolled down and grazed his forehead, making him yelp in surprise. He saw he would have to clear the lesser debris away over a wide area, to prevent it from filling up the opening. It was slow work, reaching between metal bars and boards, and he spent almost an hour on that.

Afterward came more dangerous work. With the hole widened, he had room to half sit and push through the rubble. His first attempt brought masonry and wood tumbling all around him, while he guarded his head with his hands. A metal pole crashed down, its end landing in the middle of his stomach, knocking him breathless. For a moment he thought he had been run through.

Duskin crawled in and freed him from the pole. When he had recovered they found the hole had widened, though a wooden post still lay across its middle. Together, they raised themselves on their elbows and tried to push it aside, but it withstood them. Finally, they could do nothing but use the knives from their packs to carve their way through it. There was only room for one to whittle at a time, and they had to work with arms outstretched, tiresome labor. By switching off, they finally severed it after more than two hours.

Carter was then able to rise to his knees and push more of the debris aside, lighter materials that gave way easily.

He pulled himself up by his arms where he could finally see out. The roof of the corridor had completely collapsed and he looked onto the story above, its doors opening almost comically into empty space. As he pulled himself out, a piece of heavy masonry slid toward the hole. He threw his weight against it, bringing it to a halt, and crawled from the opening.

As his brother pulled himself up, the masonry slipped again, and Duskin was pinned at the waist for a terrifying moment, until both men brought their weight against the stone. They pushed it away, and he climbed out. Steadying one another, they scrambled to the side of the corridor where they rested on a heavy timber lying atop the ruin.

They wiped their brows and looked around. The sunlight entered the corridor through broken windowpanes along the left wall. The rubble lay as far as they could see in either direction, as if some great explosion had ripped the ceiling away.

"It goes on forever," Duskin said, awe in his voice.

They looked at one another, their faces begrimed with dust and sweat, and Duskin began to laugh softly. The mirth was suddenly contagious, and Carter chuckled as well, even as he said, "We are two very stupid and lucky men."

There was nowhere to camp in the ruined corridor, and they stumbled across the rubble another hour before reaching an archway partially blocked by debris. They lugged a heavy cornice aside and squirmed through the narrow opening at the top, into a pristine corridor undisturbed by the anarchy at its threshold. Despite frequent examination of the map, they had found no recognizable markers to indicate their position. Though it was early afternoon, the passage was windowless dark, and they agreed to camp. Discouraged, exhausted, they flung themselves beneath a stair, ate an indifferent meal, and crawled into their bedrolls. Carter scarcely remembered lying down before falling into a slumber disturbed by dreams of crawling through tunnels. He woke more than once to find his hands digging the air.

An unfamiliar voice and a soft tapping against his boots

roused him the next morning. "Terribly sorry," the stranger said. "But you must move along. We are scheduled to polish here this morning."

Carter sat up in alarm, and pulled himself from beneath the stairs, his hand on the revolver in his pocket. He faced a short, barrel-chested man, old but stout, who held himself with military stiffness. He wore the dark blue trousers, jacket, and cap of a uniform, though one adorned by neither marks nor insignia, and for an instant Carter thought it might be the Bobby. But his round face displayed the candid authority such as might be found on a railroad conductor. His hair and handlebar moustache were silver, his eyes flat brown. "I am truly sorry," he said again, "but it just isn't done. We brook no vagrants in Kitinthim. If you need food and shelter for a night we can provide it, but loitering is out of the question. Looks bad, you know."

Duskin awoke with a start, rose up, and banged his head against the stairs. He clutched his wounded skull, moaned, and growled, "Who are you?"

"Spridel, Guild-Guide for the Order of Dusters and Burnishers of the Seven Halls of Kitinthim, appointed by the king himself thirty-four years ago, and still serving to the best of my capacity. But I should ask the questions. After all, you would want to do so if you found me bounding about in your country without an invitation. Who are you? Where do you go? Honest answers for honest inquiries."

Carter and Duskin rose to their feet. "Carter Anderson, Steward of Evenmere," Carter said. "This is my half brother, Duskin."

Spridel looked them over carefully, ignoring Carter's outstretched hand. "Steward of Evenmere is it? Quite a claim. Quite a claim indeed. I'm the Queen of Fis and Amithaine myself. Does the Steward always travel in such elegant garb?"

Carter glanced down at his tattered clothes and shrugged. "He does if he has crawled beneath half a mile of rubble."

"You came through the Fallen Way? If that was possible, it would explain your appearance. And what would the Steward be looking for in Kitinthim?"

"We want to reach Arkalen, but the main doors out of Kitinthim are blocked. Frankly, we have lost our way." Carter drew out his maps and showed Spridel their course.

"Ah, but the map, fine as it is, is wrong," Spridel said. He indicated two corridors. "These do not intersect as it shows, and the Fallen Way has changed many of the old routes. There was a fire, long ago, and if the firemen of Ooz hadn't come, all of Kitinthim would have gone to the flames. Things aren't as they once were. You'll have to come with me then. I will set you on the proper course."

Sensing no deception in the man, Carter and Duskin quickly packed their things and followed.

"We haven't seen anyone else in Kitinthim," Carter said.

"You won't see many. Mostly the workers are left, the carpenters and plumbers, the servants and the blacksmiths. And, of course, the Guild of Burnishers. We run things now, and try to keep everything in tip-top order for the return of the king."

"When are you expecting him?" Duskin asked.

Spridel paused in the hallway so quickly that the men nearly ran into him. He arched his eyebrows from beneath his cap and said, "Why, never, of course. Do you think we're fools?" then turned and continued on his way while Duskin and Carter exchanged puzzled glances.

They passed a pair of men scouring a wooden stair on their hands and knees, both dressed in the same uniform as Spridel, who spoke a few words of encouragement, though they neither looked up nor responded.

Soon, they met other workers patiently restoring lustre to the drab boards. The woodwork already buffed shone brilliantly, while the portions yet undone marked decades of neglect. The men themselves seemed wholly dreary, their faces pale, the hair of even the youngest thatched gray, their eyes gray as well, drained of all color, as if in burnishing the wood they had stripped their own glow away. They did not speak while they worked, nor sing, and Carter thought a prison sentence no worse than being among them. Only Spridel seemed cheerful, humming a soft, tuneless song that his workers ignored.

They marched up a flight of steps, then along a shining corridor. "This will take us over the Fallen Way," Spridel said. "You will be able to see it all from above."

They soon intersected the destroyed corridor, and Spridel brought them to its brink so they could witness the rubble below. They thought they recognized the place where they had exited the tunnel. A wooden walkway bridged the span, and they crossed it and continued on.

"It's as if the whole floor was simply cut away," Carter said. "What caused it?"

"Surely the Steward would know," Spridel said.

"I haven't been Steward long."

Spridel pondered a moment, his eyes searching the past. "It was the anarchists, as you might imagine. They unleashed a Dark Beast from a hidden door, a creature never meant to walk beneath the sun. I was a young man then, recently come to the Guild, but I was on the floor when it reached these halls, and I saw. The king himself met it where the way is now fallen, armed with Narchaldeth, an enchanted blade from old. The force of their combat was like two gods; the light was fantastic, streaks of color unlike any I saw before or since. But I fled, as did we all, when the house shook and the plaster crumbled, so I never saw the corridor collapse, but they say it went with heat and fire, and those too close were slain. When it was done, both the king and his enemy were gone, taking the entire corridor with them. Things were never the same thereafter, as if a bit of darkness had fallen into Kitinthim. People began to drift away. The members of the king's court disappeared with him, and what became of them none know, but others began departing after that. The kingdom fell into ruin, and the Guild of Dusters and Burnishers runs it now."

"How do you live?" Duskin asked. "Men cannot eat pol-ish."

"Folk still farm the Terraces in the west, and we keep the marketplace well burnished in exchange for meat and corn. They still feel loyalty to the palace, though it is mostly a sham now."

By noon they reached quarters more richly arrayed: white marble busts in the halls, heavy, braided curtains on the windows. The corridors were polished mirrors, banners of azure and argent draped the walls depicting a silver bear silhouetted against a blue moon. Yet the banners were soiled, frayed at the edges, and there were cobwebs in the corners. That, and the sparsity of servants, spoke of too much labor for too few workers.

The passages were curled maple from floor to ceiling. Carved bears marched along the windowsills, and the travelers soon stepped into a chamber with long tables and low benches, reminiscent of Viking halls, but resplendent with more gold and jewels than the northmen could have known. The centerpiece was an enormous sculpture of ebony, tinged in darkest blue, covering a wall fifty-feet broad and just as tall, depicting in intricate detail the lives and times of the Kitinthim people. The figures themselves were each less than a foot tall, so that without a spyglass the highest were only dim outlines. A golden glass dome etched with flowers and bears illuminated the chamber and warmed the dusky timbers. After a moment, Carter realized that two enormous doors stood nearly hidden in the intricacies of the carving.

"Drath!" Spridel called to a servant fussing about the tables. "We have company! Lunch for three."

Spridel flung himself down upon one of the benches and bade Carter and Duskin do the same. Drath vanished but soon reappeared with another servant carrying steaming bowls of potato soup and hunks of freshly baked bread. There was butter and honey, and hot tea over all; the men fell silent, giving all their attention to the meal.

Spridel himself took meager mouthfuls and watched as they dined. "Have you not eaten in a while, then?" he asked.

Carter and Duskin, suddenly aware of their slaughter of the meal, looked at one another and burst into laughter. "We've had little hot food the last few days," Carter said. "Dried meat, stale bread, and moldy fruit. They promote scant appetite. But this is a marvelous hall; Kitinthim must once have been great indeed."

"At the very top of the Kingdom Carving, as we call it, is depicted the coming of our ancestors, the Laubenthal, into Kitinthim. We drove out the barbarians who lived here then, and our first king, Abcell the Illustrious, set up his palace in this very place. As you can see, we have been here a long time, and there have been wars and deeds done. Though few of us remain, we were once a proud people."

Then Spridel spoke of the history of his race, and his pride in them made his speech long, so that he told of histories and legends, pointing out their depictions on the Kingdom Carving, and to Carter his words were sorrowful, for Kitinthim had been a Power once upon a time, but had fallen into disrepair over the years, as is the way of the kingdoms of men.

He ended with the story of Ithril, the last king of Kitinthim, who fought the Dark Beast and vanished thereafter. "He was the greatest of all his line. The legends say he will return someday and renew Kitinthim, raising it to a grand state once more, and he will make alliances with the Master of the house, and Kitinthim will be part of the White Circle as it was in the days of my grandfather's father's youth. But it is only a tale; some of the people still cling to it, and perhaps because of it, my guild is still given honor, for we control the palace. And on New Year's Day, we all stand at the top of the White Stairs, light seven candles, and pray for his return."

"Why do you do it," Duskin asked, "if you don't believe the legends?"

Spridel cocked one eye. "Well, it doesn't hurt anything,

after all. And it would be nice if he did come back. It would be real nice."

"So you are the ruler of this country?" Carter asked.

Spridel gave a broad wave of his hand. "If one could call it that. I am guild leader for the polishers, and the dust-men answer to me. I live in the palace and my wife and I sleep in the chamber beside the old king's room. If there is a quarrel I am called upon to solve it, and I negotiate for what we need. They do not respect me much, of course, and we are few, but I am as much a leader as they need."

"Bring me a sheet of paper," Carter said.

Spridel raised an eyebrow, but called to Drath, and a rough-bound notebook was produced. Carter took it, and wrote with careful hand the words: *I, Carter Anderson, son of Ashton, who was Master of the High House, and I the Steward after him, do make covenant with Spridel, acting Lord of Kitinthim, and declare he and all his people friends of the Inner Chambers. I vow to do all within my power to return Kitinthim to the ranks of the White Circle, and I confer to him the title of Baron of Kitinthim in the absence of the true king.* Carter signed the document with a flourish, had Duskin witness it, and handed it over to Spridel.

The man looked the writing over slowly, irony and amusement on his face. "Why, thank you," he said, his eyes twinkling. "It appears I have entertained angels, and starving ones at that."

"We may seem like vagabonds," Carter said, "but I would keep that safe."

Spridel shrugged, still smiling, and stowed the paper in the inner pocket of his jacket. "In the old days it is said the Master came to Kitinthim often, and our kings sat as equals in conference with him, for our country was the bulwark of the defense of Evenmere, and no stranger crossed the northern hallways without our leave. Those were glorious times, but we will not see them again. If you are ready, I will escort you to the border and set you on your way."

Seeing the man remained unconvinced, Carter said no more, and Spridel led them along winding hallways for another hour, until at last he brought them to a gray door with a knob cast in the shape of a bear's head.

"Beyond this door is the ring of the White Circle. Follow it until you reach Veth. Go through that kingdom, which is not large, and make your way into Arkalen. The people of Veth are kind, but shy; they will not harm you. Arkalen is empty; you will not like it. It gnaws the soul."

They thanked Spridel and made their way through the doorway, leaving the man grinning and shaking his head at the deranged strangers who thought themselves the royal stewards of the High House.

Veth

Carter and Duskin made their way through the door out of Kitinthim, down a short passage that led directly into the Long Corridor, a comforting sight after their wanderings. They were far beyond the portion of the hall that was always gray; the zinnias on the wallpaper were orange, the carpet peach. The passage lay quiet. They proceeded to the right.

Almost immediately, they reached a fork, with a black, wrought-iron gate stretched across the left branching. A wooden sign hung on the gate, depicting a green tortoise with a brief inscription beside, which said: *Peaceful Travelers, Welcome to Veth, Country of the Porcelain Duchess. Let None Come Here in Malice.* Beneath, in small letters, was written: *Carved by Jasper, in the reign of Moompis.* The gate was secured by a rusty padlock on a rusty chain. Carter called for the watchman, but received no reply, so the men straddled the barricade, which was little taller than their waists, obviously intended to keep no one out.

Veth was a kingdom of small rooms and narrow corridors. It had been built by additions, for the style changed almost at every chamber, and sections of various woods: oak, mahogany, cherry, and beech trailed one another down the passageways, past wallpapers likewise divergent, so that the quarters were a crazy quilt of patterns. The sparse furniture wore the second hand expression of worn fabrics and scuffed legs. The doorknobs were dull, the baseboards lackluster from hard use followed by neglect.

They became lost almost at once, for many of the crooks and turns within the convoluted passages were not shown on the map, and they spent the afternoon tracing and retracing their route, each step won at the cost of unwinding the puzzle of the halls. The inhabitants they met were few, and curiously frightened by their coming, rushing to hide behind bolted doors. Only once did they see a child, a boy about eleven, but when they called to him, his eyes widened and he sprinted up a stair, screaming for his mother in a high voice.

Toward evening, frustrated from unraveling their course, with Duskin complaining of a headache, they tramped into a series of small, interconnected rooms, determined to go no farther that day, and discovered a fireman sitting on the hearthstone, polishing his black boots before the flames. Beneath his red, wide-brimmed helmet, his pale face was smudged with soot; his heavy gray jacket was smeared with charcoal. He was a man of singular appearance, his face pitted and worn as if smoky winds had scored it over centuries, his brow a beetled carapace, ponderous with the knowledge of cinders and sparks, kindling and combustion, embers and arson, pyres and pyromania. His nose was a hook like the end of a ladder. He looked thoughtful and wise, like a sleuth who could read a history from dying coals. His eyes, which smoldered in the firelight, widened in alarm upon seeing them, though he did not rise, but picked up the stout axe by his side.

"Hello," Carter said.

The man looked down, then spoke in a deep voice that matched his face. "If you presume to kill me, I have neither food nor money, and I handle this axe well."

"Why ever would I want to kill you?" Carter asked.

"Aren't you some of Rooko's lads?" The man squinted up at them.

"Never heard of him. We are traveling to Arkalen. We certainly mean no harm."

The man sighed. "Good! I'm too tired to get up to defend myself, anyway. But you've come at a bad time. Fire has swept Veth; half the country is cinders. Women and children murdered. All because of Rooko. I am Nunth of the Firemen of Ooz. We have fought the blaze for three days and finally have it under control, assuming Rooko doesn't start another."

"Who is this Rooko?" Duskin asked.

"You must be strangers to Veth."

"Carter Anderson," Carter said, "and my brother, Duskin." After Spridel's scorn he had no inclination to identify himself as the Steward.

"Forgive me for not rising to shake hands," Nunth said. "I am exhausted. As for Rooko, he is a native to Veth, but the people here say he joined the Anarchy Party two years ago. He was a rabble-rouser, going about making speeches, saying there would be no more Master. The younger men started listening to his anarchists' jabber, about everyone being a leader, and no one at all. He had more supporters than anyone guessed, and last week, the Bobby himself showed up. Gave a rousing speech, but it was all a cover for Rooko to start the fires. Maybe they were intended to be small, to frighten people, but when we arrived from Ooz, the Bobby's boys blocked our way. Half the kingdom is ruined, the duchess is hiding, and Rooko and his ruffians have taken Petite Hall and are calling themselves Masters of Veth."

"Always the anarchists!" Duskin said. "We have to do something."

Carter turned to his brother, surprised by his vehemence. "I hardly think we can. We haven't any troops."

"You are the Steward of the house," Duskin said. "Father said the duty of the Master was to maintain the balance between Chaos and Order. Chaos is clearly on the offensive here, thanks to the Bobby. It is our duty."

"But don't we have a greater duty?" Carter asked. "The Inner Chamber is in danger—"

A clattering interrupted their discussion as the fireman rose stiffly, removed his helmet, then, joints popping, climbed down on one knee before Carter. With his eyes averted, he said, "I beg your pardon, sir. I did not know you were the Steward. This is wonderful news. We must take you to the Porcelain Duchess at once."

Carter flushed and helped the man to his feet. "None of that, sir. You needn't bow."

There were tears shining in Nunth's eyes. "But the Firemen of Ooz pledge fealty to the Master and his representatives. This is such an honor! They said there would be no more Masters, but I knew they were wrong. You must come, sir, and help the people. Many have died; many are injured; all need the hope you can bring."

Carter looked helplessly at Duskin, who said with a grin, "Of course we will come."

Despite his weariness, Nunth waddled off at a brisk pace through the narrow halls, his gear rattling. The men followed.

"Why did you volunteer our services?" Carter asked in a low voice.

"You may become the Master someday, but you are still somewhat dense about it all," Duskin said. "Don't you see? This is what the Master does. We can't leave them to suffer."

"But what can we do? I know Father was asked to perform such acts, but he had the keys, the mantle, and the Lightning Sword. And we have little time. We could easily lose the war for the sake of a single skirmish."

Duskin shook his head stubbornly. "It is the right thing to do."

"I suppose so," Carter said, unconvinced and a little stung. Yet he saw in Duskin an idealism he himself had lost while away from Evenmere, and he admired his brother for it.

They began to smell smoke and water, and soon found puddles standing on the floorboards beneath scorched walls. They discovered a long firehose hooked into a wide pipe protruding slightly from the wall; Carter had seen many such in his journeys, though he had never known their purpose. In such a great house, where fire could be catastrophic, the Firemen of Ooz were undoubtedly indispensable.

They quickly reached the ruins swept by the conflagration. Steam rose from tepid puddles; the husks of furniture hung against the walls like scarecrows. Stairs were consumed, walls and ceilings collapsed, floors burnt through, leaving gaping holes. In those areas where the ceiling had held, they could see for yards across the gutted remains, the rooms enlarged by the destruction. Weary firemen shuffled about, axes and shovels in their hands.

With professional grace, Nunth led them across the wreckage, steering them away from dangers, moving obstacles with his axe.

They traveled through the ruins for over an hour, and as he followed the miles of devastation, Carter raged inwardly at the cold, calculating minds capable of plotting such pointless destruction. Duskin had been right; he had to stop the anarchists wherever they struck.

At last they came to corridors untouched by the flames, unscathed save for the smell of soot. Nunth led them into a cul-de-sac with doors on either side and knocked two longs and three shorts on the final entry to the right. A brisk shuffling came from the adjacent room, and after several moments, a stern, unshaven soldier opened the door, his pike before him. By the torn cloth of his uniform, he had recently been in a fight.

"Ah, it's you, Captain Nunth," the man said. "But who are these?"

"Someone the Porcelain Duchess will want to see," Nunth replied.

"Hsst!" the guard warned. "No names here! Come in quickly."

They entered a small room occupied by seven more soldiers, four standing, wielding pistols and swords, and three seated on strawberry couches. The identity of the duchess could not be doubted; she sat apart from the others, swathed in sky-blue robes, a tiny woman, with hands like a child and enormous blue eyes, resembling nothing so much as a porcelain doll, no older than fifty, but aged by the sorrow of the last few days. She stood when Nunth approached, an act of humility Carter found unusual for a woman of her station, and the fireman dropped to one knee until the duchess bid him rise. "How goes the fire?" she asked in a sad but unexpectedly low voice.

"Contained and extinguished, unless more are set," Nunth said. "I have brought these two men to you, because I thought they might help your cause."

The woman's eyes were keen as she looked at the newcomers. "I am Mélusine. What aid can you offer my tormented kingdom?"

"Of that I am uncertain," Carter said. "Nunth said we should come."

"He is Carter Anderson, Steward of the house," Nunth said. "And his brother, Duskin."

Mélusine's eyes lit, but then doubt glazed them over once more. "You do have the name of the old Master," she said, after a moment.

"He is our father, and we came this way seeking him," Carter replied.

The duchess studied them a moment. Despite her size, she was a sturdy woman with a fearless chin and laugh lines around her eyes, though she did not laugh now. "Why, I believe you are! I met Lord Anderson more than once, and there is indeed a resemblance. If so, you have arrived at a fortunate hour. Come with me."

"For what purpose, my lady?" Carter asked. "What can we do that your soldiers cannot?"

The duchess gave him an odd look. "You need do almost nothing, sir. The fact you are here is sufficient. Nunth, as you go about your rounds be good enough to tell everyone you meet that the Steward has come to put down the rebellion."

Without further words, the lady led them through a back exit into a dimly lit corridor lined with doors on either side. The duchess's servants knocked on each of these as they went, repeating the same phrase to those inside: "The Master of Evenmere has come. Prepare yourselves for battle."

Men began pouring from the doors, pulling their boots on as they came, men grim of mien, silent in their resolution, the sorrows of their ruined homeland upon their faces, carrying swords and crossbows, pistols and pikes, some in armor, others in woolen cloth. The duchess did not pause to address them, but within moments a battalion followed her, and Carter and Duskin found themselves urged forward by the press.

Thus they marched through the desolation of Veth, the army growing with every step. Scouts went forth, and soon came running back, reporting Rooko's men encamped near what was called the Great Square, warning that they outnumbered their own forces, whispering that the dark-cloaked anarchists were among them.

"The Bobby's lies have spread too far," Mélusine said. "Stories of grandeur and glory, of Veth becoming a great empire, as Lorrimon of old."

They came to a canal, sixty feet wide, built of red marble, which brought the water supply from the mountains beyond the Terraces into Veth. The entire area was of white and vermilion stones, so that the flames had not touched it, and Carter saw the splendor of Veth, not as the massive carved palace of Kitinthim had been, but with a beauty of marble sculptures and cool, ivory pillars, and depictions of butterflies cut with such skill that light could be seen through the thin sheet of their marble wings. Glass globes, like colored Chinese lanterns, hung from poles all along the walkway beside the canal; sunlight drifted down from high skylights in the domed ceiling, and parrots of many hues sat on the poles, eyeing the men knowingly.

The company wound its way beside the canal, and still their numbers grew. An anger was building within them, and words were spoken, threats of punishment and death for those who had sided with Rooko. Yet, a dread was upon Carter, for he knew these men had rallied around him, as if he were their commander, and he did not know how to help.

On the opposite shore they saw clusters of rebels, some soldiers, most dressed as common men, though many carried bludgeons and bows. None bothered to fire arrows, but fled upon seeing Mélusine's forces, undoubtedly to warn Rooko.

They quickly came to a wooden bridge, wide enough for four men to walk abreast. Upon its far side a company larger than Mélusine's own were gathered, and at their head stood a man in a red cloak, slightly taller than his fellows, with hair dark as crow's feathers. The distance was such that a voice could carry easily, and as the duchess halted at the end of the span, a silence fell upon both sides.

The red-caped leader spoke first, in the accent of an unlearned man. "What are you doin' out of your hidin' place, old woman? Have you come to surrender to the will of the people?"

"And have you burned down the duchy at the will of the people?" the duchess demanded. "Did you strike the flint for the good of the children?"

"It weren't me as did it," Rooko cried. "Don't try to blame me. It was your soldiers, to ruin what you cannot keep. But we will build anew, when you swing from the high balconies, and Veth will become great, so that we bow and scrape no more to those from Gimry and Knoll."

"Will your new friends make it so?" the duchess asked sadly. "In one respect you are correct—I am not a great woman and Veth is not a great kingdom. But war will not change that. I have heard your plans; we are not strong enough to fulfill them. Has the lure of treasure blinded you? You are serving the will of the anarchists. They do not care that the White Circle will crush us if we invade our neighbors. We are farmers and blacksmiths, crafters in wood and stone, not warriors."

"If you do not share our vision of glory, you better step aside," Rooko said. "You have nothing to offer us."

"I have this," the duchess said, her voice rolling across the bridge. And though she looked very small among those tall men, every eye was upon her. "The Master of the High House is come, though you said he never would, and he stands here with me."

The announcement caused a reaction Carter would never have expected, exclamations of wonder followed by awed silence. Rooko appeared stunned, and he stared wordlessly across the span for a dozen heartbeats. Then he gave a slow, rolling laugh.

"Do you think we will surrender so easily to an impostor?" he asked. "The Master has been gone for years."

But Carter stepped forward a pace, feeling scarcely regal in his tattered clothing. All during the confrontation, he had focused on the Words of Power, and now held one at the ready. He spoke it, guessing little its result.

The canal water paused in its course, and all heads turned at its sudden silence. First the bridge, then the entire hall shook violently. Men fell to their knees in fear; several on both sides threw down their weapons and fled. The duchess stood her ground, tiny hands on hips, chin thrust forward, but her face was ashen.

In the silence that followed Carter cried, "My father was Master of Evenmere, I serve until his return! What has Veth done to itself? Do you become mighty by burning your homes? Do you become lords by obeying the anarchists? You serve only Entropy. Rooko has deceived you. This is but one of many fronts where the anarchists have struck."

He began to walk across the bridge, the Lady Mélusine beside him. The whole force followed a few steps behind their duchess.

"Archers!" Rooko called. "Show these mongrels we have no need for a Master of the High House."

A few of the men nocked arrows to their bows, and a murmuring ran through all of Rooko's troops.

Carter did not slow his pace, but kept his eyes on the leader of the rebellion.

An arrow struck at his feet; he strode over it, not allowing his step to falter. He could see the glint of the shafts aimed at his heart. His pulse beat at his temples.

Something flashed to his right, and he saw an anarchist behind Rooko collapse, a knife embedded in his chest, the pistol he had aimed at Carter fallen from his grasp. He thought it was over then, that the rebels would cut him down with return fire, but they only stared dumbly at the slain man.

Suddenly, one of the archers flung his bow to the ground and dropped to his knees. And then all of them were discarding their weapons, and falling to obeisance, some with tears in their eyes, some openly weeping. *The Master has returned* passed in whispers up and down the whole band.

Carter stopped four feet from Rooko. This close he perceived an uncouthness about the man, who was scarcely older than twenty, his pale eyes close together, his face lean like a hungry fox. Here was one who had found a following at an early age, and had reveled in his own prominence. But all arrogance had fled from his eyes; he looked imploringly from face to face, like a trapped animal, saw nothing that could help him, and tried to back away, but the press of the crowd prevented it.

"What is the law of Veth for a traitor and an arsonist?" Carter asked softly.

"Death, my lord," one of Rooko's prostrate followers said. "By hanging."

Carter knew this was no moment for leniency. "Then hang

him, and the anarchists with him, and your duchess will surely pardon those of you who were misled."

Men from both sides rushed to seize Rooko, and his lieutenants with him, who had deceived the people as well. The duchess quickly took charge, and had soon dissipated the crowds, some to the work of finding shelter and food for those who had lost their homes, some to rounding up the anarchists, who had all mysteriously vanished, and some to repairing what could be repaired.

"We will have to purchase wood from North Lowing, and stone from Keedin," she said.

"How did you know the people would relent when they saw me?" Carter asked. "They might just as well had me skewered."

"I knew once we rattled their leaders the people would turn," Mélusine said. "They are a good folk, led astray. Mostly they are fond of me, I think; we just needed to get their attention. Respect for the Master is great in our land. One of the few women to serve in that position was from our country, and it is said when Veth was first built, that Uzzia, who was Master then, brought the red marble you see around you all the way from Merimna, and donated more besides."

"Then if the word of a Steward has any meaning, tell those who would sell you wood and stone that I request fair dealings and more," Carter said. "Veth is but the first to falter before the Bobby's forces; all the White Circle must work together to restore the peace."

"If I could I would prepare a banquet for you, in gratitude for what you have done," Mélusine said. "But half my people are hungry and homeless. I cannot feast while they famish."

"If you can point us toward Arkalen, that will be gratitude enough," Carter said. "We are in some haste. But if you require shelter, there is much room in Kitinthim, and I do not think Spridel of the Guild of Dusters and Burnishers would refuse those in need."

"That is a good thought," Mélusine said. "I will contact

him. But as for your journey, if you could remain with us the rest of the day, so the people might see you, I would be grateful. If you leave too soon, they will misdoubt all that has occurred here. Tomorrow, guides will lead you to the Arkalen door."

Carter hesitated, torn by his desire to complete his mission, but Duskin said, "We can stay the day, but no more." He gave Carter a significant look, and the Steward nodded.

"Wonderful!" the duchess said.

They spent the afternoon accompanying Mélusine through her duchy, and Carter learned much from watching her deal with her countrymen. If men were hungry, she found food, if weary, a place to rest; if angry, she calmed them; if sorrowing, she comforted them. She was a woman of the people, and it was clear they loved her, though they had forgotten for a time under Rooko's persuasion. And always, wherever they went, the people treated Carter with awed wonder, as if he were one risen from the grave, or a great king of old. He spoke to them, and tousled the hair of their children, and though he promised them nothing and made no speeches, it was as Mélusine had said, that he brought them hope. And he saw how wise Duskin had been, to make them stay.

A girl of about eight, brown-haired and blue-eyed, came to him during the afternoon, and looking up solemn and sad, said, "Are you really the Master?"

Because she was a child who would not understand the difference between Master and Steward, he said, "I am."

"Will you find my lost brother, sir?"

He looked at the duchess, but Mélusine shook her head. "Her brother, Nicholas, was in the rooms nearest the fire. He hasn't been seen."

"Please, sir, you are the Master."

Carter knelt beside her, speechless before those innocent eyes. But before he could think of what to say, a lad of twelve rushed up to her, and taking her hand, cried, "Penelope, he's been found! Nicholas has been found! He hid beneath the wreckage and he's all right. Come quickly!"

She gave the reassured smile of a child, looked at Carter gratefully, and said, "Thank you, sir. I knew you would."

Then she was gone, while Carter still knelt, dumbfounded.

But Mélusine laughed heartily. "Good news! And that was good fortune indeed! Forever after, she will think the Master returned her brother to her."

"Yes," Carter said, but his face was pale. "And what would I have done if he had not arrived when he did?"

They slept in Petite Hall that night, brightly lit apartments with low-beamed ceilings, Morris patterns in every shade, blue and white china lamps, plates, and vases, and stained-glass windows with sunflowers in every square. Mélusine's husband had died fifteen years before, and the chambers held the cheerful look only a woman living alone can bring to such dwellings. The rebels, who had occupied the hall for a time, had done surprisingly little damage, further evidence that they respected their duchess more than even they had known. Those larders not empty the duchess distributed among the needy, so supper was not elegant, but adequate. They ate late, then the brothers went almost immediately to the room they were to share, for the day had been long, and the duchess appeared exhausted. They fell asleep on feather beds, too weary to talk.

Mélusine woke them early the next morning, and they breakfasted together. Someone had found eggs and day-old biscuits, but there was enough, and the men were satisfied. They spoke to the duchess of friendships and alliances, and she promised to do what she could to help the White Circle once order was restored. Midway through the meal, two tall, slender men appeared, bearing the insignia and blue mail of soldiers of Veth, ready to lead Carter and Duskin to Arkalen as Mélusine had promised. The Porcelain Duchess had a kingdom to put to rights, so they did not tarry, but bowed to her and departed.

Their guides seemed to hold the pair in awe, for they were extremely polite, and said nothing unless questioned. As the brothers followed them through the burnt, disfigured halls, Duskin said, "I never got a chance to ask, but I'm curious— what Word of Power did you use on the bridge, that disarmed the rebels and kept them from cutting us all down?"

Carter chuckled, but spoke softly so their guides could not overhear. "It was the Word of Secret Ways. I didn't know if they would shoot us or not, but I knew the use of any of the Words of Power could shake the house. It was an effect, nothing more, and it provided no defense. They could have killed us all on the bridge. I gambled that even Rooko's followers were shocked by the burning of Veth, and that they held to him only from pride. They couldn't have thought the duchess would torch her own kingdom; one need only look at her to know otherwise. All they needed was an excuse to desert the villain."

Duskin was silent a moment. Then, finally, he spoke, "You say you are only the Steward, but yesterday I think you were the Master, whether you wished it or not."

"Does that anger you?"

The young man looked pensive. "No, though once it would have. I am no coward, but I would not have led those men across the bridge."

Carter gripped his arm. "Yet you followed me, which was brave enough, and I won't forget. I acted on behalf of the Master, but I am still only the Steward. We will find Father and bring him home."

The guides brought them to lower levels that revealed an increasing neglect, for they led to the back door of Veth, a way none ever took. Neither did anyone live nearby, for the door to Arkalen had an evil reputation—it was said its people had been destroyed by a mysterious catastrophe. The guards grew more anxious with every step, even as the stairs and corridors narrowed to single file, as if seeking to enfold them.

At last they came to an ebony door, not even wide as a man's shoulders, carved with scowling devil faces. One of the guides produced a rusted skeleton key; the lock turned after great effort, and the door creaked open only when the soldiers pulled together.

"This is the way," one of the men said. "We know nothing of the passage beyond. The old tales say marauders used to come here, and perhaps will again, so I will lock the door behind you. Certainly no good comes from this witchy place."

"Fair enough," Carter said. "Thank you for your service."

"Do not thank us until you have passed beyond Arkalen's borders. Then you will know if we did well or ill. God protect you."

The men stepped through the door into a gloomy stone corridor, illuminated by spears of light cast from small squares cut in the right-hand wall. The door shut behind them with a groan, the lock turned, and they heard fleeing footfalls.

"They wasted no time," Duskin said. "What ancient fear drives them?"

"Perhaps none, or a terror of the unknown. Glis told me Arkalen was accursed, its inhabitants destroyed because they committed a great evil now forgotten."

Duskin peered down the corridor. "It looks grim enough."

Upon the walls and stone doors were carved symbols in heavy ocher paint, of vultures and wolves, beetles and spiders, handprints and hunting men, and writing in dead tongues. The skulls of bulls hung in the corners, the sharpness of their short horns gradually flaking away to dull ends. Carter was reminded at once of pictures of archaeological digs in Turkey and Iraq—these tokens had that same primitive quality. He suddenly felt as if he stood in a prehistoric cave, as if he had stepped backward into a primitive age. A shiver ran along his spine.

They spent the afternoon and early evening following the

corridor, which had neither intersections, nor doors to either side. This inevitable course they counted as blessing, since the passage was not on their maps. They passed unhindered, meeting no one, but as the day crawled on and the sunlight gradually deserted the portals, the dimness brought with it a preternatural foreboding, for there was a liquidity about the shadows, a flowing beyond any trick of the eye.

Before the last light had fled they reached an iron door standing half-opened, rusted into position. They lit a lantern and squeezed through the gap into a room at the bottom of a stone stair. Carter gave a gasp, for the whole chamber seemed to be moving. He raised the lantern. The walls, floor, and back of the stairs were covered with moths, large as men's hands, which rose in a cloud, surging toward the flame, flapping into the brothers' faces, leaving the taste and smell of rotten wool, while the men battered the velvet assailants in frightened disgust. The brothers fled up the stairs, but the moths followed, and more descended from the heights, until the air swarmed and danced with them. The companions halted at the second landing, checked by the pelting.

"Douse the light!" Duskin cried. "Before we drown in them."

Carter did so, which made things worse for a time, the moths landing all over them, fluttering in their faces like bats, climbing up their legs, leaving the men blindly kicking them away, a futile task since they swarmed across the stones.

"This is ridiculous!" Duskin said. "What do we do now? We can't lie down to sleep, nor relight the lamp. Defeated by giant moths?"

Carter gave a weary laugh. "It would be funny, if I weren't so tired. We either stand where we are, or continue without light."

"Either way we get no sleep. Let's try the climb."

"I agree. I never like to wait," Carter said.

He went first, feeling his way along the wall to his right, which was sticky and covered with the insects. He crushed dozens with every step. Duskin kept one hand on his back for guidance. A landing lay every twelve steps, and the stair zig-zagged from side to side, a repetition the men soon found comforting. Still, to Carter, it was little better than crawling through the rubble of the Fallen Way; he felt like a child, feeling his way in the dark, never knowing when evil might strike, being constantly startled by the repulsive touch of the insects.

They had reached the sixth landing when Duskin tugged at Carter's arm and whispered, "Did you hear something?"

Carter stood frozen, listening, perceiving only the fluttering of the wings against the stones. But then there came a whisper, so soft he could not understand the words at first. He strained to hear. *Go back.*

Carter drew his revolver. He could see nothing.

Go back, the voice said again. It seemed to emanate from the steps above them, and there was a familiar quality about it. Pistol raised, he crossed the landing and placed his foot on the first step.

You will die here.

Carter kept silent, but continued climbing. At the third step the voice spoke again, softer, as if it had retreated a pace. *Go back.*

Step by step, his brother behind him, Carter ascended to the next landing. Still the voice threatened, but he thought he recognized it now. "I know you," he said, trying to keep his tone level. "You are the Thin Man."

A heavy object whizzed by Carter's head and bounced down the stone steps, the noise of its fall like a thunderburst in the silence. *You think I don't mean it? Flee, or I will slay you.*

Carter kept as close to the wall as possible, brushing the moths away with his shoulder, climbing while the stranger threatened and retreated. No more objects were thrown, and the voice changed, becoming suddenly wheedling. *Don't make me harm you. I will, you know.*

"I don't doubt you can," Carter replied, his own voice quaking, hating the dark, the moths, the harsh stones, most of all hating his own fear. He wanted to fire at the unseen assailant, but he could not, because the Thin Man had aided him in the past. And there was something else, something just beyond his grasp, that restrained him.

"Who are you?" Carter asked. "What do you want?"

I want you to go back. Leave this place.

"Why?"

You must depart.

So it went, as they ascended, yet never did the threatened attack come. And finally, though he did not know how he knew, Carter felt certain the Thin Man would never harm him.

There rose a surge of light, a brilliance that subsided quickly to a golden glow tinged with prismatic color, as the Thin Man drew a jagged sword from its scabbard. The moths did not seek its light, as if they could not see it, and Carter stood dumbfounded in its radiance, for it was the Lightning Sword of his father.

The planes of the Thin Man's face, which Carter had seen only in shadow before, stood defined by that brilliance, the flash of the eyes, the line of the jaw, the slight lift of the lips. Then Carter knew why the voice, cloaked in hoarse whispers, had always seemed familiar.

"Father?" Carter gasped.

"Leave this house," the Thin Man said. *"It is too dangerous. Don't force me to stop you."*

"Are you our father?" Carter cried again.

The figure turned, fled up the final landing, and vanished through a half-opened door, slamming it shut behind him. With the sword gone, the men were plunged again into darkness. They stumbled after him, but reached the door and found it locked.

Beside the Rainbow Sea

They slept that night with their backs against the locked door, a fitful slumber distressed by moths' hooked feet and their own troubled deliberations on the Thin Man. They kept to their own thoughts, as do those confronted with the prospect of pain. To Carter, it was dreadful thinking of his father as a tattered vagabond, a phantom, wandering the boundless halls of Evenmere. And to what purpose? He could not banish the remembrance of the flash of light, those clear features made bare, wonderful, and terrifying at once, his own father's face, but haggard, and hardened, bereft of hope. It was nothing as he had imagined their meeting.

The new morning came with a rush—as pink light paled through an overhead portal the moths departed, swarming like slow bats, sullying forth to moth-jousts in fields of honeysuckle and clover. For half an hour they darkened the single window, while Duskin and Carter sheltered their faces with their coats. At last, when only a few stragglers flitted along the ceiling, they arose, exhausted but unwilling to stay.

The locked door remained adamant, but they soon found another beside the second landing, overlooked in the night, which led through a passage to a parallel stair. After some winding, they came to the top floor and the other side of the locked door, to corridors beamed in dark oak, with baseboards covered in brass, purple carpets spun in wool, wallpaper embellished with gold leaf, but dust thick all around.

Ardently, they yearned to pursue the Thin Man, but knowing nothing of his direction, they elected to follow their own course. "He has always managed to find us," Carter said. "And if he is truly Father, perhaps under some curse or spell, he will be drawn to us."

Arkalen's former splendor still stretched down the hall, in oil paintings bordered in gilt frames, ebony panels inlaid with lapis, and jade carvings of mantis circling the silver lamps.

"Do you smell the scent of the ocean?" Carter asked, breathing deeply. "We are close now."

Whatever destruction had come upon its inhabitants, Arkalen seemed hardly cursed, but rather, the ornate quarters of kings, whose subjects had spent the languid hours reading and making sport among its tranquil chambers. Save for the dust, the rooms remained oddly pristine; thieves had not looted the golden tapers on the walls, or the silver shields in the high-vaulted chamber where delicate bells tinkled with the rising breeze.

They saw no one, and they remained pensive, their thoughts ever upon the previous night, so that Carter scarcely heeded their approach toward stained-glass doors at the end of a wide hallway until the companions stood directly before them. Then he saw how bright the light shone through them, how clouds, made multihued by the stained glass, floated behind the pane, and with them, white crests and thundering waves.

They opened the doors together and stepped out onto a wide, white marble porch. Sunlight, diffused through heavy clouds, blinded them, leaving them blinking solemnly like owls. As their sight returned, they saw that the stained-glass colors had not been an illusion, for the cumulus formations and the sky beyond reflected prismatic hues—jade, crimson, azure, and gold—upon a bright green sea flecked with orange fire. Gushing winds troubled the waves; a storm hovered far beyond the shore, casting forks of tangerine lightning down upon the swells. The white-foamed breakers, like tiny fingers, clutched vainly toward the coast.

There was a power in that ocean; a calling that gripped Carter's heart, and he stared, mouth agape, wanting only to sail upon her. Scarce wonder his father had fantasized of finding his perished love across her boundless ways; surely some shore of heaven lay beyond that vermilion horizon, a strip of land leading to the Everlasting. He restrained himself from kicking his shoes away, bolting down the beach, and flinging himself into the depths. For an instant he struggled, feeling the urge wound him even as he triumphed.

"The Sea No Man Can Sail," he said, mouth dry. "The sea Father mentioned."

Beach began where the porch ended, gray sand fine as powder, with diamond slivers reflecting the sun. The outlines of Evenmere followed the shore in either direction, curving backward for miles, finally lost from sight. In places the coast was wide; at others the water nearly lapped the stone walls.

They strode together across the sand, and on that beach were neither gulls nor terns, but the most wondrous sea spawn lay washed upon the shore, iridescent spider crabs, bright blue prawns, silver anemones, rainbow jellyfish—and other creatures more mysterious and unique, as if these waters bred with a variety lost to mortal seas. They marched or flowed across the sand, depending on the number and kind of their legs, over seashells deep and rich of bloom, dazzling as gemstones. Duskin scooped up one of the shells, a sea mussel red and translucent as a ruby, its ridges fine as a child's comb. He examined it, then slipped it into his pocket.

As if their march to the waterside marked the end of the day, twilight fell, and by this they knew they were in an enchanted land, for it had been midmorning when they entered

Arkalen. Since they did not know what to expect, or even where to begin their search for their father's things, they combed the beach until they found enough driftwood to build a fire in a pit scooped from the sand. Then they sat and watched the fading of the light, a spectacular sunset of cold beauty, the colors like icicles, sparkling and frozen, majestic, so many hues all gradually draining away to deep emerald and brown, trailing on the scarecrow clouds.

The roaring of the breakers attended their meal, while a growing luminescence from the cloud cover to the east betrayed the rising moon. Beneath its light the whole beach took on an eldritch beauty—the sky became jade, the same color as the waters, shot with silver when the distant lightnings flashed. The rumble of the thunder was lost to the sea.

They huddled close to the fire, chilled by the wind over the water. Taken by the mood of the place, Carter said, "Father used to tell marvelous stories of countries like this. As a child, I thought them only make-believe."

Duskin smiled. "I remember. Of Numinor and Poseidonis, enchanted kingdoms both lost to the ocean's depths. In my mind I can still see the tall princes, chalk-white of skin, in mail of bronze, the sun gleaming on their shields."

"Do you recall Lud-in-the-Mist?"

Duskin grinned. "It was a village lying just beyond the Debatable Hills, where waited Fairyland."

"Was Alveric prince there?"

"No, they had no prince. You're thinking of the story of the witch Ziroonderel."

"Ah, you're right!"

"What about Aviathar, the warrior of Khymyrium, how he came to Glasgerd and the things he did there?"

"I used to dream of him, his armor shining."

"I remember Babbulkund and how it fell."

"Now that was a story! But I don't recall all of it."

Duskin proceeded to tell the tale, and as Carter listened, he heard in the tone and emphasis the voice of his father. For a time, it was indeed as if he sat by Lord Anderson's side once more, listening to a bedtime tale. When Babbulkund perished again, its towers crumbling to ruin, the mist of memory fell from his eyes as well, and he sighed and studied the fire. "Do you think they were true, the stories he told?"

Duskin laughed softly. "I didn't then, but I do now, after what we've seen. Even if they were only stories, they were probably legends he heard in the kingdoms he visited."

Carter drew a letter from his pocket, and handed it, tattered and stained, to Duskin.

"What is it?"

"The last letter Father sent me. He spoke of his desire to cross this sea. He thought he would find Mother there."

Duskin read it, and his eyes were moist as he handed it back. "Do you think he is really the Thin Man?"

"Perhaps I saw what I wished to see. If it is him, he must be ensorcelled. Perhaps he tried to sail the sea and this is the result. Have you heard its beckoning? It called to him as well, trapped him perhaps in the end. I do not believe anything goes there and returns the same."

As if in answer to their thoughts a lone cry drifted across the waters, barely audible above the waves. Carter and Duskin stood. At first they saw nothing, until Duskin pointed far over the water, where the moonlight shone through the clouds onto the sea. It was difficult to discern, but Carter finally realized it was a yellow boat, large enough for two or three, with a triangular sail. A single figure, tall and thin, wearing a high hat, stood beside the mast; even from so great a distance, Carter saw he contended against the wind and the sea.

"Is it him?" Carter asked.

"Could it be another? He isn't seeking the shore—see how he battles the waves? They are too strong."

They watched him struggle, slipping to his knees, bailing water from his craft, tacking against the wind, but it availed him nothing. Gradually, though he fought every moment, the boat was driven back. It all ended with the tearing of the sail and the breaking of the mast, which knocked him into the water as it fell. He clamored back on board, but remained half lying, no longer rowing, as the wind pressed his craft rapidly toward shore. The boat passed from sight behind a low hillock some distance down the beach.

"We should catch him, now, when he is too weak to flee," Carter said.

"I'll bring a lantern," Duskin said.

They left their fire and hurried along the shore, guided by the lightning flashes and the shrouded moon. The silicate reflected emerald beads off the jade sky, like galaxies of green stars beneath their feet.

They were breathless by the time they reached the hillock, where they saw the boat lying on the sand. They redoubled their efforts, sprinting along the shore just beyond the reach of the waves.

The yellow boat was little more than wreckage; where the mast had broken the boards had come away, leaving a hole in the bottom. It lay on its side, half-filled with water, but its occupant had vanished. They hurried down the coast. For an instant the moonlight penetrated the cloud cover, and they saw him sitting on the beach, his hands covering his face, his hat still somehow clinging to his head, a raggedy man, all shadows and darkness.

Carter approached him carefully, and halted while still several feet away. The Thin Man looked up, but did not rise. As Duskin lit the lantern and the light fell upon the spent face, the brothers gasped, for this was indeed the eyes, the square jaw, the very face of their sire.

"Father?" Carter cried. "Is it you?" If not for the spectral quality of the forlorn figure, he would have rushed forward to clasp the man, but he hung back, doubt and hope warring within him.

"Why have you come here, my sons?" the voice, no longer

disguised, was both like and unlike Lord Anderson's. But it had been so many years. "I warned you to stay away."

"But why?" Carter asked. "And why have you hidden yourself so long? You sent no letters. I thought you had died . . . or . . . forgotten me."

The Thin Man's eyes bobbed rapidly back and forth, as if Carter's words confounded him. "It was like dying," he finally said. "And I had to return, across the sea. Each night I try. I rebuild the yellow boat, but I cannot reach her. I cannot go back to him."

"Her? You mean Mother?"

"Oh, yes." The voice quivered in sorrow. "Oh, she of the bright eyes! She was so beautiful. I thought so the first time I saw her; I thought it always. She waits beyond the sea, I know, upon the shores of heaven, but I cannot go unless I die myself, for the waves are too strong. And I am afraid to die. If I did, I could not return to the Other Place."

"What place?" Duskin asked. "And what did you mean when you said you could not go back to him?"

"I can never go back to him, though I seek that as well. But you should not be here. I know why you have come—the Lightning Sword, the Tawny Mantle. It will make you Master."

"But, Father, why should I be the Master when you are here?" Carter asked. "You could come back. We would help you—"

"I, the Master?" Horror flickered across the Thin Man's face. "No, not I, but he. Do not suggest it! But I will not give you the sword or the cloak. There is only pain in being Master; I will not have that for you."

"We don't understand," Duskin said. "What torments you? How can we help?"

"Help? You can help by going away, far from Evenmere. Depart! I saved you before, when the Bobby stormed the library, when he sought you in your dreams, but I cannot always be with you. I have to cross the sea!" Tears sprang to his eyes. "But I cannot, for I must return, back to the place. It calls me already."

Carter stepped forward, but the Thin Man waved him back. "Come no closer! I must away! Can't you see I am of the damned? Thus goes the Master of the High House. I lost her, I lost you, and now I have lost myself."

With an anguished cry, he sprang across the beach, his patchwork coat flapping behind him. His speed surprised the brothers, for though he did not seem to run swiftly, his long strides carried him far down the beach before they could think to follow. In the obscurity, he fled with a certainty they could not match, though they pursued with all their hearts.

Carter's mind reeled as he desperately followed; he had found his father, yet it was not as he had expected. This pale man, wan and tormented, was he truly the strong, loving sire he had known? Could even the years do so much?

The wind rose as they ran along the beach, its goblin voice cackling, its imp claws delaying them. The swirling clouds made patchwork of the moonlight; where it shone they saw the silver reflection of their quarry, dancing far before them like a wraith, sliding over the beach, untiring, always farther away. Carter prided himself in his physical condition, but as one mile turned to two, and two to three, both men panted heavily, and he began to wonder: Ashton Anderson was more than sixty years old, yet he outstripped them as if they were still boys.

I was proud of my father's strength, yet this is beyond belief, he thought, even as he and Duskin slowed to a trot. *It is as if I am still twelve.*

"A moment," Duskin gasped, stopping, bending down to breathe. "He . . . can run."

Carter was too breathless to answer. Despair ran through him, that he would never catch up. Tears suddenly sprang to his eyes, and he stifled a sudden sob. All his life, it seemed he had sought his father, when he had been away on his journeys, when he had sat at table with his guests, finally when he had sent Carter from Evenmere. The unfairness of it all struck him like a blow to the chest, that he should pay forever for losing the Master Keys, that no reconciliation could ever be made, that forgiveness and his father's companionship should elude him forever.

They walked a moment, then ran with renewed effort. Soon, there rose before them, black in the dark, a curving arm of rock into the sea. They hurried to its base and Carter thought he saw a form scrambling over the crest. The sides were smooth this low, worn by the rising tides; farther up the rocks rose in cruel spikes like a crown, thirty feet above them.

"There's no help for it," Carter said. "I could go alone, if you would rather stay."

"We go together, or not at all," Duskin said.

Carter had always been good at climbing, the result of an adolescence spent searching for the High House among the mountains and foothills. He quickly found a purchase in the shallow cavities pocking the stone face, and pulled himself up. The first few feet proved effortless, until he reached the portion where the rock bent slightly backward, forcing him to cling with all his strength, bearing much of his weight on his arms. He was nearly past the smooth segment when the left foothold crumbled beneath his weight, leaving him scrambling for another. For a moment he flailed the air, until his toes found purchase once more. He continued upward and reached the plentiful handholds of the rough crags above, propelled himself onto an upcrop, and waited until Duskin joined him. They rested a moment together, then Carter led once more, and soon crossed over the rough rim between the dark spires. Beyond the jagged lip the rock top was twenty feet wide and relatively flat. Its granite reach extended into the sea, and at its farthest position, a dim light glowed golden. Duskin clambered over the side; Carter gave him a hand and pointed wordlessly toward the distant luminance. The younger brother extinguished the lamp, and they groped their way toward the radiance, banging their knees against jagged stones, cutting their hands as they steadied themselves.

As they drew near, they saw the Thin Man, kneeling on a low mound, hugging a large, rounded marker, all his limbs convulsed. "They mustn't come here," he murmured. "They mustn't go back to the house. I can't cross the sea, though I must; I can't leave here, though I must. Someone help me!"

Beside him, lying on the mound, lay the Lightning Sword and the Tawny Mantle. It was the blade itself that cast the glow.

"Let us help you," Carter said.

He turned toward them, and the agony on his face was nearly more than Carter could bear. "You!" he cried. "Haven't I warned you. You can't have his things! You can't be the Master!"

He stood suddenly, menacing, his features contorted, exposing the rough-hewn marker and the words written thereon: *Lord Ashton Anderson, Master of Evenmere*, and Carter saw it was a grave.

Despite the venom in the Thin Man's eyes, Carter lost his strength of limb, and collapsed, reeling, to his knees. The action had a peculiar effect upon the Thin Man, who said, "Carter, are you all right? Have you hurt yourself?"

"Are you his ghost, then?" Carter asked. "A specter left behind?"

"I never wanted to hurt you," the Thin Man said. "You shouldn't have come. I didn't want you to see. He isn't here, of course. There is no body beneath the mound. But he departed from this place, to cross the Sea No Man Can Sail."

"Could he yet live?" Duskin asked.

"He died upon the waves. And with his dying breath, he sent me here. But there is only torment. I cannot leave this place, yet I am drawn to find *her*, across the waves. And I must protect you; he made it clear. The sons of the Master were to be protected."

Still on his knees, staring at the grave mound, Carter asked, "What are you?"

"I never wanted either of you to be Master; I love you too much. But when I tried to protect you from harm, it only drew you to rule. Will this house ever cease tormenting the Andersons? She was so beautiful; her hands were fine as porphyry. I loved her so."

"Was it the Bobby who tempted him, who made him cross the sea?" Carter asked slowly, his tongue ashes.

"We used to stand here, Ashton and I, and sometimes, in the twilight, when the colors had dimmed, we thought we saw her, walking on far lands, her hair blowing in the wind. At the last he followed, and I with him. We were already parted from you, Carter, and Murmur kept Duskin from me as well. She hated me, for still loving your mother, for not wanting Duskin to be Master. I thought we would find the keys there as well, over the sea. I don't know why we thought it; we just did. No man can sail there and live."

"He is a Sending," Duskin said, staring hard, his voice shaking. "As Father was dying he sent forth a piece of himself."

"A scrap," the Thin Man said. "Only a scrap. He made me before the jade waves overwhelmed the boat, before the mountainous waters crushed him. To protect you. His last thoughts were of you both. But I couldn't find Carter, not until he returned to the house."

"That explains it," Carter said softly. "Why you drove us away, yet still tried to protect us. Father's emotions, all mixed up together. But you're not him. He's truly gone."

Suddenly Carter could contain his disappointment no longer; he burst into long, slow sobs. "He is truly gone," he gasped out. "Papa is gone. All because I took the keys."

The Thin Man went to him and placed his hands upon his shoulders, his visage all compassion. "Don't cry, son. It's all right. I never blamed you for the keys. You were a child. I loved you both so much. The mistakes were mine; you were innocent. Even death could not stop me from coming to tell you."

Carter looked up into the eyes, and they were indeed again the eyes of his father, the features suddenly sharpened. "What could you ever have done that I would not forgive?" he said. "And where I have gone, I see all clearly now. Even Murmur I have surely forgiven."

"Then why did you send me away?" Carter asked with a sudden vehemence that surprised himself.

"I never intended to be long. I thought I would soon find the keys so I could return you home. I sent the White Circle Guard, and placed all the resources of Evenmere toward that end, to no avail. The years went by, and my longing for your mother brought me here, to this sea. So I spent the days I should have spent with both of you. I am sorry, my sons, that I proved a poor father. But I loved you the only way I knew."

He stood abruptly and strode to stare across the sea. The planes of his face subsided, becoming less Lord Anderson, and more a hunted animal. "It is never long; she calls me again. I will have to rebuild my yellow boat; I will have to seek her."

Carter rose slowly to his feet. He spoke with quiet determination. "Since you are . . . not my father . . . I require the Tawny Mantle and the Lightning Sword."

"Noooo!" the Thin Man roared into the night, his expression melted away, transfigured, alien. He stepped forward, menace in his eyes. "Go away! Go away! You can't have it! Can't!"

Duskin stepped between the specter and Carter. The Thin Man halted, but bellowed again, six inches from Duskin's face, a deafening shriek. "Go awaaaay!" Again and again he cried, screaming like a child. For an instant, Duskin quailed beneath the affront, his fists knotted, sweat streaming down his brow, but then a light entered his eyes, his face grew impassive, and he stood firm as the Sending went on, screaming always the same words. Carter would never forget how firm he stood.

Failing to quail the younger brother, the Thin Man side-stepped Duskin, placed himself between Carter and the objects lying on the grave, and focused his tirade toward the eldest son. He raged, waving grasping hands before him, foam running down his face like a winded horse. "Go away! Leave here! You can't have them. He doesn't want you to be Master! He doesn't."

"I must," Carter said, his voice little more than a whisper, but the whisper silenced the pitiful creature. The Thin Man looked about him, bewildered, then his features hardened again. In a clear, still voice he said, "Carter, Duskin, I could never hurt you. If the house needs you, you must obey, even unto sorrow. It is the highest calling. The very highest."

The face slipped away. The Thin Man burst into sobbing tears. "You can't have it. Can't, can't, can't. You'll be harmed. Oh, I know you will."

Carter placed his hand gently on the specter's shoulder and slowly drew him aside, away from the path to his father's things.

The Thin Man collapsed as if his feet had been cut from beneath him, and lay weeping on the grave.

Carter turned to Duskin. "Now is the time, brother. The sword and the mantle are before us. We could pick them up together."

Duskin shook his head, the stronger at that moment. "Only one can be Master. The High House has chosen; it will be you."

"Are you certain? Once you dreamed of being Master, and I never desired it. I have learned to love you these past few days. I don't want to lose that."

"And I you. And I tell you, those ambitions are gone, purged by our journey together. We are both our father's sons, and mine is a calling as high as your own; every king must have a trusted counselor."

Carter nodded, greatly moved. He took up the Lightning Sword first; Duskin served as his squire, and helped him buckle it about his waist. As he touched its ornate hilt, small electrical charges coursed through his body, surges of power as if he tapped into an unseen dynamo. Duskin placed the Tawny Mantle about him, a dusky cloak, almost no color at all, with black spots like a leopard; it lay heavy, though it appeared light, and his shoulders felt broad as twin peaks, able to bear any burden.

He drew the blade from its sheath; it blazed golden in the night, its serrated edge circled by bands of smoke. He held it high, first toward the Rainbow Sea, then over the kneeling form of the Thin Man.

"The Master's things have become mine," he said, his face suffused with light and power. "I did not wish it, but it is so. One thing only do I lack. Answer me, then, with the mind of my father; the Master commands it. The Bobby holds the keys in his possession. Where can I find him?"

"Even Lord Anderson did not know that," the Thin Man replied. "But the Bobby cannot always keep the keys upon his person; they were not meant for him; their power would eventually devour him. He must store them most of the time. If he wanted them kept safe, it would be where the Master could not reach, a place of peril and fear."

"I understand," Carter said. "Thank you. You have aided us greatly. I would help you in return. My father summoned you, a shadow of what he was, filled with his conflicting feelings for his wife and sons. What the Master has summoned, the Master can dismiss. I grant you peace. Be gone, gentle shade."

Carter touched the specter's shoulder with the tip of his sword. The Thin Man gazed at them one last time with Lord Anderson's beautiful eyes, and spoke in his old voice. "Thank you, boys. I am very proud."

Then he was gone, with only the whispering wind and the imprint of his knees on the mound to mark him.

Carter dropped down beside the grave, ran his hands upon the earth, and wept there, saying, "He was so strong. I thought he would never die."

Duskin came and laid his hand upon his shoulder, and his voice trembled, though he did not weep. "I never really had any hope, I suppose. He has been gone so long."

"Then I gave you false hope," Carter said.

"No," Duskin said. "You gave me the chance . . . to say good-bye."

So they sat by the grave together, and because he had nothing else to offer, Carter drew a heart in the earth, as a child might do, and pressed his hand into the soft soil, leaving his print there. And they kept vigil throughout the night.

When the first traces of morning paled the sky, Carter stood, and Duskin thought he looked changed—a resolution lay upon him, and he spoke in a crystal voice. "Our path is clear. Now we will seek the Master Keys."

"But do you know where they are?"

"Of course. The place where the Bobby thinks them safe. The one place I fear most. I must seek the Room of Horrors."

Innman Tor

Midafternoon found Carter and Duskin traveling the halls of Arkalen, far from the grave of their father. As the morning sun, peeking behind the storm clouds, had set the Rainbow Sea shimmering iridescent, they had returned through the stained-glass doors, exhausted, and thrown themselves upon the carpet to sleep in the sunbeams until noon. Once awakened, they had eaten breakfast and made their plans. Carter had lost none of his resolve to reach the Room of Horrors, though he trembled when he thought of it. The day of his abduction he had been carried facing backward to the loathsome chamber, slung over the shoulder of the Bobby's lackey, and though he had seen the way he recalled nothing of it. He determined to return to the library, to consult the Book of Forgotten Things, or failing that, to brave asking the dinosaur in the attic.

The door from Veth had been locked behind them, preventing them from retracing their route, and the only other road back to Kitinthim led far out of their way. But Glis had described a path to the Inner Chambers from Naleewuath, if they could reach that country. To do so, they would have to cross the western boundaries of Arkalen and pass through the country of Innman Tor, of which they knew nothing.

With the Tawny Mantle upon his shoulders and the Lightning Sword at his side, Carter truly felt like the Master of Evenmere, but it grieved him to wear these things, since it meant his father would do so no more, and the hours spent wandering the fading splendor of Arkalen were dark to him. He did not heed the blue porphyry lions carved beside the doorways, the basalt pillars lining the great halls, the curtains tinged in argent, shining like teardrops in the light from the high oval windows. Until Duskin spoke of it, he failed to see the stabs of sunlight crisscrossing the marble floors, a sign of the dwindling of the storm, as if the taking of the sword and mantle had diminished the anarchists' power.

Despite their late start, they were weary by early evening, worn by the night's vigil and their grief, and they made camp with the waning sun, in the shelter of a narrow sitting room off one of the main halls. By mutual consent, they avoided the bedchamber two doors away; sleeping in the dusty berths of long-departed men made them uneasy. Better to lay their bedrolls beside the mantled hearth, before a blaze fueled by a broken chair. They ate in silence, Carter's face ashen as the cinders. The night wrapped itself around the room.

"Will you be all right?" Duskin finally asked.

Carter gave a mirthless laugh. "I wonder. My heart is empty; there is no hope for it. I thought him immortal and now he is gone. I will miss his smile most, the wolf's grin. He smiled a lot, you know, even through his sorrow. And I keep seeing his eyes. I know now I could never have said good-bye enough times; there is always more I would have said, and things I could never say though I stood beside him a thousand lifetimes. It is all regret. So many years my only hope was in finding him. What have I now?"

Duskin shrugged. "At least we know. When he had been gone several months, Mother told me he was dead. I was too young to question the information; perhaps she was in league with the Bobby even then, and knew he had perished on the sea. I remember mourning him a long while, alone in my room. I have missed his strength, his goodness, most of all. As I grew older, I used to ask Chant about him. He usually quoted Hamlet: '*He was a man, take him for all in all, I shall not look upon his like again.*' I suppose his enemies thought him terrible, but I think that says it well."

"More than well," Carter agreed. But then he remembered Lord Anderson standing before the Room of Horrors, the door shattered, the Lightning Sword in his hand. "Yet, you are right; he could be dreadful to his foes."

They said good night soon after, but late in the night, when the fire lay in embers, Duskin awoke to see Carter sitting before the mantel, the Lightning Sword drawn less than an inch from its sheath, its golden light barely shining upon a face streamed with silent tears.

They woke late the next morning and traveled through a long, uneventful day. Near evening they reached a lightless passage so narrow their shoulders brushed the plaster walls. By lantern light they walked an uneasy hour, all cobwebs, creaking floors, and the threat of assassins at every turning, before they came to a dead end within a low chamber of rough-hewn stone.

"The map shows a doorway," Duskin said.

Without hesitation, Carter strode to the left side of the room, and felt his way beneath the protruding stone edge until he depressed a small button. Part of the wall groaned inward, revealing yellow-green light beyond.

"How did you know?" Duskin asked. "You spoke no Word of Power."

"I'm not certain," Carter said. "It is something that has been growing within me. It began when I was trapped in the dream by the Bobby, imprisoned by Lady Order, when she bound and gagged me, to prevent me from using the Words of Power. Yet I brought the Word forth, not out of my mouth, but from my soul. Since then, the Words have seemed a part of me. It was nothing more than that, though sometimes I would see them, suspended, their letters aflame within my mind. But since I took the mantle and the sword, it is as if the maps of the High House are within me as well. At first I thought it a fancy, that I could summon them to mind, whole portions, in detail more accurate than the maps we carry—Wait, what are you doing?"

Duskin had dropped down to one knee, his head bowed, the sallow glow from the opening turning his blond hair olive. "I am certain now. You are no longer Steward. The house has taken you; you are the Master. I want to be the first to offer you fealty."

Carter's face grew hot. "Duskin, stand! You are my brother! I want no allegiance, and I will have no such nonsense between us."

Duskin raised his face; it looked like an angel's, suffused with conviction, partaking of breathtaking serenity. "I will not rise until you accept my fealty. The mark is upon you and cannot be denied. It is better to serve in the house of the Master than to rule without right. And all my life I have wanted only to know my proper place. I see it before me."

Sudden tears sprang to Carter's eyes. He drew his Lightning Sword and laid Duskin's hand upon the pommel. "Whether I am Master or not, I know now you are the better man. But offer your allegiance only to the good of the house."

"To the house, but to the man as well, or not at all."

"Very well. I accept your allegiance. Rise, brother."

Then they embraced, and saying no more, passed through the doorway to the base of a stone stair.

The glow issued from the landing above; the light prevented them from seeing what lay beyond. The stair itself appeared half-ruined, the mortar worn away by time and water, the steps weary and leaning.

They heard alarmed voices, followed by heavy footfalls descending, and a man in plate mail approached, pausing three steps from the bottom to aim a crossbow level with their chests. "Who comes by the Narroway Gate?"

Duskin stepped between Carter and the weapon. "Strangers seeking safe passage."

"You look like shabby men to me, tramps and castoffs," the man said.

Another soldier appeared, a heavy man made larger by his armor. "Stay your hand, Capecot! No one has come down this passage since our father's day. Let's see what they want."

The second soldier descended the stair to meet them, followed by the first, a young, lean fellow. Despite their differences, both men were dun-eyed and chestnut-haired, older and younger versions of one another. The portly man was obviously in charge.

"I'm Peelhammer," he said, with an air of importance. "All strangers must be brought to the Main Station for registration."

"We are only passing through your country," Carter said. "And our mission is urgent."

"Them is the rules," Peelhammer said.

"Very well. I am Carter Anderson, and this is my brother, Duskin."

Peelhammer nodded. "This way, then."

He led them up the stair. All the halls of Innman Tor were brown—not chestnut, dun, ginger, mahogany, or sienna—but brown: brown carpet, newly laid; brown walls, freshly painted; brown curtains, recently cleaned; brown pictures of brown figures playing on brown hills. Even the woodwork was painted brown. The soldiers wore brown capes over their dull armor.

"Why is it called Innman Tor?" Carter asked.

"Extraneous conversation is forbidden until after registration," Peelhammer said. Then, with a sudden sorrowful look, he added, "Them's the rules."

"You have considerable rules, sir," Duskin said.

The brothers exchanged glances, and Carter laid his hand lightly within the pocket where he kept his pistol. He saw Duskin nod and move his own hand near his weapon.

The corridors were without windows, and the lamps, defying the care shown to the rest of the hall, cast their light through age-yellowed glass. They passed other inhabitants, all resembling the soldiers, the men dressed in colorless robes, the women in brown dresses, devoid of baubles or embroidery. The young girls hacked their hair in a short, shapeless fashion, and neither skipped nor smiled as they traipsed the halls. Strangest of all were a group of children no older than six, all bedecked in brown robes like somber monks, their faces wise as monkeys, silently following a grim, ancient crone, their apparent teacher, likewise clad.

After marching an hour through the gloom, they reached a passage built of brown stone, where the men were ushered into a room Peelhammer called a way station, consisting of stone walls and a half-dozen cots covered with dirty blankets.

"We rest here for the night," Peelhammer said.

Carter tested the bed and found it uncomfortably soft. "I prefer my own bedroll," he said, laying it out on the stone floor.

"We will sleep outside," Capecot said.

"Are we your prisoners, then?" Carter asked. "Do we require a guard?"

"Just regulations," Capecot said. "We have some food, if you would like it."

"We would," Duskin replied. "Our own supplies are meager."

The soldiers did not offer to eat with them, but gave them a flask, a sack of brown bread, and a bronze fruit they called oboa before retreating beyond the door, which they left open. Carter and Duskin moved to the far wall so they could speak without being overheard, and sat on the floor to eat.

"We should take turns keeping a watch tonight," Carter spoke in a low voice.

"Better to tie them up and be on our way," Duskin replied.

"I've considered it, but we've seen too many people, and our dress marks us."

Duskin bit into the brown bread and blanched. "This is like chewing mud!"

Carter took a sip from the flask, then sniffed it. "No more bland than this. It tastes neither of water nor wine. Our own supplies are better."

All the food was equally insipid, and they reverted to eating dried strips of meat from their pack. Thereafter, Duskin took the first watch, while Carter flung himself into sleep, refusing to deliberate the intentions of their captors.

The next morning the guards made no haste to depart and the brothers were awake and ready before Capecot summoned them. They breakfasted together, a cheerless affair, the soldiers still close-mouthed, yet were it not for regulations, Carter thought Peelhammer might have proved companionable. Studied closer, he had the expression of a fearful man overburdened by a harsh master.

They set off at once, following the nondescript corridors deeper into Innman Tor. By noon the passage had widened, and they stepped suddenly through double doors into open air beneath a rainswept sky. Lightning flashed above their heads, the thunder rolled; a light drizzle misted their upturned faces. They stood upon a field miles long and equally wide, an inner court despite its size, bounded on all sides by the High House. In its center stood a jagged, sandstone hill sculpted into a watery face like a shrouded ghost, with cave openings marking its empty eye sockets. A dusty town surrounded the hill, its houses the same color as the bare stone. There were crops in the fields all around, but even they lay brown as grass after frost. A gravel road led to the town from the passage the men had exited.

"This must be the tor where the country gets its name," Carter said.

"A bleak country it is, then," Duskin said.

Forgetting himself, Peelhammer replied, "It wasn't always so. Before they carved it, it was a beautiful hill."

"Who are 'they'?" Carter asked.

"Never you mind. You'll see in time."

They followed the gravel road to a train station, where a pale yellow engine puffed black soot. A score of brown-garbed men and women were being escorted into boxcars by armored soldiers. Standing beside the engine were two men in the dark coats of anarchists; they were half turned away, their attention fixed on those boarding the train, and Carter and Duskin ducked their heads and shuffled past.

"Worse and worse," Carter murmured. "I think you were right. We should have bolted when we had the chance."

But it was too late for that, with soldiers all around. Their very numbers were a wonder; they far outmanned the towns-people. The brothers were led through the garrisoned town, down squalid streets displaying not so much poverty as a meanness of spirit, always filled with soldiers laughing, talk-ing, sitting, and eating. During the journey, Carter abruptly halted, staring intently at a line of warriors marching past.

"What is it?" Duskin asked.

Carter continued to stare, then abruptly withdrew from his trance. "Eh, did you speak?"

"What were you looking at?"

"Something that may help us." But Capecot was beside them by then, and Carter only said, "I'll explain later."

Up they went, to the tor itself, along a rough-cut stair that left them at the mercy of the rising wind. Breathless, they en-tered the left eye socket into a smooth tunnel. The air was dry, despite the rain, as if all the moisture had been sucked from it, and the wind passing through the cave mouth gave the spectral head a moaning voice.

The tunnel led into a large chamber, where an old man sat on a wooden throne atop a thin dais. He wore the conventional brown garb of his people, and looked more clerk than king, his white, thatched hair sticking out all around, his spectacles slipping down the bridge of his nose. Old and soft and afraid he seemed. He did not remain on his niggardly throne, but stood, gave a half bow, and directed the men to a rough-hewn table. "Good day, gentlemen." His voice was thin and quivered when he spoke. "I am Settlefrost, Administrator in Charge of Distribution, Redistribution, Procurement, and Relinquishment for the High Kingdom of Innman Tor, and of Querny, Lippenhost, and the Downs of Gen. Word has reached me of your coming."

Carter glanced at Peelhammer and Capecot. "Your soldiers are efficient. I am Carter Anderson, this is my brother, Duskin. I am Master of Evenmere."

Settlefrost's face went pale. "My soldiers are . . . not as efficient as I would like. Sergeant Peelhammer, you may return to your post."

Peelhammer hesitated, studying Carter wistfully, as if he wished to speak, but he only nodded and tramped away, Capecot at his heels.

Once they were gone, Settlefrost stood up and paced the floor. "I knew you would come, I just knew it," he said, wringing his hands. "I told them it couldn't be done, that they'd never get away with it. And here it is and you've come to punish me and I deserve it. It's death, I suppose. At first I thought it was good. We were organizing, and they said it would make everything better for everyone. We would all be part of the Brotherhood, all equal, man, woman, and child, and everyone would be happy. And it went well at first. After they took our king away we built the train, and painted all the halls, had work for everyone and all sorts of managers and administrators. It was going to be grand. You do understand we meant well?"

Carter was baffled by this string of words, but he said, "Such things usually begin that way."

"Yes," the man said, relief in his voice. "We were doing something lofty, and there were banners and festivals and plenty of food for everyone. And then the men in their low hats and greatcoats came, and all the soldiers recruited from our own people, though I don't know how there could be so many. Things began to happen. All the money spent on festivals never seemed to bring in any revenue. We tried work programs, economic reforms, but the more we struggled, the worse things became. We raised taxes time and again. We set up gambling houses to generate income to increase the wages of the teachers of our schools so our children could grasp the anarchists' Grand Design, and they learned less and less. We had studies and commissions and endless rhetoric, all part of what the Bobby called the 'Great Chain of Communication,' and much was said and nothing done. In the name of intellectual freedom, under the anarchists' insistence on the realistic portrayal of human suffering, our writers and artists described the basest depravity of man, until our people considered it customary. There seemed to be no help for it. When we ran out of colorful paint we used brown, and when we ran out of dye for our clothing, we used brown again. And one morning we awoke and found Innman Tor this glowering ghost, the whole tor changed overnight! It wasn't our fault! There were too many soldiers!"

Carter stared hard at the frightened man. "You built it all on sand, knowing the anarchists were stripping your land of its wealth. Wouldn't anyone stand up to them? Was there no substance within the people themselves?"

"Once, oh, once there was! I swear it!"

"You're a prisoner here, aren't you?" Carter asked.

Settlefrost looked around wildly. "Don't say it loud," he whispered. "I'm supposed to be the Leader."

"How long have they kept you here?"

Settlefrost propped his soft face in his hands. "Almost from the beginning. They let me out sometimes to give speeches, but the anarchists and their soldiers run it all. They came five years ago, and there was no Master to appeal to once we saw our mistake. They guard all the ways in and out of the country. And lately they've grown stronger, locking doors that can't be unlocked, unlocking doors we thought forever shut. At night things creep up from some foul basement—living things, but not human. People have begun to disappear. We're all afraid."

"Do the anarchists know we are here?" Duskin asked.

"Ah—that is, we had orders to inform them if strangers appeared. Word was sent this morning. You must understand, no one told me you were the Master."

Duskin slammed his palm against the table, his eyes afire. "You speak of mercy and plot treachery!"

"Forgive me!" Settlefrost cried.

"How can we escape?" Carter asked.

"There is only one way down."

They rose, and hurried back through the tunnel, Settlefrost at their heels. Looking out from the top of the stairs they saw the dark coats of anarchists crossing the fields in groups of five and six, approaching the town from all directions. Within the village itself other anarchists led hundreds of soldiers toward the tor.

"You are lost!" Settlefrost cried. "If I had known you were the Master—"

"You would have betrayed us anyway," Carter said. "You have deluded your own people."

"But the anarchists will have it all their way," Settlefrost said. "Is there nothing you can do?"

A group of soldiers were climbing the stairs, waving and shouting at them. "There is one thing I might try," Carter said. "If it succeeds, it may cost you much of what you have built."

"Anything!" Settlefrost said.

"What do you plan?" Duskin asked.

"I will use the Word of Hope, which is a Word that heartens and ends confusion, to separate the true from the false."

"What do you mean?" Settlefrost demanded.

Carter looked upon him with pity. "You poor fool. Your people have deceived themselves. Have they seen nothing around them? I noticed it when we arrived. Half your soldiers have no shadows."

A gunshot powdered the sandstone to their left and ricocheted into the sky. The men retreated into the shade of the opening. "Be ready," Carter said. "I do not know how much will fade."

He drew the Word of Power, *Rahmurrim*, from his mind, and held it before his imagination, until he thought he felt the heat from the burning letters. Each time he used the Words it became easier to wield them. It rose within him like magma against mountain-stone, but he restrained it, containing its force, allowing it to build pressure. When he could do so no more, he released it, and it erupted like flowing iron, the pent energy more potent than he had ever experienced before. Both Duskin and Settlefrost had withdrawn from him, and he was glad, for when he cried the Word, the mountain shook, sending the ascending guards tumbling backward like wooden soldiers.

It resonated across the dry fields, and for an instant after its last echoes fled, nothing occurred; then the surface of the ghastly tor began to tremble and bubble, and the face to melt as candle wax.

"We have to get down!" Carter cried.

They scrambled down the stairs, its steps rapidly turning to mud, until all that remained was a slope too slippery to support them. They tumbled helplessly through the evaporating muck, which refused to cling to their bodies, but blew away like vapor.

They slid to the bottom and landed at last on hard earth. Carter picked himself up, found himself surprisingly unharmed, and helped Duskin and Settlefrost to their feet. Behind them, the hollow eyes of the tor had nearly melted closed; already it was half its former height. Before them the soldiers who had not fled were writhing upon the ground; steam wafted from them, as they, too, melted. They did not appear to suffer, for they made no outcry, but dissolved like burning toys, soulless, impassive, and Carter noticed Capecot among them. He neither saw nor expected Peelhammer, who had possessed a shadow, to be with them.

The town was dissipating, the roofs steaming and sagging, the cobblestone streets sinking into the earth. Only the older buildings, built before the coming of the anarchists, remained whole. A filthy, brown residue of smoke billowed into the sky, while a bell sounded continual alarm from a tower near the train station.

An anarchist, gun in hand, appeared from around the corner of a dwindling house. As he aimed toward the brothers, Carter unsheathed the Lightning Sword. As if in response to danger, it shone brilliantly. Though Carter could look upon it without harm, Duskin and Settlefrost hid their eyes; the anarchist hurled his gun away and bolted down the street.

The three fled south, away from the base of the tor, in the direction where Carter had seen the least number of approaching anarchists. Soldiers scattered all around them, terrified by the destruction of their comrades. A pair of anarchists rushed by as well, heedless of the men, as panicked as the rest. In the confusion, the three companions soon crossed the outskirts of town. Carter glanced over his shoulder, then stopped in astonishment. "Look!" He pointed toward the hillock.

The entire, ghastly tor was sliding in upon itself, vanishing into a deep cavity, the noise of its crumbling like paper being crushed. It was gone in seconds, leaving a deep, steaming pit.

"How?" Settlefrost cried.

"The ghost image of the tor was fabrication, like the soldiers," Carter said. "Beneath its cover they destroyed the real tor. But for what purpose?"

"The treasure of the tor," Settlefrost said sadly. "There were said to be great riches, powerful magics hidden beneath the mound. We thought it legend. It must be what they sought all along."

"I wonder if they found it?" Duskin said.

Carter shrugged. "I hope we never find out. The name of the country will be Innman Crater from now on, I suppose."

"I have to go back," Settlefrost said, sudden determination on his brow.

"If the anarchists don't kill you, your own people might," Carter said.

"Yes, that's true. But I failed as a leader and now they need my help. I have to rally them for a stand against the anarchists. Now that there are fewer soldiers, we might have a chance."

"Be careful what treaties you found," Carter said. "When all is done I will bring the forces of the White Circle here. If the country is not in proper order, you will answer to me, Settlefrost."

Settlefrost quailed and slipped away between the houses, too frightened to say good-bye.

"Will he barter with the anarchists again?" Duskin asked. "We should have taken him with us."

"No. I believe he will do his best. He had conscience enough to know his wickedness, and he was, after all, truly a prisoner in his own high estate. If he shows courage his people may yet follow him. If he doesn't he will not survive."

They hurried across the fields that had been stripped by the anarchists, their desolation no illusion. Neither was the train, for its tracks remained whole and the sallow engine stood beyond the brown smoke covering the vale. The Bobby must have needed it to take the plundered goods from the country, and perhaps to transport the people themselves, undoubtedly to some horrible fate. Beyond the train, Carter caught sight of the anarchists, opposite their own position, hurrying toward the town. To the south, the fields were clear, but more than twenty armed men were rushing to intercept them from the east. The brothers broke into a run toward the distant gables.

Immediately, Carter knew the race would be close. The two men veered to the left, angling away from their adversaries, forcing the band to travel farther to intercept them. A hail of bullets ripped the earth behind them. Carter pulled his own pistol and fired, a careless shot to provoke their caution, but to his wonder a man fell. He chuckled humorlessly at his luck, thinking they might yet escape, then groaned as three other anarchists plunged out of the house from the southeast. The brothers veered even farther west and redoubled their efforts, but by the time they were within a hundred yards of the gables, the three pursuers had drawn close; one of them, apparently a gifted runner, had pulled far ahead of the other two, and his bullets whizzed by the men. Both Duskin and Carter returned fire, and the man fell, clutching his side. The companions were among the white terraces of the house before the other two came within range.

They slipped behind a stand of tall oaks, losing themselves among the boughs, doubling back to the right along the tree line. As the two anarchists reached the house, they met the brothers' waiting gun sights, and were downed at once. The respite gave Carter and Duskin time to clamber onto a wooden porch and reach a tidy white door. Bullets tore at the posts and door frame as they clambered into a large kitchen, bolting the door behind them.

They sped between aisles of pots and pans, cutlery and low ovens, through a storeroom filled with sacks of flour, where a pair of aproned men, struggling with a heavy box, called after them to halt. Heedless, the brothers came to a rickety stair at the end of the room, leading down into darkness. They hurriedly lit a lamp and descended into a dirty, unpromising basement scarcely likely to have another exit, with dirt floors and cobwebs crisscrossed through the middle of the room. Worse, the cooks would probably report them to the anarchists.

They passed through two empty rooms, forced the only remaining door, and found themselves in another deserted chamber, their only company a pair of squeaking rats squinting at the glow of the lantern. In the corner Carter spied a dumbwaiter; its box had deteriorated into shards over time, leaving the shaft open. Light streamed down from a large opening above.

Duskin used his hands for a stirrup to boost Carter up to the higher bracing boards in the shaft, which he could use for footholds. A score of thoughts ran through Carter's mind as he gripped the timber and pulled himself up, of the collapsing tor and the melting soldiers, of his own doubts about whether he should have stayed in the town and rallied the soldiers against the anarchists, or, if not, made a stand against them himself. Yet, Master or no, he doubted he could have commanded the troops in time. And even with the Words of Power and the Lightning Sword, he did not believe he could hold off a garrison.

As his fingers tightened over the lip of the opening and he struggled to pull himself up, he also realized he would never be truly lost in the High House again, for even as he pushed the half-closed dumbwaiter door aside, the maps came to mind, and he knew where he was. He had bypassed the kitchen altogether and entered an upper corridor.

Duskin followed quickly after, bracing himself against both sides of the shaft to climb, and in a moment they were reunited. The passage was dirty from neglect, uncarpeted, its wooden floors bare of finish. Far off, they heard the shouts and running feet of their pursuers. Carter led them, without hesitation, toward a metal stairs.

He considered using the Word of Secret Ways, and a new realization came to him, that it would do no good because there were no hidden passages anywhere nearby. Where the knowledge came from, he did not know, except that it was part of being the Master. He wondered, with vague uneasiness, what other powers he would eventually claim if he survived to come into his full inheritance.

They spent the remainder of the day in cat and mouse, fleeing the footfalls of their enemies, climbing ever higher into the house, for Carter intended to rise nearly to the attic, before descending again to the outer boundary of Innman Tor, where it connected with the White Circle. It was a circuitous route, but an unexpected one, and he hoped to outmaneuver his enemies. He also sensed he would find secret ways in the upper reaches.

By the time twilight fell across gray, moth-eaten curtains, they had attained to the highest portions of the house, and peered from smudged windows overlooking the crater where the tor had stood. Having heard no sign of the anarchists for the past hour, they chanced a few hours rest, exhaustion demanding nothing else. The rooms had been deserted many years; all the furnishings had been taken; the closets lay empty; only the soft prints of mice disturbed the dust; and Carter remembered a proverb his father often used: "as few as the men in Innman Tor," a homily no doubt common in the house.

He took the first watch. The moon, obscured by the clouds, transformed them to sullen Chinese lanterns while Carter fretted. He wondered if the rain would ever end, or if all creation were to be swept beneath the torrents, covered by the darkness. The anarchists would surely expect the brothers to seek the Long Corridor, and would muster their forces at the border. As the night wore on, and the strands of moonlight sought to break through the cloud cover, Carter cast ever for a way to escape.

Duskin relieved him near one o'clock, and he slept till four, when they rose, ate a mouthful of food, and continued on their way, going ever upward, having no other plan, though despair had crept into Carter's heart.

His one hope lay in the hidden passages he sensed in the

upper stories, and they labored until noon to reach them. Finally, in a musty corridor, in the pinnacle of that portion of the house, he spoke the Word of Secret Ways, and the mansion trembled at its speaking. A blue rectangle appeared on the wall to his left, and a blue square in the ceiling. Momentary surprise crossed his face.

"What's wrong?" Duskin asked.

"Through the maps within me, I sensed the panel on the wall, but not the trapdoor above. Why should that be?"

"I don't know; which should we take?"

Carter thought a moment. "The trapdoor. Surely our enemies cannot subvert the Words of Power; there must be something unique beyond it."

They searched the vacant halls until they found a surviving dresser to use for a step. As Carter pushed against the door, a spring mechanism released, dragging it aside. He set the lantern on the floor above before pulling himself through. Though momentarily blinded by his own light, he saw well enough to determine that no one waited in the gloom.

He helped Duskin up, then looked about.

"There's something strange about this," Carter said, as his lantern revealed the beginnings of a large chamber. An odd familiarity swept him, along with a half-remembered fear, and as the sloping walls, the tall ceiling, the bare wooden floors, and the dust told their story, he drew a sharp breath.

"This is the attic of the Last Dinosaur!"

"But we should be miles from there!"

A flame roared over their heads from a source not fifty feet away, illuminating the whole attic in a blazing flash. Jormungand towered above them, eyes gleaming red as the fire.

The flames died, leaving the men half-blind and helpless.

"Little steward, is this a young morsel you've brought me, a wrapped but uncooked hors d'oeuvre for an old friend?"

"Do not touch him!" Carter cried, drawing his Lightning Sword. Its light leapt upward, restoring their sight.

"Ahhh," Jormungand said. "You have the jagged blade,

and I see all the Words of Power within you. You have become the Master, indeed."

Jormungand stretched on the floor, resting on his short, front appendages, an act that brought him nearer the men, sending them dancing backward. He sniffed at them like a hound.

Carter placed himself between the dinosaur and Duskin. "Your attic must extend over the whole house."

"Simply because you find it in an unexpected place? It moves occasionally, though the stair always leads to your bedroom. If you come this way again, do not seek it above the trapdoor; it will have migrated."

"Then we have shortened our journey many days," Carter said. "And bypassed the anarchists. But, I do not understand."

"Never question miracles and the turns of fate and you will live a happier life," Jormungand hissed. "So it was when you sought your father; it only cost you pain to learn of his demise. Better not to have gone."

"You told me you didn't know if he was alive or not."

"Technically, part of him, the Thin Man, still lived, so I told no untruth. Did you expect wishing-well answers, a fortune cookie with a prehensile tale, your pet Oracle, domesticated and docile, waiting for a treat and a tummy pat to give you all the world's wisdom? Life is harsh, ho-hum, so what; do you know how many beetles will perish in this attic today? Do they come to me, wanting the name of the spider that will eat them? Do they ask if their hatchlings will grow up great warriors, mated to females with comely chitin, winsome mandibles, and great leg segments? Don't waste a dinosaur with questions unless you can interpret the answers."

"Then tell me this, how can I recover the Master Keys?"

Jormungand snorted, startling the men. "Looking for a game plan, are we? Tea leaves read? The keys are in the Room of Horrors; you know it, and there is no escaping it, regardless of how you phrase the question. The Bobby cannot carry them with him until he has completely mastered them, for they are not easily bent toward evil, and would destroy him. Go there and take them if you can; the Book of Forgotten Things will show the way. No sleight of hand, mummers trick, wave of the wand, can do it for you."

Carter went pale, thinking of the Room of Horrors.

"Is there anything else I can do for you? Manicure? Take a little off those toes? No? If you did not come to be eaten, feel no need to stay. I have grown wise enough to find only my own company satisfactory."

Carter recovered and said, "Two questions more. What is the High House?"

Jormungand gave a low rumbling noise that Carter eventually recognized as laughter. He blew fire through his nostrils, and the flames beat hot on the men's faces. "Tedious, tedious. Every Master comes around to ask that. And is that all you want to know? Would you rather I answered how to catch Leviathan on a hook? Do you wonder where the wind comes from, or the nature of the soul? Would you capture rain in a net? Have you a millennia for me to draw you a rough picture? Thumbnail sketch? Jormungand is amused. If we stood here till the end of the world, you and I, the explanation would not be done, for I could tell you mathematically, philosophically, theologically, scientifically, artistically, a thousand different ways: theorems and angles, proofs and disproofs, solve for X and solve for Y, Kant and can, Roger eats Bacon, Newtonian Adam's apples, thermo-and-aero-hydro-electro-dynamics. It would all mean nothing—pictures with words painted in mud, tinfoil copies of precious jewels, oil-slick dabbings with watercolor easels. Never close to the real thing.

"But I will tell you this, the High House is shooting stars and children's tears, rainbows and the small tiny cracks between the bricks where the young grass grows; cold graves and gooseflesh, clear water when drowning, gray dust when dying of thirst, ancient engineers in railroad yards, mad ladies mumbling in the street. Is that clear? No? It will have to do. What is the next question?"

"What are you, who live in this attic?"

"At last, an engaging topic. I am glad you did not ask me what I eat. Isn't the attic where the last of anything old goes? Brooms and dolls, old toys broken and discarded? All the old dinosaurs live in attics now. I spoke of Leviathan; once I was him, as well as dragons, and long ago, on a summer's day when the flowers were pink, the monster who lived in the Loch. You could think of me as the inner manifestation of the Wise Man; the Devil's Advocate; the four angels bound at the great river Euphrates, prepared for an hour and day and month and year to kill a third of mankind; or the Ultimate Evil Biting Through the Root of the World Tree if it pleases you. I prefer to consider myself a Jungian nightmare, a Freudian slip with jaws, waiting to be unleashed. I am as much a force of nature as the wind. All clear now?"

"I see," Carter said, certain he did not. "Thank you. We will go to my room now."

"Just don't expect to use my attic anytime you fancy a shortcut. This is not the posy path. You are the Master; to some degree I will obey you. But understand, even so, you are never far from death when you speak to Jormungand, in ways you cannot even comprehend. And those who accompany you, even more."

Keeping himself between the dinosaur and Duskin, Carter moved toward the stair, a path that forced him to walk right before Jormungand's massive jaws. The red eyes followed them, the white teeth glistened. When they were nearly beyond his reach, there came a flash of movement, as the dinosaur's head sprang past Carter and struck at his brother. Both men shouted; Carter heard a ripping sound and swung his sword, too late, connecting only empty air.

Jormungand lay back in his place, as if he had never moved at all, except that a dark material hung from his jaws.

Carter turned to his brother in wild fear, but Duskin stood

whole, save only his coat had been deftly sliced from his back, leaving the pockets and sleeves. The pair bolted for the stair, while Jormungand roared his laughter, bellowing, "Only a quick movement of the head is required."

Evasions

The brothers caused abundant wonder as they clambered down the stair, Duskin's jacket in tatters, Carter's clothes little better, both men uncombed, unshaven, utterly hall-worn, their hearts fluttering from their encounter with the dinosaur. One of the boys of the house spied them first; his eyes flew wide and he bolted through the transverse corridor crying, "Master's back! Master's back!" through every doorway, alarming the entire mansion, putting everyone astir. Hope strode from the drawing room, looking worried and annoyed, a reprimand upon his lips, but broke into an astonished smile when he saw them. He scurried to meet them at the bottom of the stair and gave a furious handshake to both. "Where in the heavens did you come from?"

The brothers exchanged glances. "Were we believed dead?" Carter asked.

"Or worse!" the lawyer said. "But we expected you to return using the passage from the Towers. Glis sent word of your journey to Arkalen, and we even received a report of your progress from Lady Mélusine, but after that, nothing. The last few days have been endless waiting."

"Find us some decent food, and we will tell the whole tale," Duskin said.

"I'll arrange it at once."

The hall boy came rushing back just then, Chant and Enoch trailing behind him, and Hope sent the lad to alert the cook. Enoch embraced the brothers, but Chant stood aloof, saying softly, "*Home is the sailor, home from the sea*, but the Lion of Ithaca is Master no more. *Long live the King.*"

Then Carter realized the Lamp-lighter had recognized the Tawny Mantle and the Lightning Sword, and knew Ashton Anderson was dead. With Chant's words, Enoch understood as well; a mist covered the Hebrew's eyes, and for a moment he could not speak. Finally, he smiled and said in a hoarse voice, "But wouldn't he be proud, to see his two sons standing side by side? And I see there is love between you now."

"The journey was hard, but we passed the trials together," Carter replied.

They told their tale over a veritable banquet, though how the chef prepared the meal so quickly Carter could not guess. There was Russian-style sturgeon soup and freshwater fish cooked in Bordeaux wine, followed by ham roasted on the spit, covered in Madeira sauce, surrounded by entrees of steamed macaroni and grated cheese layered with forcemeat, a ring of coney-breast fillets, and stuffed chicken quenelles with béchamel sauce. They gorged themselves. For the first time since learning of Lord Anderson's death, Carter felt a twinge of happiness, sitting in the black leather chairs, the heavy arch above the inglenook, the carved squirrels bounding round its borders, the oak panels on the wall, the cheerful fire, the Persian rugs, and his familiar friends. He was home again.

When their story was done, Enoch beamed at them. "Together you have done what neither might have alone. How you have both changed! Carter is the Master. But is there envy on Duskin's face? No. Not even a trace. I, who have known him since a child, see only respect in his eyes. It shines from his heart. But your father's ghost must have been very terrible."

And Carter realized they had indeed both changed and that Enoch knew it was the Thin Man who had changed them.

"You will be comforted to know we've kept ourselves busy since you and I shared that wretched dream," Hope said. "Glis has been in and out, and has restored our links with our allies by finding a shorter route to the White Circle. I've spent most of my time conferring with ambassadors and envoys. At Enoch's urging I've assumed more authority than was given me, and you have every right to send me packing for promises made or implied."

"He has devoured his fingernails lamenting: *'I haven't the right! I haven't the right!'* up and down the halls," Enoch said. "But who could make the decisions?"

"Too many decisions," Hope said. "When news came of the burning of Veth, troops had to be dispatched. From what Duchess Mélusine told us, we were fortunate you arrived in time to put down the rebellion, or we might still be in battle. And that was but the beginning; the Bobby has sown discord throughout the White Circle. Since his theft of the Master Keys he has built his power, and many of his works are just now bearing fruit. In some countries he has even claimed to *be* the Master. All of his plans are intended to keep us off-balance while he consolidates his position. The Tigers of Naleewuath report a massing of the gnawlings; anarchists are seen everywhere, recruiting whoever they can. And in the west portion of the house, beyond the White Circle, darker, older creatures are stirring, creatures hoping to avenge themselves against the Masters who drove them out at the beginning of the world, into the black lands of Abchaz and Broodheim."

"You have kept up your research, however busy you were," Carter said.

"All part of the work," Hope said. "I am forever scrambling back to some old volume to discern the importance of this diplomat or that lord, while they drum their fingers outside the door. I have several appointments this afternoon, which you might want to see. Your presence will add an assurance my words cannot."

"If I'm to meet guests, a bath may be in order," Carter said. "And a change of clothing. We've slept in these too long."

"And I thought a rat had died beneath the table," Enoch said.

Carter grinned. "Such cheek!"

"Your baths are being drawn even now," Hope said. "And your garments will be ready. What do you plan to do next?"

"I need to rest today," Carter said. "Tomorrow I will consult the Book of Forgotten Things. After that I must seek the Master Keys in the Room of Horrors."

After refreshing himself, Carter spent the late afternoon hours in conference with various dignitaries; after days of wandering and peril, he found the work less tedious than he would have thought, though somewhat draining. Stepping from danger into the drawing room all seemed a bit unreal, but Mr. Hope sat beside him, steering the course of the conversation when necessary, offering suggestions and information, proving himself in all ways indispensable, thus allowing Carter to cover his lack of experience under the guise of a thoughtful Master, wise and slow to speak. He met two ambassadors from Himnerhin and the Bridle of Sooth, pleasant, grandfatherly gentlemen, who wished to renew ties with the house and the new lord; a fiery, red-headed farmer from Port Keen seeking aid against wolves—Carter promised to send help when he could, though he dared not yet go himself—and a petitioner claiming to be an exiled prince of Fiffing, deposed by his second cousin, who wanted Carter to declare him the rightful heir, and to send a battalion to support his title. Carter could do nothing until he finished his dealings with the

Bobby, but vowed to soon review the history of Fiffing. The prince, deeply offended, stalked from the room in indignation, rattling the doors behind him.

"No wonder he lost his kingdom," Hope said.

Carter arched his brow. "I hope his second cousin is more even-tempered."

"Only one more today, if you have the strength."

"I can manage. Who is he?"

"A messenger from North Lowing, a country lying north of Aylyrium, and a member of the White Circle. He came in while you were conferring with that last fellow. I don't know what he wants. He seems very anxious. His style of dress is common to that people, so don't be amazed."

The man who entered the drawing room was thin, and red-faced and panting as if he had run all the way from North Lowing. His clothes were white, with black strips wrapped in a seemingly random fashion all around, as if he were a mummy or a tramp. His eyes were feverishly pale. He knelt on one knee at Carter's feet, head bowed.

"Please, sir, you must come," his voice like a pleading child's. "You must come to North Lowing."

"Rise, man, take a chair and tell me your story," Carter said.

But the newcomer remained kneeling. "As it please you, sir, North Lowing was known as the land where the rivers run, a beautiful country, watered by streams coming down the mountains, all lowlands, and so its name."

"You said 'was,' " Carter said.

"The Black River has come there, flowing between the halls of the house, cutting its way to the deepest parts of Evenmere, and where it washes it destroys. You must help us."

Carter sat silent, a quiet horror upon him. "I did not know it had gone so far," he said. "Duskin and I saw it on our journey. How is it escaping the cellar?"

"We don't know," Hope said. "Not through the doors."

"It seeps, my lord, it seeps," the man said. "We have tried

to contain it, but it eats whatever it touches, and it goes where it will, as if with mind and purpose. My people have become refugees. What can I tell them?"

Carter clenched his fists. "What kind of men are the anarchists, full of their own intentions, following their cause, and destroying the whole world with it? What kind of men?"

"I do not know, my lord."

"Tell your people I will send what help I can, though it may be scant enough. Tell them I will not come myself—"

"But, my lord—"

"Tell them I go to stop the Black River. Tell them if I do not, it will be because I am dead. You have my word."

"Thank you, my lord." The man suddenly burst into tears.

"Hope, get him something to eat and a place to sleep if he will have it."

Carter spent the evening brooding about the house, thinking before the fires, visiting with Chant and Enoch, and following the increasing ferocity of the storm. The clouds boiled; the rain pelted; the thunder rolled. The sky was ink. The Bobby was marshaling his power.

As he sat in a high-backed chair before the hearth, eyelids half-closed, he mentally rehearsed the Maps of Evenmere, his new talent granting internal visions of a unique duration and clarity, imparting an intimate familiarity with the house, as detailed as if he held the charts in his hands. He began to understand the power of the Master, to go where he would, to be wherever needed, daunting, outmaneuvering his enemies with his presence. But nowhere could he find the Room of Horrors.

Hope brought him tea in the drawing room at eight o'clock, but the lawyer seemed to sense his mood, and withdrew after only brief conversation, leaving Carter once more to himself. He became aware of his own weariness, and guessed he looked the part. The journey had been arduous, and its end, terrible. Surrounded by the old, comfortable things, he found he missed his father with a welling despair from the center of his chest, a passion so powerful he felt it must annihilate him, and he wept dragon's tears into his steaming tea. And in his mind he followed his sire across the Sea No Man Can Sail, far beyond the rim of the horizon. He imagined Lord Anderson standing upon the boat, paddling, whistling as he often did, the wind upon his face, sailing into that multicolored sky . . . and to what end? Would he could have followed.

The rain fell and he rested, dozing in the chair, dreaming of that sea, and of Innman Tor, Jormungand, Duskin, the Porcelain Duchess, Spridel, all the small things he had done on the journey, his mind patching itself, sowing together the fabrics of his life, covering him with the blanket it made.

Despite his determination, two more days passed before he felt strong enough to face the Book of Forgotten Things, and he grew miserable applauding his wisdom while ruing his delay. Mornings he spent in further conferences, made mostly enjoyable by the often foreign, always intriguing nature of the inhabitants of the White Circle. He passed his afternoons with Mr. Hope, discussing strategies and old histories, and sometimes Duskin joined them, though boredom soon drove him away, for he was indeed yet a young man.

On the morning of the third day, the Bobby reappeared beside the lamppost, and Carter knew the anarchists no longer searched for him at Innman Tor, but had mysteriously learned of his return to the Inner Chambers. He determined to delay no longer, and after lunching on truffled roast chicken with Chant, Enoch, Hope, and Duskin, he went alone into the room beside the library, unlocked the bookcase, and drew out the Book of Forgotten Things.

He sat at the desk with a pencil and pad at his right hand,

drew a jagged breath, and turned to page six. Slow colors rose from the volume, patches of forest-green, too indistinct for identification. Gradually, the scene coalesced not into a wood, but a gray hall, with a tall man, dressed in black, looming above a boy of twelve. He recognized the scene; it was the moment of his abduction. His pulse raced, his fists clenched as he watched his younger self pursued, overtaken, cast over the shoulder of the Bobby's assistant, and carried helpless down the halls. He moaned at the anguished cries. For several minutes, his captors followed the Long Corridor, then on through a doorway leading through endless halls, twisting stairs, through rooms great and small. After a long while they passed down the unforgettable, ebon stairway, where the diabolical adornments, vulture-winged and red-eyed, glared at the boy.

Despite Carter's distress at watching the scene replayed, his right hand sketched a rough map of the path taken. He made marks to number the doors at each landing, which were illuminated by green gaslights, carved as skulls. Finally, the company reached the bottom, the heavy, black marble door of the Room of Horrors. His skin went clammy as he watched the Bobby twist the sable key in the lock, heard the clatter of the latch, felt the low rumble as the door rolled open. The edge of the desk bit into his hands where he clutched it, as his younger self was cast carelessly into the chamber. He gave an involuntary shout of despair as the door slammed shut, leaving the child wailing in the dark.

The image faded. He sat, fingers still clenching the desk, gasping for breath, trembling, terrified and enraged, aching to return to the vision, to unlock the door. It took several moments to master his passion, to recall himself to the quiet room, the butterfly lamps, the stained-glass angel watching from above. He glanced at the marks he had drawn on the paper. Though irregular, they would serve for a map.

"Thank you," he said, though whether to the book or the angel he was uncertain. When he sought to rise, his limbs were as feeble as when he had learned the Words of Power. He locked the volume back in the bookcase and crept out of the library, where he found Hope pacing the corridor.

"All right?" the lawyer asked, hurrying to him.

"Well enough. I have what I need, but I am as drained as ever." He stumbled, and Hope caught hold of his arm to steady him. "One would think it would become easier."

"One would," Hope said, "if one understood the forces we were tapping."

Carter gave a ghostly smile. "I intend to leave tomorrow, if I have the strength. I don't know how long I will be gone. If the Green Door was unlocked the journey would be brief; as it is I must take the long way around, and avoid the anarchists as well."

"Are you adamant about not taking a war party? Glis himself could lead a company. Others could be brought in from the White Circle."

"No. The anarchists would meet us in full force."

"But our intelligence shows their numbers are small, though growing. We could surely defeat them."

"But at what cost? Not just in men's lives. The Master Keys are kept in the Room of Horrors because the Bobby believes I dare not go there. If an army appears and he realizes the objective, he will simply move them to another location. Then we would have to seek them again. But our time is short; with the river of darkness swallowing whole kingdoms, we cannot afford to seek the keys twice. I cannot take an army."

Hope sighed. "Your argument is sound, but I don't like it. A handful of men, perhaps . . ."

"Stealth will be my tool. There is more to it, too. It is the nature of this house that the Master often go alone, walking the secret ways, feeling the rhythm of Evenmere upon the floorboards, seeking the mysteries before him. I cannot put it into words; it is beyond words. I must do the task."

"And would there be room for just one other?" Duskin said

from behind him, having entered the corridor moments before from upstairs.

Carter hesitated. "It will be dangerous, and I would not allow even you to enter the Room of Horrors. Only one should face that fate."

"But I could accompany you until then. We did well together before."

Carter smiled. "Together, then. It was more than I could ask, but your company makes it all a bit less ominous."

They slipped off early the next morning while the house still slept. Enoch was away winding clocks, but Chant and Hope were present, the Lamp-lighter his usual stiff-lipped self, the lawyer fussing and obviously worried. Carter spoke the Word of Secret Ways, and opened a slender passage hidden behind the built-in sideboard in the dining room.

Standing before the shadowed corridor, untrod for decades, a fear fell upon him that he might never return.

"Godspeed," Chant said. "Remember, though it appears bleak, not all the power lies with the anarchists. *We are the music makers, And we are the dreamers of dreams, Wandering by lone sea-breakers, And sitting by desolate streams; — World-losers and world-forsakers, On whom the pale moon gleams; Yet we are the movers and shakers Of the world for ever, it seems.* And they have no poetry. How can they prevail?"

Carter shook the Lamp-lighter's hand briskly, saying: "Standing here, this moment, it seems I've never truly known you. Enoch has told many tales, while you have said nothing of yourself. You say you were a doctor. What else did you do before you came here?"

Chant gave his quiet laugh, his rose eyes sparkling. "I taught metaphysics at Oxford for a time, but my demeanor seemed to disturb the faculty. Before that, I lived . . .

somewhere else. It is a long story, for *I have trod the upward and the downward slope; I have endured and done in days before . . .*"

"I will have that tale one day," Carter said. "I think it would be worth hearing."

He turned to Hope, who was trying to ascertain if they had everything they needed. "You've done a remarkable job," Carter said. "I could have accomplished nothing if you hadn't been back here helping me."

"On that you may be correct," Hope replied, "simply because there is so much to be done. I will try to keep it operating until you return."

"And would you consider a more challenging position as well?" Carter asked. "Perhaps one with an extraordinary raise in title, say to the position of—butler?"

Hope broke into a wide grin. "I was wondering if you would ask. I can't do Brittle justice, but I would like to try. We can discuss particulars when you return." The lawyer suddenly stiffened, standing quite tall, and said, "Will that be all, sir?"

"It will," Carter said, shaking the man's hand. Duskin did likewise, and they stepped into the passage, the younger Anderson holding a lamp aloft. The sideboard silently closed behind them, cutting off the light.

"I trust you know where we're going," Duskin said.

"More than ever before. This passage will take us into a set of secret ways called the Curvings, which wind not only from side to side, but between floors. I've chosen them because they offer several routes to the Long Corridor. From there we have to find the stair leading to the Room of Horrors. There are risks; we can't take the Curvings all the way. Eventually we will be out in the open."

The passage led straight a short distance before reaching what appeared to be a dead end, but Carter searched the floor until he found a trapdoor. They had to pry it up with their knives and it opened with a long groan, revealing a rickety wooden ladder.

They descended into another passage with exposed wall studs. The low ceiling brushing against their heads made them stoop; their boots clattered across the bare boards. The walls were too close to walk abreast and Carter felt the touch of his old claustrophobia, but he mastered it by keeping his eyes on the edge of their lamplight. The Curvings arched gradually to the left.

Carter led. Their path slithered back and forth, rising and falling as if following some unseen contour of the house. Two hours passed in this manner before they came to a spy-hole, marked by a headrest for the forehead and chin. Carter covered the lamp, looked through the opening, and saw the intersection of two corridors, with three black-clad anarchists standing at its center, speaking in sepulchral voices, their words unintelligible. Duskin looked as well, then they crept down the hall, wary of the creaking boards.

Once safely away, Carter said, "We will see many such; the Bobby must have guards posted throughout this area, to catch any attempting to leave the Inner Chambers."

"But they already know we have access to the White Circle."

"Yes, but the anarchists can easily watch that way, to see who comes and goes; it is riddled with places for a spy to hide. So they know any clandestine movements will be on other roads."

They soon came to another spy-hole, revealing a portion of a carpeted corridor lit by a candle in a single brazier. At first Carter saw no one, but soon a pair of anarchists strolled into sight, speaking in subdued tones, smoking short, curved pipes. They strolled past the spy-hole and down the passage, but soon returned, so that Carter perceived they were sentries guarding two or more intersections. With his pocket watch he timed their schedule through two full rotations.

"They come by every two minutes," he whispered. "Half

that time, this corridor is probably still in their sight. There is a secret panel at this wall and another across the hall. We have to cross."

"For promoters of anarchy they're terribly organized," Duskin said.

Carter located the mechanism to open the panel and, at the proper moment, gently pulled the lever. The wall slipped outward with a soft click.

After insuring their adversaries were beyond view, they stepped into the hall and shut the panel, which had been concealed by a floor-length portrait.

They crossed quickly and silently as possible to the opposite wall, where hung an identical painting. Seconds passed as Carter ran his hands beneath the bottom of the frame, seeking the spring mechanism, only to find nothing. He glanced up and down the corridor, assuring himself that there were no other portraits, then dropped to one knee and peered beneath the frame, knowing where the lever must be, but not discovering it. In the distance, the soft talk of the anarchists drifted down the passage.

At last his fingers struck upon it. He pushed without success, but when he pulled outward, the lever moved, and the portrait swung away with a perilously loud groan. A small block of wood, placed inside the opening for some unknown purpose, toppled against the baseboard with a solid *thunk*.

Carter swooped up the block and both men stepped into the hidden passage. The door shut behind them with another moaning protest, wafting the smell of tobacco into their sanctuary. Carter groped his way to the spy-hole. One of the anarchists hurried into sight, his revolver drawn, peering uneasily down the hall.

The other soon joined him, saying, "Undoubtedly rodents."

"Enormous ones, then. I tell you, I heard a door."

"There aren't any doors in this passage. You heard the wind."

"You heard it, too. Do you deny it?"

"I heard something, but the house is ancient, full of creaks and moans, always settling."

The other man scowled. "The Bobby won't like it if anyone slinks past us. And what he dislikes he casts into the Room. Those who go there return changed, all eaten up inside."

"Then we should speak no more of it. If there was something it was quick, and we have nothing tangible to report. Let's go about our business."

After ascertaining the anarchists' departure Carter turned away satisfied and relit the lantern. This new passage was identical to the first, being still part of the Curvings.

"When this is over, remind me to carpet these floors," Carter whispered as the floorboards groaned beneath their boots.

"How does one carpet a secret passage? Do we kill all the workers afterward to keep it confidential?"

Carter snorted in amusement. "Enoch claims God built the house, or at least had it built."

"And does He do remodeling, then?"

"I suppose He might if we could send Him a work order. All jesting aside, Enoch's explanation makes as much sense as any. A house that runs the universe, mechanism unknown, and I its Master. We don't really even know who the anarchists are, much less the Bobby. Fallen angels?"

"Risen devils, more likely. I don't know about the Bobby, but the rest are men. Chant says they serve Entropy, as if that were a person."

"Lucifer himself, I suppose. I wish I knew."

"We may know as much as we ever will," Duskin said. "We've been given a job, and the tools to do it. Nothing more may be required or offered. We don't always have to know the whole story."

Carter nodded, thinking Duskin wise beyond his age.

They followed the Curvings all the rest of that day, tedious labor made unnerving by the obscurity and the need for silence. To save oil, they doused the lantern to eat their cold rations, and slept that night in their bedrolls on the hard floor. Carter awoke many times, sweating, suffering from a recurring dream of being imprisoned in a coffin. Each time he opened his eyes the unrelenting darkness gave no reassurance until he thrust his hands out to dispel the illusion of being contained. Then, still half-asleep, he remembered he was going to the Room of Horrors, and sheer dread clawed at his chest.

So overwhelming were his passions he could return to sleep only by playing a mental game, telling himself he would either die before reaching the room, or simply refuse to go. Then he would drift back into a slumber uneasy as mice in moonlight, only to dream and start the cycle all over.

The whole night passed thus, and he was relieved when a struck match revealed six o'clock on his pocket watch. "These halls are always dark," he murmured huskily as he tapped Duskin on the shoulder. His brother replied at once, as if he, too, had scarcely been asleep: "A warm bath, if you please, and a nice breakfast."

"You'll have neither, I'm afraid. I'm going to light the lamp. I'm sick of the dark."

They ate dried fruit, dry bread, and tough strips of salted meat, and were soon on their way. Almost at once, they came to a cul-de-sac. Carter found a spy-hole, but could see nothing for want of illumination in the room beyond.

"This will be difficult," he whispered. "The Curvings continue a floor above us and several corridors away. I don't know what's out there and we dare not use the lamp, but I think I can lead us even without light. Remember, we must not be seen."

Duskin nodded. Carter twisted the knob and the panel slid soundlessly to the side. Once in the passage, he fumbled several moments before locating the closing mechanism, a small knob at the bottom of the baseboard. Though blind, he knew they should be standing in a corridor with passages leading to either side and straight ahead, and that the next branch of the

Curvings could be reached either by going forward or to the right. After some mental calculation, he took the right-hand way, a slightly shorter route.

Carter felt Duskin grasp the soft-leather edge of his Tawny Mantle for guidance. Though he had a clear mental map of the corridors, he did not know the furniture, and immediately banged his knee against a low table. He stifled a grunt of pain, and determined to stay arm's length from the right wall, his fingers barely touching.

Thankfully, the corridor was carpeted, cushioning their footfalls. A breeze drifted from somewhere, smelling of roses and sweet showers. Within the Curvings they had been isolated from the noise of the storm, here they heard rolling thunder, the patter of rain, the water rilling down the eaves. He proceeded slowly, longing for silence, listening for voices, hoping he was not leading them into the hands of the anarchists. He knew the passage was long, with no doorways to either side, but it was difficult to estimate how far they had come. He counted his steps as he went.

It took over an hour to cross the corridor—the noise of the storm, the settling of the house, gave a hundred separate noises to spur his imagination, so that he paused often, straining to hear—and at its end he thought he detected soft, scraping sounds. He froze, certain it was simply a fancy, this low gurgling, but the longer he waited the more he believed it to be the soft buzzing of human voices, made unintelligible by the rain. He chanced another step forward.

Men were murmuring in the darkness, lurking in the absolute ebony. They could only be anarchists. Gradually, bitterly dismayed, with Duskin following, he retreated, recounting the steps, feeling his way, moving more swiftly. They returned to the intersection much sooner than he expected, and turned to follow the alternate path. If there were sentries down this corridor as well, he vowed to slip past them.

Again he kept to the right-hand way, arm's length from the

wall, counting the steps once more. This corridor was shorter, but he paused often to listen, made wary by the presence of the enemy. Eventually, they reached a turn to the right, and there they stayed a great while, attending every noise, straining to hear past the rhythm of the storm. When nothing extraordinary occurred, they moved around the corner, and almost immediately Carter felt a slight pressure against his shins. He stooped, feeling with his fingers until he discovered a thin cord stretched across the hallway, obviously either an alarm system or a trap. He dared not even whisper for fear of warning any anarchists lurking nearby, but took Duskin's hand with infinite care, and placed the back of it against the cord. Alerted, Duskin ran his hand along its surface, examining it.

With his brother aware, Carter stepped slowly over the line, one foot at a time. Less than ten inches from the first, his left leg touched another.

He had to dare a whisper in order to warn Duskin, speaking as softly as possible directly into his brother's ear, saying, "There are more." Then he stepped over the second line while Duskin straddled the first.

Again Carter's leg touched a cord, again he warned Duskin, this time by tapping his three fingers, one at a time, against his sibling's hand. He stepped over the third.

When he discovered a fourth, he could have wept, imagining a corridor filled with trip strings, and anarchists at every side. He controlled his fear and helplessness with an effort, informed Duskin of the new danger, and stepped carefully over.

He moved forward by inches, feeling for another line, but found none. Duskin crossed the fourth cord.

Carter felt no relief; there might be many such snares before them. Slowly, deliberately, he groped his way, mentally ticking off each second. It was difficult to concentrate with nothing to see; bursts of color, deep emerald and crimson, flashed before him, hallucinations from eyes starved for light.

They met no more alarms, but an hour passed before they reached another intersection, where they turned back to the left. Only then did Carter feel any relief. Beyond doubt, they had passed within a few feet of one or more sentries, but only a short corridor lay between them and the stair leading to the secret panel that would bring them back to the Curvings. Once inside, they would be safe. With his newfound powers he also sensed two secret panels within that corridor.

As they felt their way down the passage, Carter perceived the secret doors to be along the right wall, though he could not be certain of their exact location. Yet, when they were past, he knew it, as if a heat that had been before him was now behind. He had sensed many such secret ways all along their journey, but had felt none so strong as those in this utter darkness.

They had gone nearly half the distance when a dim glow appeared before them, the light of a lantern, illuminating the floral prints and baseboards at the far end of the corridor, approaching from around the corner. They froze. Only a moment more, and they would stand revealed.

Carter thought desperately. He could not reach the stairs in time, but he might reach one of the secret doors. He turned quickly; by the dim light he saw the wall was paneled, with only two of the wainscots covered with carvings of bears, the nearest a few feet away. He strode to it quickly, with only an instant to locate the opening mechanism. A brazier hung on the wall nearby, and he grasped it, hoping he had chosen well, thinking the catch as likely to be hidden among the bears. But the brazier turned easily to the left, and the panel opened at once. He stepped in, Duskin behind him. An instant's fumbling and the wainscot slid shut, leaving him staring out through a spy-hole.

The light had not fallen full upon the passage when the voices of the anarchists drifted to the companions' ears.

"A lovely conundrum, strolling about with a lantern, hoping to catch skulkers, warning them of our approach at every turn. A marvelous plan for getting ourselves skewered."

"Protestations are ineffectual," the other replied. "You should have been in the Yellow-Room Wars, back in 'fifty-eight. I was at Dannershot when the tigers came; ghastly it was, all corridors and torches, and the big cats ambushing us from the dark. The Bobby wasn't commander then; I don't believe it would occur under his leadership. He is more circumspect."

The full glow of the lantern lit the walls as the two anarchists passed before the spy-hole.

"Spare me the war stories. I only want to relieve the sentries so we can sit quietly in the darkness, where we won't be targets."

The footfalls continued down the corridor. The voices faded. When all trace of light had fled Carter opened the panel.

"Quick thinking," Duskin whispered.

"The maps are so strong in me now, I seem to keep track of the secret ways even when I'm not thinking of them," Carter replied. "But we better hurry; the sentries they are relieving will probably return this way."

With the assurance that the corridor was deserted, they quickly found the steps, a narrow, servants' stair. This, too, had to be traversed in darkness, and it protested their intrusion by creaking at every footfall. They covered two landings before reaching the top, where stood a full-length picture frame.

Carter discovered the secret stud behind its right side, and the latch clicked open as a light appeared at the far end of the corridor. But long before it revealed their position, they were back in the Curvings, the portal secured behind them.

Once down the way, they lit their lantern and settled wearily to the floor.

"That was a trial," Duskin said.

"It was indeed," Carter said. "Congratulations."

"And to you."

They suddenly broke into grins and shook hands. The meal was only dry biscuits and salted beef, but such was their relief that they ate it as if it were a victory banquet, and for a time Carter forgot the Room of Horrors. It strengthened them, and they followed the Curvings for another two hours, pausing occasionally to check the spy-holes. The anarchists seemed to be everywhere.

Eventually, they reached a series of landings leading down to an empty room, with fireplace brick leading up one wall. Carter quickly located a spy-hole, and finding their way unhindered, pulled a long lever on the floor. The fireplace swung inward, opening into the gray mist of the Long Corridor.

They came out from behind one of the mantels scattered all down the passage, and the entryway rolled silently back into place at the turning of a marble bust of a peculiarly coiffured noble identified by a placard as *Athammaus, Chief Headsman of Commoriom.*

As ever was the way in that part of the Long Corridor, the mist, like fluffy clouds, obscured the source of illumination, which drifted down from the ceiling, and the gray walls and the gray carpet cast a gray silence all along the passage, leaving the men's voices subdued, as if they stood by a bog.

"We go to the left," Carter said. "We must make haste, lest we be seen."

They followed the gentle curve of the passage, Duskin gripping his revolver, Carter with his hand on his Lightning Sword. Less than two hundred yards down the path they heard voices approaching before them. They exchanged glances, then retreated to a portal they had noticed earlier. No sooner had they found concealment than a pair of merchants strolled by, pushing a heavy cart before them, gossiping happily on the news of the house. Once the sounds of the cart wheels faded from earshot, the brothers returned to the corridor.

"At least they weren't anarchists," Duskin said.

"Quite right, but I don't want to be seen by anyone. Who knows who may be in their service?"

They traveled the rest of the passage without incident, for they had to go only a few hundred yards before exiting through a doorway leading to a white stair, which they ascended into a hallway with a marvelous portrait of the winning of the lovely Zehowah by the genii, Khaled. This proved to be the entrance to another secret way, and Carter found the mechanism easily.

This passage, lit by opaque skylights, was wider and more cheerful than many of the hidden halls, but Carter looked upon it with trepidation, for it meant he was nearing the Room of Horrors. Besides his fear of the room itself, he knew the stairway leading to it would be guarded, and he could not conceive how they might pass. He intended to part company with Duskin before then, and that saddened him as well.

They journeyed an hour along the corridor before twilight paled the walls. Carter called an early halt, too weary, too apprehensive to go on; they ate in silence as night descended, and did not bother to light the lamp, but lay down immediately. Despite his fatigue, Carter slept fitfully once more, unmentionable dreams dancing across the borders of his slumber. The night lasted a lifetime, and they rose when the morning sun drifted through the skylights, disclosing dust motes spinning like remote galaxies. Breakfast was a morose affair; Carter's bleak mood had subdued them both, and they departed at once.

Within half an hour they found an exit that brought them into a series of rooms, all painted drab-brown, with malachite-green curtains, threadbare carpets, and an odd assortment of pummeled furniture. Cigars in the ashtrays and half-empty whiskey glasses showed signs of occupancy.

"Is this the lair of the anarchists?" Duskin asked softly. "I would have expected otherwise; laboratories for making bombs, posters, slogans and such. These rooms could belong to a Gentlemen's Society."

"They are far beyond guns and bombs," Carter said, "though they can use them well enough. Evil is no less so for appearing civilized. We must move swiftly."

They passed through a drawing room, a small library, and into a hall, where they made their way forward by concealing themselves behind a series of flying buttresses. Once, as they peered out, they saw an anarchist pass between two doors far down the corridor. When he did not return, they went on, until they came to a white door with a brass knob. Carter opened it gently, his hand at his sword. He heard the murmur of voices, though he saw no one.

His heart pounded as he led Duskin into a foyer, with doors standing ajar to the right and left and a stair leading upward straight before them, the voices ushering from behind the left door. They did not investigate, but climbed the stair, taking the steps two at a time, but softly. The gentle creak of the floorboards sounded to their ears loud as sawed lumber; Carter's hands, slick with sweat, slipped on the banister.

The stairs extended to the floor above, where a gallery spread before them permeated with every manner of debris. They had no time to contemplate it, for no sooner had they rounded the banister when a voice called up: "Hello! Is anyone there?"

Numerous alcoves pocked the gallery, and they slipped quickly into the shadows of the nearest, even as the stairs groaned beneath a heavy tread. They stood pressed against the wall, their hands to their weapons, scarcely daring to breathe. It was hard to judge, but Carter thought the man had stopped halfway up the steps, and was looking between the rails. Finally, after what seemed a long age, they heard a sigh and receding footfalls.

They crept out. The stair was empty. They regarded the gallery, stacked high with books and old newspapers, boxes and trunks, machinery and chemicals, all covered with layers of dust from countless decades. A banister ran along the inside edge of the gallery, and by peering over a pile of vile forbidden volumes: the *Necronomicon*, *The King in Yellow*, the *Book of Eibon*, even the dreaded *Krankenhammer*, Carter saw three more floors below, each with its own gallery. A massive mosaic skylight provided light, depicting a skeletal, black-robed figure, his face hidden in shadows, holding in his hands a scroll with the words *Mundus vult decipi* emblazoned upon it, an inscription indicating the world wishes to be deceived. Despite the sunshine streaming through it, it was a grim portrait, all ashes and death.

They slipped along the gallery, passing between the rows of paraphernalia, hidden from the sight of those on the floors beneath, staying low to escape detection from any on their own level. When nearly halfway, approaching voices sent them scampering behind the ragged rows of boxes. From their concealment, while they crouched in silence, they saw, above the cartons, the hats of two anarchists bobbing by, and heard their voices passing out of the gallery, engrossed in a conversation on "placing the pylons."

They continued making their way between the trunks and cases, and despite the fear of discovery, a joy overtook Carter, a sense that he was indeed the Master of Evenmere, outmaneuvering his enemies as if it were only a game played in the yard among the privet. He became aware of the dirt and oils upon the floorboards, the dust motes drifting down between the barrels, the wood grain on the boxes, the paint on the trunks. And he smiled, even as he chastised himself for smiling in this precarious place. Yet, in the brief moment before the gravity of his position overtook him once more, he would not have traded this adventure for all the warm, safe hearths in the world.

A soft click, not twenty feet away, tore his smugness from him. Something was moving among the cartons to their right. The companions drifted deeper among the debris, back into the shadows. A soft tuneless whistling told them that whoever had come was not seeking them, yet he was approaching. They dropped to hands and knees, and scuttled silently behind a large wardrobe.

Footfalls and the whistling came nearer. Carter drew a short knife and steeled himself to attack, hoping to disable his enemy without arousing the others.

The whistling stopped. Just to the left of the wardrobe,

inches from their position, a pair of hands reached down and picked up a gray box. "Here it is," the anarchist muttered to himself. Carter could have turned the wardrobe corner and stood face-to-face with the man, but the whistling resumed and the anarchist returned the way he had come, leaving the brothers' hearts pounding in their throats.

They waited several long minutes, half expecting the man to sound an alarm, but as the gallery lapsed into silence, they found their courage, and worked their way onward.

Finally, they came to the end of the gallery and made their way back to the railing, where lay a wide stair leading downward. They would have to descend without being seen, and it was all a gamble. Drawing his Tawny Mantle over him, Carter crawled the last few feet to the top of the stair, and raised his head enough to peer down.

The way was vacant though voices wafted from the floors below. He signaled Duskin, who hurried up, and together they started down the steps.

And just at that moment, footfalls approached from below.

They flung themselves back to the landing on their stomachs and crawled hastily to a hiding place. But the footsteps seemed to halt at the bottom of the stairs.

A voice called, "We need everyone! Rally everyone! I have assignments."

Carter and Duskin slipped deeper into the debris as several anarchists came from behind them in answer to the call. Within moments there was a general murmuring of voices, and it became apparent that a score or more were gathered on the floor below.

A plan came to Carter at once. "We can reach our destination one of two ways," he whispered. "Come, back the direction we came."

They retreated beside the gallery banister, hoping that "everyone" was indeed gathered at the bottom of the stair. What had taken an hour to cross before took mere seconds.

They peered cautiously down the back stair, found it deserted, and hurried down.

Upon reaching the doors leading to the left and right, Carter hesitated only an instant before choosing the left-hand way. Even as he did, an anarchist stepped through it.

Carter reacted without thought, striking the man a solid blow in the face. Before he could do more than reel in surprise, Duskin caught him in the forehead with the butt of his revolver, sending him sprawling.

They dragged him out of the foyer into the room beyond. Carter wished to bind him, but there was no time, so they left him heaped behind a fainting couch. They hurried through a sitting room, but did not go onto the gallery on that floor, for a spiral staircase took them two flights down. They crept through an empty hall and from the concealment of the doorway, looked out upon a corridor, leading to the right and left, and across it, in the midst of a wide burgundy-carpeted room, a black stair leading down.

Carter shuddered. It was as he remembered—the stairs to the Room of Horrors. Five men stood at its threshold, carrying rifles.

"I have to get there," he whispered to Duskin. "But how? At best, we might get three of them before they took cover, and we can't cross that room against Winchesters."

Duskin looked about. "See the door on the other side of the room? I'd guess this corridor leads around to it."

Carter consulted the maps within him. "It does."

"I'll slip around to that side and draw them off. When I do, you rush the stair."

"They'll kill you!"

Duskin grinned. "They won't. I'm a fast runner and handy with a revolver. Anyway, you said you wouldn't let me enter the Room of Horrors. I'll return to Glis and bring an army to fetch you out."

Despair wrenched at Carter's heart, despair of leaving his brother to the anarchists, despair of going alone to the room.

But he put on a fierce grin. "That's all there is for it, then. Good luck."

"Godspeed." The two clasped hands, a lingering grip, and then Duskin was gone down the passage. And Carter suddenly knew he loved his brother very much.

An anxious eternity passed before he saw Duskin step into the room from the other side. He put on a good act, as if he were surprised to see the guards; they shouted and raised their rifles as he downed one with his revolver, then dodged back behind the doorway as a barrage of bullets whizzed past the place where he had stood.

Of the four remaining sentries, three immediately gave chase, leaving a single man to guard the stair. This one crossed to the door, to see how his fellows fared.

Carter saw his chance, and scurried across the room, revolver drawn, aimed at the anarchist's back. Still, the man did not turn to see him. Shots and the shrieks of men roared out in the hall; Carter prayed Duskin had not been hit.

He reached the stair and bounded down it, his boots squeaking as he rounded the railing. As he descended, he looked back over his shoulder to see the head of the guard rising above the top of the steps. He fired without aiming, and the fellow went down, clutching the left side of his face.

He plunged wildly down that dark staircase, and it was as if he relived his kidnapping in double time, for the ebony stair, with its carved ghouls and fallen angels, its ghastly green lanterns, its darkness and dolor, sped by him while his fear grew, until he whimpered as he ran.

Sooner than he would have thought possible he stood before the imposing, black marble door. For a moment, paralysis took him. *I am truly a coward*, he thought. *There can no longer be any doubt.* Yet he put his hand upon the knob and turned.

It was locked, but that, at least, did not give him pause. He had seen it destroyed before.

He felt every bit like his father as he drew his jagged sword and shattered the door with a single blow.

The Room of Horrors

The last sparks of the Lightning Sword withered; the splinters from the sundered door fell away. Beyond lay the room,
its revolving darkness heavy with nebulous forms. Sepulchral
winds, bitterly cold, moaned across the portal. Carter's satis-
faction at destroying the door faded. With trembling hands, he
lit the lantern, holding it aloft as he crossed the threshold. He
cried out at the first touch of those shadows, the involuntary
whimper of a boy, as the whole weight of malice pressed
against him. It paralyzed; it crippled; it consumed him. His
courage was gone; he dropped to his knees and could not rise.
All the terror, sublimated so many years, returned. He
clenched his eyes tight; from his frozen lips issued a half
prayer.

Thus he remained for endless moments, wrapped in an an-
nihilating horror, plunged too quickly into utter ruin. And outside his closed lids, not inches from his face, he felt the terrors
gathering, the unholy nightmares pressing toward him. He
could not run; he could not open his eyes; he could not leave
them closed.

There is a fear beyond all fears, and faced with it, a human must confront it or cease altogether. A child, knowing no defense, having no power, might flee endlessly; a man cannot.

For him, reason must either hold or shatter completely.

Behind his closed eyes, Carter's rationality struggled to reassert itself. A soft voice whispered within him, reminding him he was no longer a lad, but Master of Evenmere. How could he have forgotten? He ceased his muttering; he drew deep breaths. Yet he did not dare open his eyes, not without some weapon to aid him.

The Word of Hope came to his mind, a Word designed to end confusion and despair, its letters burning silver with heat. Using it would diminish his strength, but without it he could not go on. He brought it to his lips, the power surging around him. He spoke it: *Rahmurrim.* The room shook.

He felt no great change, no lessening of the fear; the terrors still murmured around him, proving they were truly real, and no illusion for the Word to dispel, but he found the courage to press forward. With an effort he opened his eyes.

A leering face bobbed before him, ghost-white, hideous, with writhing tentacles growing from it; the lips bright red, the hair green; its fangs glistened.

Shouting in terror, Carter swung at it with all his strength, a blow that overbalanced him, sending him onto his side as the monstrous head bobbed backward, avoiding the sword. He leapt to his feet, facing the creature, and in the midst of his panic, an odd realization occurred. As a child he remembered dreaming of such a nightmare, a thing too horrible to gaze upon. But in his dream he had dared to look a second time, and what had at first seemed terrible, had appeared no more than a clown's face. So it was with this, for he suddenly saw that it was but a childhood apprehension, a face pressed against the windowpane, no more than a caricature. And this, he knew, the Word of Hope had shown him, so that, there, in the Room of Horrors, he did what he had never thought to do. Before the dead face, he laughed.

The monster vanished at once; the room became deathly still; the evil withdrew, perplexed.

The first time, he had not had a lantern, now he held it high. The floor was dirty; boxes and staring doll faces lay scattered, common things.

He began his search for the Master Keys. The room was vast, its walls invisible in the dark, yet he moved unerringly forward, as if he *felt* the pull of the keys, sensing their presence now that they were so near. This did not surprise him; he was their master as well.

Just at the edge of sight flitted ghostly forms, shrouded figures with skeletal hands and empty eye sockets. They crowded innumerable beyond his circle of light, but drew no closer, perhaps fearing his sword, if such can fear. And though these, too, were the phantoms of childhood, he felt his pulse pounding at his throat.

For perhaps twenty minutes he continued, and the ghosts were joined by monsters and devils of every kind, yet his fright lessened as he perceived they would not approach him, though they moaned and cried with hideous voices. Through their clamor a single, soft groan caught his hearing, a pleading note different from the rest, and he turned toward its source.

Amidst heaps of garbage, its legs chained to the floor, lay a human form, bedraggled, hair matted, the once-fine garments shredded rags. As the circle of light touched it, it looked up with feral eyes. Carter gasped; it was Murmur.

"Carter!" she cried, her voice broken, ancient. "Are you real, or another come to torment me?"

"No, lady. It is I." But he did not approach her. "Did the Bobby do this?"

Her eyes glistened with hatred. "Him! He promised everything, but when Duskin betrayed us, he cast me here. Called me 'of no further use,' I, the lady of the manor, friend to the lord of every kingdom in the High House! How could he be so blind? I am the most important woman in Evenmere. Help me, Carter! I've seen horrible monsters, demons with my own face, all accusing. They all accuse me. I can't stand the accusations anymore." She burst into tears.

Moved by compassion, Carter drew near. "Dear Carter," she muttered. "Sweet Carter. You were always a good boy."

He drew his sword and struck the chain, which shattered with a thunderous crash. As he bent to help her rise she raked his cheek with her sharp fingernails, barely missing his eye, sending blood rilling down his jaw. She hissed like a snake and, crouching, backed away, her pleading glance turned to malice, her eyes wild.

"Stand back! Stay away!" she cried. "I know what you want. Revenge or nothing! With me gone you think you'll become Master. But you won't take it away from me. Duskin will rule, and I beside him. All the great house."

"And did I ever seek your harm?" he cried.

"Because you could not!" she sneered, triumphant. "We had you sent away before you could. And you never should have returned! Why did you?"

Carter's whole being trembled, as if he had suddenly fallen into a great void. His voice shook. "You . . . knew I would take the keys. You were working with the Bobby even then." He gripped his Lightning Sword tighter. "You didn't just leave the gate open for him. You planned it all."

She became suddenly frightened. "Now, Carter, it wasn't like that at all. Your father—"

He exploded with rage. "It wasn't petty jealousy! Planned! Contrived to exile a child!" Nearly blind with anger, he lifted his sword.

She fell at his feet, weeping, cowering like a dog. "Then slay me. I deserve it! I never had what I desired. The house was never mine. I should have been a queen. But your father would not! He had the power and he refused to use it! Slay me and I will die in ruins."

The rage ran through him, turning to pity and disgust.

"No," he said, lowering his sword. "My father would not. Nor will I. Follow me and I will lead you from this place."

Still clutching his feet, she looked up at him. "Then perhaps together, the three of us could govern Evenmere. I could be very useful. And Duskin—"

"I am the Master of Evenmere, Murmur. The house has chosen and nothing will change that. You never understood. And Duskin is my brother, though you did your best to separate us. He supports me in all things. He may have given his life to see me reach this room. If he still lives, he will indeed have a place in the house. But I can never allow you to dwell there again. That, too, is the responsibility of the Master."

She pulled herself away from him, hissing, her hands claws, utter venom in her face. "Stay away from me!" she screamed. "Keep back!" She suddenly bolted into the darkness, remarkably agile, and faded into the shadows before he could respond. He did not call to her, but turned and continued toward the Master Keys.

He could think of no reason besides cruelty for the Bobby to imprison Murmur in the chamber, except she might delay someone seeking the keys. So she had done, and would have done more, if Carter had been obligated to escort her to the entrance.

He passed through a part of the room where every form of torture was displayed, where dying men hung on crosses and women sobbed on racks. He looked but once into the eyes of those sufferers, and wished he had not, for though he knew them to be delusion given flesh, still he pitied, and would have helped each if time had allowed. Between the crosses he went, holding his light low so those suspended above him were left in shadow. The groanings filled all the darkness and he was glad when he left the tormented behind.

Still the keys called him, and he came at last upon a gaping hole in the floor, perfectly circular and six feet across. He walked cautiously around it, hoping the trail would lead farther on, fearing it would not, but when he sought to walk away, he felt the Master Keys as a lodestone drawing him back.

He stood at the edge and peered down, but the lantern light did not penetrate the darkness. Slowly, he lowered the lamp past the edge, where it vanished altogether in the deep pitch. Carter drew it swiftly back and examined it, to ascertain it was still there, and found it undamaged.

Time was precious, but still he stood staring into the abyss, mortally afraid, more frightened than he had been by the monster faces, more frightened than he had been by anything. And far below he heard the sound of rippling water.

Darkness, closed places, and drowning. He knelt on his haunches and trembled. He had called them silly fears and childish; they did not seem childish before that void.

He looked around. Once inside the well it would be easy for an enemy to trap him. Yet, even then he would not be helpless, so long as he possessed his Lightning Sword and the Words of Power.

As he stared at the chasm a slow resolution overtook him. "This is where it leads," he half whispered. "All those years ago, when I stole the keys. Oh, bitter consequence." Yet, he knew it was *his* consequence, and he found it suddenly ironic that the darkness was a circle, for only by restoring the keys could he close the circle begun so long ago. There was justice in that.

He groped his way along the edge, reaching into the darkness, working his way around the rim until he found metal rungs, for he knew the Bobby must have a way to descend. Cold sweat ran down his back as he placed his foot on the first step. The lantern would be useless below, and he left it burning at the edge. Rung by rung he descended, but while his shoulders and head were still above the lip, a pistol cracked, and a bullet ricocheted off the floor just to his left. He ducked down, leaving only his eyes above the darkness.

The Bobby charged from the shadows with a velocity suggesting a furious flight to reach the room before Carter regained the keys. His revolver blazed again and again, and wooden splinters grazed Carter's face, blinding him. By the time he recovered, his enemy was directly above him, aiming at his head.

Carter drew his Lightning Sword. In answer to the danger it flashed like its namesake, a brilliant golden bolt. It did not affect Carter's sight, but the Bobby reeled backward as if struck, his hands before his face, his shot wild. He fired twice more, sightless, and then the gun was empty. Carter clambered back up the ladder, and was half over the rim when his foe kicked blindly at where he thought he must be, catching him a bad swipe to the head. His sword clattered to the floor as he seized the Bobby's leg and shoved him backward. Though dazed, Carter leapt at his enemy, but fell short.

The Bobby sat up quickly, and catching Carter beneath the arms with amazing strength, carried him back toward the abyss. In that brief second, Carter had a flashback of being thrown into the well in the yard, and he fought with all his might against those cold hands, the double fury of child and man within him.

Then they toppled, both together into the darkness.

They struck the water hard and separated. Carter pulled himself to the surface, racked with coughing, clearing his lungs.

The darkness within the well was thick as a mantle. A panic swept through him, greater than any he had ever known. He would die here, in the cold night, trapped in the well, forgotten. There was nothing to cling to and he could not touch bottom. His enemy awaited him somewhere in the narrow confines.

He reached forward, seeking his foe, and received a solid blow to the chin that reeled him backward, dazed. He heard the splashing as his enemy followed after; Carter swung blindly and connected against solid muscle. Arms like bands of iron gripped his waist; he struck again, a pitiful, glancing blow. The Bobby threw him against the side of the well, driving the breath from him, and as the anarchist paddled even closer he saw the faceless head, glowing faintly, ghastly green like a hobgoblin, just visible through the murky air.

The Bobby's strength was unbelievable; Carter clearly could not face him without help. All in a moment, a Word of Power sprang unbidden to his mind, the Word Which Gives Strength. Desperation gave him the will to invoke it quickly; the entire well shook as he spoke it. New power rushed through him, filling his limbs, even as the Bobby pounded him in the ribs. Though he felt the impact, it did not conquer him; he returned with a jab to the eye, and the Bobby grunted in surprise at its force. At last, Carter could harm his enemy. They separated, distance extinguishing the luminescent face.

They circled, each trying to disguise his position, a task made impossible because of the noise of the water. Carter backed into the side of the well, but could gain no fingerhold for support.

The Bobby leapt at him with a liquid rush, the face rising like a demon from the dark, the gloved hands finding purchase around his throat, powerful fingers closing his windpipe and forcing him beneath the surface.

He struck out savagely, pummeling the Bobby's abdomen and chest. For an instant the gloved grip held, then the anarchist broke away, leaving Carter gasping for breath.

He knew this trial must end soon; already his legs were strained from staying afloat. He searched for his revolver, but it had slipped from his pocket during the fall. His hand chanced upon his knife, but even as he took it he heard the soft snick of another blade being opened.

He dove beneath the water, going deep, then drifted upward, searching for his foe, hoping to rise under him. Groping, he found nothing, and was finally forced to return to the surface. He took a deep breath and dove again.

So they played their game, maneuvering in the dark, and the well, such a small place, still hid them from one other. But Carter knew he would soon drown.

He came up again, and this time his hand brushed his enemy's leg. Immediately, the Bobby kicked hard, a glancing blow to Carter's head. He stabbed furiously upward, driving the knife into the anarchist's thigh, but the Bobby pulled away in pain, and Carter's blade was ripped from his grasp to tumble to the depths.

Carter swam forward, hoping to take his enemy while he was still stunned by the wound. The ghastly face appeared; he clutched for the Bobby's knife, but as he slammed his foe's right hand against the side of the well he found it empty—the anarchist was left-handed.

He turned inward, so that the thrust caught only the edge of his inside shoulder; he felt skin separate, blood run. He screamed in pain, captured the knife hand, and hammered it against the side of the well, disregarding the blows to the left side of his face. His head was ringing by the time the knife fell, clattering.

He wanted to break away, to flee, but his time was short, and he knew this must end soon. He blocked the blows to his head with his left hand, while jabbing hard into his enemy's kidneys with his right. He had trained in boxing at university, and the knowledge came to the fore. So, too, did his anger: here was the author of all his pain, the initiator of all the schemes against him. His blows became sledges, while he ignored the few return jabs and battered away at his enemy's face.

Then the Bobby had his hands before his head, defending himself against the punches. Carter kept up a merciless pace, his anger swelling.

Suddenly the Bobby pushed out from the side of the well with his legs, coming down over Carter, dragging both of them deep. Then Carter knew he had weakened himself with his attack, wasting his strength while the Bobby protected his head and rested. His arms felt leaden; his anger fell from him, replaced by fear.

They were sinking deeper, and he had not taken sufficient

air. The Bobby was hoping to outlast him. Carter brought his legs up against the other's stomach, and kicked upward furiously, daring all his breath in the attempt. His struggles pushed him away from his enemy, and he darted toward the surface. He broke gasping into the air, and slipped quickly to the side, exhaustion overtaking him. He had never been a strong swimmer, and there was nowhere to rest.

He heard the Bobby break the surface to his left. Because he could do nothing else, he dove for his enemy, determined that this would be the last encounter, for well or ill.

This time it was he who was on top, driving the Bobby downward, guided by the glowing face. He squeezed his enemy's throat, even as the anarchist's hands encircled his neck—Carter vowed to stake all on his ability to outlast his foe. He felt his throat closing, and he gripped tighter himself. They drifted deeper into the well.

The moments dragged on, an eternity of seconds, while darkness crept to the edge of Carter's sight. He was losing consciousness, losing the battle, yet he dared not relinquish his grip.

Bursts of light exploded before his eyes; the thrashing of the water was like crashing waves on a far shore. His arms and hands, the well and the darkness, the Bobby's face, all seemed far away.

Distantly, he felt the Bobby kicking at him. Even through his stupor, he clung tighter. His father's face suddenly appeared before him, the kind eyes, the ready smile; he wondered vaguely if he were about to join him in death. His vision narrowed, everything closing down, until Lord Anderson was only a distant speck at the end of a long tunnel.

And then, before the tunnel dwindled completely, he saw a Word of Power dancing through it, the letters flaming, sparking with a vigor Carter no longer felt. The Word Which Manifests. He had used it before, in the attic, to drive the Bobby back. Now, this close, it might be damaging indeed. His thoughts began to wander, but he refocused on the Word, until he saw it alone, standing as if miles high, huge, unrelenting, the symbol of a Power that would never submit, never surrender, though Carter himself should fail.

He spoke it, though whether in his mind or beneath the water of the well itself, he never truly knew. The letters were all he could see, but he felt the water steaming all around him, as if the heat of the Word had brought it to a boil. The whole world seemed to shake.

Then, he was looking at the face of the Bobby once more, not a blank face, but a face with terrified eyes and snarling lips, a face confronting death and dark defeat. The legs flailed, the hands drifted downward.

Suddenly a pressure ceased. For an instant Carter did not know what it was, then, through the mist of his thoughts, he felt cold air filling his lungs. Still he did not loosen his grip. Gradually, he found himself treading water. The Bobby had gone limp; his face no longer glowed. The darkness was absolute. But Carter did not relinquish his stranglehold for many long moments, until he was certain his enemy was truly dead. Then he pushed the corpse aside, and swam to the wall, seeking some purchase where he could rest.

He managed a tenuous hold upon the stones, though it did little to relieve his weariness. His shoulder throbbed where the Bobby had cut him, and he knew it must be bleeding. Desperately, he worked his way around the circle, searching for the ladder, leaping out of the water in an attempt to grasp it, but he found nothing. Exhaustion and despair overtook him; though he had destroyed the Bobby at last he could remain afloat only a few moments more. With his death the anarchists would still have the Master Keys. They would raise a new leader and the game would continue.

Thinking of the keys, he realized he could still sense their presence below him. He doubted they were simply lying on the bottom; the anarchist would have secured them, perhaps in some compartment within the well itself. The Room of Horrors was not on the maps he carried in his mind, and thus its secrets were hidden. A thin hope struck him: since the ladder provided no means of exit, could such a compartment lead to a way out? It seemed too fantastic, too illogical. He hastily reviewed his other options.

He could speak the Word Which Brings Aid, but he doubted anyone could come in time, not through the Room of Horrors. He would escape on his own or not at all. He thought of the other Words. He had already used three; he would only have strength for one more, if that.

Finally, he decided to cast all upon the Word of Secret Ways. At that he chuckled grimly, thinking it a fool's hope, yet as his paddling slowed, and his muscles stiffened, he determined to make the final effort, to go down fighting.

It took a long time to raise the Word into his mind, and longer to find the strength to speak it. *Talheedin.* The well shook; the water rippled.

Far below him, a dim blue glow rose from the bottom of the shaft. He gave a sob of despair. Even if he could reach it, how could he open the door without the water pouring in? The horror of the well, of drowning, closed in upon him. The sides seemed to lean over, as if they would shortly draw closed, smothering him. This was death and he was not prepared.

Yet he saw he would soon perish anyway, that eventually he would slip into the water and drown. And perhaps whoever placed the hidden passage at the bottom of the well had provided some ingenious method of escape.

He took several deep breaths. Each passing moment lessened his strength. With a prayer on his lips he plunged beneath the surface.

Immediately, he realized how little of his vitality remained, how slowly his arms moved. The blue square was far away. He tried to swim with steady strokes, rationing his power and his air, but by halfway, he knew he would never return to the surface alive; either he would reach the opening and pass through, or he would drown.

His desperation gave him new resolve. He saw nothing but the light. It occurred to him that he was doing the one thing he feared the most; the irony of it beat through him, imparting a sliver of courage. He redoubled his efforts.

He found himself suddenly before the opening, but to his surprise he saw no panel. The light seemed to form a transparent barrier, covering an otherwise open portal that was only a shallow bowl. And lying within were the Master Keys.

Instinctively, he reached toward them. He had no more air; the opening could offer no escape, but he would touch the keys before he died. He would triumph in his own defeat, and the anarchists would find him clutching the bronze ring even in death.

His hand slid through the blue light as if it were no obstacle at all. He grasped the Master Keys.

And suddenly the well was gone, and the water with it. Sweet oxygen filled his lungs. He was lying on wooden floorboards, his lamp and his Lightning Sword beside him, the body of the Bobby to his left. Fearing his enemy still lived, he fumbled for the sword, but then saw the staring, dead eyes. The faceless mask was departed, leaving the pale features of an ordinary man, the man the Bobby must once have been, before he donned the role of Supreme Anarchist.

Carter looked around. He was in the Room of Horrors, but it was empty, its terror gone. And in his hand he still clutched the Master Keys.

He stood slowly, his benumbed brain trying to comprehend what had occurred. His clothes were dripping; the well had been no illusion, or at least, no more than any of the fears within the room. Yet by passing through the fear, he had stripped it of its power over him. At that moment, he did not think he would dread the water or the darkness ever again.

As he stumbled toward the lance of light that was the door leading from the room, he heard footsteps clambering down the stair. He clutched his sword. Even in his exhaustion, his enemies would not take him without a struggle.

A crowd of men rushed through the door, bearing lanterns and rifles. Arm trembling with weakness, Carter raised his sword.

"Carter!" a voice called, and he saw it was Duskin, leading a company of men to his rescue.

"You're alive," Carter muttered gladly as he fell into his brother's arms. For he discovered he could no longer stand.

THE HIGH HOUSE

The Angel

Carter was kept quite busy in the days following his struggle with the Bobby, for now that the Master Keys were finally back in his possession there were doors to unlock, which never should have been locked, and doors to lock that never should have been opened. The Green Door was secured once more and the doors into the cellars of Naleewuath were unbolted, where the gnawlings dwelt. And shortly after, another hunt was organized, and the men and tigers drove into the depths and put an end for a time to the ravening of the chameleon beasts.

The worst task of all was the closing of the Door of Endless Dark, and it took all of Carter's strength of will to order the river of blackness back to its proper place, for even it would obey him now. For two days it flowed into the basement, and Carter neither ate nor slept during all that while, and Duskin, Hope, Chant, and Enoch all took turns keeping vigil with him, preventing him from succumbing to slumber, least the dark tide reverse itself.

At last, the task was done, and he slammed the door shut with a mighty heave, and the noise of its closing rang throughout the great house, so the very foundations shook. Afterward, Carter slept for a day and a night, and that was the end of it.

So he was finally Master of the High House and there was no one to gainsay him, for old Murmur had been found dead within the Room of Horrors, lying stiff before a tall looking glass, her eyes wide in terror. Whatever fears the mirror had shown her it no longer reflected even ordinary light thereafter, but showed an impenetrable gray, and Duskin smashed it with the handle of his knife.

They buried Murmur to the left of Carter's mother, and erected a headstone in-between in honor of Lord Anderson, whose body was never found. This Carter did not mind so much, as in the end he had pitied the woman her petty evil, and because her death was a hard blow for Duskin.

Together, Carter, his brother, and Mr. Hope accompanied Captain Glis and his knights to those parts of the house hardest struck by the anarchists. Everywhere they went the people cheered the new Master, and he set all things in order, bringing comfort and aid where he could. And he made certain to bring his entourage to Kitinthim, to greet Spridel and thank him for feeding the brothers beneath the Kingdom Carving. The old burnisher stood stunned to discover that Carter's claims had been true, and wept openly when the Master declared him before all men baron of that land.

As for the Society of Anarchists, with the loss of both the Bobby and the Master Keys, they fled the White Circle, and it was many years before they dared to rise again.

So the days fell into routine, with Chant lighting the lamps and Enoch winding the clocks. The sun shone on the yard, the beetles wandered the rim of the old well, and the servants went about their duties.

Carter found he liked to sit at the desk in the Room of Forgotten Things, though he never took the key from the drawer to unlock the case and open the book. He watched the patterns of sun upon the angel mosaic and he thought of all that had been. Sometimes Mr. Hope joined him, and they drank tea and discussed many things.

One day, in the midst of their conversation, the sunlight through the angel brightened, until it was nearly blinding, and a figure appeared in the shaft of brilliance. When the radiance waned they saw it was Brittle, standing before the door, looking no different than ever, except that his eyes were keen as swords and his smile bright as a country lad's.

Both men sat speechless, until Carter finally rose and said, "Is it really you?"

"It is, young master," Brittle replied. "Do not be afraid. Come, shake my hand, so you know I am authentic."

They approached him unsteadily. His grip was solid, if somewhat warmer than might be expected. "But you were dead," Carter said. "We saw the coffin."

"I think of it rather as a promotion. But I can only stay a moment. I have other duties now."

"Duskin will be sorry he missed you," Carter said, his voice choking. "Of us all, he loved you best. We all miss you, of course. If I had not abandoned you in the library you might live yet . . ."

"Let us speak only of happier things," Brittle said. "I did my work here and it is completed. I have no regrets, nor should you. You have done a great task. When you restored the balance of the house all the universe was brought to equilibrium as well. Failing suns will flame brighter; planetary rotations will steady; catastrophes of cosmic import will be averted, all because you did the work for which you were meant."

Carter stood astounded. "But how can that be? Are all the worlds, every creature, subject to the house? Are we mere puppets, our every action governed by forces beyond our ken?"

Brittle laughed. "Would you settle the question of volition and destiny in one hour, here in this room? I cannot give an answer you would understand. I will say only this: we are free to choose our way, yet all is ordained."

"But, what then is the High House?" Hope asked. "A mathematical concept as I once suggested? A physical manifestation of the entire universe? God's blueprint? Which is correct? And did God really build it, as Enoch claims?"

"None, and all of these are correct. But, closest to anything you might comprehend, like all of Creation, the High House is a Parable. As for who built it, some say God is the Great Architect; some say the Grand Engineer." Brittle gave his wry smile. "And some say He was once a carpenter as well. I can explain no better."

"Is that why you have come, to tell us this?" Carter asked.

"No. I was sent, as messengers have been sent to those throughout the ages, because when certain men are appointed a great task, they need a moment of utter magic in their lives, a moment they can recall, to know beyond doubt that their mission, and their faith, is true. You have touched my hand; we have spoken together. Know that you are the Master of the High House, as your father before you, and that you, Mr. Hope, are its butler. For this work you were conceived."

"And . . . is my father . . . with you, then?" Carter asked.

"Your father and your mother. You will see them in your time. Do not ask for that now! It is only by special dispensation I have come, and I must leave you. Just remember that they both love you. Go with God, Carter, and you, good William."

"Good-bye, Brittle." They shook hands once more, and through a mist of tears, Carter saw the light brighten again, and then Brittle was gone.

"I think I should like some tea," Hope said.